ELLEN FANNON

DON'T BITE THE DOCTOR
by
Ellen Fannon

Copyright © 2021 by Ellen Fannon
Published by Forget Me Not Romances, an imprint of Winged Publications

Editor: Cynthia Hickey
Book Design by Winged Publications

All rights reserved. No part of this publication may be reproduced, stored in a retrieval system, or transmitted in any form or by any means—electronic, mechanical, photocopying, recording, or otherwise—without the prior written permission of the publisher. The only exception is brief quotations in printed reviews. Piracy is illegal. Thank you for respecting the hard work of this author.

This is a work of fiction. Unless otherwise indicated, all the names, characters, businesses, places, events and incidents in this book are either the product of the author's imagination or used in a fictitious manner. Any resemblance to actual persons, living or dead, or actual events is purely coincidental.

All scripture is from the New International Version.

Copyright TXu002240577   01/20/2021

ISBN: 978-1-952661-65-5

ALSO BY ELLEN FANNON
Other People's Children
Save the Date

If you love animals, you'll enjoy this humorous book written by veterinarian Ellen Fannon. While this book is fiction, the story is full of details about the many different animals the heroine deals with and comes to love. Well, most of them. Set in the eighties when women animal doctors were a rare thing, the story addresses the attitude of that time, and has a wonderful romance that will make you smile. If you need a break from humans, you'll love *Don't Bite the Doctor*. It made me laugh from the first page.

Lenora Worth, author of more than seventy novels, including, *Deadly Connection*, Carol Award finalist, and a *New York Times, USA Today, and PW* bestselling author.

Don't Bite the Doctor is a very entertaining and engaging story about a young, female veterinarian who encounters all kinds of stressful (and humorous) situations with pets and their quirky owners. This book kept me smiling and laughing as the pages flew by. It's a fun read and highly recommended.

Cara James, author of several novels, including *Love on a Dime,* and award-winning author from Romance Writers of America and the American Christian Fiction Writers.

If you need a laugh-out-loud adventure in reading, you must read *Don't Bite the Doctor* by Ellen Fannon.

With Fannon's years of experience as a veterinarian and her unique sense of humor, she tells entertaining stories about her interesting variety of animal patients and their sometimes unreasonable owners. I have a greater appreciation for veterinarians and the work they do from reading this book. *Don't Bite the Doctor* is like *All Creatures Great and Small* but ramped up a few notches, with much more excitement and humor. If you like animals, I promise you'll enjoy this book.

Marilyn Turk, award-winning author

This book is dedicated to the doctors everywhere who treat more than one species—those who care for all God's furry, feathered, and scaly creatures. May you be showered with puppy kisses, warm nuzzles, and grateful clients who always follow your advice and pay their bills.

"But ask the animals, and they will teach you, or the birds in the sky, and they will tell you; or speak to the earth, and it will teach you, or let the fish in the sea inform you. Which of all these does not know that the hand of the Lord has done this? In his hand is the life of every creature and the breath of all mankind." **Job 12:7-10**

"A righteous man cares for the needs of his animal." **Proverb 12:10**

Chapter 1

"I haven't had this much fun since we neutered the squirrel!" I laughed, leaning against the sink, trying to catch my breath.

"Oh, I forgot about that!" Kelly, my long-time technician, laughed with me.

Cara, a second technician, looked up from the phone she cradled against her shoulder. "Wait. You actually neutered a *squirrel?*"

I shrugged. "You know me. I'll neuter anything." Well, except for that pig a few weeks ago. But that was from my firmly entrenched PTSD from my first and only pig neuter in veterinary school, rather than true unwillingness to perform castration surgery. It's a long story.

"Why would you neuter a squirrel?" Cara persisted.

"It belonged to someone who kept it as a pet," Kelly answered. "Remember how it got loose and we chased it all over the surgery room?"

"That was quite a challenge." I smiled at the memory.

Squirrels, it seems, can not only climb trees, they can climb walls. And ceilings. And they are *fast*! They do not corner well, as opposed to other pets with which I am more experienced. This little bugger zinged over our heads, under our feet, and up and down the walls, leaving a trail of upended equipment and surgical supplies in his wake.

"Catching him in midair was pure luck." I didn't like to brag, but I had made an impressive squirrel interception, if I did say so myself. As the creature sprang from one surgery wall to the opposite side of the room, I reached up and fortuitously nabbed it at just the right second, like a squirrel flyball. Even more fortuitous was the fact I happened to have a towel in my hand and didn't suffer sharp incisor teeth embedded into my sensitive palm from a panicked rodent who was not too keen on parting with his nuts. Pun intended.

Until today, I hadn't seen an animal with moves like that. Then came Sadie. It wasn't as if I didn't *know* Sadie. For years, I'd had the dubious pleasure of chasing her down in the cat room of the no-kill pet rescue shelter where it was Sadie's fate to live out her nine lives because nobody in their right mind would ever adopt her. Or get near her, provided, of course, that were possible, which it wasn't. Because I am such an accommodating soul, I made the three or four visits a year to the shelter to vaccinate the cats so the unpaid staff didn't have to load them up in crates and truck them to the clinic.

I always saved Sadie until last. That's because I could generally round up and capture everybody else on the list who needed vaccinating. Granted, some were easier than others, but vaccinating Sadie invariably posed a challenge. She would sense me looking at her and race out the doggy door to the screened-in catio (cat patio) and back into the main cat room before I could react. All I ever saw of her was a gray blur. I had to bide my time, waiting until she lit on one of the overhead ledges, then climb gingerly onto a flimsy plastic chair, hoping Sadie felt trapped and wouldn't bolt—or the chair that was not designed for standing wouldn't topple over with me on it.

Sometimes it worked. But more often than not, I had to chase her outside, inside, up on a chair, down off the chair, back outside, up on a chair, down off the chair, back inside

... well, you get the drift, while the volunteer assigned to me largely stood by helpless. This is why I get paid the big bucks. Hah, who am I kidding? I never charged for my time at the shelter. Eventually Sadie would freeze in one place and this was when my several years of expertise and quick reflexes came into play. Not to mention luck. I usually had one chance at getting this done. With lightning speed, I would reach out and snatch her by the nape of her neck, praying for a good grip the first time. If I missed, it would either be another ten minutes of playing "chase Sadie," or I would be the recipient of Sadie's quick teeth or razor-sharp claws. With the other hand, I would impale her with the needle in some vague area of hopefully-nothing-anatomically-important, and wa-lah! Done. For another year!

On Sadie vaccination days, the uncomfortable thought always reared its ugly head in the alarmist region of my brain, *I dread the day Sadie gets sick and I have to actually get my hands on her.* I generally managed to push this troublesome thought into the easily-forgotten corner of my mind where I wouldn't have to deal with it. Besides, I'm an optimist. I figured a lot of things could happen before that day ever came, such as getting hit by a bus, moving to Africa, or the shelter firing me—well, that's unlikely, since I do their work for free—and I wouldn't have to deal with Sadie if and when that day came.

That's why when Arlene, the cat coordinator at the shelter, called a few weeks ago and said Sadie was drooling excessively and would I mind coming by the shelter to look at her, my heart plummeted.

"Well, I don't mind," I told her. "But *looking at Sadie* is probably the best I can hope for. If you want me to actually examine her, you'll need to find some way of getting her to the clinic, because there's no way I can do that without sedating her." *Yeah, good luck with that.*

Arlene agreed, and once again, I pushed Sadie back into

the cobwebbed area of my cluttered brain and forgot about her; that is, until the day some brave volunteer managed to get her into a carrier and present her at the clinic. To make matters worse, it wasn't my day off.

It wasn't as if Sadie was my first fractious cat rodeo. I'd been down this path many times, so Kelly and I barricaded the surgery room, readied the plexiglass anesthetic induction box, and prepared to dump Sadie directly from the carrier into the box. The transfer went flawlessly. After about five minutes of inhaling the gas anesthetic, Sadie's body went limp. We pulled her out of the box, placed an endotracheal tube, hooked her up to the anesthesia machine, and proceeded to examine her mouth. Aha! There on the upper right side was an abscessed molar.

We moved Sadie onto the dental table where I easily extracted the offensive tooth. After a more thorough exam, I could see extensive gingivitis and resorptive lesions on the crowns of many other teeth, a sure indication that future problems were coming—and I didn't particularly want to see Sadie back anytime soon.

"Drat, Sadie needs a full mouth extraction," I muttered.

"We don't have time blocked off for that," Kelly pointed out.

"It doesn't matter. She's already asleep and it's too difficult to get her back later." I donned my face shield and head loupe and went to work sectioning roots and removing stubborn, but unhealthy teeth that were sure to flare up later if not attended to now. Of course, this put me way behind schedule. Since Sadie was under anesthesia, I asked Kelly to draw blood to be sure there wasn't anything else going on with Sadie's health we should know about.

Certain I had fixed Sadie's problem, I sent her back to the shelter with antibiotics, pain medications, and a soft diet, and put her out of my mind, again. Three days later, in the middle of the treatment area, there sat Sadie in her carrier with a note attached. She hadn't eaten since leaving the clinic.

Shoot! These are the cases I dislike the most. When I have done everything right and the animal is supposed to get better, it is frustrating when the patient doesn't seem to realize this. Why couldn't Sadie just read the book and get with the program? Well, for one reason, she was a cat, and cats do what they darn well please. Second, not only was she a cat, she was *Sadie*.

And that brought me up to today. I reviewed her blood work and found no reason for her lack of appetite, other than a painful mouth. Foolishly I thought, *if Sadie hasn't eaten since the dental, surely, she is weak. Maybe I can just remove the top from her carrier and get a quick look without having to sedate her again.* Now truly, I should have known better. And truly, I *did* know better. But every once in a while, my flawed logic works, so I gave myself (and Sadie) the benefit of the doubt. Big mistake.

At least Kelly and I had the foresight to close off the surgery room. We unsnapped the clips latching the top to the bottom part of Sadie's carrier and popped the lid. I no sooner attempted to touch her than Sadie sprang vertically from the box and across the room in one swift motion. Now I had seen the squirrel climb the walls, but never had I seen a cat do so. All the supplies on the surgery cart toppled over and clanged to the floor. I held my breath as the big glass bottle of penicillin fell over and rolled precariously to the edge of the cart, stopping just short of going over the edge. Sadie let out a screech like a banshee, which brought everyone to the surgery window.

"Stay back," I ordered. "We've got this." All I needed was for some helpful hand to open the door and release Sadie into the clinic, where she would evade capture forever.

Sadie rebounded off the ceiling and landed on the floor in front of the large, green oxygen tanks chained in the corner. She immediately retreated behind the two tanks, hissing and spitting. Kelly and I converged on her, but there was no wiggle room to reach in to grab her—assuming we didn't want to draw back a shredded hand. Kelly gently maneuvered one of the tanks laterally, but before I could make a move, Sadie bolted to the other end of the room and squeezed under the heavy surgical supply cabinet that had an approximate two-inch gap between its bottom and the floor.

"Get a broom!" I shouted to nobody in particular.

A minute later, my third technician, Lexie, rushed into the room, wielding the broom like a weapon. I snatched it from her and got down on my hands and knees, prodding the recalcitrant feline, who refused to budge.

"Do you want me to move the cabinet?" asked Kelly.

"It's too heavy," I replied as Sadie managed to resist all efforts to shoo her out. "Where's the rabies snare?"

Lexie ran in search of the elusive snare while Kelly and I surveyed the situation. Neither of us wanted to poke our hand under the cabinet, assuming both a hand and cat could be removed together from those close confines.

After what seemed like an eternity, Lexie located the missing-in-action rabies snare. I passed the loop under the cabinet, where Sadie batted at it and howled. After several missed attempts, I slipped the noose around her neck and tightened. And pulled. Out came the "sick" cat, contorting her body in ten different directions at once, all claws bared and emitting such an unholy scream I feared the waiting room would clear. Just as her rump cleared the bottom of the cabinet, she slipped out of the noose and retreated once more under the cabinet.

"I'm too old for this," I grumbled. "I just had the Medicare birthday."

Kelly and Lexie shoved on either side of the cabinet, managing to shift it slightly. Sadie emerged, and Lexie plopped the induction box over top of her. Finally! Then, very carefully, Kelly eased the lid between Sadie and the floor until she was trapped. The latches were closed, the box inverted, and Sadie once again breathed anesthetic gas.

I left Lexie to monitor Sadie while I washed up. The whole fiasco reminded me of the "great squirrel chase," and how crazy and unpredictable my job was. Also, how happy I was to still be able to do my job at my advanced age. This thought brought about a case of the giggles. Who would ever believe the things I did in the course of my regular workday?

You're probably wondering how the Sadie saga ended. Well, after the three-ring-circus of "catch Sadie," it was rather anti-climactic. Once she was sedated, I got my second look in her mouth. Although healing nicely, the mouth still appeared painful. I gave her another pain injection and some fluids, along with an appetite stimulant. Then I prayed God would miraculously heal her and leave me out of it next time.

ELLEN FANNON

Chapter 2

I wish I could say I was one of those people who knew from the age of five I wanted to be a veterinarian. But the truth is I never knew what I wanted to be when I grew up. I still don't.

No, as a child, I never aspired to a profession where I would be underpaid, underappreciated, and misunderstood—a profession in the top ten in the U.S. for injury on the job. That decision came later, about the time I had to declare a major in college. Since I had no idea what major to declare, I blurted out biology, for no other reason than I liked biology in high school. Sometime during my first year in college, I started toying with the idea of going to veterinary school. Then, when I found out how difficult it was to get in, my stubborn streak kicked in and acceptance became my unassailable goal.

Why didn't I go to medical school instead, you might ask? Two reasons, really. One, it was much easier to get into medical school than veterinary school. This might seem odd, but the reason for that is there are relatively few veterinary medical schools in the country compared to the number of human medical schools. Two, I can't stand the sight of human blood. Or human anything, for that matter. People are gross, disgusting, icky. My patients might bite and scratch, and they occasionally do stupid things, but nothing on the order of spying a poisonous snake and saying to their inebriated friends, "Hold my beer and watch this!"

I won't bore you with the details of how difficult it was getting into veterinary school, despite the fact I graduated summa cum laude with my B.S. in Biology. Suffice it to say I did; and I managed to survive four years in veterinary school and graduate. Then came the hard part—the real world.

At the time I graduated, jobs for new veterinarians were few and far between, particularly because I had my heart set on moving to Florida. I vowed I had spent my last miserable Ohio winter shivering in a barn, stomping my frozen feet to restore circulation, and dreaming of climbing back into a warm truck, leaving the sick patients to fend for themselves. I had exactly one job offer, from Dr. Drew Spangle, owner of Spangle Animal Clinic in Pinewood, Florida, a small, still largely rural community on the northwest coast of the state. Thrilled to have a job, much less in Florida, I packed my new Camaro—my graduation present to myself—and headed south the day after receiving my diploma.

I was incredibly naïve. I thought I had been hired because Dr. Spangle's practice had grown to the point where he needed to add a second veterinarian. He failed to disclose the fact I was the latest in a long line of predecessors who had come and gone through his revolving door. Little did I know what I had gotten myself into.

~

A few days later, I faced a distraught older lady and a tiny, limp black kitten across the exam table.

"I just don't know what's wrong with her. She hasn't eaten for two days."

The fact that the fleas were deserting the lifeless body in droves did not bode well. I raised the patient's lip. White as a ghost. Instant diagnosis.

"Mrs. Nelson, your kitty is severely anemic due to fleas," I explained. "Fleas suck blood, and they have just about drained her dry."

"Fleas?" The woman looked aghast. "Simone doesn't have fleas."

I gestured to the table where the reddish-brown insects hopped away from the dying kitten like drowning rats abandoning a sinking ship. I suddenly itched all over.

"Well, she must have gotten them from here! I can't imagine where else they would have come from!" Mrs. Nelson's incensed "flea-nial" (flea denial) railed at me. She absently scratched at her left arm.

If I had a nickel for every case of flea-nial I have seen over the years, I would be a rich woman.

"I'll have you know I keep a clean house." Mrs. Nelson's nostrils flared with indignity, but she did seem to realize she had been scratching her arm and abruptly stopped.

This condition called for diplomacy and tact. "It has nothing to do with your housekeeping," I assured her, scratching my head. Did a flea just jump into my hair? "Fleas are quite prevalent in Florida, and in the black fur you probably just didn't see them." Although I had to wonder how this woman failed to notice her kitten was infested with fleas, there was nothing to be gained by making her feel guilty. "It doesn't take many fleas to kill a kitten this size."

"Kill? You mean she's dying?" Mrs. Nelson not only suffered from flea-nial, but denial, as well. A cold, lifeless kitten with the gum color of freshly-fallen snow generally had the prognosis of three feet in the grave and one on a banana peel.

"Yes, I'm afraid without aggressive intensive treatment, Simone is going to die. Even with aggressive care she may not make it."

Tears welled up in the older lady's eyes and trickled down her cheeks. She reached out a thin, blue-veined hand to stroke the moribund little body. "I've only had her two weeks, but I can't bear to lose her. You have to save her."

My gut clenched. Mrs. Nelson placed her pet's fate solely into my hands, and I'd *better* not fail. This pressure only added to my already stressed state. I was young and inexperienced, and if Simone died, it would be *my* fault, not due to her owner's negligence.

"I'll do everything I can, but I have to caution you. Simone is deathly anemic, her body temperature is dangerously low, and her blood sugar is undoubtedly critical. Just handling her to treat her is risky. She may not survive."

Mrs. Nelson nodded. "I understand. Do what you can." I relaxed just a tad at the thought I had finally gotten through to the woman; then she added, "Just don't let her die."

My heart started thudding with dread. I gave Mrs. Nelson's hand a reassuring squeeze and scooped up the half-dead kitten.

In the treatment area, I ran the faucet until the water turned warm, then immersed the little kitten under the gentle stream. Rivulets of bloody water ran from the inert body. At the indignity of being thrust into water, the kitten began to squall, pitifully, mustering what little energy she still possessed.

Tess, the kennel helper, appeared at my side. "What happened? Is it hurt?"

"No," I said. "The blood is from flea dirt. When fleas suck blood, whatever they don't digest is expelled in their feces. Those are the black specks you see in the fur. When the flea dirt becomes wet, it dissolves, releasing the ingested blood."

"Oh, gross." Although Tess' duties mainly consisted of cleaning and feeding the boarding animals, she often wandered into the treatment and surgery areas to observe the action. "Can I help?"

Several fleas jumped onto my arm as I attempted to separate them from their victim. Repulsed, I shoved my entire arm under the faucet.

"Yes. Turn on the incubator and fill some gloves with hot water. This baby is really cold and needs to warm up before I can give her a blood transfusion." Make-shift hot water balloons utilizing old surgery gloves came in handy in a pinch to warm up a patient quickly.

Tess scurried to attend to her assignment while I scrubbed the weak, protesting kitten with flea shampoo. At long last, I left a load of dead and dying fleas in the sink, bundled Simone into a warm towel, and placed her in the incubator.

"Would you bring Tigger up?" I asked Tess. "I need to draw some blood from him for this little one." Tigger's free room and board as the clinic cat sometimes exacted payment in terms of parting with his blood. I rooted through the supply drawer for a ten-cc syringe.

"He just ate. Do you need to sedate him?"

"No. I only need a few cc's of blood." When larger quantities of blood were required for adult patients, I could not count on Tigger's kitty minutes to hold out. But he generally cooperated for a syringeful of blood, which was all I needed for Simone. I pulled up a small amount of anticoagulant into the syringe to keep the blood from clotting.

Tess returned carrying Tigger, a huge gray tabby, and plopped him onto the treatment table. Despite the fact he knew what was coming, he butted his big head into her shoulder, demanding petting. His rumbling purr could be heard across the room.

"You're a good boy, Tigger," I said, rubbing his massive head. "How about saving someone's life today?"

Tigger's purr continued to rattle in his throat. I lifted his head to search for his jugular vein. "Poor baby, your hair just grew back and now I have to shave it again." I reached for the clippers and cut a patch of fur from the underside of Tigger's neck, making it easier to find his deep vein.

I let Tess hold him for the blood draw, confident Tigger would comply. But for the transfusion, I needed more expert hands. This procedure would be difficult enough without entrusting the kitten to an inexperienced restrainer. I only had one—two at best—chances of getting this done. Hitting a vein on a half-pound seriously ill patient was always challenging. Keeping a needle *in* that vein long enough to deliver blood over a period of a few minutes was even *more* challenging. Blood transfusions could not be done too quickly for fear of overloading the heart, causing acute heart failure. Unfortunately, our IV catheters were way too big for this pediatric patient.

I sighed. I needed to enlist the help of Myra, the technician, who was assisting my boss, Dr. Spangle, in surgery.

I poked my head into the surgery room. "I need your help." I told her.

She flattened her lips. A few years older than me, Myra had worked with Dr. Spangle for ten years and knew how veterinary medicine was *supposed* to be practiced. I was a new vet, young, and *female*, at a time when women were just starting to make inroads into veterinary medicine. Where Myra was concerned, I had come to my first job with three strikes against me. The resentment she held toward me was palpable. She made it clear she could do my job better than I could without the inconvenience of actually having gone to veterinary school. Myra, after all, worked for Dr. Spangle who could do no wrong, and she was his number one fan. She only condescended to assist me when she absolutely had to, leaving me to rely on the inexperienced Tess or fend for myself the rest of the time.

Dr. Spangle did little to alleviate the situation. His ego, continually fed with Myra's adoration, acquiesced to her tattling on my incompetence.

"What is it?" Myra asked, her tone surly. Her narrow, pinched face and upturned nose always gave the impression she smelled something unpleasant when in my presence. She pushed a stray lock of blonde hair with dark roots off her forehead.

"I need help transfusing an anemic kitten."

Myra let out a beleaguered sigh and stepped out to assist.

Simone's body temperature had increased to the point where it registered on the thermometer, but was still critically low, at 94.2. As Myra cradled the little body, I shaved the fur over Simone's jugular vein and searched for the tiny vessel. Despite the fact she was half-dead, Simone fought like a tiger.

"Can you hold her still?" I asked, nicely.

"I can't hold her any tighter without crushing her," Myra snapped.

I knew it was possible to properly restrain the kitten without crushing her, but I held my tongue and my breath. After all, Myra knew everything, and was not going to take instruction from *me*.

Inserting the smallest gauge needle I could find through the thin skin, I breathed a sigh of relief when I was rewarded with the sight of blood slowly oozing into the hub. Simone squirmed and meowed piteously. If the transfusion didn't kill her, the stress could. The next few moments literally meant life or death.

Adrenaline ratcheted my heart rate, and I willed my shaking hands to steady. Gently, I attached the syringe full of blood, so as not to drive the needle through the delicate wall of the vein. Then I tentatively pushed the plunger just the least little bit. Relief washed over me as the blood flowed easily, with no ballooning of the tissue around the vein. If the vein blew, or the needle went through the venous wall, the blood would be deposited in the soft tissues around the vein and would do Simone no good.

Simone squirmed even harder. Against everything I knew to be the proper way to give a transfusion, I sped up the delivery of the blood.

"You're giving it too fast!" warned Myra.

"I don't have a choice. If I don't get this blood into her, I'm going to lose the vein." I emptied the syringe, followed by a quick flush with saline and IV glucose, as Simone screamed and writhed in Myra's hands. Then, as if someone had thrown an off switch, Simone's body suddenly went limp.

"Oh no!" I snatched the baby from Myra and rubbed her gently. "Please, little one, don't die. Hang in there!" Simone's tiny chest rose and fell sluggishly.

I risked a peek at Myra. With her lips compressed into a thin line, her eyes accused me of once again not knowing what I was doing. She turned and stalked off.

I swaddled Simone in a towel and laid her back in the incubator. At least she was still alive, if only just barely. I had done everything I could, hadn't I? It wasn't my fault she was half-dead when Mrs. Nelson brought her in. So why did I feel so guilty? How would I break the news to Mrs. Nelson that I had let her beloved kitten die?

What was I doing here? I felt like an imposter. I wasn't qualified to be a veterinarian, despite what my license to practice said. Myra's open hostility and Dr. Spangle's refusal to support and defend me only heightened my feelings of inadequacy and tendency to second-guess every decision I made. Tears stung my eyes as I watched the kitten and willed her to live. But then I heard Heather, the receptionist, escort a client to an exam room. I had to go back to work. Besides, there was nothing more I could do.

I temporarily forgot about Simone for the next couple hours as I stayed busy seeing patients. Then I heard Tess' excited voice.

"Dr. Bennet! Come see!"

I hurried back into the treatment room where Tess stood in front of the incubator watching Simone devour a bowl of canned food.

"She was crying, so I gave her some food. I hope that's okay."

For a moment I couldn't speak. I could only gaze at the little miracle before me. "Of course, it's okay," I said over the lump in my throat.

Pure joy washed over me as my brain processed the transformation from the dying kitten of just two hours ago to the robust little creature chowing down like there was no tomorrow. I had succeeded in saving a life!

"I need to call Mrs. Nelson."

That afternoon, I sent Simone home with a very happy owner, and my heart sang with the knowledge I had snatched the kitten from the brink of death. Not surprisingly, since I had triumphed, rather than failed, Myra didn't say a word.

~

Several months later, I faced Mrs. Nelson again across the treatment table with a different cat. I was relieved to see that this patient wasn't actively trying to die. It only needed vaccines.

"Do you remember Simone? The kitten you gave the blood to?"

I felt my whole face light up with a huge grin. "Yes, of course."

I just knew Mrs. Nelson was about to sing my praises again for having saved Simone's life. But that was okay. I could use all the pats on the back I could get. After all, it was hard for me to reach back there to pat myself.

"Well, I just wanted you to know that blood you gave her turned her mean!" the woman informed me.

Dumbfounded, I stared at her.

"I don't know what kind of blood you used, but it must have been bad blood. It made her mean." The dissatisfied look on Mrs. Nelson's face reinforced the fact she wasn't kidding.

How was I supposed to respond to *that* accusation? Should I introduce her to sweet Tigger, the blood donor? Nothing I could possibly say would convince her Simone's disposition had not come about as a result of Tigger's "bad blood."

I sighed and turned to the patient on the table, who hissed and spat at me. Surely this cat hadn't also received bad blood. The thought crossed my mind that perhaps Simone had become a product of her environment, rather than the victim of "bad blood." But as they say, "no good deed goes unpunished."

Chapter 3

"Don't use the bathroom," Myra ordered. "The plumber is fixing the toilet."

I hadn't planned on going to the bathroom the minute I walked in the door from my lunch break, but even if I had, I could probably have seen for myself the plumber was in there.

"And Dr. Spangle wants to see you in his office right away." She gave me a "you're in trouble" smirk and walked off.

I headed up the hall and stopped in the doorway to Dr. Spangle's office. My boss, a paunchy, middle-aged man with a receding hairline leaned back in his expensive leather chair, nervously twirling a pen between his thumb and index finger. He looked up, then gestured frantically for me to enter.

"Evelyn Slone is on the phone about her dog," he hissed. "How is he?"

My eyes cut to the desk where an insistent red light blinked on the telephone. Ah. Mrs. Slone, one of the "Dr. Spangle *only*" clients was calling to check on Rudy. Her beloved miniature poodle had been hospitalized yesterday with a raging bout of vomiting and diarrhea no doubt brought on by the fact that she indulged him with all kinds of forbidden table food. As usual, whenever an animal was admitted to the hospital, it became *my* responsibility. Also, as usual, my boss remained clueless of the pet's condition until I briefed him. And, lastly, as usual, the "Dr. Spangle *only*" clients believed the man personally and tenderly stayed up all night attending their cherished pets. In their eyes, the man walked on water. He did his best to maintain this image.

"He's doing much better, sir," I answered. "No vomiting or diarrhea overnight, and he kept down his breakfast."

"Do you think he can go home this afternoon?"

"He should be able to."

"Good." He snatched up the phone and sang, "Evelyn, so sorry to keep you waiting. I just got out of surgery."

The lie caused hot indignation to rise up from my belly, and I huffed out a loud sigh of disgust. But my boss didn't notice, as he had swiveled in his chair with his back facing me. Angrily, I lingered on the threshold, in case he needed further clarification on anything.

"Oh, Rufus is doing fine, just fine." He laughed. "What's that? Rudy, yes, of course, so sorry, I meant Rudy." He turned and shot me a nasty glare over his shoulder. It was my fault for not reminding him of Rudy's name. "Yes, he should be able to go home this afternoon. Why don't you check back with me around four o'clock?" A long pause followed, during which time Dr. Spangle smiled profusely. "Of course, Evelyn, it's a joy taking care of Rudy. He's one of my favorite patients. Now don't you worry about a thing. I have everything under control."

After another pause, he said, "You're very welcome, Evelyn, I'll see you this afternoon."

He replaced the receiver and his smile immediately disappeared. "Why didn't you update me this morning?" Two deep creases furrowed his brow. "The woman's been on hold for ten minutes waiting for you to get back from lunch."

Why, indeed, had I not briefed him earlier? Perhaps the fact that he kept telling me, "later," when I tried to talk to him had something to do with it. I refrained from rolling my eyes and muttered, "Do you want me to get Rudy's go-home medication ready?"

"No, I'll have Myra take care of it. Is there anything else I should know about the hospitalized cases that you've failed to tell me?"

"No, sir, the rest of them are mine."

"Good. In the future, please do a better job of keeping me informed."

It was on the tip of my tongue to instruct him not to use the toilet, but the sarcasm would have been lost on him.

As I turned to go, I almost collided with Myra, hovering in the hallway behind me for no good reason, other than to eavesdrop. As I pushed past her, I heard her ask, "What would you like me to send home for the Slone dog?"

I sighed. Myra had rarely prepared medication for *me*. But then she didn't worship me as she did Dr. Spangle. And Dr. Spangle loved being idolized by staff and clients alike.

It was only natural that certain clients preferred to see the vet they had been seeing for years rather than the new graduate. That didn't particularly bother me. What did bother me was Dr. Spangle's taking credit for my work. Mrs. Slone, case in point, refused to give me the time of day, while gushing on and on about what a wonderful man my boss was.

Yet I was the one who had placed Rudy's intravenous catheter and stayed late last night, cradling him in my arms while the rehydrating fluids dripped into his vein. I had also checked on him in the middle of the night when I came back to check on two of my own patients. The dog had soiled his cage, so I cleaned it and put in fresh bedding.

I didn't do it for Mrs. Slone or even for Dr. Spangle, for that matter, although he did sign my paycheck. I did it for Rudy.

This undying allegiance to my boss' healing abilities was brought home to me in an ironic way on a particularly busy Saturday morning. To my surprise, I found my boss already there when I walked into the office.

"I took in a hit-by-car cat on emergency last night," Dr. Spangle told me. "He has a fractured femur and a fractured humerus that both need to be pinned. I have to get started in surgery as soon as possible."

I nodded, only because I had no choice. With Dr. Spangle in surgery, that left me to cover all the morning's appointments, which were already double-booked for two doctors. Saturdays were busy enough without the added shortage of a doctor unable to see his patient load due to unexpected surgery. My head began to throb as the morning's mayhem began. I could already hear the non-stop ringing of the phones up front.

Myra rushed to set up surgery as Dr. Spangle pulled up the injectable anesthetic.

"I'm sorry, Doctor." Heather appeared in the treatment room. "Mr. Crabtree is here with Spike and he only wants to see you."

Dr. Spangle spat out a bad word and threw the syringe on the table. "Have everything ready and I'll do the cat after I see Spike."

I assumed he was addressing Myra, although he could have just as easily been addressing me. I chose to believe he meant the former and left the more-than-capable Myra to set up surgery.

Not wanting to fall behind from the get-go, I picked up the first chart and ushered the owner and patient into the second exam room. As I finished up, I heard Heather once again. "Mrs. Smythe is here with Buttons. She was on the schedule specifically for you."

The boss let out a groan. "Bring her back to room one."

For once I was grateful some of the clients only wanted to see Dr. Spangle. After quickly disinfecting the exam table, I grabbed the next chart from the top of a rapidly growing pile, stepped into the waiting room, and called Mr. Kilmer's name. An older gentleman with a cat in a carrier rose from his chair in the already crowded waiting room. A little band of tension worked its way up my neck and lodged at the base of my skull. *How am I going to take care of all these patients by myself?* All these people couldn't have appointments. Some must have been walk-ins. But Spangle Animal Clinic never turned anyone away, regardless of a full schedule. Extra patients meant extra money.

Fortunately, Mr. Kilmer's cat only needed vaccines. I did a brief physical exam and administered the injections. As I walked Mr. Kilmer back to the lobby, Heather thrust another chart into Dr. Spangle's hand.

"Sorry, Doc, but it's Mr. Miller. You know he won't see anyone but you."

"Myra!" bellowed the boss. "Get up here and help me. Confound it, at this rate I'll *never* get into surgery."

I secretly welcomed the reprieve from double-duty doctoring for as long as possible. The rest of the morning flew by, with one delay after another for the boss to get to his surgery. Finally, only two clients sat in the waiting room, both of whom understood that Dr. Spangle had an emergency surgery waiting, and they both graciously agreed to see me.

The boss disappeared into the back, yelling for Myra to bring up the cat. A few minutes later, I finished up the morning's appointments.

"Mrs. Westermeyer is on her way with an emergency," Heather said, as I handed her the last chart. The tension headache that had my neck in a vise all morning broke free, sending tendrils of stabbing pain behind my eyeballs.

Oh, Dear God, not Mrs. Westermeyer! Not today! Although I tried to maintain a Christian attitude in my workplace, some clients almost made me lose my religion. Of all the high-maintenance clients patronizing Spangle Animal Clinic, Mrs. Westermeyer stood head and shoulders above them all. A formidable woman in her late forties, she bred show dogs; and as an accomplished authority on her subject, she knew how she wanted and expected her veterinary visits to go. We were to agree to everything she said and do what she wanted without question. If we did, all would be fine. If not . . . well, it was best not to open that Pandora's box.

My first encounter with Mrs. Westermeyer had been on another busy Saturday morning when she brought in a sick two-week old puppy. She had insisted on barging ahead of the other clients because, after all, *she* was Mrs. Westermeyer, a breeder with a sick puppy.

Dr. Spangle had nabbed me in the hallway and dumped her on me because he didn't want to deal with her. "Just go in, introduce yourself, and give her whatever she wants," he instructed.

The unfairness of the whole situation made my blood boil. I stepped back into the exam room where I had been with another client. "I'm so sorry," I said, "but I have an emergency. I'll be back as soon as possible."

"Oh, of course, dear. I completely understand." Dear sweet Miss Hooper. She truly thought there was a life and death situation and didn't realize she and her Pekingese were being shoved aside for a bully.

I gave her a half-hearted smile and left her sitting there, while inwardly seething. It took every bit of willpower to force myself to walk into the last exam room where Mrs. Westermeyer waited impatiently.

"Where is an electrical outlet?" she demanded as I entered. "I need to plug this in." She held up the cord to a heating pad which lay under a green towel in the bottom of a small cardboard box. I could see a tiny black nose poking out of the towel.

I took the cord from her and moved a jar of Q-tips aside to expose an outlet, while secretly thinking where I would like to tell her to "stick" the end of that plug.

A tall, large-boned woman, Mrs. Westermeyer oozed intimidation. Her air of superiority enveloped her like an invisible cloak. I plugged in the heating pad while she looked down her patrician nose at me.

"We've been waiting ten minutes! Puppies are very susceptible to cold, you know. Where's Dr. Spangle?"

"I'm afraid he's tied up at the moment. I'm Dr. Bennet. I'm working with Dr. Spangle." I held out my hand, which she ignored. "What can I do for you today?"

The woman pursed her lips and scrutinized me as if I were a bug under a microscope. "Do you know *anything* about puppies?"

I blinked. The question completely caught me off-guard. A number of unsuitable answers sprang to mind, none of which I could verbalize.

Well, I did graduate from vet school. Surely, I learned something about puppies.

Puppies? Hmm. Aren't those baby dogs?

Nope, don't know anything about puppies, but I'm willing to learn. After all, there's a first time for everything.

My flabbergasted brain refused to come up with a satisfactory reply. I just stood staring at the woman, hoping my astonished facial expression didn't appear too rude. Even though Mrs. Westermeyer had just treated *me* with the utmost offensiveness, I still did not want to come across as unprofessional. But I realized that forcing my services on her was not going to work. Finally, I swallowed and said, "I think it would better if you saw Dr. Spangle, after all." With that, I turned on my heel and left the room.

Hearing my boss's voice in exam room one, I knocked once, then poked my head in. "She wants to see *you,*" I said, and shut the door before he could respond.

That first encounter with Mrs. Westermeyer and her sick puppy had been several months ago, and surprisingly, she had actually condescended to see me a couple of times since then when Dr. Spangle was unavailable. But our encounters were always uncomfortable. After the morning we had just finished, dealing with this difficult woman was the last thing I needed.

Lord, give me patience. Now! In fact, give me all *the Fruits of the Spirit! I need all the help I can get.* I took a deep breath and prayed for the fluttering in my stomach to settle. In the back, I heard Dr. Spangle scrubbing for surgery. There was no way he would wait for Mrs. Westermeyer. She would not be happy.

Speak (or rather think) of the devil. In came the woman, herself, announcing in a no-nonsense tone that Taffy needed to be seen *right now.* I peeked in the back to see the boss donning his surgical gown.

"Dr. Spangle's in surgery," I heard Heather say, "but Dr. Bennet can see Taffy. Come on back."

Was it possible to hear disdain without someone speaking? If so, I could swear I heard disdain dripping from the pores of Mrs. Westermeyer's body and pooling in a puddle around her feet, although the woman hadn't uttered a word. She passed me in the hallway and shot me her "stink eye." I followed her into the room, where she grabbed a paper towel from the dispenser on the wall and a bottle from the supply cabinet, wiped the stainless-steel exam table, and gingerly deposited a beautiful blonde cocker spaniel on the area she had just cleaned.

I mustered up the energy to appear cheerful and anxious to help. I didn't enlighten her that she had just disinfected the exam table with ear cleaner. In a glance, I ascertained that Taffy did not appear to be in any life-threatening situation. In fact, as her owner placed her on the exam table, Taffy wagged her stumpy tail and took in her surroundings with large, curious brown eyes accentuated with long, pale eyelashes.

"We have a *huge* problem," Mrs. Westermeyer informed me. "One of the other dogs scratched Taffy and as you can plainly see, she has a deep cut under her eye."

I had to look closely. But yes, with some imagination, I could envision the tiny, more-of-an-abrasion-than-a-cut, hidden in Taffy's fur under her left eye.

"As you can also plainly see, this injury is potentially quite disfiguring. We can't have that. Taffy is a show dog, you know."

Pointing out that the miniscule blemish was hardly visible would be a waste of breath. So, I did what I had learned to do best when dealing with Mrs. Westermeyer. I remained quiet and let her tell me what needed to be done.

"She'll need stitches, obviously. Very tiny ones so as not to tear the skin any more than it already is."

I nodded. "Okay, I can take care of that right now, if you'd like to have a seat in the waiting area."

The woman's lips flattened. "I'd *prefer* Dr. Spangle do the surgery. And I *prefer* to be with Taffy while she has the procedure."

Although Mrs. Westermeyer had said "prefer," what she *meant* was "demand."

A lead weight lodged in my chest. There was going to be a battle of the wills which I did not feel up to fighting. "I'm terribly sorry, Mrs. Westermeyer, but he just went into an emergency surgery."

Mrs. Westermeyer's nostrils flared. "Well, *this* is also an emergency, and *I am* one of his most *loyal* clients."

"Yes, I understand." I avoided looking at her piercing gaze. "I'm sure he'll be happy to take care of Taffy as soon as he's finished."

"And just how long is that going to take?" Her cantankerous voice rose, as her narrowed eyes challenged me.

My throat constricted. "I really can't say." I forced the thin words past my clenched vocal cords. "He has a double orthopedic procedure. It could be a couple of hours."

Her eyes widened. "*Two hours!* Well, that's simply not acceptable." Two splotches of pink indignation rose in her cheeks.

"You can leave Taffy with me and he can call you as soon as he's finished."

"*Leave Taffy!*" The unhappy client shook her head as if she could not believe the depth of my ignorance and insensitivity. "One does not simply *leave* a show dog at a vet clinic. Who knows what kind of diseases Taffy might be exposed to!"

We were at an impasse. I squared my shoulders and braced for another onslaught. "Mrs. Westermeyer, I understand, but there's really nothing else I can do. You can either leave her here for Dr. Spangle or I can suture Taffy's laceration for you now."

She closed her eyes and blew out a huge, slow breath, obviously teetering on the edge of a meltdown. "Dr. Bennet," she uttered, carefully enunciating each word, her soft voice somehow more ominous than her loud one. "You are acceptable when my show dogs just need vaccines. But for a *procedure* I need Dr. Spangle." She opened her eyes and challenged me to a stare-down.

My chest heaved with frustration. What did the woman expect me to do? Wave a magic wand and produce Dr. Spangle? There was nothing more exasperating than having to tell a client who didn't want to see me that they were stuck with me because the vet they demanded to see didn't want to see *them*. And was Mrs. Westermeyer truly so selfish as to care so little for the poor cat with the two broken legs? Well . . . *that* was a silly thought. Of course, she was.

I lost the stare-down by looking away first. "Let me go talk to Dr. Spangle and see what he suggests."

I left the room, closing the door behind me because I didn't want her to hear the inevitable avalanche of manure about to hit the proverbial fan.

Please don't shoot the messenger. Please don't shoot the messenger. The mantra repeated itself in an endless loop in my head as I moved slowly toward the surgery suite, feeling as though I walked toward my own execution. I looked through the window and saw that Dr. Spangle had just finished draping the back leg and was reaching for his scalpel.

Before he could make his first incision, I burst through the door and blurted out, "I'm sorry, Dr. Spangle, but Mrs. Westermeyer is in exam room two with Taffy who has a cut under her eye and she insists on seeing you and refuses to leave Taffy until later." There. I had spit it all out in one huge breath, leaving me somewhat winded. I drew air into my oxygen-deprived lungs and risked a peek at my boss from under my lashes.

Dr. Spangle stopped, scalpel poised over the surgically prepped leg. His face turned the color of an over-ripe tomato, but he uncharacteristically laid the scalpel gently back onto the surgery tray. I was immensely relieved he hadn't thrown it, as had been the case with numerous other surgical instruments. He snatched off his mask and gloves, and threw them toward the trash can, missing the mark.

"I'll take care of Mrs. Westermeyer. *You* pin this leg!" With that, he walked out of the surgery room, his angry footsteps echoing off the tiled hallway.

I stood for a moment, gawking after him. Then I turned to Myra. "Would you please get me a gown and gloves?"

For once, she complied without an argument, probably realizing her refusal to assist me in surgery would not go over well with her beloved boss.

Forty-five minutes later, I drilled the bone pin through the two ends of the fractured femur, pulling the pieces together into an almost perfect alignment. As I contemplated how to approach the surgery on the fractured humerus, I had to laugh at the irony of this whole situation. I had been relegated to major orthopedic surgery due to the fact I was too incompetent to place a stitch in a tiny laceration.

~

"The plumber is asking to see you," Heather told me, as I finished checking my two hospitalized cases.

"Me? Why does he want to see *me?*" I didn't have anything to do with clinic maintenance. "Are you sure he doesn't want to see Myra?" In addition to all her other duties, such as making sure I did my job correctly, Myra was also the self-appointed office manager.

"No, he asked specifically for Dr. Bennet."

"That's odd." I quickly jotted down a note in one of my patients' records and headed to the bathroom where the plumber was putting away his equipment in a big red toolbox.

He turned when I stepped into the small enclosure, and his face immediately infused bright red from his neck to the tips of his ears.

"You wanted to see me?" I asked, confused. Was he going to tell me he had found feminine hygiene products that weren't supposed to be flushed in the plumbing? If so, I wasn't the only young female who worked at the clinic and I prepared to take offense.

"You probably don't remember, but I had my dog in to see you a while back."

Oh. I was either going to be asked for free veterinary advice while he charged an arm and a leg for plumbing services, or he was going to tell me how I messed up with his dog. I tried to place him, but couldn't.

"Flash? The yellow Lab? The one who ate the sock?"

Oh! Of course. I often had difficulty remembering clients when they weren't with their pets—well, with the exception of certain ones, like Mrs. Westermeyer—but once they told me the name of their animal, it immediately clicked.

"Yes, I remember. I hope he's doing okay." The big, goofy Labrador retriever had a habit of ingesting inedible items, but had been fortunate in that they had all miraculously passed through his intestinal tract without causing a blockage.

The man chuckled softly. "Yes, he's fine. Everything came out in the end, so to speak."

I smiled at his little joke. "I'm glad. I was worried I was going to have to do surgery to remove that sock."

There was a long moment of silence.

"Is there another problem with Flash?" I finally asked.

"Oh, no, no, nothing like that." He glanced at the floor.

I needed to get back to work. I wished he would come to the point. "Well, Heather said you needed to see me about something. If it's about the plumbing job, you'll need to talk with Myra."

He looked up. "Oh. No." He cleared his throat. "I was wondering. I mean, if you're not doing anything . . . I mean, if you are, I understand, but . . . I didn't know if you were seeing anybody, and, I mean . . . if you're not . . . do you think you might like to . . . to have dinner with me sometime?" His terrified eyes briefly met mine before darting back to the floor.

Oh. *Oh!* He was asking me out! On a date! In the bathroom where the toilet seat was still up and I could hear water gurgling through the pipes. How romantic! Wait. Was it permissible to date a client? I mean, technically, his *dog* was my patient, not him, so this didn't cross some doctor/patient ethical line, did it? I guess I took too long answering.

"That's okay, I under—" He still stared at the floor.

"Sure, I'd love to," I said at the same time.

"Oh." His relieved eyes met mine for a brief second and a huge, lopsided grin broke out on his face. His blush deepened. "Oh, okay. Good. Well, how about Saturday night?"

"Saturday's good." I reached into my pocket and pulled out a note pad and a pen. "Here's my number. Call me."

"Yes, okay. I will."

I smiled at him and turned to go.

"Oh, and Dr. Bennet?"

I turned back. "I think you can call me Jill." It suddenly struck me I didn't know *his* name. Surreptitiously I glanced at the name stitched across his uniform pocket. Jack. *Jack what?* Never mind, I would figure it out later. Then it hit me. *Jack and Jill.* I almost groaned out loud.

He offered a shy smile. That lopsided grin was actually quite endearing. "Oh, okay. Uh, Jill?"

"Yes?"

"It's okay to use the toilet now."

Chapter 4

"Dr. Bennet, can you come? Horatio is colicky." The anxious woman at the other end of the phone didn't realize the anxiety she had just instilled in *me* with those last three words.

For at least two years after graduating from veterinary school, I couldn't hear the word "colic" without breaking out into a cold sweat. Even after giving up equine practice almost thirty years ago, that word still has the ability to evoke a strong visceral response in me. I blame this on my time as a veterinary student when we saw only the worst of the worst colic cases, as these were the ones referred to the university. The word "colic" simply means abdominal pain. For some reason, horses, being somewhat delicate animals, are subject to all sorts of abdominal maladies—often as the result of their own stupidity for doing things like getting into excess amounts of grain or eating sand. For some reason, God endowed them with a complex gastrointestinal tract, but without the ability to vomit; hence they frequently have belly pain. And colics almost always occur at inconvenient times.

I glanced at my watch. Yep, five o'clock. Dinnertime. Colic is aptly nicknamed "the cocktail hour disease" for good reason. Except when it is a middle-of-the-night event, in which case I dare not repeat what I call it. Night calls had certainly enhanced my prayer life.

"Yes, of course," I responded, trying to sound professional and reassuring. *Please, God, don't let it be serious. I'm too tired to stay up all night with a sick horse.* My mind flashed back to another equine all-nighter when I was a student.

~

I stood under the bright surgery lights, having been on my feet for eighteen hours. Equine rounds in veterinary school started promptly at eight o'clock, and my patients all had to be evaluated and treated prior to rounds. It seemed like days, not mere hours, since I had bent over Bob, cleaning out the debris in his enormous hooves with my hoof pick. A Clydesdale gelding, Bob was a gentle giant, other than when I tried to administer his eye medications. Bob, a draft horse for Budweiser, had recently undergone cataract surgery, and required frequent eyedrops, which he intensely disliked.

"Hey, can you help me with Bob?" I called to Craig, a harried, fellow student who was trying to get his own cases done before rounds.

"Sure." Thankfully, most of us bottom-of-the-totem-pole vet students helped each other out. Craig stepped into Bob's stall and pulled the sliding door closed. "You pull his head down, and I'll put in the eyedrops."

"Okay." I handed the medication to Craig and grabbed onto Bob's halter, trying to bring his eye down to Craig's level. Bob simply raised his head higher, leaving me hanging onto his halter, my feet dangling in the air.

"Pull his head down!"

"I'm trying!"

Craig added his muscle to mine, and between the two of us, we managed to administer the first of Bob's four-times-daily dose of eyedrops.

That was seventeen-and-a-half hours ago. I had to treat Bob one more time tonight. *If* we could ever get done with this colic surgery, which had shown up at six o'clock, right when I was getting ready to take a dinner break. It had been my luck to be one of the students on call. I bounced from foot to foot, trying to relieve the pressure from my aching feet. It wasn't as if I could see anything on the surgery table, anyway. With two equine surgeons, two residents, and two interns packed in, my assistance was not required. My job was to replace the scalpel blades each time the surgeon made a cut and hand instruments to the increasingly cranky team, who took out their fatigue on me. After four hours of surgery, the intern finally placed the last stitch—the higher echelons of equine gods having departed the surgery suite a good forty-five minutes earlier.

"Once you recover him, you'll need to stay with him to be sure he doesn't hurt himself," the intern instructed. Unfortunately, there was only one "you" to whom he referred, and I was it.

Beyond exhausted, my morale took a nosedive. "For how long?"

I don't know what possessed me to ask this ill-advised question. It must have been lack of oxygen to my brain for having stood on my feet for so long. No blood flowed north. It pooled at my aching feet and gave me a whole new appreciation for horses suffering from laminitis, a painful inflammatory condition of the hooves.

"All night!" he barked, giving me an *I can't believe you asked such a stupid question* look. "You can page me if there's a problem." He threw his instruments on the dirty tray, snapped off his gloves, and strode from the room.

It was just me and the horse in a padded stall. The padding ensured if the beast became violent while waking from anesthesia, he wouldn't hurt *himself*. Vet students were expendable. As soon as the horse regained consciousness, I coaxed him up, gently walking him in ever larger circles to keep him from collapsing back down again. Mercifully, after a long, uneventful night, the patient was transferred to the regular ward and to another student.

I was late getting to Bob. After hastily finishing my treatments, I joined the others on rounds. There was no time for breakfast. I hadn't slept in over twenty-four hours. I hadn't showered, brushed my hair, or even my teeth. My greasy hair hung in limp strands down my tired shoulders. Although I hadn't so much as glanced in a mirror since yesterday morning, I could feel puffy bags under my eyes—which I knew were bloodshot from the sandpaper scratchiness that came with the pure effort of holding them open. I felt like the walking dead.

"Listen up," announced Dr. Gossling, the head of equine medicine and surgery, and a legend in his own mind. Behind his back, the students referred to him as "Goose." This nickname came more from his childish temper tantrums and inflated ego than his surname. My sole objective during my time in the equine rotation was to make it through without having to scrub into surgery with Dr. Gossling, who made life in surgery a living nightmare for those unfortunate enough to be stuck with him. His theatrics and meltdowns in surgery were legendary. I didn't want to become another victim of his air-born instrument projectiles when his anger erupted. "The Ohio State Fair queen candidates are going to be touring the vet school today, so be good representatives of the university."

No sooner had the words left his mouth than a parade of chattering beauty queen wannabees emerged through the doors separating the small and large animal clinics. Dressed in completely inappropriate apparel for a tour of the stables, each young woman sported an expensive, form-fitting dress, hi-heeled boots, and, yes, cowboy hats perched on impeccably teased and sprayed hair. Each perfectly made-up face glowed with youth and freshness.

Goose's evil twin retreated as he rushed forth to greet the envoy. "Ladies," he gushed. "Welcome. If you will just follow this way . . ." His voice trailed off as he led the gaggle of giggling girls away from our knot of students and instructors.

"Oooh! Can we pet the horses?" I overheard, as the last of the Barbie Brigade trotted after Goose.

"There but for the grace of God go I," I muttered under my breath, as I watched them depart, painfully aware of just how unfeminine I appeared at that moment.

~

I shook my head to clear it of the unpleasant memory. *Please let this be an easy one,* I pleaded with the good Lord. Since being in practice, I'd had my fair share of difficult colic cases, but, thankfully, none compared to the nightmares that showed up at the veterinary teaching hospital. That knowledge still didn't stop the rise of panic just below my calm exterior.

As I drove out to Metcalf Farms to check on Horatio, the sun began its dip below the horizon, a blazing red ball quickly disappearing into the softer pinks and purple hues of twilight. My car turned onto the gravel road leading to the stable, tires crunching loudly as I slowed my speed. I really should have taken the time to swing by Dr. Spangle's house to pick up his truck. Although my boss had pretty much given up horse work except for a few favored clients, his truck was top-of-the-line and outfitted with every necessity to attend to an ailing horse. My 1980 arrest-me-red Camaro was not the proper type of vehicle in which to conduct horse calls. However, I had the few supplies I needed in my trunk, and for now, it served the purpose and didn't cost me an extra thirty minutes in time. I pulled up to where a group of people huddled around what had to be my patient, Horatio. I couldn't actually *see* Horatio for the mass of humanity crowded around, but I knew he was in there somewhere.

There is an unwritten rule in horse practice that when a horse gets sick or injured, it always attracts a small crowd of people—all of whom know way more than the vet. This begs the question, "Why did they call *me*?" Tonight was no exception. I exited my car, immediately struck by the pleasant, earthy odor of horse, mixed with the slightly sweet smell of manure. Regardless of the reason I had been dragged away from my impending dinner table, simply being outside in the balmy evening, breathing in the scents of the stable carried in the light breeze, filled me with a sense of euphoria. My feet kicked up dust as I attempted to part the Red Sea of humanity.

"Oh, thank God you're here!" cried Courtney, Horatio's owner. "He keeps trying to lie down and roll."

Sometimes I have to wonder at the naivete of people who apparently believe I am more omnipotent than I truly am. I wished I had the confidence in myself that the young owner had in me. Nevertheless, I stepped forward and smiled.

"Hi, Horatio," I soothed, as I reached up to stroke his velvety nose. A handsome, sorrel animal with a magnificent white blaze, Horatio leaned into my caress and closed his mahogany eyes. "I hear you have a tummy ache."

Horses can be strange creatures. You never know if they're going to stand stoically or suddenly lash out for no reason and try to kill you.

Horatio, thankfully, stood stoically, and I flipped his top lip up to examine the color of his gums. Healthy pink. Good. I pressed my thumb gently against his gum to see how long it took for the blanched color to return. Less than two seconds. Good. Moving down his jawline, I located the mandibular artery just below the angle of his jaw and took his pulse. A little high, at fifty. I pulled my stethoscope from around my neck and listened to his heart, which sounded fine, then his abdomen. An abundance of gurgling gut noises assaulted my ears, and I took that, too, as a good sign.

"I need to do a rectal exam," I said, returning to my car and popping the trunk. I donned a plastic sleeve that fit up to my armpit and proceeded to slather on a liberal amount of lubricating jelly. At that, the crowd moved way back. There is nothing quite like having someone's arm thrust up a horse's south end to make him go berserk. A horse in the throes of berserk-ness doesn't care who it tramples.

"Would you mind raising a front leg for me?" I asked Courtney.

The theory is if a horse's front leg is off the ground, he can't kick the daylights out of you with his back legs. Theoretically, of course.

"I never seen Ole' Doc Potter do that," observed one grizzled bystander, a piece of straw stuck between his front teeth.

I ignored him and nodded to Courtney, who dutifully bent and raised Horatio's left front leg, holding it steady against her knee.

"Yeah, Ole' Doc Potter was the best horse vet I ever seen," agreed a balding man with a fringe of unruly gray hair encircling his pate, standing next to the old-timer. "He could do anything." He crossed his arms and frowned at me.

Except live forever, obviously. Gingerly, alerting Horatio to my presence, I made my way across Horatio's rump to his more personal area and pulled his tail to one side. Rectal palpation in horses carries risk to both patient and doctor, so I always approached this part of the exam with a healthy degree of trepidation. I gently inserted my lubricated hand into Horatio's anus and slowly slid it forward. He responded by dancing sideways on his back feet and clamping down with all the bone-crushing musculature at his disposal in his terminal digestive tract. I paused a minute, waiting for Horatio to let up and for the feeling to return to my hand. Two preteen girls standing a few feet away giggled. There were always gigglers in the crowd. I suppose a rectal exam is funny to those who aren't direct participants. After a moment, Horatio relaxed, and I swept my hand around the confines of his caudal abdomen—at least as far as my short arm would allow. Aha! There was the problem. At the pelvic flexure I felt the distinct heaviness and slightly displaced segment of the right dorsal colon.

"It's a sand impaction," I said, removing my arm.

Courtney released Horatio's leg. "Can you fix it?"

"I'll give him something for pain and some mineral oil to try to move it out."

"How did he get that?" asked another bystander.

We live in Florida, the sandbox capital of the world. Duh! Besides, you're not the owner and legally, and otherwise, I don't have to discuss his case with you. "Sand colic is very common where we live," I explained, nicely. "Every time he picks up a mouthful of hay from the ground, he ingests some sand."

I walked back to my car to retrieve my supplies. After drawing up ten cc's of Banamine, an anti-inflammatory medication, I approached Horatio once again and rubbed his neck. The crowd looked on as I tried to find a vein in the gathering darkness. On a brown horse. No pressure. *Don't think about the fact that everyone's watching to see if you can hit the vein and you can't see squat.* Fortunately, the jugular vein stood up nicely and I hit my target first try.

I gave the medication a few minutes to work while I prepared the mineral oil. There are few things messier than mineral oil, unless it's mineral oil and sand—which is inevitable because we were in Florida. As cleanly as possible, I poured a gallon of oil into my stainless-steel bucket and set it well out of the way in case Horatio objected to having a stomach tube passed and kicked the bucket—so to speak. I lubricated the first few inches of the stomach tube, threw it over my shoulder, and walked back to where Horatio stood, looking at me with a guarded eye.

"Hello, boy," I cajoled. I reached up to pull his head down, placing one arm over his nose, and started to thread the tube into the floor of his left nostril. Horatio jerked his head upright, catching me square in the jaw. This brought a bit of comic relief to the onlookers, and stars to my eyes.

"I'm sorry," I told Courtney. "We'll need to use the twitch." I went back to my car and fetched my plastic pole with the rope loop.

"Will that hurt him?" asked one of the preteens, wide-eyed.

"Not really," I replied. I loved having to justify my professional decisions to pre-pubescent *non-owners* who didn't really have any business being there in the first place other than idle curiosity. *Stop.* My inner-voice chided me. *You're just hungry and tired. Use this as a teachable moment.* My stressed brain did battle with itself.

I took a deep breath. *Lord, I need patience and compassion.*

"It might look a little scary, but the twitch is used to temporarily restrain a horse for a procedure he doesn't like when you don't want to sedate him. It distracts him from what's going on." I glanced around and noted a few people actually listening to me and warmed to my lecture. "And studies have shown twitching actually releases pain-relieving chemicals called endorphins, which help to calm the horse. Sort of like acupressure."

The grizzled old man spat in the dirt. "Sounds like a bunch of hooey to me," he mumbled under his breath, but still loud enough for everyone around him to hear. "Ole' Doc Potter didn't use no new-fangled gadgets. He just done what needed to be done and that was that."

His friend nodded in agreement.

I wished I had met Ole' Doc Potter, the legend. The man was not only a miracle worker and horse-whisperer, he must have been a saint. More than that, I wished Ole' Doc Potter were here right this very second—and I was home eating my dinner.

I placed the rope around Horatio's upper lip, twisted it with the pole, and handed the pole to Courtney. She bit her lip and held on with dogged determination. This time, Horatio accepted the stomach tube with only a mild snorting and head tossing. I watched the tube slide down the esophagus on the left side of his neck, but to be absolutely sure it was where it was supposed to be, I let one of the preteens blow in the end of the tube while I listened with my stethoscope for the telltale sound of air moving in the stomach. There was nothing more disastrous or deadly than accidently inserting the tube into the windpipe rather than the stomach and pumping the lungs full of mineral oil.

Giving the preteen a thumbs up, I had her hold on to the end of the tube while I fetched the bucket of oil and pump. She beamed. My stomach pump was a bit tricky, in that the stomach tube didn't seal well over the end, which meant I had to hold it in place to keep the tube from flying off under pressure. Holding the tube onto the pump with one hand, I proceeded to pump the oil with the other. This maneuver required a bit of manual dexterity and would probably have been more easily accomplished had both my hands not been slippery with mineral oil. An assistant would also have been handy, but there were no volunteers, and I didn't want to recruit anyone else—although the crowd had grown.

I pumped in the last of the oil, kinked the tube to prevent oil from dribbling down the trachea on its way out, pulled it out of Horatio's stomach, and told Courtney to release the twitch. Then I gathered up all my oily supplies and returned them to the trunk of my poor Camaro, which should never have been subjected to such disgusting cargo.

The show was over, and the group dispersed. I was left with Courtney and Horatio. "Thank you so much," Courtney said. "What should I do now?"

"Just watch him and make sure he doesn't get worse."

I said a little prayer, and for added measure, crossed my fingers, because colics could be simple, or they might turn ugly at any time.

~

The ringing of the phone jarred me awake at 4:30 am. Stifling a groan, I mumbled into the receiver, "Hello?" Calls at 4:30 am were never a welcome thing. Nobody ever telephoned at that hour to see how I was doing or if I wanted to go to lunch that day.

"Dr. Bennet, it's Courtney. Horatio's trying to roll again."

I said a bad word in my head, immediately asked the good Lord for forgiveness, and asked, "Has he passed any stool?"

"A little, but there was no oil in it."

Drat! "Okay, I'll be out in thirty minutes."

Forgoing my morning shower and other good hygiene, I climbed into my dirty, horsey-smelling coveralls, which lay on the floor from where I had stepped out of them the night before. I had a full schedule of appointments starting at 8:00 am. I tried not to think about it as I drove back to the stable on autopilot.

Despite the early hour, dense, humid air hung heavily over the stable as I exited my Camaro. No welcome breeze stirred the still air, as it had last night. The sun made a feeble attempt at poking through the gray clouds covering the horizon. If and when it succeeded, the day would be a scorcher. Hopefully, I would be out of here before the sun prevailed. As it was, I could already feel sweat beading on my brow, threatening to run into my eyes.

If at all possible, Courtney looked worse than I did. At least that was some consolation.

"I've been up all night with him," she said, as I approached the equine who refused to get better.

To my dismay, the old man and his crony were already up at this unholy hour, ready to pontificate with unsolicited commentary. Several other early birds wandered over to where the action was. Didn't *anyone* sleep past the hour of five o'clock?

I completed another exam on Horatio and, thankfully, found him not much changed for the worse.

"Let's give him another gallon of oil and see if we can move that impaction. If he's not improved in a few hours, I'll need to give him some IV fluids."

Wearily, I fetched the bucket, stomach tube, and pump, which I had not had the energy to clean from the night before. Horatio received another pain injection, made easier by the daylight, and I poured another gallon of mineral oil into the greasy bucket. The stomach tube went down easily with the use of the twitch, and, while still holding onto the twitch, Courtney blew into the open end to assure correct placement. The helpful and inquisitive preteen appeared to be the only one engaged in blissful sleep and unaware of Horatio's ongoing medical malady.

"These new vets don't know much about colic," observed the old man, still chewing on his piece of straw. "Ole' Doc Potter woulda' had him galloping across the field by now."

You do realize I can hear you? Maybe Ole' Doc Potter was deaf as well as old, and therefore, this gentleman assumed all veterinarians were hearing-impaired. My indignation rose as I attempted to attach the greasy end of the stomach tube to the greasy pump. Granted I wasn't Ole' Doc Potter, but I was the only available option at the moment, and I was doing my best at this ungodly hour.

"Yeah, he sure had a way with horses," the crony chimed in.

My greasy hands slipped as I lifted the handle of the pump and attempted to deliver the mineral oil. Just as I pushed down on the handle, the end of the hose flew off the pump, spraying slimy mineral oil down the fronts of the

Ole' Doc Potter fan club. The two men jumped back, eyes wide, mouths agape.

There are few things as miserable as being covered in oil, unless it's being covered in oil in a hot, sandy stable.

"I'm so sorry," I half-heartedly apologized. "My pump is a little loose."

Without another word, the two stomped away and climbed into a rusted, blue pick-up truck. The engine sputtered to life, belching out a cloud of black smoke in its wake as the two disgruntled horsemen drove away. I turned to the stunned crowd. "I didn't mean to do that," I offered, in my own defense.

A middle-aged man in a tan cowboy hat chuckled. Removing his hat, he took a handkerchief from his front pocket, wiped his sweaty brow, and said, "Serves 'em right. Those two old buzzards are always shootin' off their mouths. Besides, Ole' Doc Potter was a quack."

ELLEN FANNON

Chapter 5

On Saturday night, I found myself seated across the table from Jack, the plumber, at McCormick's, a popular local restaurant, sipping my iced tea and trying to think of something to say. Jack had picked me up in his work truck, which read *Hill and Son Plumbing* on the side. I couldn't help but think this relationship was doomed before it ever got off the ground with *Jack* and *Jill* and *Hill*. I fought the urge to giggle—or worse, yet, chant "Jack and Jill went up the hill."

Jack fiddled with his napkin. "So," we both said at the same time.

He grinned. "You first."

"Oh, I was just going to ask how Flash was doing." When my uncooperative brain refuses to throw a hint of small talk to my lips, asking a pet owner about his animal always broke the ice. "He hasn't eaten any more socks recently, I take it."

Jack smiled that lopsided smile, which I was finding more and more endearing, and shook his head. "No, for the most part he has been on his good behavior, 'good behavior' being a relative term for Flash."

"Well, he's almost two," I said. I had reviewed Flash's record before my date with his owner so as not to appear ignorant. "Most Labradors' brain fairies come by the time they're two."

Jack chuckled. "That's good to hear. Flash is a bit of a knuckle-head. He's always into something. But he's a happy soul."

"Most Labs are. That's why they're such great family dogs. Nothing phases them."

Jack's face became somber. "Well, actually, Flash is my first dog—ever. My parents aren't really big on dogs, and especially not in the house. I had to wait until I moved out on my own to get a dog. Then it's been one thing after another with his puppy stages. My parents are constantly reminding me how much trouble he is."

Huge red flag. His parents weren't big on dogs. What kind of people were they? I had long since deduced there was something not quite right with people who weren't "dog people." And if Jack's parents weren't big on dogs, how would they react to their son dating a vet? This relationship was definitely doomed.

"So, you never had any pets growing up?"

Jack shook his head. "Not unless you count the goldfish I won at a carnival. You know that game where you try to toss a ping-pong ball into a goldfish bowl?" His questioning eyes met mine and I nodded. "Well, I managed to land one, much to my mother's chagrin. It didn't last long. One day I came home from school and she told me it had died. I always secretly believed she flushed it."

My heart went out to him. He fell quiet, fiddling with his napkin again, and I took a moment to study him over the edge of my iced tea glass. When I saw clients in a professional capacity, I generally didn't appraise them all that closely, as I was more concerned with appraising their animals. Jack was a nice-looking young man, nothing extraordinary, but he had an honest face and sensitive brown eyes. His dark hair, a little long, curled around the neck of his collar. Of average height and weight, there was nothing physically imposing about him, yet he radiated a shy, sweet strength. Intuitively I knew Jack was dependable.

"So," he started again, "you had to go to school to become a vet?"

The warm, fuzzy feelings I had started to develop for this man evaporated in a cloud of annoyance. What *was* it with people who didn't realize that it took just as long to become a veterinarian as it did to become a physician? Besides, veterinarians had to know the anatomy, physiology, behavior, and idiosyncrasies of several different species, not just one. We literally held lives in our hands. We performed surgery on our patients with the same standard of care a human would receive. We were just paid a lot less for the same procedures. *A lot less.* The medical tests we ran were the same, most of the drugs were the same, and many of the diseases were the same. We had to be proficient in internal medicine, surgery, dentistry, cardiology, neurology, dermatology, pharmacology, radiology, anesthesiology, pediatrics, and geriatrics— and in a variety of species. We had to know what drugs could be given to dogs, but not to cats, and what diseases were specific to rabbits, but not to birds, and what diseases were communicable from animals to people. Plus, our duties extended to more than just private practice. The safety of the meat we ate and the dairy products we consumed depended on veterinarians, not to mention our role in disease surveillance and research in the public health field.

I sat ready to give him a thorough tongue-lashing, along with a much-needed education, when Jack said, "That didn't come out right at all. I mean, of course you had to go to school."

I waited for him to continue, as my temper gauge slowly drifted out of the red danger zone. Maybe he thought veterinarians went to a six-month trade school, or we obtained our license through a correspondence course, rather than having to pass rigorous national and state boards. He looked at his hands again.

"I'm making a mess of this," Jack sighed. He raised his eyes, obviously realizing he had highly offended me, and plowed on, "What I *meant* was you had four years of pre-vet, and then four more years of vet school."

I pressed my lips together and nodded. Where was he going with this?

"And you told me you've been practicing a little over a year."

"Yes, about a year," I replied, tersely.

Jack inhaled an audible breath through his nose and blew it out slowly through his mouth. "I guess what I'm trying to figure out without actually coming out and asking, is how old you are. I mean you look so young, and . . ."

I burst out laughing. "I'm twenty-six, Jack. Almost twenty-seven. Why?"

"Well, I didn't want you to think I was too old for you."

I couldn't help teasing him a little. "So, how old are *you*? Fifty? Sixty?"

Jack's lips quivered into a smile. "Twenty-nine."

"Well, it's a relief to know you're not robbing the cradle. Here I thought you were old enough to be my grandfather."

The blush that rose in Jack's face tugged at my heart. He breathed out a soft laugh. "I'm sorry, Jill, I just seem to be a little intimidated by you. And it's making me nervous so I'm putting my foot in my mouth. I didn't go to college or anything. I learned plumbing from my dad."

I reached across the table and touched his hand. "I may have eight years of college, but I can't fix a clogged toilet. I *can*, however, fix a clogged Labrador who is stopped up with socks. But I don't bite. Too bad I can't say that about some of my patients."

~

Jack called the next night. "I was wondering," he began, in a hesitating manner, "I didn't really have much dinner. Would you like to get some ice-cream?"

"Sure," I agreed. "But I'm on call. If my beeper goes off, I may have to leave to see a patient. Shall I meet you?"

"No, I can pick you up. If you get called in, I'll go with you. If that's okay."

I sat for a moment, stunned. Jack would go with me on an emergency?

"Well, sure, if you want to. But sometimes I get stuck until all hours at the clinic." I had regaled him with several stories of my late-night emergencies the evening before. He had listened with rapt attention, somewhat intrigued, while at the same time horrified. I had probably rattled on way too long, caught up in sharing my world with a captive audience, yet I apparently hadn't scared him away.

"That's fine. I don't mind." He paused. "Besides, I don't like the idea of you being out by yourself late at night."

A delicious warmth spread over me. We'd only had one date, and he felt protective of me? I wasn't used to chivalry. In vet school I had fought hard to pull my own weight in order to prove I could handle the job just as well as a man. Despite the fact more women were entering the field, veterinary medicine was still considered a man's profession at the time I entered school, and there were still those who didn't think women had any business becoming veterinarians. Myra, for example. Displaying any sign of feminine weakness was sure to tank the career of a woman veterinarian in those early days of my work.

"That's very nice of you, Jack. Hopefully I won't get a call."

Of course, I got a call. The moment I took my first bite of rocky road, my blasted pager went off. I groaned and set my spoon down. "Sorry, I need to find a phone." Cell phones would not become readily available for another twenty years.

Jack gestured to a pay phone just outside the ice-cream shop and started to get up to accompany me.

"You stay and eat your ice-cream before it melts. I'll just be a minute."

Jack watched as I made my way outside to the phone. Sometimes I could talk to a client, make the determination the situation could wait until morning, or just give advice. This wasn't one of those times. As soon as I connected with the answering service, they patched me directly through to Mrs. Bellamy, who was so hysterical I had a difficult time understanding her. Mrs. Bellamy, a frail, elderly widow who had recently lost her husband, lived alone with her scruffy little terrier. The dog was all she had.

"That nasty dog next door attacked Muffy," she screeched, between sobs and sharp intakes of breath. "Her whole insides are hanging out."

"Wrap her in a clean towel and bring her straight to the clinic," I said. "And be careful how you handle her. If she's badly injured, she could bite you unintentionally."

"There's blood everywhere! I don't think she's going to make it!" Great choking sounds came from the other end of the phone.

"Mrs. Bellamy, I need you to calm down and do what I'm telling you."

"She had just gone outside to do her nightly potty. She was in her own yard minding her own business."

"Mrs. Bellamy, you need to get her to me *now*. Is there anyone there with you? Someone who can drive you to the clinic?"

The woman babbled something I couldn't make out.

"Give me your address," I said. "I'm coming to pick her up."

Mrs. Bellamy rattled off an address. "Please hurry," she begged, before the line went dead.

I hustled back into the ice-cream shop where Jack had polished off his sundae and had snuck a bite of mine. I caught him in the act. Ordinarily I would have teased him, but I couldn't think of anything but the urgency to get to Mrs. Bellamy's house as quickly as possible.

"Jack, do you know where 415 Sycamore Street is? I have to pick up an injured dog. The owner is too distraught to drive."

"I know my way around most of this town," he replied. "Whose house is it?"

"Mrs. Bellamy. Her dog, Muffy, was attacked by another dog."

"Edith Bellamy? I've been to her place lots of times. She's forever putting things down her garbage disposal she shouldn't. Come on, let's go."

Relief flooded over me as Jack hustled me out to his truck. Being directionally-challenged sometimes made my job doubly hard when I had to find an unfamiliar barn, or made the rare house call. Jack's calming confidence beside me in the dark settled my frazzled nerves, as we sped through the mostly deserted streets. Emergencies were always emotional roller-coasters because I never knew for sure what I was going to encounter. An owner's description of a problem and the reality of the problem were often two very different things.

A short time later, Jack pulled up in Mrs. Bellamy's driveway. The little woman stood in the front doorway hugging her arms around her waist, silhouetted in the light from deeper inside the house. I raced up the dimly lit front porch steps, Jack right behind me.

"She's in here," Mrs. Bellamy said, opening the door to admit me. Her wrinkled face was streaked with dried tears, which started afresh when I stepped into her small living room. Muffy lay on the chintz sofa wrapped in an enormous bright red towel. Her eyes were closed, and I could see her breathing heavily, but I couldn't tell much more from this vantage point. I figured the best course of action was to hurry her back to the clinic where I could do a proper exam.

I placed one hand on Mrs. Bellamy's shoulder. "I'm going to do everything I can for Muffy. Let me take her back to the clinic and I'll call you as soon as I know more." Gently scooping up the injured dog, I stepped past the old woman on my way to the door.

She turned, and noticing Jack, standing in the foyer, her whole face lit up. "Why, you have Jack Hill with you!" Suddenly a wicked smile played with the corners of her mouth. Muffy's predicament momentarily brushed aside, she continued, "Hello, Jack. Are you keeping company with our young lady veterinarian?" Before Jack could respond, she rubbed her hands together in delight. "Oh, you are, aren't you? And I've interrupted your evening. Oh dear."

"That's quite all right, Mrs. Bellamy," Jack assured her.

I got the impression the elderly widow would have loved for us to stay and enlighten her further as to our budding relationship, but then she seemed to remember her little dog. She reached out a gnarled hand and laid it on Jack's arm. "You won't let anything happen to my Muffy, will you, Jack?"

Jack shot me a helpless look.

"We'll do everything we can," I answered for him, indicating with a nod of my head that we needed to go.

She still clung to Jack, smiling up at him, her keen eyes glistening with tears. "Please take good care of my baby, Jack. She's all I've got, now, you know, since my Ned passed."

It would do no good to remind her that *I* was the doctor and *Jack* was the plumber. In her world, the men had always taken care of things.

"We need to go, Mrs. Bellamy," I said, grabbing Jack's other arm and wrestling him away from the old lady, while trying not to drop Muffy.

She followed us onto the porch and stood staring after us as we climbed into the truck and pulled away. Jack seemed a little bewildered by what had just happened, but I didn't feel up to discussing gender inequality at that moment. I didn't like the way Muffy lay so still and I really needed to focus on getting to the clinic so I could evaluate her.

We drove in silence. Finally, able to get a look at Muffy's injuries, I laid her on the treatment table and unwrapped the towel. Then took a deep breath, as my heart plummeted. Mrs. Bellamy had been right. A large hole had been torn in Muffy's abdominal muscles, and her insides, were indeed, hanging out, covered in hair, grass, and dirt. Her muddy gum color indicated shock.

I quickly clipped the hair over her front leg in order to locate a vein and placed an intravenous catheter, the task easily accomplished by virtue of the fact that my patient was pretty much unresponsive. Then, largely forgetting Jack's presence, I hooked Muffy to an IV drip, and zipped around preparing the surgery room. In no time, I had Muffy anesthetized and hooked up to an ECG monitor; I then set about cleaning the contaminated wound. For a good ten minutes, I flushed the abdomen with warm saline, cleaning out as much of the dirt and debris as possible.

Finally, I donned a surgical cap, mask, gown, and gloves, and went to work repairing the damage. Fortunately, most of the bleeding came from the torn muscle, not from vital organs, so the blood loss had not been as extensive as it had appeared at first glance. But there were a couple of punctures through Muffy's intestines. The damaged intestines would either need to be sutured, or if not deemed viable, resected. I methodically pulled out the several feet of small intestines and laid them on the surgery drape for closer inspection.

"Jack, would you mind squirting some saline on these guts to keep them moist?" I asked, suddenly remembering I had a helper. I looked up from the surgical table. "Jack?"

Jack leaned heavily against the wall in the furthest corner of the surgery room, his ashen face and sweat-covered brow an indication of impending blackout.

"Jack!" I cried. "Sit down. Now!"

"I'm fine, really," he slurred, right before he slid down the wall and landed in a heap on the floor.

I abandoned Muffy and flew to Jack's side. "Jack, are you okay?"

His glazed eyes struggled to focus on my face. Fortunately, he hadn't banged his head too hard, as his body had the wall for support. I helped him into a sitting position and went to fetch him a glass of water. *Jack and Jill went up the hill to fetch a pail of water. Jack fell down . . . stop it!* My rattled brain wouldn't let go of the silly nursery rhyme. The crazy scenario of my patient's guts laid out on the surgery table while Jack was laid out on the floor—forcing me to leave my patient to attend to him—caused an involuntary giggle to force its way up my throat.

"Here," I said, thrusting the water into his shaking hand. He took a couple of quick sips and handed the cup back to me.

"So sorry, don't know what happened. Never done that before." His speech still came out slurred, but some color slowly seeped back into his face.

"It's okay, Jack. Lots of people faint when they see surgery for the first time. And this one is particularly gory."

He shook his head. "Maybe I'll just wait in the other room." He fought to get his wobbly legs under him. I steadied his arm and guided him into a chair in the treatment area. He slumped over and placed his head in his heads. "Some help I am."

"Don't worry about it. You just sit here. I'm afraid I may be a while, though. Do you want to go home and lie down?"

"No. I'll be fine. You do what you need to do."

An hour or so later, I finished up with Muffy, and by the time the surgery was over, both her and Jack's color had improved considerably. I debated on taking her home with me for the rest of the night, then decided both she and her owner would probably be better off spending the few remaining hours of the night together. Mrs. Bellamy could return her in the morning.

Jack drove me back to Mrs. Bellamy's house, where the delighted old woman met us on the porch, tears streaming down her cheeks. I started to hand the dog over to the grateful owner, when Mrs. Bellamy threw her arms around Jack's neck. "Oh, thank you, young man. I don't know what Muffy and I would have done without you!"

ELLEN FANNON

Chapter 6

Hector the beagle was stoned. There was no doubt about it. As I shined my penlight into his sluggish, dilated pupils, he didn't even flinch. Hector, usually a ball of endless energy, stood listlessly, wobbling on the exam table. Every few seconds it appeared he was on the verge of falling over before catching himself.

"I just don't know what's happened to him," Mrs. Riley lamented. "He was fine this morning. Do you think it's that Provo virus?"

For some reason, people could never properly say the name of the dreaded Parvovirus, which causes a sudden onset of vomiting and bloody diarrhea. For some other reason, whenever a dog was poisoned, people always jumped to the conclusion it had Parvovirus. And for still *another* unexplainable reason, when a dog truly *did* have Parvovirus, people refused to believe it, insisting it had obviously been poisoned.

"No, Mrs. Riley, Parvovirus doesn't look like this. Hector has gotten into something." The only other possibility besides marijuana was antifreeze, which could cause similar symptoms and more fatal consequences. "Could Hector have gotten into antifreeze, by any chance?"

The prim and proper middle-aged lady shook her head and wrung her hands. "No. He's never out of the yard. He's always supervised. I just can't imagine what he could have gotten into."

I glanced at her teenaged son, who worked hard to make himself invisible in a chair in the corner of the exam room.

"Okay, then. I will need to keep Hector for a little while. Do you think your son could carry him into the treatment area for me?" Not that I wasn't perfectly capable of carrying Hector to the treatment area by myself. I needed to confront the boy alone.

The teenager jumped.

"Of course," Mrs. Riley said. "Dylan, carry Hector for Dr. Bennet."

The boy slowly rose and swooped the beagle under his arm. Without meeting my eyes, he followed me to the back, deposited Hector onto the treatment table, and turned to make his escape.

I deliberately closed the door separating the treatment area from the exam rooms, effectively blocking Dylan's exit. The gangly youth towered over me, but I had the advantage of age and experience, plus the power to intimidate a hapless child trapped in an adult's body.

"Now, then Dylan," I said, as the boy still struggled to avoid eye contact. "Is there anything more you can tell me about what Hector might have gotten into?"

The boy's eyes went wide and he shook his head vigorously, his shaggy brown hair falling over his eyes.

"I need the truth," I stated in an authoritative tone. "Otherwise, I'm going to have to subject Hector to a lot of painful and expensive tests to try to figure out what he got into. And by the time I get results, it may too late to save him."

This was pure nonsense, of course. There is no test that will rule out every known toxicity on the planet. Toxicity testing is very specific, and you have to have a general idea of what you're looking for before you start.

"Is there any way Hector could have gotten into marijuana?"

The blood drained from Dylan's face.

"It's okay, Dylan. You can tell me. I'm not going to report you to the police. Or even to your mother, for that matter. But if you want to help Hector, you need to be honest with me."

"It wasn't mine!" the boy blurted out. "I was just keeping it for a friend."

Of course, you were. And I fell off the turnip truck yesterday. "Thank you for leveling with me, Dylan. That makes my job a lot easier."

"Is he going to die?"

"No. I'm going to give him some fluids to help move the drug out of his system and keep him quiet."

The boy's shoulders relaxed. "Good. I didn't mean to hurt Hector, honest."

"I know that, Dylan, but dogs are very curious. They get into a lot of things that can hurt them. You have to be very careful to keep harmful things out of their reach."

"I won't do it again, I swear."

"I hope not, Dylan. Marijuana isn't good for you, either."

His faced flushed. "I told you—"

"Oh, that's right, I forgot. Well, tell your friend marijuana's not good for him and because you have a dog, you can't keep his stash at your house again." I moved so Dylan could access the exit door.

"Yeah, sure, I'll do that," he promised, as he quickly fled.

Fortunately, Hector's vital signs were stable, so I didn't have to worry about hypothermia or a dangerously slow heartrate. Still, I would have to monitor those parameters throughout the day to be sure they didn't change. I was reluctant to try to induce vomiting, as Hector was a little too stoned and I didn't want him to aspirate stomach contents into his lungs. Besides, most of what he had ingested had most likely already been absorbed. I started an IV drip and settled Hector into a dark, quiet cage.

By late afternoon, I heard Hector's typical beagle baying coming from the kennel. Apparently put out at being cooped up in a cage, he wanted everyone in the vicinity to know of his displeasure. I entered the kennel, relieved to see the goofy beagle, still a bit wobbly, but furiously barking and wagging his tail.

"Well, then, Hector," I said, "have you slept off the effects of your adventure into the dark side of illicit substances?" He gave my face a thorough licking when I knelt down to rub his ears. I removed his IV catheter and called Mrs. Riley to come pick him up.

The next morning, Mrs. Riley called to update me on Hector's condition. "He's back to his old self," she reported, happily. "I don't know what you did, but when he got home, he ate like there was no tomorrow!"

I laughed. "I'm glad." I didn't mention she might want to have a talk with Dylan.

A few weeks went by, then I happened to see Hector in the waiting room with his obviously distressed teenaged owner.

"Dylan! What's wrong? Hector didn't get into—"

"No!" the young man assured me. "No, I learned my lesson after what happened last time. I don't have any of that stuff around the house. But Hector got out of the yard a little while ago and I found him in the neighbor's garage licking antifreeze off the floor."

I glanced quickly at Hector, who seemed unbothered by the whole situation. He wagged his tail and raised his lip, giving me a silly doggy grin.

"I remember you asking us about antifreeze before and figured I should bring him in right away."

"I'm glad you did. Antifreeze is very toxic and without immediate treatment is often fatal. Where's your mom?"

"She's at work. I called her and she told me to bring Hector in."

"Well, you did the right thing. Bring him back to the treatment area."

The worried teen reached down and picked up the dog, cradling him against his chest. When he got to the treatment table, he stopped, and choked out, "Will Hector be okay?"

"I think so, Dylan. Luckily, you caught him in the act. A lot of times we don't know a dog has ingested antifreeze until the damage is already done and it's too late."

Dylan's Adam's apple bobbed in his throat.

Of course, Myra was nowhere to be found, so I had no choice but to enlist the help of the young owner, as I so frequently had to do in those days. Nowadays, allowing an owner to hold a pet during examinations and treatments can result in nasty lawsuits if an owner gets injured. But back then, I did what I had to do to get the job done, and most owners were more than willing to help.

"The first thing we need to do is make him vomit. If there is any antifreeze left in his stomach, this will keep him from absorbing it into his body." I spoke as I prepared a syringe of apomorphine, a powerful emetic generally guaranteed to cause a dog to toss his cookies within seconds.

I quickly felt for Hector's cephalic vein and injected the drug directly into his bloodstream. Hector stood stoically for a brief second, then he shot me a look of betrayal as his stomach began to heave. How dare I make him feel so lousy? Wasn't I his friend?

"Put him down, *now*," I instructed Dylan.

Dylan set his pet on the floor just as Hector let loose with a massive retch, bringing forth a gargantuan pile of partially digested kibble, white foam, and a few various unidentifiable particles. He hung his head in misery, clearly bewildered by what had just overtaken him. Hector barely caught his breath when the second wave of nausea assaulted him. This time the stomach contents he produced weren't quite as impressive. He retched mightily with dry heaves for another agonizing half a minute.

"I think he's done," I told Dylan. "You can put him back on the table."

I let Hector's stomach settle for a few minutes while I cleaned up the mess and tried to ascertain if there was any antifreeze in the vomitus. But it was hard to tell.

"Okay, now what we need to do is give him some activated charcoal to try to keep him from absorbing any antifreeze that might have already emptied from his stomach."

Activated charcoal is a nasty, thick, black substance that animals hate having shoved down their throats. But it is a standard treatment in many poisonings, as not only does it absorb a number of toxins, but also speeds up their passage through the gastrointestinal tract. I just needed to be sure Hector's nausea was past so it didn't all come back up. There was nothing worse than seeing that black material a second time, especially if vomited onto something that can't be washed.

I filled several large syringes with the charcoal and draped a towel around Hector's neck. There was no way to administer this stuff without making a colossal black mess that stained everything and everyone associated with the process. In reality, the towel would likely do minimal damage control.

"Okay, hold his head still," I told Dylan.

The teen did as he was told, and I inserted the tip of the syringe in the large fold of cheek skin between Hector's upper and lower teeth, depositing a few cc's of the murky liquid. Hector balked and flung his head, spewing the tarry substance back in my face. The rest dripped from the corners of Hector's lips, staining the beautiful white areas of his face an ugly black, as it made its way down the front of the towel and onto the treatment table.

"You need to hold him tighter," I said, wiping my eyes on my lab coat sleeve. That hadn't been the smartest thing to do, I realized, belatedly. My pristine white lab coat now had permanent black smudges on the sleeve.

I excused myself and stepped into the surgery suite, returning with two gowns, caps, and masks. I donned one set for myself and handed the other to Dylan.

"Sorry, old boy, but you're going to have to take this," I told Hector, as I held his head firmly and injected another several cc's of charcoal. Hector held the slurry in his mouth for a moment, then reluctantly swallowed. "There's a good boy," I cooed to him, as I syringed more and more of the nasty concoction down his throat. With a maligned sigh of resignation, Hector submitted, and the deed was accomplished.

I removed the towel from Hector's neck, wet it, and tried ineffectively to clean some of the charcoal from his face. I had forgotten about cleaning my own.

"What are you doing?" Myra shrieked.

I looked up to see her hovering over me.

"Look at this *mess!*" She put her hands on her hips and flattened her lips.

Dylan looked as if he had been caught with marijuana again.

"I'm trying to save this dog from antifreeze poisoning," I snapped.

Myra, a longstanding thorn in my flesh, huffed and stomped off.

"Wait!" I called after her. "I need some vodka!"

Dylan gaped at me as if I had lost my mind. I could almost see the wheels turning in his impressionable young mind. *Yes, this is stressful, but shouldn't you wait until after office hours to imbibe?*

I couldn't help laughing. "This is going to sound crazy, but we use vodka to treat antifreeze poisoning."

"You're kidding, right?" The look of sheer incredulity on his face was priceless.

"No, it's true. You see the vodka combines with an enzyme, called alcohol dehydrogenase, which converts the antifreeze into its toxic metabolite. If the enzyme is all tied up with the vodka, the antifreeze will be excreted unchanged and won't harm the animal."

Dylan's mouth hung open. "You're going to get Hector *drunk?*"

I nodded. "I know it sounds strange—"

"So, Hector can get drunk, but he can't get stoned."

I burst out laughing. "Yes, that's basically true. But only for medicinal purposes." I excused myself and stuck my head into the kennel area. "Tess?"

There was no response. Myra reappeared in the treatment area. "She's at lunch. What do you want?"

"I need someone to go to the liquor store and pick up a bottle of vodka."

"Fine. How much do you need?"

By her apparent willingness to help, it became clear to me that the great Dr. Spangle had, in fact, resorted to this treatment at some time in the past. Otherwise, I would have had to make the trek to the store myself. I couldn't send Dylan because he was underage, and I didn't want to waste precious time running this errand, as I needed to get an IV placed in Hector for his induced bender. Not to mention the other patients waiting to be seen.

"Thank you, Myra," I said, relieved. "I think a fifth should suffice." It occurred to me, not for the first time, that I shouldn't have to cajole and pander to Myra in order for her to do her job, which was that of a veterinary *assistant*.

A short time later, Hector had a nice buzz on, as he rested, once again, in a dark kennel. I couldn't help wondering what, if anything, was going through his confused little doggy brain as to the strange things that happened to him whenever he came to the clinic. Or was he too inebriated to care? One thing was for sure. He was going to have one heck of a hangover, and the hair of the dog was not going to help him.

ELLEN FANNON

Chapter 7

One of the aspects I love most about my job is the diversity of patients I get to see. On any given day I may see half a dozen or more different species, all of which have their own unique anatomy and physiology, health issues, nutritional and husbandry requirements, and temperaments. Even within the same species there are tremendous variations. For example, it is rare to see bloat and stomach torsion in small breed dogs, whereas dislocating patellas are quite common. Squashed-faced dogs, such as Pekingese, pugs, and bulldogs have an exclusive set of respiratory issues known as "brachycephalic syndrome" simply based on their shortened facial anatomy. Manx (tail-less) cats are more prone to congenital spinal disorders, whereas Himalayan and Persian cats suffer more than their fair share of allergies.

Birds present even more complex variations. While one doesn't necessarily expect to see the same problems in chickens versus cockatoos, even within the parrot species one needs to be aware of differences; feather picking in an African Gray parrot is often associated with behavioral issues, whereas in a parakeet, plucking is almost always secondary to an underlying disease process.

While physicians only treat one species, veterinarians are provided daily with an unlimited variety of creatures, which can easily branch out into more exotic species, such as marine mammals, reptiles, and zoo animals.

One lesson I learned at Spangle Animal Clinic was that there was no species of animal we wouldn't tackle. It didn't matter whether or not we had any expertise with that species. I suppose this is one reason why today, when I hear that an emergency clinic refused to treat my patients because "they don't treat ferrets, or birds, or guinea pigs, or whatever," I become angry. In an emergency, a veterinarian should have enough knowledge to provide basic care to any species. And, of course, today, one can find enough information on the internet to at least try. After all, if a patient is bleeding or having difficulty breathing, it really doesn't matter whether it is a bird, a goat, or a cat. One can always do the basics.

But we didn't have the advantage of the internet back when I started out in practice, nor did we have specialists at our fingertips, so I learned a lot by "seat of the pants" and "trial and error." At least I tried. Still, when Dr. Spangle sent me out to see Mrs. Cole's sick monkey, I harbored a healthy degree of apprehension. Suffice it to say, I had had exactly zero hours of primate medicine in veterinary school and felt quite outside my comfort zone in providing medical care for such creatures. My trepidation increased exponentially when I arrived at the Cole home and Mrs. Cole informed me that Chico, her spider monkey, was not tame, and had, in fact, put her in the hospital from bite wounds requiring multiple stitches. As if that weren't alarming enough, a little warning bell sounded in my brain that primates carried a number of deadly diseases that could be transmitted to humans, which is why I didn't especially have any desire to treat this particular species.

My first inclination was to say, "Sorry, I don't know anything about primate medicine, and more importantly, I don't know the proper way to safely restrain a monkey, and most importantly, I don't want to end up in the hospital needing multiple stitches." But that simply wasn't an option back then. If Dr. Spangle ordered me to see this monkey, then by golly, I had no choice. I had to fake it and hope for the best.

Mrs. Cole met me in the big circular driveway that ran in front of her palatial home. A striking woman in her late forties, she ushered me directly through a gate leading to a large, lush, fenced-in back yard. I quashed down a slight disappointment at not being able to set foot in the mansion, but quickly reminded myself of my mission.

Under different circumstances, I might have enjoyed the surroundings. Off to the side of her screened in back patio, sat a deeply-sunken fishpond filled with vibrantly colored orange and white koi. The pristine water circulated through a filter that hummed in a mesmerizing melody, as bubbles periodically rose and burst on the surface. Across the vast expanse of perfectly manicured lawn (a rarity in our part of Florida) beautifully maintained flower beds displayed an astounding assortment of vivid colors. An eight-foot privacy fence separated the Cole's expansive property from the neighbors, whose back yard (from the small area I could see) appeared every bit as beautifully landscaped as my client's. Several trees, whose species I couldn't identify, provided ample, but not excessive, amounts of shade, and I noticed a hot tub tucked away under a massive magnolia tree to the right of the patio. I spied several citrus trees blossoming in colorful flowers, and wondered if the Coles harvested fresh oranges, lemons, or grapefruit from their own back yard.

In contrast, my back yard consisted mainly of weeds and sand, and the dissimilarity prickled at my awareness, while the ugly seed of "yard envy" planted itself into my sub-conscience. *Lord, help me not to covet.* But how peaceful it must be to come out here on a warm evening and enjoy a drink on the patio or in the hot tub while overlooking this serene view. Had it not been for Chico, I could have happily plopped down and spent a care-free, leisurely hour conversing with Mrs. Cole.

But although the exquisite back yard seeped into the periphery of my awareness, its beautiful tranquility was marred by both Mrs. Cole's worried monologue over Chico, as well as the unworldly chatter coming from the enclosure of my patient, himself. I tried valiantly to listen to the complaints, hoping to gather some clues as to a direction in which to proceed, but my own anxiety occupied too large an area in my overloaded mind.

". . . so we don't really know how old he is," I was aware of Mrs. Cole speaking, but had to force myself to back up and hit "replay."

"I'm sorry, I didn't quite catch what you said."

Mrs. Cole stopped in her advance toward the monkey enclosure, seeming to realize she walked ahead of me as she talked and perhaps I had difficulty hearing.

"So sorry, I'm rambling." She paused, took a deep breath, and started over. "We acquired Chico from one of those horrible traveling circuses. His accommodations were appalling, and I told Mr. Cole to see if the owner would sell him to us." She huffed out a brittle laugh. "They were only too happy to let us have him for the price we paid."

"And how long ago was that?"

"That was twenty years ago, and from my understanding, spider monkeys can live up to thirty years. The people we got him from didn't know his age, but he is probably old."

"And you haven't ever been able to handle him?"

The edges of her lips curled into a sad smile that didn't quite reach her eyes. "We tried. When we first got him, my husband and I spent hours trying to make friends with Chico. But he would have none of it." She shook her head. "He must have been so traumatized." She started walking slowly toward the enclosure again, this time making sure to stay by my side. "The most we were ever able to do was to get him to take treats from our hands."

"What happened that caused him to bite you?" I had to know, since I would most likely need to handle him in order to do an examination.

She waved a dismissive hand. "Oh, that was my own fault. I was giving him a treat, and just as he reached out to take it, I held on, rather than let go, in an attempt to try to get closer to him. Then I reached up to try to pet him and he just went crazy." Mrs. Cole showed me her left hand and wrist, which still bore ugly scars. "After that, we just decided to let him be content and stopped trying to force him to accept us."

We had reached the cage where I got my first look at my patient. My initial impression was that Chico was much larger than I had anticipated, probably a good fifteen pounds, and at least two feet tall. He grasped a low-hanging branch with his long prehensile tail and swung directly in front of us, where he gripped the wire of his enclosure with two black hands and feet. His wary black eyes stared at me with an expression of both curiosity and apprehension. I gathered Chico must not get many visitors. At least, from this distance, I could easily get a good visual. His dark brown haircoat appeared unkempt, but his eyes and nose were clear. His breathing looked normal. It was hard to assess his muscle mass, but his easy movements in swinging from the branch and planting himself against the front of the cage ruled out neurological dysfunction or severe muscular weakness.

"What exactly is he doing that has you concerned?" I asked.

Mrs. Cole turned worried eyes to her pet. "He has barely eaten anything for several days. And he has been listless. I know he looks alert right now, but that's just because you're someone new. Do you have any idea what might be wrong him?"

Since I knew exactly nothing about monkey diseases, I had to rely on what I *did* know. If Chico were a dog, cat, horse, bird, pig, or any other species with which I was more familiar, I would start at the beginning. It always came down to one thing. The first order of business would be to get my hands on him and do a physical examination. I sighed.

"Unfortunately, Mrs. Cole, in order to do a proper exam and work up on Chico, I'm going to need to sedate him." Even as the words left my mouth, I wondered how the heck I was going to manage *that*. I didn't have any tranquilizer guns or darts like other veterinarians who worked on dangerous, uncooperative animals.

"Oh dear, isn't that risky?"

I couldn't lie. "There is always risk in sedating a living creature, whether it be animal or human. Plus, since I don't know for sure what's going on with him, sedation could affect his heart, his liver, or his kidneys, and possibly cause other complications. But I don't think we have a choice."

Mrs. Cole chewed on her lip for a moment, then slowly nodded. "All right. We need to find out what's wrong with him. We've been so fortunate since we've had Chico in that he's always been so healthy."

My mind churned. First, I would have to make an educated guess as to Chico's weight and how much injectable sedative to use. Too little and I would have a loopy patient, but one I still couldn't examine. Too much sedation and I might not have a patient at all. Second, how was I going to get the injection into him?

"I'm going to go back to my car and get my bag. If you could get some of his favorite treats to distract him, I'll try to inject him through the wire of his cage."

I prayed as I unhurriedly returned to the car. I tended to pray a lot when I was in tough situations and reminded myself to talk to the good Lord on other occasions besides those in which I needed divine intervention. Returning to

Chico's cage, I opened my bag and removed a three-cc syringe and bottle of ketamine. After rough calculations, I drew up ½ cc and prayed again.

Mrs. Cole emerged from the patio bearing a smorgasbord of delicious-looking fresh fruits in a large plastic bowl.

"Okay, this is what we're going to do," I said. "You try to distract him and keep his head turned toward you and I will try to sneak in behind him and give him the shot."

She nodded, her head bobbing just a little too vigorously with nerves. Her Adam's apple moved up and down in her throat as she repeatedly swallowed, clearly as nervous as I was. Nevertheless, she put on a brave, cheerful face and, holding a large ripe strawberry between her thumb and forefinger, approached the enclosure and wheedled, "Chico, look! Mama's got a nice strawberry for you. Do you want a nice strawberry? Come, on, that's a good boy."

The monkey's interest was immediately piqued, and he came down from a leafy branch where he had been perching to investigate.

Keep going, keep going, I mentally urged him. Ever so slowly, he crept to where Mrs. Cole dangled the bait, seemingly to have forgotten about me standing off to the side. As unobtrusively as possible, I edged closer to Chico's turned back, and just when he reached out to grab the treat, I jabbed him in the buttocks. But before I could drive the contents of the syringe home, the monkey whirled around, a look of pure disbelief on his face. For a brief second, the monkey stared at the syringe, still impaled in his behind. Then with one swift motion, he pulled it out and threw it back at me. The projectile miraculously sailed effortlessly through the wire fencing and landed at my feet, landing needle down in the dirt, just barely missing the toe of my shoe. I jumped back at the last second.

Bending to pick up the syringe, I grumbled, "Well, that didn't go very well, did it?"

"Oh dear. Now what?"

Now what, indeed? Nothing in my career to this point had prepared me for this event. I thought quickly. "Do you think we might be able to throw a blanket over him and subdue him?"

Mrs. Cole wrung her hands. "I don't know. Maybe my husband can help."

She left to summon the up-to-this-point conspicuously absent Mr. Cole. A few moments later, a small, wiry, much older man came out of the house carrying a thick comforter. The fleeting thought ran through my mind that Mrs. Cole was, perhaps, a "trophy wife." I immediately dismissed the intruding thought as none of my business. Besides, she was a compassionate and caring lady.

"Don't know how you're going to manage to catch him in this," he said.

Well, that's helpful. "Perhaps if you and Mrs. Cole can go into the enclosure with Chico and distract him, I can capture him in the blanket."

Mr. Cole snuffed. "*I'm* not going in the cage with him. You should see what he did to my wife a few years ago."

"Never mind, Edward, we'll manage without you," his wife spat out.

"Now Sylvia . . ." He stopped, took one look at his wife's stony expression and said, "Oh, all right. What do you want me to do?" I knew a defeated man when I saw one.

Our plan, such as it was, finally worked, after much chasing, cajoling, and sweating. The Coles pursued the monkey all around the large cage, dodging hanging branches, toys, and shrubbery. In the end, I think the little fellow wore out. I managed to snag him as he clung to the side of the enclosure, wrapping him as thoroughly as I could, praying my hands were nowhere in the vicinity of his vicious, razor-sharp teeth. He fought hard and with incredible strength for an animal his size, especially one who was supposedly sick. Just as I dug into my pocket to retrieve the syringe, a hairy little arm thrust itself out of the blanket-wrapped straitjacket. I took full advantage of the exposed body part and injected it with lightning speed. Then I left the wrapped monkey, frantically trying to free himself, and retreated to safety outside the cage.

Now it was a waiting game. As the Coles and I looked on, our chests heaving from the exertion, Chico threw off the blanket, glared at us, and climbed up into the highest branch he could find. This was not ideal, as I didn't want him to become woozy and fall when the sedative began to kick in. After a few moments, it became apparent Chico did not want that for himself, either, as he began to make his unsteady way down to the dirt floor. It can be heart-wrenching to watch an animal struggle when it doesn't understand why its body is suddenly behaving so oddly, and all it wants to do is get back to normal. Chico fought the effects of the ketamine for several long, tense minutes while silent tears streamed down Mrs. Cole's cheeks. Mr. Cole, for his part, apparently thought his job was finished and returned to the house.

At last, the little monkey gave up and lay in a heap on the ground, breathing deeply. I waited a few more minutes to be sure he was fully under before venturing back into the enclosure. Some of the worst injuries veterinarians receive are from partially sedated animals who aren't conscious enough to know what they're doing. At the same time, I monitored his respirations from afar, grateful that they were strong and regular. Grabbing my bag, I made my way to Chico's side, and cautiously touched him. Relief flooded through my tense body when he continued to lay limp and unmoving.

Finally, I was able to do my exam. I checked his eyes, ears, mouth, and gum color, listened to his heart, and palpated his abdomen. He seemed rather thin, once I had my hands on him, but then again, I didn't have anything to compare to what his weight had previously been. I didn't find anything out of the ordinary. The whole time I examined him, I had the creepy sensation I was working on a little hairy person, so human-like were some of his features, like his hands and his ears.

Finding nothing on his physical, the next step involved lab work. I easily found his cubital vein in the crook of his elbow and filled several tubes with blood. I also procured a urine sample by aspirating it directly from Chico's bladder with a syringe. Then, after giving him fluids under the skin to help dissipate the anesthesia, and not knowing what else to do, I wrapped Chico in the blanket, and left him to sleep off the sedation.

"I'll send this blood to the lab," I told Mrs. Cole. "It may take a few days, but I'll let you know as soon as I get the results."

"Thank you, Dr. Bennet," she replied. "Will he be okay here, do you think?"

"Yes, he'll start to come around in a few hours." I packed up my lab samples and, relieved I had finally gotten what I needed without ending up in the hospital, I took my leave.

A few days later, my fears were confirmed when the blood results showed Chico was in kidney failure. I had suspected as much after checking his urine sample and finding that Chico was not concentrating his urine. Unfortunately, when the kidneys wear out and fail to do their job of filtering waste products from the blood, there is little that can be done. If Chico had been a human, he would have been started on dialysis and perhaps put on a list for a kidney donor. But not only was this not an option for veterinary patients back then, Chico's temperament would have made it impossible. Sometimes we can prolong the lives of our terminal kidney failure patients by having owners give them fluids under the skin at home and putting them on a low-protein kidney-friendly diet that reduced the workload of the kidney. This worked fairly well in dogs and cats, but again, this was not an option for Chico.

With heavy heart, I called Mrs. Cole and broke the news. She informed me that in the few days since I had seen Chico, he had gone steadily downhill. He now refused to eat his favorite treats, and on several occasions, she had observed him vomiting. He didn't even try to climb and play, but lay listlessly curled up in one corner of his cage.

"So, there's nothing that can be done for him?" she asked, and I could hear the tears in her voice.

"I'm afraid not. The kindest thing to do at this point is to put him to sleep so he doesn't suffer."

I could sense her mental struggle as she fought for composure. Putting a beloved pet to sleep is always a heart-wrenching decision, but in the end, it becomes the last act of love we can give a suffering pet with no hope.

"I suppose it would be wrong to just let him die naturally," she said, a hint of a question reflected toward the end of her statement.

I have heard this question many times over the years. Everyone wants their sick pet to just die a quiet death at home, but in reality, few animals go peacefully into the light. Letting a terminally ill pet linger for days waiting for the inevitable does nobody any good, least of all the suffering animal.

"Chico will just continue to get sicker," I told her. "And he's suffering. He has no quality of life."

She sniffled loudly into the phone. "Then I guess we'd better get it over with. Can you come out today?"

"Yes," I said. "I'll be out this evening after the clinic closes."

As I drove out to the Cole's house for the second time that week, I dreaded the upcoming ordeal. I knew we were doing the right thing, but losing her pet after twenty years was bound to leave an aching hole in Mrs. Cole's heart. Plus, I fretted over having to capture the little monkey again. He would be much more on guard this time and chasing down a sick animal in order to euthanize it was doubly unpleasant.

I needn't have worried, however, because as Mrs. Cole led me through her beautifully manicured back yard toward Chico's enclosure, I saw, with horror, just how much he had deteriorated. The poor creature lay lifeless in a corner of his cage, and barely looked up to acknowledge my arrival.

"He won't feel anything, will he?" pleaded Mrs. Cole, tears spilling down her cheeks. Mr. Cole suddenly materialized by her side, and blew his nose loudly into a large white handkerchief.

"No," I said. "I'll give him a sedative again, and when he is asleep, I'll administer the euthanasia injection.

I drew up the ketamine and the three of us entered the cage. But this time, Chico just lay staring listlessly at us, making no attempt to escape. Still, I had to be cautious. The absolute worst-case scenario is when a pet who is to be euthanized bites someone; then, by law, the animal has to be quarantined for ten days, dragging out the dreaded ordeal, or the head has to be cut off and submitted for rabies testing. Neither of those situations is conducive to making the ordeal of euthanasia any easier on already stressed and grieving owners dealing with the most gut-twisting decision in their lives.

The Coles converged in front of Chico, murmuring tenderly to him. He raised his head and regarded them briefly before letting it flop back against his chest. As before, I snuck up quietly behind him, a large blanket slung over my arm. When I threw the blanket over him, he barely moved. I quickly administered the injection, then backed off to wait, while the Coles continued to talk soothingly to him.

It didn't take long for the sedation to kick in this time, as Chico was already so sick. When I was sure he was adequately sedated, I readied my euthanasia syringe and crept back toward the inert little body.

Mrs. Cole looked up at me through tearful eyes. "Could we have a few minutes with him first? I'd really like to hold him, if possible."

"Of course," I said. "Take as long as you need."

Mrs. Cole sat cross-legged on the dirt floor of the pen, no doubt ruining her designer pants, and pulled the limp little monkey onto her lap. She cradled his hairless head against her chest and stroked his dark fur. "This is the first time I've ever been able to hold him and pet him."

Mr. Cole stretched out a hand to caress the sleeping animal. I don't know how long we sat there. When owners are saying their last goodbyes to a beloved pet, time is immaterial. I never wanted people to feel rushed in these moments, which is why I often scheduled home euthanasia for after work. All I know is that while we sat there, the sun slowly made its descent below the horizon, illuminating the graying, twilight sky in soft pastels against the growing darkness. Still, we sat in unhurried silence.

Finally, with the last vestige of daylight, Mr. Cole spoke. "Sylvia, we need to let Dr. Bennet finish up and go home."

As if she suddenly remembered I was still there, Mrs. Cole's head shot up. "Oh, of course. I'm so sorry. You must be tired after a long day."

I was, but I would never admit that to the bereaved woman. "I'm fine, Mrs. Cole. There is no hurry. You just let me know when you're ready."

"We're ready," Mr. Cole said, softly, starting to lift Chico from his wife's arms.

I held up my hand to stop him. "No, that's okay, you can hold him. I'll work around you."

"Thank you," breathed Mrs. Cole, and she cradled the little monkey even tighter against her body.

I liberated Chico's left arm from her embrace, located the antecubital vein from which I had drawn blood a few days before, and, again, the eerie sensation of working on a small human sent shivers down my spine. Fortunately, I hit the vein on the first try, which, considering the blackness that had enveloped us over the last several minutes, was a triumphal feat. It took less than fifteen seconds for Chico's respirations and heartbeat to stop. Taking out my stethoscope, I listened to several areas on the monkey's chest before pronouncing him gone. Mrs. Cole wailed and rocked the little monkey's body as if he were a baby.

I turned to Mr. Cole, who was only barely holding himself together. "Do you want me to take care of Chico's body for you?"

He shook his head. "We have a wooden box we're going to put him in, and we're burying him right here, next to his pen."

City ordinances prohibited the burial of pets on private property, but seeing as how I wasn't a law-enforcement officer, I always chose to keep my mouth shut in these situations, unless asked. I squeezed Mr. Cole's shoulder, then reached down and wrapped Mrs. Cole in a hug, Chico's body mashed between us.

"He was one blessed little fellow to have found you," I told them.

"We're the blessed ones," Mrs. Cole choked out. "I don't know what we'll do without him."

"I'll walk you out," Mr. Cole offered.

"No, that's okay. You stay here and say your final good-byes. I'm sorry I couldn't do anything more for him."

"You gave him a peaceful end. We appreciate that."

As I walked back to my car, I reflected once again on the vast diversity of patients I had the privilege of treating. Although Chico is not the most unique creature I have ever treated over the years, he is certainly one of the more memorable. And, I'm relieved to say, Chico was my first and last primate patient.

Chapter 8

"I just have to vaccinate some birds, then we can go," I told Jack, who had called to see if I wanted to spend a few hours at the beach.

"You vaccinate birds?" Jack's voice conveyed his surprise.

"Not individual pet birds. This is an aviary I recently started working with."

"I'll go with you," he volunteered.

I loved that about Jack. He was always game to accompany me on calls, and after his indoctrination as my assistant with Mrs. Bellamy's dog, Muffy, he didn't do a bad job at restraining animals for examination and treatment. He showed promise as a veterinary assistant. Maybe he could leave Hill and Son Plumbing and come work for me! Then I wouldn't have to fret over getting the technical help I needed from the reluctant Myra. Wouldn't his family love that!

"Okay, I'll be ready when you get here."

Jack pulled up to my house a few minutes later and took the small cooler containing the vaccines from my hand. I held a folded sheet over my arm.

"What's that for?" he asked.

"For catching the birds."

"Why a sheet?"

"Because macaws don't have feathers on their faces and they bruise easily with restraint. I like to catch them with something smooth and soft, like a sheet, rather than something more abrasive like a towel."

"Grab another sheet for me and I'll help you."

I laughed. "Jack, these are macaws. They can bite off a finger. You have to know what you're doing when you handle them."

He clearly didn't believe me. "You can show me what to do."

I figured it would be best to let him see for himself. We took off down highway 40 which led out of town and into the country. The change in the landscape never failed to thrill me as we left the buildings and parking lots of civilization behind us and ventured into a vast panorama of nothing but grassy fields and farmland. Jack's truck didn't have air conditioning, and the hot breeze blowing through the open windows carried the sweet aroma of freshly cut hay. I breathed in deeply and let out a contented sigh. Where else in the world could I live where I had the urban conveniences of a small town within a few miles from rural countryside, and then within another few miles in the opposite direction, the powdery white sand beaches and azure waters of the Gulf of Mexico? Feeling blessed, I thanked God, yet again, for bringing me to this beautiful part of the country.

"Turn at that dirt road up ahead," I told Jack.

He complied. There had been no rain for several days and the tires of the truck stirred up the dry dirt into a dusty cloud as we bounced along the uneven road. I coughed and cranked my window up part-way. We continued down a desolate country lane, lined on either side by huge pine trees intermixed with live oaks.

"How much farther?" Jack said.

"You'll know when we're close."

He looked at me quizzically, but drove on, until we came to a thick overgrowth of trees forming a dense canopy, blocking out the sunlight. As we emerged back into the sunlight, the raucous sound of squawking macaws drifted into the open windows of the truck, becoming louder and louder until we stopped in a clearing. To the right, about fifty yards away, sat a massive aviary, in which several macaws announced our presence in a cacophonous greeting.

I have always loved macaws. Of all the birds in God's creation, I found macaws, the giants of the parrot world, one of the more fascinating species. Arrayed in vivid colors, ranging from blue and gold, scarlet and yellow, crimson and green, various hybrids, and up to the largest hyacinths, with their dark blue plumage and bare yellow eye rings, macaws captivated me with their versatile beauty and strength. But as striking creatures as they were, one did not undertake interaction with them lightly.

The rowdy reception signaled our arrival to the owner of the aviary, Ray Boone, who came out of his Silverstream motor home and walked toward us. Retired and relatively new to the area, Ray had acquired a few acres of land with the intention of pursuing his dream—breeding parrots, and he had started out in a big way, with ten pairs of the massive birds. Although not physically imposing, Ray exuded strength and confidence.

"Doc," he greeted, extending his hand. "Thank you for comin'." He smiled, and his eyes disappeared into slits in his darkly tanned face. "I appreciate you makin' the trip all the way out here."

I squeezed his hand, briefly, and replied, "I'm happy to do so. You know how much I love your birds."

Before I could introduce Jack, Ray turned to him and held out his hand. "Ray Boone. Welcome."

"Jack Hill, Jill's boyfriend. I came to help with the birds."

I shot Jack a dubious look. Then it hit me. Had he said *boyfriend?* Or had I heard wrong? No, no, I had heard correctly. He had, most definitely said *boyfriend.* Up until this point, though we had been spending quite a bit of time together, our relationship had been largely undefined. A little tingle of excitement ran down my spine and I felt a smile light up my face. But I couldn't bask in this moment for too long. I had work to do. Picking up the cooler, I said, "Shall we get started?"

Ray led the way to the aviary, where a multitude of macaws eyed us with suspicion. As breeding pairs, the birds were not tame and immediately took off flapping in all directions as we entered the enclosure. Large, wooden nest boxes hung from the upper reaches of the wired compound, just waiting for pairs to lay eggs and raise young.

I set down the cooler, slid open the lid, and removed the first filled syringe. "Do you have the records ready so we can identify who we've done?" I asked Ray.

"Yep, right here." He extracted a small spiral notebook from his back pocket and flipped it open. "Okay, ready when you are."

I reached for the sheet and slowly approached the first bird, who clung to the wire at my waist level. I quickly threw the sheet over it and, in one swift movement, grabbed its head with my left hand positioned just behind its massive beak, wrapping the rest of the body loosely in the sheet with my right hand. Cradling the bird against my chest, I fished the syringe out of my pocket, administered the vaccine, and read the number off the leg band for Ray to record. Then I let the bird go. It immediately flew up to one of the nest boxes and glared down at me.

"It'll be a little harder now that the others have caught on to what's happening," I said, as I stalked my next victim, a gorgeous blue and gold who had just landed on the dirt floor. Although I had to chase it a few steps, I cornered it against the side of the aviary before capturing it and repeating the process.

The other birds scattered. Unexpectedly, I noticed out of the corner of my eye, Jack had picked up a blanket that had been left in the enclosure and was attempting to move in on another bird. He didn't stand a chance. His slight hesitation allowed the bird to easily escape, where it flew to the upper corner of the aviary, a difficult place to access.

"Jack, just let me do it, okay?" I suggested, as diplomatically as possible.

"No, I've got it. Really," he assured me, as he pursued a scarlet macaw close to the feeding station. That bird, too, easily eluded him, and he set his sights on a third macaw.

Looking up, I noticed a green-winged macaw on a long, rope perch above Jack's head running back and forth in a frenzy, and screeching, *"Stop it! Stop it!"*

I burst out laughing. "Did that bird just say, 'Stop it?'"

Ray nodded. "Yep, some of these guys have quite a vocabulary."

Usually, my patients don't talk to me. Parrots, however, are often good talkers, and I have heard a lot of funny things from them. People say birds don't really understand what they are saying, they just mimic. But I don't believe that. This bird knew *exactly* what it was saying, and it was hilarious.

"Stop it!" the bird cried again, as Jack stood bewildered. Without warning, the agitated bird swooped down and landed on Jack's shoulder.

"Uh, Jill?" Jack's voice verged on panic. *"Jill!"* Jack's face turned ashen as his eyes darted sideways at the massive bird perched two inches from his head.

"Here now," reproved Ray, prodding a large dowel rod against the bird's feet. "Step up, now. Be a good bird."

The macaw refused to budge, digging its claws deeper into Jack's shoulder.

"Stay still, Jack," I urged, as I moved slowly to his side holding the sheet. I didn't want to spook the bird into taking a chunk out of Jack's ear. Or worse.

Other than his frantic eyes, Jack stood stone still. I snuck up behind the bird—not an easy thing to do. Because of the strategic positioning of a parrot's eyes at the sides of its head, it can see almost 360 degrees, making it difficult to catch a bird by surprise. The macaw turned just a fraction of a second too late as I threw the sheet over it, restraining its head firmly with my left hand. Now, at least, it couldn't bite. But the claws were still embedded in Jack's shirt, so I couldn't just jerk the bird off his shoulder. I methodically peeled each claw away with my right hand until the bird lost its grasp. Then I wrapped it in the sheet, reached for a syringe and administered the vaccine.

Jack heaved a sigh of relief. "I think I'll just wait for you outside," he said, as he headed for the aviary door on shaky legs.

"Yes, I think that would be a good idea," I agreed, waiting for him to clear the door before I released the green-winged macaw who had obviously taken a dislike to my *boyfriend*. The thought of that word and the implications it held caused my heart to beat a little faster. On the other hand, maybe the bird had taken a *liking* to Jack. Sometimes it was hard to tell with birds, and they could pretend to be friendly and then nail you with a vicious bite.

The rest of the round-up proceeded in a mostly uneventful fashion. I had to climb a ladder a couple of times to reach reluctant patients, and I had to chase down a few others, but the process went fairly quickly. Ray and I exited the aviary and I walked over to an outside sink to wash my hands.

Jack paced back and forth as Ray and I finished up. Then Ray turned to Jack and slapped him on the back. "Well, young man, I admire your pluck. Not many people will venture into an enclosure with big birds, let alone try to help."

Jack nodded, obviously embarrassed. "Jill tried to warn me. I didn't listen."

"Say, I see from your truck that you're a plumber. I wonder if while you're here you'd mind takin' a look at this faucet. Drips all the time. I think it needs a new washer, but I don't know a lot about these things."

Jack brightened. "Of course, I'll be glad to."

Ray turned and winked at me while Jack went to fetch his toolbox from the truck.

I watched Jack quickly assess the problem and fit a small rubber ring into the end of the unscrewed faucet cover. "You were right," he told Ray. "Just needed a washer. It should be fine now."

"Excellent, thank you, young man. Send me a bill."

"There's no charge," Jack replied.

"Well, that's mighty nice of you. I'd say between the two of you, you can tackle just about anything." Ray winked at me again and walked us to the truck.

As we drove away, Jack said, "You know the only reason he had me look at that faucet was to make me feel better after making such a fool of myself."

"No, he didn't, Jack," I objected.

Jack shot me a skeptical look. "Anyone could have fixed that faucet."

"Not anyone, Jack. Ray couldn't. I couldn't."

"Well, I do know one thing. I'm not cut out to handle birds."

I grinned. "Maybe not yet. But I'll make a bird assistant out of you in no time."

"No thanks. I'll leave the birds to you, if you don't mind. And next time a bird tells me to 'stop it,' I'll do what it says."

DON'T BITE THE DOCTOR

Chapter 9

One of the lessons ingrained in veterinary students in the seventies was that they could and should do anything and everything. It never occurred to us we weren't qualified to handle certain situations, and even if we weren't, there was nobody else to do it. It often came down to us or nothing. Specialists pretty much existed only in veterinary teaching universities, and few clients were willing to spend the time and/or the money to drive to a university several hours away.

I stood over the surgery table in Dr. Spangle's clinic, attempting to wire the jaw of a mixed-breed dog named Mojo, who'd had an unfortunate run-in with a car. I knew I could do this. Never had we been led to believe in our training that there were some procedures that were simply beyond our limited capabilities.

But this jaw was one of them. Frustrated, I asked Tess, who had mostly been watching, rather than actually doing anything, if she could find Dr. Spangle and ask him to help me. Of course, Myra was too "busy" to assist me with a complicated surgery, so Tess served as my warm body. A few minutes later, Dr. Spangle poked his annoyed face into the surgery room.

"What's the problem?" he demanded, impatiently. Myra's head popped up over his shoulder.

"I can't get these bone fragments to go together. There are just too many pieces."

Dr. Spangle scowled. "I shouldn't have to do this for you. You should have learned how to do surgery in vet school." He turned and barked at Myra. "Get me some gloves!"

I stood, mortified, as Myra hustled to do her master's bidding. Two minutes later, my boss moved me out of the way so he could do the job himself. I hovered, helplessly, not knowing whether to stay and try to assist, or scrub out and leave. Though he ignored my presence, Dr. Spangle would likely be more irate if I left the room. So I remained, quietly, not daring to offer any snippet of advice when his efforts didn't yield any better results than mine had.

After an hour of sweating and peppering the air with four-letter words, he threw his instruments on the table.

"This is impossible! You should have referred this case to the vet school." He snapped off his gloves, tossing them toward the trash can and missing. Come to think of it, I don't think I had ever seen him hit the trash can. Without picking them up, he banged the surgery door open and tromped out of the room, Myra on his heels.

I looked at Tess, who had wordlessly taken in the whole episode. "I need to call the clients and see if they will consider a referral. Would you stay with Mojo?"

She nodded and I left the room to use the phone in my office. The clients consented to a referral, so I returned to the surgery room. My failure in not being able to fix their pet still smarted, but it was not quite so devastating, since the only other alternative to referral was putting Mojo to sleep. At least now he had a chance.

"I'll need to place a feeding tube until his owners can get him to the vet school," I said, mostly to myself.

I clipped up an area on the left side of my patient's neck and made a small skin incision through which to place a tube into the esophagus. Inserting a long-handled forceps into the open mouth, I poked it as far back into Mojo's throat as it would reach, used this as a guide, and made a stab incision into the esophagus. Then I introduced a soft, red rubber catheter through the incision, slid it down the throat, and sutured the protruding end to the outside of the dog's neck. This would enable me to provide liquid nutrition until he could have surgery at the hands of a more capable surgeon.

Mojo was one of my privileged patients. Most of my clients weren't able to afford the advanced standard of care required in difficult cases, as was the case with Mr. Findley, an older gentleman living alone on a fixed income, and his paralyzed dachshund, Barney.

Like many ill-fated dachshunds, Barney had ruptured a disc in his back. The anatomy of this breed's long back, coupled with a low center of gravity, made them susceptible to back problems. We later learned there is a genetic component to disc disease in dachshunds, as well. Choosing the wrong parents to be born to contributes to a myriad of medical maladies, none of which is the patient's fault. Sometimes, with time, medical treatment, and luck, the condition improves; but in the case of acute, total paralysis, the prognosis for recovery is poor without surgical intervention.

"Barney really should go to the veterinary teaching hospital as soon as possible," I told Mr. Findley. "He needs immediate surgery."

Mr. Findley shook his head. "I just can't afford that. Isn't there anything else you can do?"

I bit my lip. Knowing the grim prognosis, I disliked presenting the small sliver of hope that medical treatment alone could work.

"I can try, Mr. Findley, but you see this?" I pinched the toe of Barney's back foot with a forcep and he didn't even blink. "He can't feel deep pain. That's a bad sign because deep pain is the last sensation to go in a spinal cord injury. It indicates severe damage to the spinal cord."

"Look, he's moving it!" cried the owner. "He feels something!"

Barney's leg had, indeed, pulled a fraction of an inch toward his body. "I'm sorry, Mr. Findley, that's just a reflex."

"Are you sure?"

"I'm sure. It's called the withdrawal reflex. You know how when you put your hand on a hot stove you instinctively pull it away before you actually feel the burn?"

The client mulled this over a moment. "Yeah, I guess that's true. I'm not sure I've actually thought about it."

"The reflex protects us in that split second before our brain registers the pain so we're already moving away from the source of danger."

"I see. So, Barney didn't really feel the pinch."

I shook my head. "No, I'm sorry." I patted the sweet dog's head. Other than dragging around his back end, Barney was perfectly happy and healthy. A fine-looking black-and-tan fellow, Barney gazed up at me with expectant eyes that said, "I know you will help me."

"I sure hate to put him down. He's only four years old." Mr. Findley rubbed his hand across his stubbly jaw. "Look, here, can't *you* do the surgery?"

I only wished I were that gifted. "I'm afraid neurosurgery is a bit more complicated than what I'm capable of."

The client's eyes brightened. "But you could *try,* couldn't you? I mean, he's not going to get better anyway, right? So, what would it hurt to try?"

I hesitated, wrestling with my decision. "I'll tell you what. Let's try aggressive steroid treatment on him first. If that doesn't work, I'll try, but I can't make any promises."

Mr. Findley's face broke into a huge grin. "Oh, that's wonderful. You hear that, Barney, you're going to be all right!"

I am all too aware that clients often hear what they want to hear, and in this case, I didn't want there to be any doubt of what I had actually said.

"Now, Mr. Findley, this is a long shot. The prognosis for Barney recovering the use of his back legs is still poor."

"I know. I just want to give him a chance, is all."

How I wished I could ship Barney off into more skilled hands. But I couldn't. It was me or nothing. But, as Mr. Findley had said, what did we have to lose?

After two weeks of high doses of steroids, coupled with antibiotics to combat the undesirable immunosuppressive side-effects of the steroids, as well as stomach protectants to prevent gastrointestinal ulcers associated with high doses of steroids, Barney's paralysis had not improved. Still, he maintained his cheerful countenance, always looking up at me with those trusting eyes as if to say he would really love to wag his tail, if only he could. It became clear that Barney simply regarded his paralysis as a minor inconvenience, rather than the life-altering crisis with which I regarded the condition.

At his three-week check, Mr. Findley placed Barney on the exam table. "He's not any better, Doc. Will you operate now?"

"Like I told you earlier—" I started to reiterate.

Mr. Findley waved my objection aside with his hand. "I know all that. I'm ready to try anything."

"—plus, the longer the paralysis goes on, the less likely it is to improve, even with surgery."

"But you'll try."

I sighed. "Yes, I'll try."

And I did. It never fully occurred to me I had no business mucking around with spinal surgery, especially without the proper diagnostics and equipment. All I had was a standard radiograph of Barney's spine, which showed a narrowed disc space between the T-13 and L-1 vertebrae, which may or may not have been the actual site of the problem. But without a contrast study, let alone an MRI, I had to make do with what I had. I also lacked a proper drill, so removing the vertebral arches using clumsy bone-cutting rongeurs made for tedious work. Locating the suspected offending disc, I scooped out as much of the gelatinous material as possible, flushed the surgery site liberally with sterile saline, and closed the incision. I performed the surgery on a Sunday afternoon, so as not to take time from our normal schedule, and I didn't charge for the procedure.

To nobody's surprise, Barney did not recover use of his rear legs. I gave him several weeks, post-operatively, in the hope that, over time, he would improve. I even tried physical therapy by swimming him in the treatment area sink, his short little front legs paddling furiously, but his rear legs useless.

"I guess I'll have to put him down," Mr. Findley said, finally resigned to the fact that Barney was not getting better. "I sure hate to. He's still got so much life in him except for his legs. Too bad they don't make wheelchairs for dogs."

An idea suddenly sparked in the back of my mind. Today, you can go online and order a doggy mobility cart from a number of vendors. Back then, such things didn't exist—or if they did, I wasn't aware of them.

Excitement and hope flooded through me for the first time since I had diagnosed Barney's paralysis. "Mr. Findley, I have an idea! I think I might be able to make Barney a doggy wheelchair."

"Really?" The old man's face lit up. "How are you going to do that?"

"I'm not sure yet. But leave Barney with me for a couple of days. I want to try out a few things."

DON'T BITE THE DOCTOR

Over the next three days, I bent metal rods used for making Thomas splints into a framework, over which I fashioned a detachable sturdy cloth sling and leather straps to go around Barney's muscular shoulders. Barney took to his numerous fittings and adjustments like the good sport he was, probably wondering what crazy thing I was subjecting him to now, but always with the sweet look in his eyes that said he trusted me. Finally, I purchased a toddler's riding toy with wheels that I removed and fitted into the ends of the steel rods. The contraption appeared to work perfectly. Now for the true test.

I took Barney home with me for the evening in order to try out his new wheels in a home setting. He took one look at Bitsy and Delilah and attempted to drag his pitiful little body around the living room so he could play with them. They didn't know quite what to make of this strange creature, but seemed to sense he was a friend. Bitsy crouched and barked at him, her tail wagging furiously from her raised rear end, daring him to chase her. Delilah, a little more subdued, contented herself with sniffing the interloper, not quite sure why he didn't behave like a normal dog.

I scooped up Barney and placed his belly in the sling, his atrophied back legs hanging out the back, and buckled the leather straps. Instantly, he took off after Bitsy, his strong front legs pulling him and the cart down the hall toward the bedroom. Delilah stared after them for a brief second before joining in the fun. I heard a crash as Barney failed to negotiate the turn into the bedroom. Dashing down the hall, I spied the plucky little dachshund overturned in the cart, trying bravely to right himself.

"Whoa, Dude, you've got to slow down," I laughed. After several weeks of not being able to run, I suppose he just couldn't help himself. I set him upright, and he took off again, his long ears flapping behind him, and, I swear, a doggy grin across his face.

The next day I returned him to his owner. "I hope you don't have steps in your house. Barney is not afraid to tackle stairs in his cart." I had learned that the hard way the previous evening when I put the girls out to do their final business before bed. With no regard for common sense, Barney had bolted down the back steps before I could grab him to take him out of the cart. No worse for the wear, he tore around the back yard, even trying to chase a squirrel up a tree. I could only imagine what the squirrel must have thought over the strange creature pursuing it.

"No, I don't have any steps in my place." Mr. Findley grinned with delight as he watched Barney race around the large treatment room, investigating every inch. Laughing aloud, he said, "I just can't believe it. He loves it! A wheelchair for dogs." He turned and looked at me, tears shimmering in his eyes.

"I can't thank you enough for not giving up on Barney." Mr. Findley sniffed. He removed a handkerchief from his front pocket and blew his nose.

"You're very welcome."

"Barney, come tell the doc thank you," the old man said.

Barney, too busy darting back and forth, exploring his new world, ignored his owner. That was okay. That was all the thanks I needed.

Chapter 10

Neutering male animals is one of my favorite surgeries. Now don't get me wrong. I'm not trying to be a sexist, here. It's just that, in most cases, neuters are relatively simple procedures, and there are many benefits to having a neutered, versus an intact, male pet. Neutered pets are much less likely to mark territory and go out looking for fights. They are less apt to roam. Plus, the obvious—reproducing, adding to an already overpopulated number of animals languishing away in shelters looking for homes.

Over the years I have tackled neuters on many species, including the reluctant and elusive squirrel. Some have been more challenging than others. But I did draw the line at mature pigs. This was due to a rather traumatic experience in veterinary school, and some things are just too deeply ingrained to ever risk opening that can of worms again.

~

Carlie, my surgical lab partner, and I stood anxiously waiting to be assigned our patient. Operative practice, our junior year, involved long days while we fumbled through our first hands-on surgeries with clumsy fingers.

Back then, during our operative practice rotations, we received a surgery dog to be used for two surgical practice labs. I'm not quite sure where these unfortunate creatures came from, but they became ours for the purpose of training veterinary students in surgical techniques. The first week, we did the required surgery, recovered our dog, took care of it for a week, then did a terminal procedure the next week, in which the animals were euthanized. To ensure students didn't become overly attached to the dogs they had cared for all week and try to sneak them out of the lab, our instruments were not sterilized for the second procedure. Some students snuck the animals out anyway, along with a bottle of penicillin, but as the quarter went on, the procedures became less conducive to allowing for that scenario. Needless to say, I hated these labs and the sacrifice of these hapless animals, but I was forced to suck up my feelings for the supposed higher purpose of being educated. And, realistically, I didn't want my first surgery to be on some unsuspecting client's beloved pet. Thankfully, times and methods have changed in veterinary teaching hospitals, but at that time, this was the norm.

In those practice labs, we used a long-acting intravenous barbiturate anesthetic for our patients. We didn't have the luxury of a gas anesthetic machine with oxygen, let alone any monitoring equipment. We basically administered the injection and the patient slept for the next ten hours or so, which made for an incredibly long recovery time for the non-terminal procedures. I remember waiting until the wee hours of the morning for my patient to wake up, long after several grueling hours in the surgery lab.

But today's surgery lab was different. Today, we were performing free hernia operations on piglets who would then be returned to farms. All baby animals have their unique charm, but there is just something particularly appealing about piglets—aside from the fact that they squeal incessantly in high-pitched, eardrum-shattering decibels when subjected to procedures they find disagreeable. No amount of soothing talk or comforting caresses will calm a frightened pig and the only way to make the squealing cease is to stop doing whatever it is you were doing to it in the first place. Or sedate it.

Nevertheless, our little patient, for the most part, was relatively cooperative, compared to the cacophony of shrieking porcines that echoed off the walls of the cavernous large animal surgery suite set up for forty students. Carlie and I were delighted to get one of the smallest piglets, an enchanting little bundle with a round, pink body, stubby legs, and inquisitive snout. Plus, a large umbilical hernia protruding from his belly. Our baby seemed to like being handled, however, as he amused us with a string of soft, contented grunts while we fussed over him. Before long, however, the unwilling patients all blissfully slumbered under the influence of their barbiturates, and the ringing in our ears gradually receded.

Even better, still, the surgery went quickly and easily. In no time, we had cut around the ballooned protrusion, dissected down through the hernial sac to the abdomen, tucked the abdominal contents back where they belonged, repaired the hernial defect in the abdominal wall, and sutured the skin. As the first team to finish our procedure, we called upon Professor Raynes, the large animal instructor supervising this lab, to inspect our work. The professor studied our effort and pronounced it a good job. And it wasn't even four o'clock! We were going to get home for dinner before midnight! Ecstatic, we began to clean up our area.

"Since you got through that surgery so quickly, there's time for you to do a second one," Dr. Raynes told us.

Momentarily deflated, we shrugged it off and philosophically accepted the opportunity for further surgical experience and learning. Despite his assigning us more work, I liked Dr. Raynes. Laid-back and casual, he was a welcome contrast to most of his colleagues in the small animal surgery sector, and my gut didn't clench every time he hovered over our surgery table, watching our inexperienced and sometimes barbaric efforts. That is, I liked him until Professor Raynes returned with a monstrous boar and instructed us to neuter it. This enormous beast was not the cute little piggy who currently slept off his anesthesia on a blanket next to our surgery table. There was nothing to do but accept our fate and seeming penalty for having finished our hernia surgery too quickly while the other teams toiled away.

Two hours later we finished up, and after another two hours of recovering the second patient, we left him in the company of his peers in a deeply straw-covered pen and called it a night. We were the last team to leave the hospital.

The next day, I went to check on our patients. We didn't often have hospitalized swine in the large animal wing, but when we did, the veterinary school housed them way down on one end, far away from the other large animal areas—the reason being obvious. The stench hit me full in the face as I opened the heavy door leading to the isolated ward. Carlie had an early elective class that morning, so I had volunteered to check on our cases. Our little hernia pig greeted me with soft grunts and nuzzled his snout into my hand for a good scratching. His vital signs all checked out normally and I watched him attack his breakfast with unbridled gusto. Then I continued onto the pen holding the large swine. As I entered, several curious hogs swarmed around my legs, nearly knocking me down. It took me a moment to locate our patient among all the others. To my unpleasant surprise, I found the boar's scrotum to be quite swollen. Uh oh. This wasn't good. Although not uncommon to have some post-operative swelling after a neuter, especially in an animal with a pendulous scrotum, this distension was way more pronounced than expected. I left to seek Dr. Raynes.

I finally located the professor at the other end of the large animal wing, where he was in the middle of supervising a couple other students working on a cow.

"Dr. Raynes," I interrupted, the worry making me rush my words. "The boar we neutered yesterday has a lot of swelling."

Of course, when one is a student, anything that goes wrong with a patient under our care is potentially disastrous. Not only is there the obvious consequence of creating a problem and causing potential harm to an animal who had been perfectly fine before we got our hands on it, there is also the distinct notoriety of being the "screwup" when the rest of the class learned of the situation, as they inevitably would. And with intense competition among a group of type A personalities, one did not want the distinction of being the student who messed up. Not to mention the remote possibility of flunking out of veterinary school for gross and irreparable incompetence.

"It's probably just some fluid," Dr. Raynes replied, distractedly, as he drew a milk sample from the cow, his head buried deep in the bovine's flank. "Take out a suture and let the fluid drain."

"Okay," I said, taking a deep breath and wishing he would come with me. But he was busy and Carlie was still in class, so I was on my own.

Returning to the pig pen, I managed to corral my patient. I squatted down behind him, grasping one hind leg to hold him still—while he shrieked bloody murder—and with the other hand snipped a suture. To my utter horror, several feet of pig intestines fell out into my arms. I had to let go of my patient's rear leg in order to catch the guts to keep them from hitting the ground. But without the restraint, my spooked patient took off dragging his intestines behind him in the straw. The other pigs, also spooked, trampled around us in confused pandemonium. I held on, the best I could, to the trailing guts, trying to keep them from being crushed under the sharp hooves of the other pigs, my own guts feeling as though someone had thoroughly trampled *them*. Unfortunately, the swine ward was completely deserted.

Panicking, I began to scream, sounding not too unlike the squealing hogs surrounding me. "Help!"

It seemed like an eternity before someone heard me and came to investigate.

"Get Dr. Raynes!" I shouted, on the verge of tears. "Hurry!"

After another eternity, Dr. Raynes appeared with reinforcements. Everything after that became a blur. Somehow, we got the boar, whose guts were now liberally covered in straw, out of the pen and back into the surgical suite where he was quickly sedated.

"Who's your surgery partner?" asked Dr. Raynes.

"Carlie Ballinger," I replied, miserably.

He grinned. "Well, we can't let you take all the blame for this." He turned to one of the large animal technicians. "Go have Carlie Ballinger paged to large animal surgery, STAT."

I was both relieved and mortified when poor Carlie appeared a few minutes later, her expression a mixture of curiosity and abject terror. There was nothing like having one's name blared over the intercom for the entire school to hear, particularly when you were being summoned to a specific location STAT. However, her questioning look quickly changed as she took in the situation. Of course, it was kind of hard to miss, what with our enormous porcine patient lying supine on the surgery table with several feet of contaminated intestines spilling out from his scrotal sac.

After having us scrub up for surgery, Dr. Raynes patiently, calmly, and methodically instructed us on how to clean the straw and debris-covered loops of bowel, examine them for injury, and thread them back through the inguinal ring through which they had herniated. Then he talked us through how to close the inguinal opening so the guts stayed where they belonged. Grateful for his cool-headed guidance, my taut muscles began to relax, and by the end of the surgery, when we knew our patient was no worse off for the potentially life-threatening ordeal he had just been through, we relaxed and exchanged light banter with each other.

"Don't feel bad about what happened," Dr. Raynes told us. "Boars often have large inguinal rings and herniation can be a complication of neutering, especially in a boar this size. Besides, you've had the extra practice of getting to do an additional hernia repair."

I did have to acknowledge this had been quite the learning experience, albeit one I preferred never to repeat. I smiled weakly at him, imagining the berating we would have gotten had this situation occurred in our small animal surgery lab.

"Plus, look on the bright side. In food animal surgery, if the surgery isn't a success, you can often eat your mistakes."

~

That event occurred over forty years ago and has provided many a laughable memory. However, to this day I will neuter pretty much any other animal but a mature boar. But, boars aside, for the most part, testicles and their removal are pretty similar across species lines.

That is, until I tried to neuter Bugs. Bugs, a small, shiny, black Netherland Dwarf rabbit came in for a pre-surgical exam by his owner, a nice young lady named Kylie Echols. The problem was Bugs was impossible to handle. Some bunnies are just naturally "goosier" than others, and when one goes to touch them, they bolt upright in an attempt to break their backs and paralyze themselves. Because rabbits' backs are more fragile than other species, handling them safely can present a challenge, particularly when it is necessary to conduct a thorough examination. I did the best I could with Bugs, but he was simply too wild. Still, I wasn't overly concerned. He was just being seen in preparation for an elective neuter, and he was otherwise young and outwardly healthy.

On the day of surgery, I still couldn't handle him, as he freaked out in his cage, ricocheting off the sides of the stainless-steel enclosure every time I drew near. After cornering him in the back of the cage, I threw a towel over him and quickly administered a preanesthetic sedative injection, then waited for him to calm down. Finally, after several minutes, I was able to scruff him by the back of the neck, making sure to restrain his back legs with my other hand so he couldn't kick and injure his back, and place him in a gas induction box. Bugs gradually yielded to the anesthesia, and Tess removed him and laid him on the surgery table, belly up.

For several months now, I had been teaching Tess to assume more technician duties, since I rarely received any help from Myra. I adjusted a face mask over Bugs' nose and mouth, after lubricating his eyes. Some animals don't close their eyes when they are under anesthesia, so we have to be careful their corneas don't dry out from exposure since they lose their blink reflex. I allowed Tess to clip and surgically prep the neuter site. Then I carefully draped the area off from the rest of the body to avoid contamination and attempted to commence my surgery.

"Hmm, that's funny," I said, probing for a testicle.

"What's wrong?" asked Tess.

"I can't find his testicles. Did you notice them while you were prepping?"

"Gee, I'm not really sure," she said.

Well, this was aggravating. I did a thorough search for where the testicles should be, then moved the drape forward to examine the inguinal rings. Some animals have the ability to retract their testicles when they are under stress. Retraction of the testicle is caused by an involuntary muscle reflex and is different from an undescended testicle that never made it into the scrotal sac at birth. Retained testicles are a whole 'nother surgical problem, as they can be found anywhere from the groin area to inside the abdomen, requiring a major laparotomy to find and remove. They can be quite difficult to locate, especially if they are lurking somewhere between the internal and external inguinal rings.

But I was positive I had felt Bug's testicles, despite the fact he had been a challenge to examine. I poked around all the places the testicles could be hiding. At one point I thought I felt something in the groin, so I made my initial incision. After dissecting through the subcutaneous tissues, the "something" became frustratingly elusive. Sometimes inguinal fat or the inguinal lymph node can be mistaken for a retained or retracted testicle. I boggled my way exploring the entire area before giving up and deciding whatever it was I thought I felt was not, indeed, a testicle. By this point, what should have been a fifteen-minute surgery at best, had turned into thirty minutes, and I still was no closer to success. I blew out an irritated breath and tried to think.

Sometimes a hiding testicle can be "pushed" out by applying pressure behind the inguinal area. I tried this approach, still with no results. I even resorted to having Tess hold Bugs vertically by the scruff and shake him, in the hope of dislodging the stubborn gonads. But finally, I had to admit defeat. Bugs had bested me. He was not going to be neutered today.

I explained the situation to Kylie, who, thankfully, was very understanding.

"Sometimes animals retract their testicles and we just can't get them to release," I said. "We can try again, later. Perhaps give him something to calm him before he comes in." Of course, I didn't charge her for the hour I had wasted.

A few weeks later, I tried again. Still no luck. I had begun to think that perhaps Bugs did, indeed, have retained testicles and I had been wrong when I thought I had felt them earlier. I believe I even mentioned to Kylie that I might have to open up his abdomen and look.

I had more or less forgotten about Bugs until Kylie had another rabbit in for me to examine. As I waxed forth with my professional wisdom concerning this bunny, Kylie casually mentioned, "Oh, by the way, Bugs had babies last week."

Astonished, I naturally assumed those stubborn testicles had finally decided to make an appearance and Bugs had managed to impregnate one of Kylie's other rabbits.

"He did? So, Bugs is a father?"

"No, Bugs is a mother," she replied. "She had four babies."

I felt the blood drain from my face. Could anyone have made a more idiotic mistake? Not once, mind you, but *twice*. Now granted, of all the animals I see, rabbits have to be the most difficult to accurately sex, but still . . .

Up until this point, I had prided myself on not having performed a "tomcat spay," a procedure in which the veterinarian fails to ascertain that he or she has a neutered male cat on the surgery table before mucking around in the abdomen looking for a non-existent uterus and ovaries. But *this!* If only the ground would open up and swallow me now. If I had been Kylie, I would have had serious doubts about ever trusting me with another of her pets. Yet here she stood—not accusing or angry—just matter-of-factly sharing the tiny detail that Bugs was, in fact, not a male.

I may have partially redeemed myself by performing Bugs' spay surgery at no charge, but the mortification of the whole ordeal still makes me cringe. Of all the things I tried in order to find those testicles, the one thing I failed to think of was to check for the presence of a penis.

~

Kylie had been gracious. Mrs. Holman, not so much. The day after I neutered her cat, Felix, she called the clinic, outraged, saying her cat was dead.

Dead! This was every veterinarian's worst nightmare—to have a routine surgery patient die unexpectedly. I racked my brain. There had been absolutely nothing out of the ordinary with Felix's neuter operation. There was no bleeding, everything was tied off neatly, the anesthesia went well, and the recovery was quick. Felix was young and healthy, his pre-anesthetic blood work was normal, and his heart sounded good.

I picked up the phone with trembling hands. What could have caused this cat's death? What could I possibly offer the owner in terms of an explanation?

"Mrs. Holman," I said into the receiver. "I'm so sorry to hear about Felix. Can you tell me what happened after you took him home?"

"I certainly can! I can tell you *exactly* what happened!" she snapped. "This morning I went out to get my newspaper and Felix bolted out the door, ran into the street and was hit by a car."

My initial panic subsided, and my flip-flopping heart settled into a more natural rhythm. As devastated as I was to hear of Felix's demise, at least it had not been the result of my surgery. At least, so I thought, until Mrs. Holman spoke again.

"And it's all your fault!"

"My fault?" I echoed.

"Yes! You're the one who told me to neuter him. Felix has never tried to get out before. He was obviously so distraught over the surgery he committed suicide!"

~

"Mrs. Holman actually believes her cat committed suicide because I neutered him," I complained to Jack that evening. After work, I had gone to his house where he had cooked a delicious dinner—spaghetti and meatballs. My boyfriend, was, in fact, an excellent cook. Much better than I. I wound a mouthful of pasta around my fork and transferred it to my mouth. "Mmm. This is really good."

A lot of evenings I didn't eat dinner until late, and by the time I had finished up at the clinic that night, my stomach had been making some rather unladylike rumblings. Flash sat next to me, his happy tail thumping against the hardwood floor, his expectant brown eyes begging for a handout.

"Can't say as I blame the cat," Jack replied. "If someone put me through that particular surgery, I would be tempted to do the same thing."

"Oh, you men," I retorted. "You're all the same when it comes to the subject of neutering."

"Well, you have to admit it's a rather delicate subject."

I set down my fork and stared pointedly at Jack. "I don't understand why neutering is always such a big deal with men, but women don't have the same reaction when it comes to spaying a female animal—which is a much more involved major surgical procedure."

"It's a guy thing," Jack offered, lamely, averting his eyes.

"Hmph." I shook my head and took another bite, mindful of a piercing gaze that was *not* averted, but rather intently fixed, with hopeful determination, on my plate. "Flash, you know you're not likely to get anything from me, so stop with the big brown puppy-dog eyes." At hearing his name, the goofy dog's tail beat even faster, and a smidgen of drool escaped his lips. "Someone has allowed you to get into bad habits," I said, pointedly.

"Flash, go lie down," Jack commanded. The dog, a look of pure rapture on his honest, Lab face at being acknowledged, immediately moved over next to Jack and took up a new begging position.

I laughed. "You have him trained well. And speaking of neutering—"

"I told you. I'm still thinking about breeding him," Jack interrupted.

We had been through this discussion many times before and this was one area in which Jack refused to concede to my professional advice.

"Well, as two men opposed to neutering, you will appreciate what happened to Dr. Spangle last week."

Flash cocked his big head as though to say, "Do tell."

Jack's expression was slightly more wary.

"One of his *Dr. Spangle only* clients, Mrs. Arthur, brought in her Maltese, Gus, to be neutered several weeks ago. She was tired of Gus getting her female dog, Gidget, pregnant, even though she insisted that she took extreme measures to keep them separated during Gidget's heats. Dr. Spangle neutered him and two weeks later he fathered another litter."

"What? That's possible?" Jack's eyebrows rose.

"Unusual, but it can happen for up to a month after the surgery. Apparently, Dr. Spangle forgot to warn Mrs. Arthur about that remote possibility."

"Good for Gus," Jack chuckled. "I guess the old guy got in one last hurrah and showed everybody."

"He certainly got the last laugh. Never underestimate the resolve of an unjustly neutered male."

Jack slipped a bite of meatball to Flash. "Sure beats committing suicide."

ELLEN FANNON

Chapter 11

"This wound just ain't getting' no better," said Bubba Barnes.
Yes, his name *really* was Bubba, and he was the epitome of the stereotypic good ole' boy. Sorely in need of a dentist, the middle-aged man graced me with a gap-toothed, tobacco-stained smile, the countenance of which said he just couldn't understand why his home remedy wasn't working. His long, thinning hair hung out of his backwards placed cap that read, "Ferguson Tractor and Supply," and Bubba suddenly seemed to realize he should remove the cap indoors. One thing about good ole' boys is they are generally well-mannered when around the opposite sex, even if they didn't put much confidence in my veterinary abilities, being as I was a woman and all.
Bubba hoisted a skinny black-and-tan coonhound named Digger onto the exam table and I got my first look. On the right shoulder was an old, gaping wound with a generous amount of unhealthy-looking granulation tissue sprayed bright blue.
"I bin doctorin' it with blue lotion, but it just ain't helpin'."
Ah, blue lotion. The cure-all remedy for everything, particularly in the hunting dog world. Located in a semi-rural area, Spangle Animal Clinic received its share of hunting dogs, and rarely in a timely fashion when our

services might have actually helped the situation. Usually, we only saw these poor beasts after the owners had tried everything else. We were the last resort when all else failed and the condition had gone completely south. I wasn't sure what exactly was in the magic concoction aptly named "blue lotion," but I do know it stained everything in which it came into contact, my hands included, a brilliant shade of blue which would not wash off for days. I had yet to see blue lotion work for any veterinary problem but the good ole' boys swore by it.

I hated the stuff. I hated touching animals sprayed liberally with the stuff. I hated walking around with blue hands. Back then, we didn't have the ever-present latex exam gloves we reach for now without a second thought. We had sterile surgical gloves, which cost dearly, and were only used in surgery—not simply because we didn't want to get our hands dirty.

"How long has Digger had this wound?" I asked, wincing as I probed the blue area around it, trying to gauge if there was enough skin to pull together to close the wound and if I could do a proper exam without once again sporting Smurf hands.

"Oh, I reckon' goin' on about ten days, give or take. He got tangled up with one of my other males over a bitch in heat. I put Neosporin on it, but it didn't help."

"That's because Neosporin is only for superficial wounds, not deep puncture wounds from a dog bite." I knew I talked only to hear my own voice, but felt compelled to continue, nevertheless. "With a deep bite wound, it's like taking a syringeful of bacteria and injecting it into the muscle."

I couldn't help but chide, "If we'd have seen him when this first happened, we could have started Digger on antibiotics and likely prevented this nasty infection."

Bubba nodded his head, absently. "Jus' didn' think it was all that bad."

"Bite wounds are always potentially dangerous," I said. "As you can see, the infection has caused a great deal of tissue damage, and it's going to take some aggressive surgical treatment to close this wound."

"Surgery?" he ran his hand through the thinning strands of hair clinging to the top of his head. "Oh, I don' know 'bout that."

"I'm afraid we don't have any choice," I insisted.

"You mean you can't just give him a shot or somethin'?"

I often had to wonder at the naivete of the general public who believed in the elusive cure-all "shot" that would fix anything from behavioral issues to cancer. How a shot was going to miraculously move the edges of the skin together to cover this wound escaped me.

"No, I'm afraid not," I said. "I need to put Digger under anesthesia, cut away all the dead tissue, and try to create clean skin edges to pull together. Even if I'm able to do all that, he's going to have to be kept quiet so he doesn't open the stitches back up. Plus, he'll need to be on antibiotics for several days."

Bubba scratched his head. "Dang. All that, huh?"

"Yes," I emphasized.

He chewed on his lower lip, then let out a resigned sigh. "I suppose you gotta' do what you gotta' do. I guess huntin' him this weekend is out."

"I'm afraid so." I hesitated, knowing very well I shouldn't broach this taboo subject, then threw caution to the wind. "While Digger's asleep, this might be a good time to neuter him. That will help stop the dog fighting."

Bubba's head shot up like I had insulted his granny, his face becoming inflamed. "Neuter him? You mean cut off his . . ." he groped for an appropriate word he could say to a woman. ". . . his manhood?"

"Yes."

Sweat broke out on Bubba's forehead and he removed a checkered cloth from his hip pocket to wipe it away. "I ain't never heard'a such a fool thing!" He snatched Digger from the table. "Come on, boy, this lady don' know nothin' about doctorin'."

Before I could open my mouth, Bubba and Digger had bolted from the room. I heard him call to Heather on his way out the clinic door, "We'll come back when we can see the man doc."

Drat, I had blown it. I knew I had to work hard to earn the trust of the good ole' boys, but despite my efforts, I simply did not speak their language. No wonder I was met with such distrust. I knew better than to utter the "N" word (neuter) to a good ole' boy, but I had gone and done it anyway. When would I ever learn?

A couple days later I picked up the top chart for the next client and opened the door to the waiting room, where Gator Clark and his bird dog, Wally, waited patiently. Yes, the man's name was really Gator, another good ole' boy who had brought Wally in due to a badly torn and infected rear dewclaw.

A burly man, probably in his mid-fifties, Mr. Clark led Wally into the exam room, eyeing me suspiciously.

"Good morning, Mr. Clark. I'm Dr. Bennet." I held out my hand.

"You're the doc?"

"Yes, I'm Dr. Bennet. I'm working with Dr. Spangle."

Gator Clark hesitated for a second, then took my hand in his big mitt, pumped it once, and grunted. "Never seen no lady doc before. Didn' know ladies could be vets."

"Yes, there are quite a few woman veterinarians now." I grinned, but Gator's apprehensive look remained firmly in place.

I waited a moment for him to bring up the reason for the visit, as most clients generally do. Although the purpose of the visit is usually listed on the appointment sheet, that doesn't necessarily mean anything. I have seen many patients scheduled for one thing that turned into something else, entirely, like the dog presented for his yearly vaccines who, the owner neglected to tell the receptionist at the time the appointment was made, hadn't eaten in three weeks. Sometimes it just doesn't occur to people to mention little details.

As Mr. Clark appeared to be a man of few words, I went on. "I see Wally has a torn dewclaw."

"I guess Doc Spangle ain't here, then?" His voice rose on a thin thread of hope and he stared at me anxiously.

"He is, but he's with another client."

The expectant look disappeared, and his worry lines deepened, but Mr. Clark didn't insist on seeing Dr. Spangle. Since Mr. Clark hadn't overtly objected to my examining Wally— although he had not lifted the dog onto the exam table—I bent down to look, trying not to groan aloud at the familiar sight of blue lotion all over the left rear leg. My hands were still blue from Digger, and I hadn't even gotten to treat him. If memory served correctly from the quick glance at the appointment book, Bubba and Digger had an appointment with Dr. Spangle this afternoon.

What the heck, I was already blue. I gently palpated the dangly extra toe, which is not normally present in most breeds, and frequently causes problems from getting caught and injured in carpets, fences, and other things. The toe pad had been torn halfway off, leaving a nasty wound which Wally had obviously been trying to cure with canine saliva. When that hadn't worked, Gator Clark had applied blue lotion with the philosophy that if a little is good, a lot is better.

"I'm afraid that dewclaw is going to have to come off," I said, straightening up and addressing Wally's owner. I dispensed with the rest of the history, such as how long this condition had been going on, which in vet school would have been regarded as a cardinal sin. A thorough history, they assured us, was of vital importance to obtaining an accurate diagnosis. But in this case, I felt the question unnecessary. The answer was "for a while."

"Come off?" Gator boomed. His shocked, doubtful eyes confronted me.

"Yes. The dewclaw is already torn halfway and is badly infected." I tried to sound authoritative, but my voice came out high-pitched and insecure under the owner's intimidating glare. I knew what needed to be done, I just didn't appear to be conveying that message very well to Mr. Clark.

"What about snakebite?" the man challenged.

Snakebite? Where had that *question come from?* I cleared my throat. "No, it's not a snakebite. Wally's just caught his toe in something and injured it."

The man shook his head vehemently and looked at me as though I were dull-witted. "No, I mean you remove his dewclaw, he won't have no protection from snakebites."

My jaw dropped. I must have missed this lecture in veterinary school. Surely, I would have remembered. Inadvisably, I asked, "What do you mean?"

Gator's eyes bugged out and his face became flushed. "Lady, *everybody* knows the dewclaws protect against snakebite!"

They did? *Everybody* knew this but *me?* I couldn't wrap my mind around this fact, let alone get into the particulars, such as, did the dewclaw only protect from snakebite if the snake happened to bite the dog on its dewclaw? Or was there a magic antidote living in the extraneous toe that didn't reside anywhere else in the body? I wisely refrained from pointing out that this was an old wives' tale—albeit one with which I was unfamiliar—and sheer nonsense.

I could not dispute Mr. Clark's logic. Fortunately, since Dr. Spangle was in the office, I decided to throw the problem to him. "Perhaps Dr. Spangle could take a look after he finishes with his room. Excuse me and I'll check with him."

Gator Clark expressed his satisfaction with this idea by returning his eyes to their sockets.

I don't know how Dr. Spangle did it, but an hour later, Wally, minus his snakebite- protective dewclaw, lay in a recovery cage, waiting to be picked up by his owner.

Shaking my head, I entered the next exam room, where a pungent odor assaulted me. What in the world? Before me stood a miserable-looking mutt who smelled like a Jiffy Lube shop. I glanced at the chart. Skeeter Jackson and his dog, Ivan. Yes, the man's name was really Skeeter.

"Did Ivan get into something?" I asked, resisting the urge to cover my nose and mouth. Maybe I should crack the door a little to let in some air. I took a step backward.

Skeeter stared at me. "No. He's got the red mange. I bin puttin' burnt motor oil on him tryin' to get rid of it."

Ah. That accounted for the overpowering stench. At least this was one old wives' tale I had heard.

"It's jus' gettin' worse. I done everythin' I can."

I really, *really* didn't want to touch this dog. For one thing, I didn't want to get lead poisoning. Okay, I admit that concern was rather far-fetched, although remotely possible for the poor dog. I could only hope the burnt motor oil had been cooled when Skeeter applied it. Secondly, I didn't want to smell like Ivan.

"Yes, Ivan does look pretty uncomfortable. Demodectic mange can be tricky to clear up. But fortunately, we have newer treatments that are much more effective than burnt motor oil."

Skeeter's face took on an expression of hopeful anticipation. "You got somethin' better than burnt motor oil?"

At last, a good ole' boy who showed a modicum of trust in my professional advice. I smiled.

"Yes. I'll need to do a skin scraping on Ivan, first, to verify that it is, indeed, demodex, although it certainly looks it. Sometimes skin conditions can look alike. If it is demodectic mange, we need to remove the motor oil from his skin, as that can do more harm than good. But there are a number of new dips available which work well for this type of mange."

"That takes a load off my mind," Skeeter said. He beamed, showing a mouthful of rotten teeth. "Thanks a lot, doc. I'll leave him with you, then."

I had finally scored a victory with a good ole' boy! I could hardly contain my joy as I carried Ivan to the back so I could give him a thorough degreasing.

"What the devil is that awful smell?" demanded Dr. Spangle, as he caught a whiff of Ivan.

"Burnt motor oil," I replied.

"Stupid rednecks and their home remedies," he muttered.

I wanted to retort that if we continued to regard our clients as stupid rednecks, we were unlikely to educate them in better ways of taking care of their animals. But considering he had somehow talked Gator Clark into removing the hallowed dewclaw, I held my tongue.

"Use the Dawn dishwashing soap. That's the best way to get the motor oil off," advised my boss.

"Yes, sir, I had planned to."

Dr. Spangle was very good about giving unsolicited advice for things I knew how to do. It was when I actually *needed* help that he became irritable, telling me I *should* have learned these things in vet school. As if vet school could possibly teach a person everything he needed to know in four short years. After forty years, I've come to realize how little I *do* know.

I sat Ivan in the deep sink in the treatment area and called for Tess. Myra, I knew, would refuse to touch Ivan unless Dr. Spangle took over his care, which was highly unlikely. But at least with Tess, what she lacked in experience, she more than made up for in willingness to help.

"Ugh! What *is* that?" Tess screwed up her face as she came into the treatment area.

"Burnt motor oil," I replied. "It's a home remedy for mange."

"Does it really work?" she asked.

"Not really. If it does any good at all, it may be due to the small amount of sulfur in the motor oil. Sulfur is an effective treatment for mange."

"Then why do people use it?"

"Because it's an old wives' tale and people don't know any better. Also, demodectic mange sometimes resolves on its own, so people think the motor oil is what cured it."

"This dog looks terrible. I don't think the motor oil is helping."

"It's not. Not only can the dog become sick if he licks the oil, but it can irritate the skin, making the condition worse. Toxic substances in the motor oil can also be absorbed through the skin."

I went into the surgery room and grabbed a scalpel blade and two pairs of surgical gloves. "Here," I said, handing her a pair. "I want you to wear these while we wash Ivan. But first, I need to get a skin scraping."

From the lab, I obtained a clean microscopic slide and a bottle of mineral oil. Then I attempted to find a relatively motor-oil-free area of skin on the poor dog. Using the scalpel blade, I scraped until the skin looked more irritated than it already was. The scraping had to be somewhat deep because the demodex mites live in the hair follicles deep in the skin. Placing the specimen on the slide, I dispersed it evenly through the mineral oil and left to examine it under the microscope.

It didn't take long. In the first field alone, numerous of the nasty, cigar-shaped demodex mites looked back at me, their squat little legs kicking vigorously in the mineral oil.

"Ivan's definitely got demodex," I confirmed, as I came back into the treatment room.

For the next hour, Tess and I scrubbed repeatedly with Dawn dishwashing soap, trying to remove as much of the motor oil as possible. Ivan stood stoically, gratitude flowing from his liquid brown eyes.

"Now what?" Tess asked, as I declared Ivan as clean from motor oil as we could get him.

"Now we're going to dip him with lime-sulfur, which smells like rotten eggs." Today, there are a variety of wonderful, easy to use products for treating demodex. Back then, we had a limited choice of foul-smelling dips, which sometimes worked and sometimes didn't.

Before long, the entire clinic reeked of the stench of rotten eggs.

"What are you doing?" screeched Myra, poking her head into the treatment area.

"A lime-sulfur dip," I replied, a little more sarcastically than was probably necessary, as I felt the answer to her question was intuitively obvious.

"We don't do those in the clinic! We send the dip home with the owners to do. *Outside!*" She shook her head at my stupidity, and for once, I saw her point.

"Sorry, I didn't realize." I sighed. I quickly dispatched Ivan to go home with Skeeter, along with a four-week supply of lime-sulfur dip, benzoyl peroxide shampoo, and antibiotics.

Several weeks later, Skeeter returned with Ivan. Ivan's skin had improved dramatically, and Skeeter was thrilled. But I still saw some live mites on the skin scrapings.

"What now, Doc?" Skeeter asked.

"We just need to treat Ivan a few weeks longer. Sometimes it takes several weeks to completely clear mange."

"Boy that stuff sure does stink," Skeeter said.

"I know, and I'm sorry, but it's the best treatment available."

Skeeter nodded. "That's okay, he stays outside most of the time anyway."

I thought we had finally cleared Ivan of his mange, but a few months passed, and once again, Skeeter and Ivan appeared at the clinic with the same problem.

A little discouraged, I ran my hands through the balding areas of Ivan's haircoat, as the non-descript mutt fixed me with his trusting gaze. A skin scraping confirmed that the mange was back—or probably never completely cured in the first place.

"I'm going to try a different dip," I told Skeeter.

Good-naturedly, he replied, "Whatever you say, Doc."

Two different dips later, Ivan still showed patches of hair loss. Although nowhere near the pitiful creature I had first encountered covered with burnt motor oil, he just couldn't seem to clear the mites.

About that time, a colleague told me about an orchard spray that was being used as an off-label treatment for demodex. She had managed to get her hands on the contraband, and generously offered to share it with me. Desperate, I was willing to grasp at any straw, despite the potential side-effects of using a commercial fruit pesticide unknown in dogs.

"This is a new treatment," I told Skeeter, excitedly. "It's not approved for use as a mange dip in dogs, but there have been anecdotal reports that it works quite well."

Bless his heart, Skeeter was willing to try anything, even if it wasn't approved for this use. Then again, he had also tried burnt motor oil, so perhaps that didn't say much.

The orchard dip, later developed into a veterinary product called Mitaban, worked well for a few months. But nothing got rid of the mange for good.

I finally had to resign myself to the fact that Ivan was one of those unfortunate individuals born with a faulty immune system. We knew that all dogs have small numbers of demodex mites in their skin as part of their normal flora, but these mites are generally kept under control by a normally functioning immune system. When the mites multiplied to the point they caused skin disease, it was often the result of an immature immune system—as in puppies— or another underlying disease-causing immunosuppression. We have since learned that genetics also tends to play a role, through a specific defect in T-cells, one of the components of the immune system responsible for cell-mediated immunity.

I ran a number of blood tests on Ivan, checking his thyroid, his adrenal glands, and his overall health. Everything came back normal. I made sure his flea control was top-notch. I even tested him for allergies. But in the end, I had to concede that Ivan had the rotten luck to be born with a lousy immune system.

I tried to explain this to Skeeter, who had been extremely patient over the frustrations and failures of the past several months.

"It's nobody's fault," I said, "Ivan just had the misfortune to be born with an immune system that isn't quite doing its job." I went on to explain about the life-cycle of the demodectic mange mite, the fact that it lived in the skin of all dogs, the role of the immune system in keeping the mite population low, and that in order to keep the mites under control, Ivan would require dips every two weeks for the rest of his life.

This was apparently too much information for Skeeter to swallow. He nodded politely as he exited the exam room, but I overheard him as he ran into Bubba Barnes and Digger in the lobby.

"So, what'd the doc say?" asked Bubba.

"Oh, she don' really know. Made up some crazy story about Ivan's moon system."

"Moon system? What the Sam Hill is that?"

"Don' rightly know. She says I gotta' keep dippin' him for the rest of his life."

Bubba grunted. "Shoulda' jus' listened to me in the first place and stuck with the motor oil. It's a lot cheaper."

"Maybe." Skeeter changed the subject. "Digger's lookin' mighty good."

"Yep! Just sired ten pups. Imagine. That lady doc tellin' me to cut off his manhood!"

ELLEN FANNON

Chapter 12

"**Jack wants me** to meet his family!" I blurted out to my best friend, Rosemary Ward, as I took my seat beside her in our Sunday school class.

Rosemary and I had met at the First Baptist Church of Pineville, shortly after I moved to Florida. Being the only two single women in a class full of young married couples, we immediately hit it off. Besides being the owner of an incredibly spoiled Boston terrier, Rosemary worked in the business office of the local hospital, so she had a fringe knowledge of medicine. Because I was on call every other weekend, I couldn't always attend church, but the second week I visited First Baptist, the young adult Sunday school class had a picnic in the park after services, and it happened to fall on one of my off Sundays. It seemed a good time to get to know people.

Being the new person in the crowd, I set my lawn chair in the middle of a group of gabbing young women. It occurred to me after a moment's observation that the men were all standing off to the side, deep in discussion of what sounded like sports. The women, engaged in their own conversations, seemed not to notice I had joined them. I remained quiet and listened, waiting for my opportunity to jump into the animated chatter.

"And then," a young red-haired woman said, "you wouldn't believe what Sarah did."

"What?" queried the two women on either side of her.

"*She went potty all by herself!*" gushed Red-Hair.

I took it she was referring to a child, not a dog.

"No!" came the surprised response from the blonde to her left. "Already? I couldn't get Hunter potty trained until he was almost three."

The woman on the other side of Red-Hair sighed loudly. "Well, at least you have a girl. I thought I was going to have to go to college with Richard to change his diapers. Boys are *so* much harder than girls."

Another woman across the circle contributed, "My pediatrician says you need to let them run around naked from the waist down."

"I tried that, but Jeffrey just peed on the floor," moaned a heavy-set woman sitting next to me, who still hadn't acknowledged my presence.

"Well, I'll sure be glad when this stage is over. It's so stressful," complained a dark-haired girl next to Blonde Lady. Dark-Haired Girl looked too young to have kids.

"You'll get through this," laughed Red-Hair. "Sarah didn't show the least bit of interest in using the potty, and then, suddenly, *bam!*"

"It wouldn't be so bad if Carson would just help out, but he's always so busy."

"Oh, don't I know it," Blonde Lady commiserated. "John is always working and when he gets home, he's too tired to help with the kids. And with number three on the way I don't know *what* I'm going to do."

My dog was housebroken in two weeks. Maybe you should stick to puppies. I tuned them out and looked around to see a lone woman putting out food on the picnic table behind us. Unnoticed, I'm sure, by the animated group of women in the circle, I stood and went to see if she needed help.

"Hi," she greeted, as I approached. "Rosemary Ward. I take it you're tired of listening to potty talk."

I laughed. "Jill Bennet. Is there anything I can do to help?"

"It's about all ready. You look so familiar. I think I've seen you somewhere before."

"Do you have a pet?"

Rosemary snapped her fingers. "That's where I've seen you. You're the new vet. I saw you at the clinic one day when I was in buying food for Ollie. I didn't get the chance to meet you, but I thought it was great to finally have a lady vet in our area."

"Thanks. I hope I get to meet Ollie soon."

"Oh, you will. He's coming due for his annual. I'll ask for you." She leaned over and said quietly, "Are you married?"

"No. Why?"

"Oh goody! That makes us the two old maids in the class. Our church is so small we don't have enough people for a singles' class. And other than some old geezers, you and I are the only singles. It's so nice to finally have someone my age at church beside the Stepford Wives."

I grinned at her somewhat unflattering depiction of the chattering women. Rosemary immediately made me feel so welcome. "I guess I don't have much in common with the young- marrieds-with-children," I admitted. "Speaking of which, where are their kids?"

"The nursery coordinator volunteered to watch them so—get this—the young couples, me excluded, of course, could have some time to themselves without the children. So, what have they been doing for the last forty-five minutes? The women have been sitting around talking about *their kids*. And the men immediately distanced themselves so they didn't have to listen to their wives talk about *their kids*."

Rosemary rolled her eyes. "Those ladies have set women's liberation back a hundred years. It's like the 19th amendment never happened." She clucked her tongue.

Giggles spilled from me. "Rosemary, you're terrible. Surely they're not that bad."

"Oh, don't pay me any mind. I'm just jealous, that's all. I'm waiting for Mr. Right to come along and sweep me off my feet so I can buy a station wagon and join the ranks of the sisterhood." She let out a self-deprecating little chuckle.

"I take it the ladies aren't all *that* bad, then."

Rosemary smiled. "Nah., I love them all like sisters. We're in different places in our lives right now, that's all. But now God has sent me *you*. You're going to be my new best friend."

And I was. Over the next couple years, Rosemary and I formed the solid friendship of two busy career women who rarely had time for outside interests, but when we did, we clicked perfectly. Rosemary was fun, smart, and outrageously irreverent. I soon found that despite the initial not-so-flattering portrayal of her fellow Sunday school classmates, Rosemary was a solid and dependable friend to them all and they teased her, good-naturedly, just as much as she did them. And once past the potty talk, I became friends with them, too. I even liked most of their children, although I had never been particularly comfortable around children. But Rosemary still remained my "go-to" soul mate.

"Meet the family?" she now squawked in mock horror. "Oh no! You've gone over to the dark side! You've become one of *them!*"

"Rosemary, this is serious! His parents don't like animals!"

Her eyes grew wide. "See, I told you to dump him," she teased. In truth, she liked Jack and he liked her. And since Jack and I had been spending most of our free time together, meeting his family seemed the inevitable next step.

"Look, Jill, they're going to love you. There's no way they won't."

~

I only wished I could have had Rosemary's confidence in myself when I stepped over the threshold to meet Jack's family for the first time.

"We're here," Jack announced, ushering me into the family room. A large crowd of people swarmed around me, all talking at once. As Jack introduced me to his large immediate and extended family, I felt completely overwhelmed. I couldn't remember anyone's name or how they and Jack were related. It seemed half the town occupied this tiny home. I would have preferred to have started out small with perhaps just his parents or even a couple of his many sisters. But nobody wanted to be left out of the first meeting of Jack's girlfriend. A bug under a microscope couldn't have felt more on display than I did. The air in the small room hung dense and heavy, and a trickle of sweat worked its way down my forehead.

I reached up to wipe away the sweat, just as Jack's mother hustled out of the kitchen, wiping her hands on her apron. She enveloped me in a crushing hug and joined in the deafening racket. A plump, matronly woman, Mrs. Hill wore her silver hair in a messy bun with frizzy tendrils escaping willy-nilly, giving her a frenzied appearance. I soon realized it wasn't just her appearance that was frenzied. The woman, herself, seemed to run on pure adrenaline. She soon excused herself to head back to the kitchen, where I watched her scurry back and forth between it and the dining room, into which had been squeezed two long tables and an assortment of chairs. Nobody else appeared to notice or offered to help.

"I'm going to see if your mom needs help," I finally told Jack.

"You can try, but Mom is in her element when she has a houseful of people. She likes to do everything herself."

Still, I couldn't stand the sight of the one-woman whirlwind single-handedly doing all the work. If I were in her place, I would be in the midst of a nervous breakdown. I eased from the crowd and made my way into the cramped kitchen, where delicious aromas battled each other for dominance. Steam wafted from several mis-matched, covered bowls lined up on the limited counter space. Stifling heat rose to mix with the already thick air in the room.

"Mrs. Hill, can I do anything to help?" I asked.

I must have startled her, because she jumped, nearly dropping a basket of heavenly-smelling rolls. "Oh, *no*, dear, you're our guest." She took my elbow, as if I were an invalid, and ushered me back out of the room. "You just relax and enjoy yourself. Dinner will be ready shortly."

"Told you so," Jack said when I returned to his side.

A few minutes later, Jack's mother appeared in the entryway to the dining room and announced, "Come sit, everybody."

A mad stampede ensued, with everyone trying to jam into the small space at the same time. Jack shielded me from the onslaught and tenderly seated me next to his oldest sister, Rebecca, about half-way down the length of the enormous table, where everyone could get a could view of me. He sat on my other side and gave my nervous hand a reassuring squeeze. The multitude of children of various ages took up places at the second table.

Jack's father said a brief prayer, and everyone dug in. My knotted stomach ruined the anticipation of the sumptuous feast.

"This all looks delicious," I said, placing a small dollop of mashed potatoes on my plate, hoping they would just slide past the lump that had taken up residence in my throat. "I wish I could cook like you, Mrs. Hill. I'm afraid I'm not much good in the kitchen." I forced out a self-deprecating little laugh, which sounded to my horrified ears like the bray of a donkey.

The entire room grew silent, even the children's table, and everyone stared at me. Good gracious, what had I said? Or was it my braying?

"Oh, don't worry, dear," Mrs. Hill assured me. "Once you get married and settle down, you'll learn to cook in no time."

The ball seemed to be back in my court, as the heads swung round to me again. *Get married and settle down? What did that mean?*

Jack, mercifully, came to my rescue. "Jill's pretty busy with her job, Mom. She doesn't have a lot of time to cook."

Mrs. Hill waved her son's comment aside with her hand. "Oh, pooh. That will all change once she's married and settles down."

Warning bells began to sound in my brain. Apparently, Jack's family thought my career was simply a means of killing time until I landed a husband. I didn't want to burst their bubble, but I had no intention of giving up my hard-earned career, even if I did manage to snag a man. I suddenly felt very much on trial. I was obviously being evaluated for suitability as Jack's future wife. With a pang of guilt, I remembered the first meal I served Jack when he came for dinner. A take-out pizza. The second time he had come for dinner I made grilled-cheese sandwiches. But at least I had cooked. Perhaps the family's unspoken misgivings were right—Jack needed to look elsewhere for a life partner.

Jack's Aunt DeeDee spoke up. "You know, we *finally* had to break down and get Lucy a puppy. She just wouldn't give up."

At the sound of her name, a golden-haired moppet at the next table raised her head and grinned.

Oh good! A change of subject to something I could relate to. A new puppy! *Thank you, dear Aunt DeeDee!*

The woman shook her head. "I had to take it to the vet the other day for its shots. And you wouldn't believe what they asked me to do."

All eyes rested on DeeDee. "They told me to bring in a sample of its *stool!*"

A collective gasp of disgust rose from the table.

"Can you *imagine?*"

Well, yes, actually I could. Testing puppies for intestinal parasites was extremely important, not only for the health of the animal, but because certain parasites could be transmitted to humans. I didn't think it would be a good idea to point this last fact out to DeeDee, however, as I spooned a serving of pole beans onto my plate. I attempted a bite of roast beef, dreading where DeeDee was heading with this discussion.

DeeDee went on. "I never in my *life!* I told them that was the most revolting thing I had ever heard of, picking up a *dog's poop* and carrying it to the vet." She glowered at the man next to her, who must have been her husband. "And since the whole thing was *Ronnie's* idea, I told them he would just have to deal with it."

"Mama won't let me bring Oscar into the house," bemoaned Lucy.

DeeDee turned to her daughter. "Of *course,* you can't bring that filthy animal into the house. That was the condition we all agreed to when we decided to let you have a dog against my better judgement." She turned back to her captive audience at the adult table. "It's bad enough outside. But I'll not have dog hair and . . . and fleas and who knows what else in my house." Her distressed hands punctuated the air in front of her. "And you wouldn't *believe* how much the vet charged me. Twenty dollars! For a *dog!*"

I glanced around at the astonishment registered on the faces at the table and decided not to defend my profession's audacity to charge for its services.

DON'T BITE THE DOCTOR

"Oscar is so cute!" Lucy piped up.

At the risk of digging myself deeper into the hole of the Hill's disapproval, I replied, "Puppies are cute, aren't they, Lucy?"

DeeDee spoke again. "I'm always on Lucy to stop letting that filthy animal lick her in the face. Who knows what diseases it's carrying?"

Well, duh, DeeDee. That's why you take it to a highly trained professional who is paid to be sure it's healthy. I restrained my tongue, but only for a brief second.

"Actually, dogs' mouths are cleaner than human mouths." I didn't know this for a fact. It might have been an old wives' tale for all I knew. I didn't remember addressing this particular issue in veterinary school. But it was something I had heard all my life and it sounded good.

The group at the table stared at me as if I had sprouted goat horns.

"Baby animals are so cute, aren't they, Jill?" Lucy persisted.

At least I had *one* member of the family in my corner, not counting Jack, who, after this fiasco of a dinner, might have second thoughts.

"Yes, they certainly are," I agreed.

"Well, just you wait until you have your own babies," Jack's granny cut in. "Then you'll want to stay home and take care of them and stop all this nonsense about working." The wizened old lady beamed at me, then reached up to adjust her teeth.

"That's right," Jack's mother agreed. "A woman's place is in the home. Once you're married, you won't need to work anymore. Then you can stay home and have babies."

My throat constricted to the point where I didn't think even the mashed potatoes could squeeze through. I didn't *dare* say aloud that I wasn't sure I wanted children.

"To be truthful," I heard my rebellious mouth say, "I'm not sure I want children."

Mrs. Hill's fork dropped with a loud clang against her plate. "Not want babies? *Every* woman wants babies!"

"And I won't be quitting my job if and when I get married. I worked very hard to get through school and I love practicing veterinary medicine."

After a very long and uncomfortable silence, Rebecca spoke up. "I just don't understand. If you wanted a career in medicine, why didn't you become a nurse? At least that's a *noble* profession."

I noticed she didn't say *a physician*. "Because I didn't *want* to become a nurse," I replied. The hackles on the back of my neck stood at attention and I was in imminent danger of trying to convert an entire room of Jack's kin with ill-chosen words. It would never work.

"You'll have to give me your recipe for this pot roast, Mrs. Hill," I chickened out.

"Of course," she smiled, a look of immense relief flooding her face.

I read in the expressions that settled on the rest of the faces that there might still be hope for me, yet.

~

"Jack, they were interviewing me for the role of your wife and mother of your future children!" I lamented to my boyfriend, as he drove me home from the disastrous meeting of the family.

He laughed, softly. "No, they weren't."

I turned in the truck seat to face him, although his eyes were on the road. "Yes, they *were!*" I insisted. "I am obviously not the woman your family envisions for you."

"Well, you're not marrying my family," he replied.

My heart stuttered. Jack had used the "M" word. I stared, wide-eyed at the side of his head.

He turned slightly, and I noticed the familiar red blush creeping up from his neck to the tip of his right ear.

I didn't dare break the silence that ensued and continued until he pulled into my driveway, but my heart flopping around in my chest like a dying fish sounded deafening to my ears. Surely Jack heard it, too. From the house came the yapping of my two dogs, Bitsy and Delilah. I could see their happy faces in the window, tongues hanging out, thrilled to see I was home.

Jack made no move to get out of the truck. I stared at my hands, which I gripped tightly in my lap to keep from shaking.

After what seemed an eternity, Jack twisted his body to face me. "This wasn't how I planned to do this, you know."

"Do what?"

"Propose." His dark eyes, a hint of merriment in them, searched mine.

Stunned, I remained speechless for once.

"What I said about marrying my family just kind of slipped out."

Still, I couldn't speak.

"You're not making this easy, you know." Jack took a deep breath and I held mine. "Jill, I love you. I want to spend the rest of my life with you." The merriment in his eyes gave way to abject terror.

I laughed. That was probably not the reaction he had been hoping for. But the timing of his proposal seemed so surreal after my miserable failure to meet his family's expectations, Lucy aside.

"Jack, are you sure?" That was probably not what he expected, either. I shook my head. "I mean, we're so different in a lot of ways and—"

He reached over and took my trembling hands. "We're alike in the things that matter."

"—and your family hates me, especially Aunt DeeDee and—"

"My family doesn't hate you. And DeeDee lives an hour away. We'll hardly ever see her. And like I said, you're not marrying my family."

I took a shaky breath as tears collected in my eyes. I bit my lip and nodded. "Okay," I whispered.

Jack let go of my hands and pulled me into a tight embrace. "I love you, Jill," he murmured into my hair. "I promise I'll always be a good husband to you."

Beyond a shadow of a doubt, I knew what he said was true. "I can't cook," I felt obligated to point out.

It was his turn to laugh. "That's okay, I can cook."

"I'm not giving up my career."

"I wouldn't want you to. Where else could I get free veterinary care for Flash?"

I burst out laughing and pulled away. "Is that the real reason you want to marry me, Jack? Free veterinary service?"

He pulled me back. "Among others."

Chapter 13

My mother flew in from Ohio to celebrate my upcoming birthday and to start helping with weddings plans. Thrilled her daughter was not going to end up an old maid, Mom immediately took to Jack, and even his family, who had still not quite come to terms with the fact I had no plans to quit my job and have babies once we were married.

I didn't want a lot of fuss over the wedding, which was scheduled in the spring, a few months away. My mother, however, didn't see things that way, and methodically went down her ever-present to-do list. Having her staying with me had its benefits, though. Every night I came home to a good dinner, and she insisted on cleaning up the kitchen, as well as keeping my house immaculate. I could tell, however, that she was growing bored, even with all the wedding preparations and domesticity, so I began taking her with me on emergency calls.

Ever the avid learner, as well as an animal lover, my mother found every aspect of my job fascinating, and I doted on her attention. So few people seemed to realize what all my work entailed, and having someone appreciate what I did, even if it was my *mother*, affirmed my sense of worth in my chosen profession. My inflated ego crashed and burned, however, the first and only time I took her on a horse call.

My birthday fell on a Saturday that year, which, of course, meant nothing. I worked the usual half day that stretched into the early afternoon. I came home tired and hungry, wanting only to collapse on the couch and rot my brain with mindless television. It *was* my birthday, after all. My mother, however, had a different idea.

"I didn't get you anything for your birthday," she greeted, as soon as I walked in the door. "So, I was thinking, why don't I take you to the mall and let you pick out something?"

Now the last thing I wanted to do was drive across town to the mall, let alone spend "girl time" with my mother shopping. I am not a typical female shopper who loves to wander in and out of stores with no idea of what I'm looking for. I'm more of a "get in, find what I want and get out" type of customer. I took no joy in prolonging the process. But my mother looked so excitedly happy at the prospect of trotting me in and out of stores searching for that perfect *something* that would tell me just how much she loved me, I couldn't say no.

"That sounds great, Mom," I lied.

"We can have lunch out, too," she suggested, or rather insisted.

Lunch sounded good. I was starving. "Okay," I agreed, and we set off.

About halfway to the mall, the inevitable happened. My beeper went off. Just because it was my birthday didn't excuse me from taking emergency calls, and there was no way I would lower myself to ask my boss to cover for me. Dr. Spangle didn't believe in foolish nonsense such as a personal life outside of work and would likely have been completely unsympathetic to the fact I happened to be born on this day and my mother was visiting from several hundred miles away in order to celebrate my entrance into the world. So, I didn't bother. Besides, I didn't have any particular plans. Perhaps a simple dinner and a movie at home with Mom and Jack. That's about all I was up for anyway.

"Sorry, Mom, I need to find a phone," I sighed, debating on whether to keep heading to the mall or turn back toward home.

"That's fine," she replied, once again simply happy to be along on the adventure that was my life.

"Maybe I can just give some advice over the phone and won't have to go in."

"That's fine," she assured me, again.

I pulled into a small strip mall and located a pay phone. *Dear God, give me a break. Let it be something non-urgent and let me get back to spending some time with my mother.* As it was, with my long workdays, I'd spent precious little time with her. Then I reminded the good Lord, *it is my birthday, after all,* as if that revelation had escaped His notice and He might show mercy upon me as a benevolent favor to this special day.

God apparently didn't quite catch my entire petition. Or maybe He did, but once again was about to teach me that my plans weren't His plans. I punched in the number for the answering service, who patched me right through to a client with a foal suffering from colic. My hopes plummeted. I had no choice. I had to go. And I wasn't dressed for an afternoon at the stable. My coveralls were in the laundry at home, which lay in the opposite direction. Giving in to a modicum of self-pity and *why me, why now*, I returned to the car.

"Is it something serious?" Mom asked, before I could close the car door. "Do you have to go in?"

I groaned. "Yes, but not to the clinic. It's a foal with colic. I have to go to a stable."

"Oh!" Mom brightened. "How exciting!"

My mind churned with the logistics. The barn was not too far from where we were, and Mom would love going with me. She hadn't observed me doing any large animal work. If the call didn't take too terribly long, we might even still be able to make it to the mall.

"The stable is just a few miles from here," I said. "We'll swing by there and see how bad it is."

"That sounds good." To Mom this was one great adventure, rather than the huge pain it was to me.

A few minutes later, we drove through the gates to Pinewood Farms, my tires crunching over the uneven gravel and dirt road leading to the front of the stables. I had long since given up on cringing in response to the dust kicked up from these rural lanes settling on my once shiny red paint. Still, the occasional kicked up piece of gravel pinging against the car's body always made me flinch.

Characteristically, a crowd of people were gathered around the sick animal. All eyes turned toward us as Mom and I exited the car. As I extracted my large animal box from the trunk of my car, a few hesitant raindrops fell from a lone, gray cloud floating just above our heads. Typical of this area, a virtual deluge could let lose in one spot, and a quarter mile away, it was completely dry. A torrential downpour often lasted for mere minutes, coming and going in the short time it took to shut opened windows against the storm. Hoping for nothing more than a light sprinkle, I strode confidently into the arena, Mom on my heels.

A nervous-looking young woman, about my age, stood trying to comfort an obviously distressed little bay filly. I guessed the foal to be approximately three months old.

"Oh, thank you so much for coming," the young woman said. "I'm Margie Pierce. My husband spoke to you on the phone." She indicated a worried-looking young man off to the side, leaning against a brown split-rail fence separating the stable area from the corral, smoking a cigarette. The fleeting thought ran through my mind that smoking in this environment was inadvisable.

"I'm Dr. Bennet," I said, extending my hand. "And who is this lovely young lady?" I withdrew my hand from

Margie's clammy one, and brushed it gently across the baby's fuzzy muzzle, eliciting a soft snort. Just then, the sky opened up and released an overflow of pent-up raindrops from the oversaturated little cloud. We scurried for shelter inside the stable—the filly balking at first—but not before getting thoroughly drenched by the unexpected downpour. Forced into protection from the sudden storm, the crowd impinged upon us even more closely.

"This is Winnifred." Margie stopped to catch her breath, patting the foal's neck as the animal tossed her head against the unanticipated soaking. "We just started her on grain and I'm afraid that might have caused the stomach upset."

"It's possible," I agreed, "or it could be totally coincidence." I raised the filly's lip, satisfied with the healthy pink gum color and quick perfusion. The pulse was strong and steady, not overly elevated. While I examined the patient, I asked about the usual history—when did the pain start, any previous illnesses, any problems with the birth, diet, other issues. All had been normal. Sticking my stethoscope into my ears, I listened to the chest, then the abdomen. I thumped the tense abdomen with my thumb and third finger, trying to ascertain a pinging sound which is often heard with excessive gas. I heard no evidence of gas, and there were good, burbling gut sounds. The small size of the patient precluded a rectal exam.

"What do you think?" Margie asked.

I folded my stethoscope back into my box and pulled out a bottle of Banamine. "It doesn't look too serious. I'll give her something for pain and we'll see how she does."

The rain stopped as suddenly as it had started, and the tight area in the stable became insufferably hot and stuffy. "Let's move her back outside. I think she'll be more comfortable in the open."

We made our exit from the barn, although the rain had done nothing to cool the muggy air. If anything, it had made things worse, as steam rose from the baking ground. My wet hair, plastered to my head, now reacted to the one hundred percent humidity by springing into frizzy coils, and my damp clothes clung hot and sticky to my skin. I could almost picture water vapor oozing from my body in an eerie mist. The onlookers, as expected, meandered back outside.

As I drew up a few cc's of medication into my syringe, I became vaguely aware of my mother doing what she did best—chatting away to the crowd of people assembled to watch the show. Unlike me, Mom had never met a stranger. I stepped back to the filly, held off the jugular vein to administer the injection, and then stopped cold when I heard my mother's voice carrying over the tense silence.

"She's so small. Is she still a *pony?*"

I almost dropped my syringe. I could feel my credibility as a horse doctor dripping away like the sweat that had instantly appeared on my brow, that was still dripping from the rain. How could anyone with a mother so dense as to think baby horses were *ponies* possibly know what she was doing? I held my breath, waiting for lightening to strike us all. It was no use pretending I didn't know the woman. I had brought her with me, after all.

Somehow, I managed to get the injection into the *baby horse, not pony,* and even managed to wait for several long minutes to see if it would do the trick. Mom appeared baffled by the chilly responses she got from further attempts at conversation with the onlookers. Thank goodness the two old geezers weren't here. Ole' Doc Potter would be rolling over in his grave if he had heard the blasphemy which had issued forth from the ignorant mouth of the lady horse doctor's mother.

I couldn't usher Mom back into the car quickly enough. Driving away, as fast as my car would bounce over the uneven terrain, I turned to her and blurted, "How *could* you?"

"What? What did I do?" She still didn't get it.

"Mom!" I wailed. "A pony is not a baby horse!"

"Well, how was I supposed to know that? I thought ponies were baby horses." She crossed her arms over her chest, her lips set in a defiant line.

"You made me look like an idiot!" I railed at her. "It's bad enough I'm not a *horse person*. I wasn't raised with horses. I don't own a horse. I'm automatically treated with distrust. But . . . but . . . *this!* Nobody will ever think I know anything about horses now!"

Mom sat, wounded to the core. "Really, Jill, I don't see what you're getting so upset about. It was an honest mistake. I'll bet lots of people think ponies are baby horses."

"Not *horse people*, Mom!"

"Well, fine. I'm sorry. But I don't see how my mistake reflects on you or your abilities." Contrary to what she'd said, she didn't sound the least bit sorry.

"Maybe it shouldn't. But your faux pax automatically extends to me as your daughter."

Mom took a deep breath. I'm sure she wanted to point out all the times I had embarrassed *her* over the years, but wisely refrained from digging up old history. "Let's just drop this discussion and go to the mall."

I really didn't want to go to the mall after this, but I felt bad about berating her. She was right. Why should horse people judge me for my mother's sin? Still, I knew they would.

I sighed. I was hot, sweaty, wet, smelled like a stable, and in a foul mood. "Okay," I agreed. Maybe a little retail therapy would actually work to relax me this time.

It didn't. After two hours of dragging through the stores and not finding the perfect birthday present, I was more than ready to call it quits. Mom finally insisted on buying me a pair of shoes I didn't need, and I agreed in order to get out of there. By that time my clothes had dried, though they hugged my body in wrinkled testimony to the earlier shower.

We drove home in silence. I was still miserable and brooding over the horse incident and wanted nothing more than to climb into a warm, lavender-scented bath and soak away the day's tensions and smells.

Pulling into the driveway, I knew I looked like something the cat dragged in, but I didn't care. I was home at last. I was only moments away from escaping the world and collapsing into a warm tub, and my mother was not going to guilt me into anything else. It was *my birthday* and I intended to spend the rest of it doing what I wanted.

Drat, I hadn't left the porch light on. Then again, when we'd left the house I hadn't anticipated coming home in the dark. Fumbling for the lock, I breathed a weary sigh of relief as my key made contact and turned. I pushed into the darkened house and groped for the light switch. Suddenly, blinding lights exploded around me and a hoard of people jumped out yelling, "Surprise!"

I'm not sure who was more shocked—me or the happy celebrants when they beheld their first sight of the bedraggled birthday girl. Someone would pay for this, I vowed.

Several hours later, when the last of the partygoers had finally left, Mom and Jack asked, "So, were you surprised?"

Weary to the point of hysteria, I laughed. "Yes, I didn't suspect a thing."

Mom and Jack exchanged conspiratorial looks. "I was so afraid we wouldn't be able to pull it off. After you got that emergency call, I was worried you'd want to come back home. Especially after we got caught in the rain. Jack still needed time to get things ready."

"I never suspected anything. If I'd had any inkling of what you two had planned, I would have insisted on stopping by the clinic to take a shower before coming home." I always kept a *just in case* change of clothes at work. Walking into a room filled with well-dressed, nice-smelling people, looking as I did, and reeking of horse stable had been humbling, to say the least. But everyone had been too polite to mention that I looked rode hard and put away wet.

"Good night, Mom," I called out, an hour later, after finally getting a quick shower to wash away the day. "And thank you for everything." *In spite of everything.*

"I hope you had a good birthday, despite some detours," Mom said.

I laughed. "I did. You and Jack did an amazing job of keeping everything a secret."

A long pause followed. Then Mom spoke again. "Jill, can I ask you something?"

"Of course, Mom, what?"

"What exactly *is* a pony, anyway?"

I laughed. "Mom, you really have no horse sense."

Chapter 14

I have found the stethoscope to be one of the best pieces of medical equipment ever invented. Not only can one sling it around the neck and instantly appear "doctorly," but it has other great uses, besides the obvious.

Yes, it is a remarkable apparatus with which to auscultate the various body organs. Using a stethoscope to listen to the heart gives the doctor information such as whether there is a heart murmur caused by a leaky valve, or an arrythmia, in which the heartbeat is irregular. The lungs can also be examined for abnormal sounds, such as wheezing, crackles, or rattles. Absence of normal heart and lung sounds point to the possibility of something in the way, such as free fluid or air in the pleural space preventing the lungs from expanding, or fluid in the pericardial sac surrounding the heart precluding the heart from contracting properly. In addition, the stethoscope tells us vital information as to the presence or absence of gut sounds and placing it over the trachea can distinguish upper airway from lower airway disease.

But one way in which almost all doctors utilize this wonderful device is to buy time. Sometimes, we just need to regroup and think, before bumbling ahead into unknown territory, and anxious owners don't give us the luxury of a quiet contemplation in the exam room. If I don't have a clue what is going on and the owner is pressing me for an immediate answer, a long, leisurely auscultation can buy me a couple of minutes to meditate on what my next step should be—aside from the fact it looks like I'm actually doing something to try to diagnose the problem. Even if the pet presents with a non-specific lameness or an odd skin disorder, a good listen to the heart is imperative in formulating a plan.

The problem comes with the "chatty" clients who, upon seeing the earpieces of the stethoscope enter my ears, seize upon this opportunity of my moment of silence to enlighten me with more and more details. Or talk about their grandchildren. Or where they went on vacation last summer. Apparently, they believe that if I am not talking to them, they need to jump in and fill the void in the conversation. And what better chance than when I am busy with my stethoscope? If I am playing for time, I let them rattle on, since this seems to make them happy. I don't have to listen to them, and it's not hampering my examination. However, it's the ones who won't shut up when I am truly trying to hear something who exasperate me.

The Duffys were such clients. They owned an ancient cat named Violet, who suffered from heart disease. For some reason, it always took all five members of the Duffy family to get Violet to her veterinary appointments. I liked Violet. She was a sweet old calico of unknown age, as the Duffys had acquired her as an adult stray sometime before the first two-footed Duffy child joined the household, and said child was now a young teenager. Despite her bad heart and the chaos in which she lived, Violet took everything in stride. Once out of her carrier, she always strutted across the exam room table, tail held regally toward the ceiling, and rubbed her head against my hand, soliciting nonstop head rubs. A loud purr usually accompanied her attention seeking; at least when she could breathe.

I noted, with a feeling of dread, that Violet was the first appointment on the schedule when I arrived at the clinic one Monday morning. I had just seen her the week before and drained more than eight ounces of fluid from her chest. Although the fluid inevitably came back due to her failing heart, the periodic removal usually bought her a few weeks of relief and some quality time with her family. For her to be back so soon meant her disease was progressing rapidly and soon there would be little I could do.

True to form, both Mr. and Mrs. Duffy and their three children took up half the waiting room when I opened the door to bring my patient back. Also, true to form, Violet initially refused to come out of her carrier. And finally, true to form, the Duffys offered all kinds of unhelpful suggestions for how to remove her.

"There's a towel in the bottom of the crate," Mr. Duffy told me, as if I couldn't see this for myself. "If you just pull on the towel, she'll come right out with it."

Now I had been doing this job for a while at this point, and never, in that time had I *ever* seen a cat slide out of a carrier on a towel, including the multitude of times Mr. Duffy had suggested I try. In fact, now that I have been doing this job for more than forty years can I say this trick has ever once worked. Nevertheless, I always kept my mouth shut and did things the owner's way. I yanked on the end of the towel and, surprise, surprise, the towel came out, leaving Violet sitting in the back of the carrier. It reminded me of the tablecloth parlor trick where one jerks the end of the tablecloth under a pile of dishes, leaving the dishes undisturbed on the table.

"Huh, would you look at that!" exclaimed Mr. Duffy. "It didn't work."

"Oh, Frank, just get the treats out of your pocket. She'll come out for them," instructed Mrs. Duffy.

This attempt at luring her out of her crate had never worked with Violet, either, or for that matter, precious few other felines.

"Oh, okay, right." Mr. Duffy withdrew a plastic bag with semi-moist morsels from his pants pocket and deposited them in front of the open crate door. "Come on, Violet, there's a good kitty, come and get the yummy snacks."

At their father's example, two of the children chimed in, positioning their faces in front of the open crate door and screeching, "Come on, Violet!"

The reticent feline withdrew even further into the depths of her crate, her body pressed to the back. This caused the children to beseech her even louder. "Violet! Come out!" One of the kids encouraged the effort further by banging on the side of the crate.

"Oh dear," lamented Mrs. Duffy, "what can we do to get her to come out?"

This might have been a perfectly legitimate question, had this scenario not replayed itself every time the Duffys came in with their cat. Ordinarily, I would have simply reached in and grasped Violet by the scruff of her neck and pulled her out. However, Violet occupied a huge crate, the depth of which exceeded the length of my short arm. Another technique I frequently employed—tilting the crate and letting gravity do the job—had upset the Duffys too badly in the past, so I opted to forego a repeat of that performance.

"We'll have to undo the top," I said. "Again." This is how I always ended up getting to my patient, and after all this time, I never failed to wonder why the Duffys didn't just skip to the chase and suggest unscrewing the top from the get-go. I didn't like having to do this because Violet had one of those old carriers with the rusted screws and wing nuts, and even after repeatedly being removed, the blasted screws and nuts still made extraction a chore. And, as usual, none of the five Duffys pitched in to help.

I painfully made my way around the entire carrier, loosening and removing ten rusty screws, then lifted the top of the carrier. Violet blinked at the bright light suddenly invading her dark corner, then head-butted me as I reached in to stroke her once lustrous multicolored fur. I gently lifted her out and placed the torn-apart carrier on the floor, where no one in the family ever made an attempt to put it back together.

"Now then, what is going on with Violet?" I asked.

"She's going like this!" The middle child, a boy about ten years old, made exaggerated gasping noises.

His older sister smacked him in the shoulder. "No, she's not, it's like this." The girl mimicked her own version of Violet's noisy respirations.

The youngest child, another girl, piped up. "No, it's like the big bad wolf that huffs and puffs and blows the house down." She blew out her cheeks for a thorough demonstration as turbulent air whooshed out past her lips.

The parents allowed their offspring to compete for dominance in supplying the history. Fortunately, after treating Violet for the past several weeks, I had a pretty good idea, even without their input. I pulled my stethoscope from around my neck and placed the bell on Violet's chest. This is when the older Duffys decided to weigh in.

"Well, you see, she's been doing this thing . . ."

Mrs. Duffy's voice was lost as her husband's boomed, "We've never seen her do this before, like she's hyperventilating . . ."

The children still competed with each other for their own voices to be heard. I held up my hand. "Please, I need for you all to be quiet so I can listen."

The family looked startled, as if I had asked them all to remove their clothes and streak through the lobby naked. But their sudden silence gave me only a brief reprieve. Within a few seconds they were all talking at once again. There was no way I could hear anything in Violet's chest with all the noise.

I tucked Violet under my arm and excused myself to the back. Once away from the exam room, I headed into surgery and closed the door, where I could block out most of the clinic noise. As I poised my stethoscope over Violet's thorax once more, Tess threw open the door.

"Oh, is that Violet again?" she asked.

I held my finger to my lips and nodded, as I attempted to count Violet's heart beats.

"Oh, poor thing. Is it the same thing as before?"

I looked up at her with barely concealed impatience. "I'm not sure. Would you please be quiet so I can hear?"

Tess looked a little hurt, but managed to briefly hold her tongue. At least until she apparently thought I was taking too long. "Well, what is it?"

"Tess!"

Chastened, Tess bit her lip. To distract herself from talking, she absently patted Violet's head, a tapping noise which carried down to the chest where I was trying, unsuccessfully, to hear something besides head banging.

I removed my stethoscope from my ears and murmured, "Would you please not pat Violet's head? I can hear the drumming through the stethoscope."

Tess withdrew her hand and stood quietly for a blessed few seconds. Just when I finally thought I heard something definitive, Violet decided to purr. All chest sounds were drowned out by the soft rumbling referred from the region of Violet's vocal cords.

"Violet, not now," I said. I tried covering her nostrils, gently squeezing her throat, and even putting rubbing alcohol on a cotton ball and waving it under her nose—a trick that usually ticked off cats enough to stop purring—but Violet's contented droning continued unabated. How I envied my counterparts in human medicine who simply ordered their patients to "take a deep breath and hold it." Except for pediatricians, of course, who probably regularly got their ear drums blasted with screaming children.

"All right, you leave me no alternative," I told the contented feline. Whipping my thermometer out of my pocket, I lubricated it and inserted it into Violet's rectum. Not that I thought she had a fever, but the intrusion into her privacy caused the purring to abruptly stop and I got a few short seconds of uninterrupted auscultation.

To my relief, I could hear Violet's heart sounds easily and her lungs sounded clear. So, I didn't think she had any significant fluid buildup. Just then, Violet made a noise that sends terror through the hearts of most owners at one time or another; that is until the benign condition is explained to them. Violet had a reverse sneeze.

To many owners, a reverse sneeze resembles an asthma attack, and they worry the pet can't breathe. The animal makes forceful, snorting inspirations, often with its neck extended and lips pulled back, which can appear alarming. A reverse sneeze is a response to an irritation in the back of the throat, and although more common in the dog, is occasionally seen in cats. Since most episodes only last a few seconds, no treatment is usually necessary.

I returned Violet to her family with the good news that it wasn't her heart this time and attempted to question them about any changes in her environment that might have elicited an allergic or irritating response in her throat. But, as usual, I heard conflicting bits of information, so I left them with instructions to try rubbing her throat when she had an episode. Then I methodically replaced all the screws and nuts on Violet's cage and placed her inside. Slinging my stethoscope around my neck, I bid the Duffys goodbye and moved on to my next patient.

ELLEN FANNON

Chapter 15

In my first encounter with the Burns, I quickly realized this would not be the simple appointment I had hoped for. With the vague description of "new patient exam" on the appointment schedule, I could be walking blindly into any one of a hundred possible scenarios.

I picked up the chart and entered exam room one to greet a pleasant looking middle-aged couple and their handsome golden retriever.

"Hello," I said, extending my hand to first the husband, then the wife. "I'm Dr. Bennet." Then I made my first mistake. "I see we don't have Buddy's age listed in his medical record. Can you tell me how old he is?"

It seemed a straightforward enough question. At least to me.

"Well, we got him when Caroline was a freshman in high school—" answered the wife.

"No, dear, she was a sophomore. Remember, we got him right after she flunked that algebra test and she was so upset."

"Oh, that's right. Getting Buddy really cheered her up." The wife went on, excitedly, "We named her after that Neil Diamond song, Sweet Caroline. We just love Neil Diamond." She laughed. "It was either Sweet Caroline or Cracklin' Rosie. Sweet Caroline seemed to fit her better. Anyway, she's a junior at the University of Florida now.

She's majoring in elementary education. She was majoring in finance, but she couldn't stand her economics professor—"

"No, Lorraine, it was her statistics professor," corrected the husband.

The wife turned to her husband. "No, Tom, it was Dr. Zimmer. Remember? He was her economics professor. He was so hard on her."

Mrs. Burns suddenly began fishing through her large purse sitting on her lap. To my dismay, she extracted a wallet, out of which a large photo collage unfolded. "This is our daughter, Caroline." She stood, laid the photo collection on the exam table, and pointed to a somewhat blurry picture at the top of the fold-out.

I mumbled the obligatory, "She's very pretty. Anyway, about—"

"No, Dr. Zimmer was her statistics professor," Tom interrupted. "I'm positive."

I took that moment to squat next to my patient and began examining Buddy.

Mrs. Burns put her hands on her hips and glared at her husband. "Tom, I'm *sure* he was the economics professor. Oh! Here's a picture of Caroline with her boyfriend, Kyle. He's the nicest young boy. He's majoring in pre-law. His father's a dentist." She dangled the collage in my face.

"Speaking of dentists," I interjected, "Buddy's teeth could use a cleaning. He has a lot of—"

"Oh, no. Our last vet, Dr. Gates, said he was too old to be put under anesthesia," Lorraine informed me.

I quickly did the math. Buddy must be about six, unless Caroline was held back. Maybe it took a couple extra years for her to get to the level of a college junior. Come to think of it, if Caroline flunked algebra, why had she originally been majoring in finance? Perhaps Dr. Zimmer had seen the issue with a math-flunker making a career out of crunching numbers; hence the problem. Shaking my head, I realized we were now ten minutes into our allotted fifteen-minute appointment, my next patient was waiting, and I had not one relevant piece of information about my current patient, who might be anywhere between the ages of six and perhaps nine. Unless Buddy hadn't been acquired as a puppy when Caroline was a sophomore in high school.

"That's right," said Tom, snapping me out of my reverie. "Our neighbor's dog died under anesthesia, you know."

Lorraine turned to me. "They were the nicest people. What were their names again, Tom?"

"Parker," said Tom. "John and Norma."

"No, I don't think that's right. Are you sure it wasn't John and Naomi?"

"It *could* have been Naomi. No, maybe it was Nancy."

"I believe you're right. I think I remember a 'Nancy.' Actually, I think I still have a picture of them with that dog." Lorraine flipped through her pictures. "The dog's name was Sparky, I believe. Or was it Spanky?"

I tried to bring up something relevant about their visit, but they were both ignoring me as Lorraine searched for that elusive picture of John and Norma/Naomi/Nancy Parker and their unfortunate canine, Sparky or Spanky. It struck me that there was nothing more time consuming and aggravating than someone searching for an elusive picture to show you that you didn't want to see in the first place.

"Excuse me a moment," I said. I left the room, grabbed Myra, and threw her under the bus. "Find out what Buddy is here for. But don't ask his age."

"I can't," she replied, crawling out from under the bus. "I'm in the middle of doing radiographs."

"When you finish, go in and find out." I threw her back, as I headed into the next appointment.

Buddy's appointment set me back thirty minutes and I ran behind the rest of the morning.

The Burns became regular clients at Spangle Animal

Clinic. They always came in together, always argued over irrelevant details, and were always incapable of doing whatever I recommended.

"Buddy just isn't any better," Lorraine Burns lamented when the couple returned Buddy for a recheck of his skin condition.

I ran my hands over the happy dog, noting the scaliness hadn't improved. Underneath his thick wavy coat, his skin was still broken out in red, circular lesions called collarettes, typical of a Staph infection. As I parted the hair on his back, Buddy lifted his hind leg and started scratching himself. A Staph infection often accompanies allergies, which are prevalent where we live, but it usually responds well to antibiotics, and I had prescribed a three-week course of Cephalexin for Buddy. The medication should have been effective. It didn't make sense.

"Cephalexin is one of the best antibiotics for treating Buddy's infection," I mused, aloud. "Did you finish the entire prescription?"

"Oh, we didn't give him the pills," Tom explained.

"Buddy won't take pills," Lorraine added.

I stared at the couple. The words, *"How do you expect him to get better if you don't give him the medicine?"* perched on the tip of my tongue, but I pulled them back before I launched them.

"Did you try hiding them in peanut butter?" I asked. Peanut butter is often a good substance in which to sneak a dog's unwanted medicine.

"Yes," said Lorraine, at the same time Tom said, "No."

Lorraine turned to purse her lips at her husband. "Tom, I *specifically* told you I tried peanut butter."

"No, you told me you tried cheese, not peanut butter."

"I said no such thing. Why would I say I tried cheese, when I didn't?"

"How should I know? That's what you said."

"You could try using cheese," I interjected, helpfully.

At least *I* thought it was helpful.

The wife inhaled sharply. "I *most certainly* did *not* say 'cheese.' We rarely even have cheese in the house." She turned to me. "Both Caroline and I suffer from dairy intolerance."

"Well, *I* don't have dairy intolerance," Tom countered. "Maybe you gave him *my* cheese."

"And then I would have had cheese on my hands and what if I accidently didn't wash it all off? I might have died."

Tom rolled his eyes. "Lorraine, people don't die from dairy intolerance. It's not like it's an allergy."

"Or hot dogs. Some people hide their dog's pills in hot dogs." I don't know why I bothered. I had already lost my audience.

"I beg to differ. It most certainly *is* an allergy." Lorraine turned her back on her husband. "Don't pay any attention to him. He doesn't know what he's talking about."

"Hmph!" came a voice behind her. I couldn't actually see Tom anymore because his wife blocked him from my view. "*I* don't know what *I'm* talking about!"

"Look, why don't I give you some medicated shampoo to try?" I offered. "You can bathe Buddy, can't you?"

They stopped arguing and stared at me as if I had asked them if the ocean was wet.

"Of course, we can bathe him," Tom assured me.

So off they went with Buddy and his new treatment plan, and, I was sure, that was that.

Two weeks later, Buddy returned, this time in the care of not only the Burns, but also their dairy-intolerant, algebra-flunking daughter, Caroline.

"Dr. Bennet, this is our daughter, Caroline," Lorraine gushed. "She's home for a while on a school break."

Caroline huffed, "It's *not* a break, Mother, it's a *sabbatical*."

Lorraine retorted, "Break, sabbatical, what's the

difference?"

"They're not the *same thing,* Mother. I've already explained this to you several times."

"What can I do for Buddy today?" I interrupted.

They both stopped, giving me an incredulous look, obviously put out by my intrusion into their debate.

Mr. Burns took charge. "Well, as you can see, Buddy still has the rash."

I sighed and bent over my patient to see that, yes, the infection was still there. "Did you use the shampoo I sent home with you?"

"Actually, no," Mrs. Burns admitted. "You see, Caroline came home from school and when she saw what you had prescribed, she advised us not to use it."

My jaw dropped as I stared at the daughter. Wasn't she majoring in elementary education or finance or pre-law or something? How did she suddenly become an expert in veterinary medicine? I couldn't even think of anything to say at that moment.

Fortunately, Caroline was quick to explain. "Yes. When I showed the shampoo to my friend, Penelope, she said it was too strong."

"Caroline and Penelope have been friends since they were in kindergarten," Lorraine told me, apropos of nothing. "Penelope works at a florist shop. She makes the loveliest arrangements."

Ah! That would explain it! Wait. Nope, still confused as to Penelope's credentials.

"She worked for a kennel when she was in high school," Caroline filled in the blank for me, "so she knows a lot about animals."

I had to refrain from a snarky comment along the lines of cleaning cages didn't qualify one to practice veterinary medicine.

"Penelope's wonderful with dogs," Tom added. "She could have easily gone to vet school if she'd wanted, except she can't stand to see an animal get a shot."

There was nothing I loved hearing about more than all the animal lovers who could have "easily" gone to vet school. Why didn't they do so, then? Oh, yes, the pesky "shot" thing.

"Her father owns a landscaping company, so that's where Penelope gets her horticultural talent." Mrs. Burns started fishing in her purse and I was afraid she was going to pull out more pictures.

I cut in quickly when all three miraculously paused for breath at the same time. "I gave you the best shampoo for Buddy's condition. There is absolutely nothing in that shampoo that can harm him."

The trio regarded me, skeptically. After all, who was I to dispute what Penelope, the floral assistant, decreed?

"Look, I'll tell you what. Why don't you bring Buddy in for a bath twice a week? I will personally see to it that the shampoo is used correctly, and I'll be here in case any problems arise."

The three exchanged dubious glances.

"I'll run that idea by Penelope and see what she recommends," Caroline said. Her parents nodded in agreement.

Fortunately, Penelope concurred with my recommendation and the Burnses brought Buddy in for twice weekly baths. His skin cleared up nicely in a few weeks. The only problem was getting the Burnses out the door when they dropped him off and picked him up. However, I left most of that business to Heather, especially if I heard them up front.

"Here's Buddy for his bath," Heather told me, as she led the golden back into the treatment area.

"Did the Burns say how he was doing?" I asked.

"No, but I did find out that Caroline dropped out of school because she developed an anxiety disorder. Penelope is engaged to Joe, who went to school with her and Caroline. Joe works for FedEx. The wedding is scheduled for next spring. And Mr. Burns is having a colonoscopy in the morning."

I held up my hand to stop her. "Please, Heather, think of me as 'Joe Friday' in 'Dragnet.' Just the facts."

Chapter 16

The tinkling of a bell sounded when I opened the door to Rucker's Feed and Seed. I had been a regular customer of Rucker's since acquiring an unwanted parakeet from a client several months before. Veterinarians seldom had to go looking for pets of their own. They just kind of "happened" upon us. For some inexplicable reason, people had the mistaken impression that veterinarians were a fount of information for sources just aching to take on someone else's unwanted pets. I suppose this was a logical assumption; the truth, however, was that for every ten owners asking us if we "knew of anyone who wanted a blind, sick, old, un-housebroken dog with skin allergies," we might find one who asked us to keep our eyes open for a French bulldog puppy. We didn't exactly keep lists of people lining up to adopt other people's problems.

Hence, I became the owner of Josie, a sweet, powder-blue, one-ounce, feathered ball of joy with the most tenacious personality ever seen in a creature her size. Josie had belonged to an older woman who died, and her daughter did not want to take on the exhausting responsibility of caring for her mother's beloved little pet. She dumped Josie at the clinic with instructions to either find a home for her or put her to sleep. Since I had procured Bitsy and Delilah—two mutts of undetermined heritage—

through similar circumstances, Josie fit right in with my growing, cast-off menagerie.

"Hel-*lo!*" called a delighted voice around the corner to my right.

The voice belonged to Monty, the store's mascot—a beautiful Moluccan cockatoo. I poked my head cautiously into the room, where I saw another customer scratching Monty under his raised left wing, much to Monty's delight. Monty had his eyes closed, a look of sheer bliss on his birdy face. Monty was a people lover. Every customer who came into the store received the full gamut of his resplendent charm. Every customer but me, that is. Monty opened his eyes, took one look at me, raised his salmon-colored topknot and let out an unearthly shriek. He spread his legs into a menacing stance, extended his wings threateningly, and screamed at the top of his lungs. The other customer stepped back in surprise, his face contorted in confusion.

"Don't worry," I told him, as I approached the still screeching bird. "It's not you. It's me. Monty hates me."

The man gawked at me. "I've never seen him like this. He's always so friendly."

"It's a long story," I sighed. "The short version is that I'm a vet."

Recognition dawned on the man. "Ah, I see. I take it Monty has had the benefit of your professional services."

I nodded. "It's been six months. He's still holding a grudge."

Mrs. Rucker appeared from the back, wiping her hands on a towel. "Monty! What in the world . . . oh, hi Dr. Bennet."

I offered her a lame smile. "Sorry for the commotion. I just need to pick up a bag of pellets and some millet trees."

"Monty!" she chided. "Stop that!" She turned to me. "He still hasn't forgiven you. The thankless little buzzard."

She scolded the bird again. "Monty! Dr. Bennet saved your life. And this is the way you treat her?"

Monty paid no attention to his mistress' reprimands. The squawking continued until I had obtained my purchases and exited the store.

The whole saga with Monty began several months earlier when his worried owners had brought him into the clinic in obvious respiratory distress. I had seen Monty once or twice when in the feedstore, and he had always been a robust and cheerful little soul. But today, his normally shiny black eyes were dull, a greenish discharge clogged his nostrils, and his whole body labored with the effort to breathe.

There is a saying in avian medicine, "a sick bird is a dead bird," and this was often more truth than adage. Birds, unlike a lot of other animals, tend to hide their illnesses; so, by the time owners realize they are sick, they are usually *very* sick. This is a self-preservation instinct inherent to many avian species, as sick birds in the wild are easy prey. I looked at my patient and my heart lurched.

"How long has he been this way?" I asked.

"We just noticed him acting lethargic a couple days ago," replied Mr. Rucker. "I started him on some antibiotics in his water—something we had in the store, but it hasn't helped. If anything, he's worse."

I pressed my lips together. So many times, when owners tried to self-medicate their pets, they only made matters worse. For one thing, sick birds often don't drink. For another, even if Monty had drunk the antibiotic-laced water, it was unlikely he drank enough to do any good. But the underdosed antibiotic might have ticked off his bacteria enough to mutate into stronger germs, besides messing up my chances of getting an accurate bacterial culture.

I ran my hand over his bony keel, an indication that Monty had been sick longer than a couple of days. He had lost considerable weight. A quick auscultation of his lungs and air sacs confirmed a distinct wheezing.

"Is he going to die?" asked Mrs. Rucker, twisting her hands around the strap of her tightly clutched purse.

I took in a deep breath and looked her straight in the eye. "He's very sick. I'm going to need to keep him and run some tests. In the meantime, I'm going to start him on some injectable medications so I know for sure he's gotten them, and I'm going to have to tube feed him."

The couple exchanged worried glances. "Do whatever you have to do," the wife finally said. "We've never been able to have children, and . . . well, we've had Monty for twenty years. He's like our baby."

"I'll do everything I can," I assured them.

Since Monty needed twenty-four-hour care, the easiest course of action was to take him home with me. For several days, I mixed up a slurry of baby bird formula and tube fed him, as well as administering broad spectrum antibiotics. When his culture came back, it confirmed that Monty had a resistant bacterial infection that was only sensitive to injectable antibiotics. Over the course of the next three weeks, I gave Monty twice daily injections. During the second week, he perked up and started eating on his own, and by the third week, he'd had enough of me and the twice-a-day shots. In fact, every time I approached his cage, he became agitated and increasingly more difficult to handle. This is generally a good thing in veterinary medicine, as it means the patient is improving.

When it appeared Monty had gained back a substantial amount of weight and was no longer wheezing, I sent him back to two grateful owners and his job as the greeter at the feedstore. The only problem was that although the Ruckers were delighted with Monty's treatment, Monty, himself, was not. And every time I entered the store after that, he hissed and pulled himself up into an intimidating posture, even going so far as to lunge at me if I got too close to his perch. I was definitely on Monty's "list," but I suppose it was a small price to pay for a healthy patient and a happy outcome.

~

Generally, Monty aside, I found that most of my patients were quite forgiving of the unpleasantries I inflicted upon them. It occurred to me, more than once, that if I were one of my own patients, I would not be a good one. I would be one of those dogs who cowers in the corner, peeing all over myself, and snapping at anyone who threatened to remove me from my corner. That would be after I had to be dragged or carried to the exam room. I would be one of those cats who hisses and swats at anything in my path. I would be one of those birds who, given the slightest opportunity, flies all around the room, forcing the doctor and technician to chase me. They would have to move furniture out of the way to get to me, by which time I would take off for another area of the room where it was difficult to get to me. Once captured, I would attempt to sink my beak into the most sensitive part of the hand holding me.

If someone tried to draw blood from me, I would squirm and screech at the top of my lungs. If at all possible, I would let loose with an explosive stream of stress diarrhea, accompanied with the emptying of my anal glands, and manage to get as much of it on my body (as well as on everyone else) as possible. If I were put into a cage, I would claw at the door and bark non-stop. If restrained for radiographs or ultrasound, I would wiggle as much as possible, rendering the diagnostic procedure useless.

That said, it is amazing how few of my patients are like this. Even though they don't understand why strange people are doing disagreeable and scary things to them, most of them cooperate with good grace; and a lot of them even wag their tails, give our faces a lick, or beg for a scratch or two after everything is over. I wonder, sometimes, why, with a few notable exceptions, animals are such good sports and so quick to forgive.

Speaking of notable exceptions, Ollie, Rosemary's Boston terrier, took his grudge to an extreme. I had been to Rosemary's house many times, and Ollie— although he had seen me on numerous occasions in my professional capacity at the clinic—always delighted in seeing me. That is until the fateful day that changed our relationship forever.

Typical of Rosemary, she had forgotten to get Ollie's long-overdue rabies vaccine updated and was in imminent danger of having to pay a fine for not getting his dog license renewed. She had scheduled a last-minute appointment, then called in a panic to tell me she was stuck late at work.

"Ollie *has* to have that vaccine today," she lamented when she called to tell me she wouldn't be able to make the appointment. "And I'm up to my eyeballs in this audit. I don't know when I'll make it home."

"Would you like me to run by your house and give him the vaccine?" I asked.

"Oh, Jill! Would you? That would be perfect. You know where I keep the spare key, right?"

"Yes, under the flowerpot on the front porch. The most obvious place where nobody would ever think to look."

She laughed. "It's worked so far. Besides, I have a ferocious watch dog."

I snorted. "Yeah, he's a killer, all right. Don't worry, I'll take care of everything."

"Thanks so much. I owe you one."

"You owe me more than one. But who's counting?" I hung up and went to collect Ollie's vaccine before I forgot.

Jack came by after work to take me to dinner.

"I just have to stop by Rosemary's and give Ollie his rabies vaccine," I said, as I hopped up into the truck.

Jack nodded, good-naturedly. He was used to plans being derailed or delayed due to my work. He made a left out of the parking lot and headed to Rosemary's house, just a few blocks from the clinic. He didn't even ask why I was doing an after-hours vaccine call.

As we pulled up in Rosemary's driveway and Jack cut the engine, I could hear Ollie barking. He kept up a steady barrage as we made our way up the cobblestones to the front porch. I located the one and only flowerpot—unadorned by any flowers—and turned it over. Ollie lunged at the window by the side of the front door.

"Good hiding place," Jack observed, wryly, as I removed the key from beneath the pot.

I gave him a shrug and a half-smile.

"Ollie, it's only me, Auntie Jill. Calm down, baby."

As I inserted the key into the lock, I heard Ollie's front feet slamming against the door and the barking became more frantic. I opened the door to greet Ollie, Jack trailing behind me. Ollie stood in the foyer, feet planted against the tile, hair erect, ears back, growling and snarling.

"Ollie! What's wrong baby? It's only me. See?" I squatted down and reached out my hand, expecting the big doofus to realize he was making a total fool of himself and come crawling on his belly for a good scratch. Instead, he turned and ran into the living room.

I looked up at Jack, bewildered. "I don't understand. He's never acted like this before."

"It must be because Rosemary's not here," he said.

"How strange," I mused. "But I have to give him his rabies shot."

Ollie had retreated to a corner of the living room, where he stood his ground, baring his teeth.

"He's cornered," Jack pointed out, "but if we trap him, he's likely to bite."

Dumbfounded, I stared at the miniature Cujo. He was like a completely different dog from the attention-demanding little rascal who wouldn't leave me alone whenever I visited Rosemary.

"Let me find a blanket or towel to throw over him." As I turned to go up the hall, Ollie shot out from his corner and followed me, yapping and lunging at my feet from just out of range for me to catch him. Every time I turned and tried to sweet talk him, he retreated a few feet, a thunderous growl emanating from deep in his throat.

"This is ridiculous," I grumbled to myself. What should have been a thirty second procedure now stretched into ten minutes. And I was hungry.

I felt a little uncomfortable rummaging through Rosemary's closets, but I had no choice. Finally, I located a thick blanket and carried it back to the kitchen, where Ollie now took up his angry vigil next to the back door. Furious, frothy bubbles issued from his mouth.

"What should I do?" asked Jack.

"I'm going to try to pin him against the door. Hand me the syringe when I have him secured."

Bless him, Jack had learned not to "get in the way" after his terrifying encounter with the macaws. Jack picked up the syringe and advanced slowly behind me. For a brief, tense moment, Ollie and I faced off with each other, neither of us conceding defeat. His incensed, unblinking eyes challenged me to try anything. I had given up trying to wheedle him with baby talk. I continued to move in, inching my way toward him. Just as I raised my arms to toss the blanket over him, he bolted from his position, jumped up and nipped at my exposed elbow. I felt a whoosh of air and the brush of teeth against my skin before I leapt out of the way. Ollie ran back through the living room, down the hall, and disappeared into a bedroom.

"Are you okay?" Jack's concerned voice jolted me from my shock.

I examined my elbow, but Ollie had made only a glancing contact. "Yes," I replied, realizing I was shaking from the close call.

"Now what?" Jack asked.

I heaved a frustrated sigh. Rosemary would never believe this. "I hate to have to do this, but I guess we need to go back to the clinic and grab the rabies snare."

Thirty minutes later, I wrestled the rabies snare under the bed and around Ollie's neck. As I snugged it down and began to pull, I was afraid his shrieking would alert the neighbors to call the police. Ever so slowly, the wiggling little body emerged from under the bed, a trail of urine behind it. I handed the pole to Jack, popped the injection into Ollie's moving target of a rear end, and released the noose. Ollie lunged once at my ankles before fleeing under the bed and burrowing to the farthest corner, where he continued to growl.

After wiping the sweat from my forehead and cleaning up the urine, Jack and I emerged victorious—if one could call the "Boston" marathon we had just endured a victory. I locked the house, returned the key to its hiding place, and collapsed into the front seat of Jack's truck.

"If you don't mind," I said, wearily, "could we just pick up something and eat at my house instead of going out?"

"Sounds like a good idea," Jack agreed.

~

"Ollie did *what?*" Rosemary's incredulous voice ascended an octave. "I can't believe it. Ollie loves you."

"Yeah, well, remember what you said about him being a watch dog? I don't think you have anything to worry about if someone does find your key in its unimaginative hiding place."

For almost two years after the "Ollie incident," the little dog ran and hid under the bed, growling all the way, every time I stepped foot in Rosemary's house. As far as grudges went, he didn't forgive, nor did he forget.

"Dr. Bennet, the Howes are on their way with Gonzo. He got into rat poison," Heather announced at the end of a long day.

I was glad I hadn't left yet. Where poisonings are concerned, every minute counts. "Did they say how long ago it happened?" I asked.

"Just now. They caught him chewing on a box which he must have knocked off a shelf in the garage."

"Thank goodness they saw him."

Rat poison was one of those nasty things that if not caught right away would cause massive hemorrhage and possibly death in a few days. Unfortunately, it presented no early warnings, and unless owners witnessed the ingestion or happened to find evidence of it rather quickly, there was no way to know the pet had been exposed until it was often too late. I headed for the controlled drug cabinet to get the apomorphine, a powerful drug that induced vomiting immediately. I always thought it was a shame apomorphine had to be kept under lock and key. It seemed to me that anyone breaking in looking for drugs would get exactly what he deserved should he seize upon the "morphine" on the label and not realize that apomorphine caused violent nausea. I drew up Gonzo's dose in a syringe and had it ready when the Howes came through the door.

Gonzo, a happy-go-lucky assortment of many breeds, came cheerfully trotting down the hall, his long, whip-like tail banging against the walls in sheer ecstasy of an adventure, a silly grin on his somewhat odd-shaped face. Gonzo was always thrilled to come to the office, despite the fact that nothing pleasant ever happened to him here. He greeted me, as usual, by planting his feet on my chest and giving me a thorough face washing with his slobbery pink tongue. Generally, I didn't encourage this behavior, but Gonzo was so sincere and honest, I allowed it for the simple reason I didn't want to hurt his feelings. I know that sounds foolish, but Gonzo was just one of those special dogs who was always delighted to see me, and in return, delighted me.

This evening, however, there was no time to waste. "Sorry, Bud, but you've gotten yourself into big trouble," I told the overly-affectionate canine, as I pushed his feet to the floor. "I hate to have to do this, Gonz, but I'm going to make you sick." I squatted next to him.

The Howes stood by, nervously, as I lifted Gonzo's front leg, balanced it across my knee, and looked for a vein. The whole time, Gonzo kept trying to steal doggy kisses, as his tail thumped furiously against the exam room wall. He didn't even flinch when I gave him the injection.

"Okay, now let's get him outside, quickly," I instructed.

The four of us, three humans and Gonzo, made a beeline for the back door, where Gonzo could be turned loose in the fenced-in yard. No sooner had we made it outside, than Gonzo's tail stopped wagging and a confused expression replaced his doggy grin. A few seconds later, when the full misery of the injection started to take effect, Gonzo shot me a look of utter duplicity. How could I do such a terrible thing to him when all he wanted was to be my friend and shower me with kisses?

He started to drool, then his sides began to heave with unrelenting force until he had deposited a considerable quantity of stomach contents in the grass. I moved forward rapidly to examine the output, relieved to see a large number of the undigested blue-green pellets of the rat poison mixed in with Gonzo's dinner. But Gonzo wasn't finished. He went into another wretched series of spasms, producing another pile of vomitus, this one not quite so spectacular, but still containing a few of the pellets. A third and fourth time yielded little more than some white foam. Gonzo stood dry heaving for another couple of minutes, occasionally stopping to look up at me with sad, accusatory eyes. He was so transparent, I could almost read his wounded doggy mind. "How could someone I trusted and considered my dear friend treat me like this?" I almost felt a twinge of guilt for putting him through such an ordeal.

Finally, the pitiful heaving ceased, and Gonzo stood quietly, drained and miserable.

"Do you think that's all the poison?" asked Mr. Howe.

"It looks like it," I replied. "His stomach is empty. But just to be safe, I need to give him some activated charcoal to help absorb any poison that might be left. I also want to put him on a few weeks of vitamin K. That will counteract any poison that might have already made it out of his stomach."

"How long will he be so nauseated?" questioned Mrs. Howe, as she ran a comforting hand over Gonzo's hanging head. His eyes were closed in his suffering and saliva dripped from his mouth.

"I'll give him something to reverse the apomorphine. He should feel better quickly."

But even the second injection to stop his miserable nausea didn't restore Gonzo's trust in me. Tail tucked between his legs, he followed his grateful owners out the door of the clinic, his mouth stained black with charcoal.

~

I was pleased to see Gonzo on the schedule a few weeks later for his yearly checkup. It just so happened I was at the front desk and saw the Howes pull in. Gonzo hopped out of the car, took one look at where he was, and his excited demeanor immediately changed to apprehension. The constantly-in-motion tail stopped in mid wag and hung listlessly between his legs, and he planted his feet firmly in the graveled parking lot. Mr. Howe tugged on the leash, but Gonzo remained entrenched in his position. After a bit of a battle, the couple managed to get Gonzo through the front door.

"Hello, Gonzo!" I greeted, cheerfully, hoping my former buddy would warm back up to me and once again, be his old, friendly self. Instead, he cowered behind Mr. Howe's legs.

I sighed. I had lost a good friend. I knew, in my mind, that I had saved Gonzo's life that day; but in my heart, I mourned the loss of our relationship. Some prices were hard to pay.

Chapter 17

The jarring explosion of the bedside phone in my left ear jolted me from a deep, blissful sleep. Momentarily disoriented, I fumbled in the dark for the receiver, dropping it somewhere in the depths of my warm comforter, where I longed to be. I hastily reached for the lamp on my end table, nearly knocking it over as I groped for the switch.

After locating the phone, I mumbled into the receiver, my voice thick with sleep, "Hello?" I glanced at the time displayed on the nightstand clock and winced. Two-eleven. How I hated these middle-of-the-night calls.

It was one thing to be awakened at eleven o'clock, when there was still a chance of grabbing a few uninterrupted hours of sleep, or five a.m., when I had already had those hours. But two a.m. calls always cut the middle right out of the night. Even if I was able to dispense advice over the phone and didn't have to drag my half-awake body into the clinic in the dead of night, I always had trouble falling back asleep. And in my sleep-addled state, God only knew what bizarre advice emanated from my mouth independent of my sleeping brain.

"Dr. Bennet? It's Gracie at the answering service. I have a Mrs. Pryner on the phone calling about a coughing dog. May I patch her through?"

My exhausted neurons screamed in protest. *No! Not Mrs. Pryner, the Whiner.* The woman sent my stress level skyrocketing. Not only was she high-maintenance, she was low-budget—a combination sure to try the patience of even the saintliest veterinarian during normal office hours. At two-eleven a.m., it would take every fiber of self-restraint to stop myself from reaching through the phone and wrapping my hand around the woman's scrawny neck. Fortunately, for her sake, that was impossible.

I gritted my teeth, resisted the urge to screech at Gracie, and said, "Yes, patch her through." After all, this call *could* be a true emergency, and I was tasked with providing professional care to a sick animal, regardless of the misfortune of the poor creature to be owned by a human who drove me bonkers.

"Dr. Bennet?" came the nasal, whiny voice of Mrs. Pryner, and my toes curled in dread. True to her usual demanding and entitlement nature, she didn't apologize for waking me up, as most clients did. She got right to the point. "Harvey has been up all night coughing and I'm worried."

I closed my eyes and grimaced. Thankfully, she couldn't see me. "Uh huh," I replied in a monotone. "And how long has he had this cough?"

"Oh, about a week. But tonight, he woke me up coughing. I think he's getting worse and I didn't want to wait."

Of course. Harvey woke *her* up, so now she had to wake *me* up. Because she hadn't bothered to bring him in earlier in the week when it wasn't the middle of the night. I resisted the urge to tell her to put Harvey in a room where she couldn't hear him coughing and go back to sleep.

"Do you think he needs to be seen on emergency?" I asked. I knew what was coming and braced myself.

"How much will *that* cost?" she asked, her voice full of concern, mixed with a whopping dose of accusation that I dared charge a fee for being roused from my warm bed in the wee hours of the morning. I knew the concern stemmed as much, if not more, from the money versus the health of her pet.

I told her and she gasped.

"That's *so* much money!" she complained. "Do you think Harvey can wait until morning?"

I asked a few more questions trying to ascertain the nature of the cough and whether it was accompanied by difficulty breathing, but her responses were decidedly unhelpful.

"Oh, I wish he'd cough for you. Wait a minute. Let me put Harvey on the phone." She dropped the phone against something hard and I jumped as the noise radiated through my end of the receiver directly into my unsuspecting ear.

"Harvey! Harvey! Come here, baby, come to Mama. *Harvey!*" I could hear scuffling sounds in the background. "*Harvey, you come here,* now!" I heard a lot of noise, but no coughing. Finally, she came back on the line. "Oh, I can't get him. He ran into the other room and crawled under the bed. Do you think I should bring him in?"

"That's up to you, Mrs. Pryner. It's difficult for me to say how sick he is over the phone."

"But it's *so* much money!" she repeated. "I really hate to spend all that money if it's something that can wait. But you know how much my animals mean to me. I would never forgive myself if I didn't bring him in and something happened to him."

I thoroughly disliked these one-sided debates in the middle of the night. I listened, without comment while she carried on her back-and-forth discussion with herself. At last, she gave up the fight and asked the most unfair question ever asked of veterinarians everywhere, "Do you think he'll die if I wait until morning?"

I was sorely tempted to make a flippant remark about my crystal ball being in the shop for repairs, but stopped myself with the empathetic understanding that, in her mind, it was a legitimate question. "I honestly can't say, Mrs. Pryner. I can't diagnose Harvey through the phone."

"But you're a *vet!* Surely you must have some idea."

I sighed, loudly, then hoped it didn't carry through to her. "All I can tell you, Mrs. Pryner, is that if *you* think Harvey needs to be seen tonight, *you* need to make that decision."

She seemed to deliberate for a moment, then announced, "That's just too much money. I'll wait until tomorrow. I just hope he doesn't die." Without further comment, she hung up without thanking me for my time and, yet again, not apologizing for waking me up. It took me a full two hours to go back to sleep.

~

If I had been any less familiar with Mrs. Pryner, it would have concerned me that she was not in the parking lot waiting for the doors to open the next morning. However, having been down the road a few times with the woman, I was not surprised. Nor was I surprised to see she had made an appointment for five o'clock that afternoon. Apparently, Harvey's condition had been downgraded to *not-life-and-death* so as not to disrupt whatever Mrs. Pryner had to do between when the clinic opened that morning and the last appointment of the day. Throughout the afternoon, I harbored the sneaky and fanciful thought of writing Dr. Spangle's name on her chart when she finally made her appearance fifteen minutes late. But he had ducked out the back and was long gone, foiling my less-than-honest plan.

My sleep-deprived body had barely made it through the long day, and the added aggravation of the source of my sleep-deprivation not being on time for the *last appointment* before I could drag my exhausted body home and get some much-needed rest rankled me. All the other clients had long since departed, and I watched through the office window as Mrs. Pryner unhurriedly emerged from her new Mercedes and leisurely extracted her ailing Yorkshire terrier from the passenger side. She paused to fiddle with something in the car for another good five minutes while her appointment time dragged into now twenty minutes late. When she finally ambled her way to the door, allowing Harvey to stop at every bush on the way in, I didn't wait for Heather to check her in. I threw open the door and told her to come right back into a room.

"I thought you'd bring Harvey first thing this morning," I said, offhandedly, hoping she would take the hint for what it was, "since he was so sick last night."

She reached up and patted what appeared to be a freshly cut and colored lock of hair back into place with what also appeared to be a freshly manicured hand. "I just couldn't get him here any sooner," she replied, without offering an explanation.

Was it my imagination, or was there a healthy glow about her face, such as might be seen after a facial? And was there the slightest reddening of her perfectly arched brows, as might occur after waxing? For someone so worried that her dog wouldn't survive the night, she seemed to have gotten over her concern when the sun came up. I suspected a spa day may have had something to do with Mrs. Pryner's decreased worry over the health of her pet.

"Anyway, he seems better," she said, as she set the shaking little animal on the table.

Harvey looked at me with wide, frightened eyes and tried to crawl up his mistress' shoulder. I unhooked his clutching front paws from the client and returned him to the table, where I placed a gentle, restraining hand on his back. The exertion caused a soft cough to issue forth from my patient.

"There! That's what he did all night, only much worse," Mrs. Pryner pointed out.

"How about today? How much coughing has he done?"

"Well, I really couldn't say," she replied, somewhat evasively.

"Why not?" I probed.

"I wasn't home most of the day," she finally admitted.

I bit my lip and held my tongue. After taking Harvey's temperature and determining he did not have a fever, I ran my hand over his throat. The slight pressure evoked a goose-honking cough, followed by a gag.

"That's it. That's what he was doing last night. What do you think it is?"

I ignored her question and, pulling my stethoscope from around my neck, I auscultated Harvey's heart and lungs. I frowned as I heard the significant whooshing noise of a loud heart murmur.

"Well?" demanded the client.

I straightened up. "Harvey's trachea is sensitive, which can be a symptom of acute tracheobronchitis or a collapsing trachea, which is common in small breed dogs. Harvey also has a heart murmur, and heart problems can also be associated with coughing. I would like to take a chest radiograph to better evaluate what is causing his problem."

Mrs. Pryner's face registered annoyance. "And how much is *that* going to cost?"

I told her and she frowned. "Is that *really* necessary?"

No, I just like staying late doing unnecessary tests and exposing myself to extra radiation for the fun of it. I folded my arms across my chest. "I would highly recommend it."

"Well, can't you just give him something for the cough?"

"I can, but it would be better if I knew for sure what was causing his cough."

"If it's his heart, then what?"

I sighed. There was nothing I hated worse than playing the "if/then" situation game with clients. They could go on for hours.

"Mrs. Pryner, there really is no point in discussing treatment for heart problems until we know for sure Harvey *has* a heart problem, which a chest x-ray can help determine."

"But I want to know. If it's his heart, how would you treat it?"

I knew the feeling of defeat. She would not let this circular argument rest until I outlined each and every possible scenario for her. Against my better judgment to stick to my original refusal to discuss the "if/thens," I briefly explained the medications we generally prescribed for heart disease.

"And how much do those cost?" she demanded.

I sighed. Once again, I had been suckered into a self-defeating conversation that served no purpose other than to waste time.

"I honestly don't know," I said. "I would have to calculate drug doses and look up the prices. But there is no point doing that unless I know for sure Harvey needs the medications."

"Are they expensive?"

I stifled the temptation to smack her. I also stifled the temptation to say, "Considerably less than a day at the spa, and *much less than a Mercedes.*"

"What about bronchitis? If it's bronchitis, how much will it cost to treat *that?*" she persisted. "And what was the other thing you mentioned?"

I bit out, "Collapsing trachea."

"Okay, what about *that?* How much will it cost to treat *that?*"

Knowing when I was beaten, I said, "Excuse me. I will put together some estimates for you." I trudged out of the room, leaned against the wall, wearily, and kicked myself for having gotten to this point with Mrs. Pryner, *yet again*. I should have handled that conversation better. I should have taken charge and told her in no uncertain terms that Harvey needed a chest x-ray. Why, in spite of my best intentions, did I let the woman get the upper hand and force me into this debacle of wasted time and energy? I couldn't even blame my exhaustion and lack of ability to think straight. She did it every time, and I always fell victim to it.

But not this time. Nope, doggone it, *I* was the professional and she would do things *my* way. Squaring my shoulders, I marched back into the exam room.

"Mrs. Pryner, it is a waste of time to give you estimates for treating conditions I can't say Harvey even *has* without further testing. I'm going to take a chest x-ray." I faced her across the exam room table and held out my hands for her to surrender the little dog.

She showed no inclination of handing over Harvey. Instead, she clutched him tighter to her shoulder, where he had once again crawled and hung like a human baby. Her chin lifted ever so slightly. Finally, she spoke. "No, I don't think he needs an x-ray. Just give him something for the cough."

I gritted my teeth and closed my eyes, taking deep breaths through my nostrils. Warning her that this might not be the best course of action would do no good. Shoulders sagging, I retreated to the pharmacy, where I counted out antibiotic and cough suppressant tablets. I returned to the exam room, thrust them into her hand, and started to give her instructions.

"Don't you have these in liquid form?" she interrupted. "Harvey won't take pills."

I leveled a piercing gaze at her and said, "Yes, but they *cost a lot more."*

If she asked "how much more," then I would have no choice but to smack her.

She seemed to wrestle with that answer for a moment, then conceded, "I'll try to get the pills into him."

I ran around to the other side of the exam table and held the door open for her to leave. It was now an hour past closing time. Bless Heather, she had stayed late waiting for the last client to be seen. As Heather added up the charges, I heard Mrs. Pryner say, "Aren't there any *cheaper* medications that could be prescribed?"

I caught Heather's eye and shook my head. Then I snatched my purse and made a hasty retreat out the back door before the woman could come up with any other possible ways to keep me late trying to pinch pennies, comforted by the fact that if Harvey woke her at 2:00 am tonight, Dr. Spangle was on call.

~

"Mrs. Pryner thought of some more questions, but you had already left," Heather relayed to me the following morning.

"I'm sorry I left you to deal with her," I apologized. "Was it anything important?"

Heather laughed and shook her head. "She said she forgot to mention that Harvey has been throwing up a lot for the last several days and wanted to know what you thought."

I slapped my palm to my face.

"This was after she had already paid the 'outrageous bill' and I had handed her the receipt."

"That little piece of information about the vomiting would have been nice to know," I grumbled. "I guess she was too busy calculating expenses in her head to think about informing me of that problem." Irritation with Mrs. Pryner, coupled with new concern for her pet, nagged at my conscience. "So, what did you tell her?"

"I told her she would have to make another appointment since you had already gone."

"And did she?"

"Yes, for this afternoon. But she requested to see Dr. Spangle. *And* she did not think she should be charged for another visit since all her concerns had not been addressed at yesterday's visit."

I grinned. There were literally hundreds of causes for vomiting, and the idea of Dr. Spangle being forced to list and specify diagnostics and treatments for each and every one filled me with no small amount of satisfaction. Somehow, though, I doubted he would allow himself to become ensnared in Mrs. Pryner's trap of unending circular scenarios. Part of me wanted to be a fly on the wall at Mrs. Pryner's appointment with my boss that afternoon, just to observe how he dealt with her, but then I decided I'd just as soon not.

I picked up the next chart—a new client—and frowned at the vague and unhelpful reason of "sick" given for the visit. Opening the exam room door, I saw an older, dour-faced man sitting with the chair tipped back against the wall, his eyes half-closed. A non-descript, medium-sized, brown-and-white dog roamed freely around the room with no leash.

"Good morning," I greeted. "I'm Dr. Bennet."

The client opened one eye, but showed no other indication that he was aware of my presence.

"Uh, I see you brought Butch in because he's sick. What exactly is his problem?"

The old man plopped his chair back onto the floor and I breathed a little easier knowing he wouldn't be flipping over backwards, cracking his head on the hard tile, and suing me.

"If I knew what his problem was, we wouldn't be here. That's what I want *you* to tell *me*. You're the vet."

Oh no, not another "stump the vet" client. I managed a small smile. "Can you give me a little more information? Is there something specific you're concerned about?"

"He ain't right."

Okay, that certainly narrows things down. Although veterinarians, in fact, have an acronym for vague changes in a pet's disposition, called ADR (short for "ain't doing right"), we can often ferret out pertinent details with a thorough history from the owner. With some clients it's easier than others.

"In what way is he not right, Mr. . . . ." I glanced at the chart in my hand, "Lane?"

"He ain't himself."

Normally when a client tells me an animal isn't "himself," I try to inject a little light humor and ask, "Well, if he's not himself, then who is he?" In this case, I decided against it.

"In what way is he not himself?"

"He's just off, like."

"Well, what is he doing?"

"He ain't doin' nothin'."

"And how long has Butch been like this?"

"Oh, for a spell, now."

"But can you tell me exactly when he started to go 'off'?"

"It's been a bit."

Well, I had gleaned exactly zero bits of useful information. Time to play the next round of twenty questions. "Is he eating?"

The old man considered this, then responded, "Sometimes he does, sometimes he don't."

"Is that unusual for Butch?" I prodded. "Has his appetite always been sporadic?" Some dogs ate intermittently, which was normal for them. Other dogs needed to be rushed to the vet if they missed a meal because not eating in those patients constituted a dire situation.

"Ever since we got Daisy, anyway."

"I see." I really didn't. "And how long ago was that?"

The old man reached up a thin, bony hand and ran it through his sparse, gray hair. "Oh, it's been a while."

Okay, moving on to the next question. "Is Butch having any vomiting or diarrhea?"

"Only when he eats grass."

Aha! Perhaps a tidbit of something useful. I brightened. "Uh, huh. And how often does he eat grass?" I stood, pen poised over the paper to record the answer.

Mr. Lane rubbed his chin for a moment. "Oh, off and on."

I sighed and laid down my pen. "Does Butch seem painful anywhere? Is he limping or having trouble getting up?"

The old man slowly shook his head. "No more than before."

"Than before what?"

Mr. Lane shrugged, but didn't answer.

"Has Butch had any injuries?"

The client shook his head again. "Not since that one time."

"What time? What happened?"

"We don't rightly know for sure. He weren't right then, neither."

Okay, another dead end. "Is he coughing or sneezing?" I asked.

He chewed on his bottom lip. "Hard to tell."

"What do you mean it's hard to tell? Either he is or he isn't."

Mr. Lane studied the wall over my right shoulder. "I'm not rightly sure."

"Could he have gotten into anything? Trash or medications, for insistence?"

"Don't rightly know. The missus takes something for her blood pressure. I'd have to check with her to see if she's missing any pills."

I knew when I was beating a dead horse, so to speak. So, I gave up and turned to the patient. Butch was an interesting combination of only God knew what breeds, with a curly brown-and-white coat, long floppy ears, and large, inquisitive brown eyes. His beautifully feathered tail whipped the air around him in a happy cadence. A friendly fellow, he gave me a face lick when I knelt down to examine him. His temperature, pulse, and respirations were normal. His eyes, nose, mouth, and ears looked fine. His heart thumped merrily in a nice, steady rhythm and his lungs sounded clear. I could detect no pain or other abnormalities when I palpated his abdomen, and in running my hands all along his body, I detected no sensitive areas or lumps. His gait appeared normal, and he held his long, curly tail erect over his back. He ate treats readily from my hand.

I stood upright and faced the client. "Mr. Lane, I really don't see anything wrong with Butch."

The client pursed his lips. "I'm tellin' you, somethin' ain't right."

I sighed. "Okay. I can run some tests on him and see if anything shows up."

Mr. Lane waved his hand, dismissively. "Do what you have to do. I don't care how much it costs. I wanta' know what's wrong with my dog."

"All right. Let me keep Butch for a couple of hours and I'll see what I can find out." I led Butch, who trotted along happily beside me—tail still wagging, tongue lolling—to the treatment area and prevailed upon Tess to help me procure some samples.

I pulled several tubes of blood and sent them to the lab. I took a stool sample and checked it for parasites. I took radiographs of Butch's chest, abdomen, and legs. The stool exam and the radiographs were normal. I even asked the boss to have a look in case I had overlooked anything. After going over the animal, Dr. Spangle grumbled,

"There's nothing wrong with the dog. Tell the owner to find a new hobby."

Mr. Lane came to pick up his pet later that afternoon. I told him I would get back to him with the blood results and walked him up front to pay his substantial bill. He didn't even blink when Heather gave him the total. I soon found out why.

"I don't have no money on me right now," the old man said. "I'll pay you next week."

I cringed. Dr. Spangle would be furious. Of course, Mr. Lane never mentioned the fact that money was an issue until *after* all the services had been performed. In fact, he had indicated just the opposite. This was my first—but unfortunately, not my last—hard-learned lesson in that when a client said he didn't care how much something cost, it was because he had no intention of paying the bill, anyway.

A few days later, I called Mr. Lane with the blood work results, which were normal, and gently reminded him that he still owed the clinic money.

He remained silent for a long minute. Then he said, "So, you didn't find out what's wrong with Butch."

"No, sir," I replied, then added, cheerfully, "but his blood work is all normal. That's great news."

Again, a long, uncomfortable silence. "And you still expect me to pay even though you didn't find out what Butch's problem is."

I squirmed under his logic. "Well, yes, sir, we did perform a number of expensive tests at your request."

"Hmph. Hardly seems right when you still don't know what's wrong with him."

"I'm sorry you feel that way, Mr. Lane, but there is no way we can guarantee—"

He cut me off. "Seems you didn't do your job, if you ask me."

I bristled. "Mr. Lane, that is not true. Butch was examined by two veterinarians and had a number of tests run. As I started to point out, we can't guarantee the results. You are welcome to take him somewhere else for another opinion."

He grunted. "And that'll cost me more money. I don't mind tellin' you, I'm not satisfied." He hung up.

We never saw a dime of what Mr. Lane owed us. But every now and then, when I was out and about, I saw the old man and his dog out for a stroll, Butch trotting along happily, tongue hanging cheerfully. Whatever had been "off" with Butch apparently resolved itself, so I didn't worry too terribly much over missing something important.

~

"You vets! All you ever think about is the money!" accused the young woman standing across the exam table. A skinny, angular girl with a huge chip on her shoulder, Darla Mundy glared at me with a disapproving scowl before taking a sip of her expensive take-out latte.

Over the course of my more than forty years in practice, I have been hit with this accusation on a regular basis. For some reason, many people seem to have the mistaken impression that vets are all independently wealthy, and practice animal medicine more as a hobby rather than a means of earning a living. It did little good to point out the exuberant costs of obtaining an education in veterinary medicine, not to mention the skyrocketing costs of running a small business. Veterinary hospitals house all the same expensive equipment as human hospitals, such as x-ray machines and processors, anesthesia machines, surgical instruments, autoclaves, and lab equipment; moreover, we have to carry a large inventory of medications. This is in addition to the overhead costs of employee salaries, electricity, water, taxes, phones, insurance, licenses, building maintenance, and other business expenses.

DON'T BITE THE DOCTOR

At the time Darla Mundy threw her guilt-inducing statement in my face, I was making less than minimum wage. This might sound strange, but I was a salaried employee, one who put in close to eighty hours a week. Figured on an hourly basis, my paltry income came up to less than minimum wage. I lived in a small, rather run-down rented house in the less affluent section of town, couldn't afford health insurance, and was overdue for a dental exam, which I also couldn't afford. My car had been making strange noises, but I didn't have the money for a mechanic, and since the vehicle was still running, I crossed my fingers and ignored the noise. And did I mention my student loan payment?

"I'm sorry, Miss Mundy, but Parvovirus is an expensive disease to treat." I cast sympathetic eyes to the unhappy little pit bull-mix puppy who lay miserably and listlessly on the exam room table, and resisted the urge to rub salt into his negligent owner's wound by pointing out that an eight-dollar vaccine would likely have prevented this, now, life-threatening situation.

"I thought you were supposed to love animals," she spat at me. "You don't care if Koby dies. You're just going to let him die because of money."

No, you're going to let him die because of money. Of course, I couldn't say that aloud. I attempted to, once again, go over the rationalization for the high cost of intensive care treatment, but she had tuned me out after being convinced of my opportunistic and uncaring greed.

"You can take him to the humane society," I offered. "They might be able to treat him more cheaply." *Seeing as how they are tax-supporter subsidized, not to mention the recipient of generous donations and grants with which to directly compete with us greedy private practitioners.* Again, I didn't voice this thought.

"I'm not taking him *there!* They killed the last dog with Parvo that I took there. They even refused to allow me to adopt another puppy."

I was beginning to see a pattern. But my heart broke for Koby, the unwitting victim of this irresponsible young woman. Mostly white, with a few brown patches, including the one encircling his left eye, he lay curled up in an apathetic ball, vomitus soiling his lips, and bloody diarrhea oozing from his rectum without his apparent awareness.

People like Darla Mundy put me in a no-win situation. There was more at stake here besides my reasonable expectation of being paid for my professional services and her blaming her own negligence in allowing yet another puppy to become sick with an easily preventable disease on my corporate greed and hard heart. Veterinarians often discounted and reduced fees for indigent clients, or flat out didn't charge at all. But it was one thing to give charity by choice and another to have it forcefully thrust upon us through guilt-tripping, entitled and irresponsible owners. If we developed the practice of indiscriminately losing money treating patients because of our great love for animals, we would soon end up declaring bankruptcy.

I sighed. "I can't promise you Koby will survive even with intensive care. But regardless of the outcome, you will be out hundreds of dollars. If you sign him over to me, I'll take full responsibility for his treatment."

She brightened, almost imperceptibly. I could see the wheels turning in her head. A way to dump her obligation on someone else and not have to feel bad about herself. Apparently, her own love for her pet only ran so deep.

"And I won't have to pay anything?"

"No. But you will have to sign a release saying you're giving up your rights to him."

She mulled that proposition over for less than five seconds. "Fine. You can have him."

I nodded. "I'll get the form for you to sign." I left the room to retrieve the required paperwork and returned to see she had already removed the puppy's collar and leash.

"You don't want to keep those," I said. "In fact, you need to get rid of everything of Koby's that can't be disinfected with bleach. Parvovirus is extremely contagious."

"I paid twenty bucks for these," she complained, depositing the leash and collar on the table.

"And please don't bring a new puppy into the home for at least three months. The virus can contaminate the environment for several weeks."

She scribbled her signature and turned to go.

"Oh, and one other thing."

She stopped and scowled at me over her shoulder. "What?"

"If you get another puppy," which I unfortunately knew she would, "be sure to get it vaccinated immediately. Puppies need a series of vaccines to prevent several deadly diseases, such as Parvo."

She opened the door and left without a reply.

I tucked a towel around Koby and carried him to the isolation ward.

Hearing Tess in the kennel, I summoned her to come help me place an IV catheter.

"Whose dog is that?" she asked, popping into the room.

"Ours," I muttered, as I tore off strips of tape.

Her eyes widened. "Oh, Dr. Bennet, you did it again. What's Dr. Spangle going to say?"

"With any luck he won't find out," I said, clutching a syringe between my teeth. "He never comes back here."

Tess shook her head. "Myra does."

In reality, I knew the odds of keeping our new acquisition from the boss were slim. But I also knew, after his initial fussing at me, he would let it slide. For all his bluster, he did, at times, have a soft heart underneath, and I know he would have done the same thing had he been in my position.

Chapter 18

"Do you know of anyone who might want a pit bull-mix puppy?" I asked Jack that evening. "That is, if he makes it." We had attended the last game in a softball tournament to cheer on his best friend, Wes, and were on our way to the victory party at the local YMCA clubhouse.

Jack groaned. "You did it again, didn't you?"

I turned to face him in the darkness of the truck. Slivers of moonlight fell here and there on Jack's face as he drove, illuminating his silhouette in a mosaic of light.

"What was I supposed to do? Just let Koby die because his owner couldn't be bothered to get him vaccinated? It's not *his* fault."

Jack's lips curled in the lopsided grin that I loved. "You can't save them all, Jill." He glanced at me briefly before turning his eyes back to the road.

I smiled back. "Maybe not, but perhaps I can save Koby."

Jack chuckled, softly, and slid his arm around me, pulling me closer. "That's what I love about you."

"*Only* that?" I asked, lifting my eyebrows and peering intently at the right side of his face, knowing he could feel my gaze.

He shot me a quick peek and a huge smile. "Well, that and a few other things."

I settled my head against his shoulder, completely contented. "I won't make you enumerate those other things just now."

We rode in silence for a moment. Then I said, "When we get to the party, don't tell people what I do for a living."

He looked at me quizzically. "Why not?"

"Because I don't know any of these people, and when new people find out I'm a vet, they always want to regale me with their cute animal stories or solicit free advice."

"So?"

"So, when I'm off duty I don't want to talk shop. Do you want to discuss clogged pipes at a party?"

"No, I suppose not. But Wes knows you're a vet."

"Try to grab him when we get there and tell him not to mention my profession."

But it wasn't meant to be. The minute we walked in, Wes spied us, and in a loud voice, announced, "Hey, everybody. I want you to meet my best friend, Jack, and his fiancé, Jill. Jill's a veterinarian."

Immediately a small crowd formed around us. "Are you really a veterinarian?" asked a freckle-faced young woman about my age.

I smiled, weakly. It would probably do no good to pretend Wes misspoke and I was *really* a vegetarian. "Yes."

"Do you know why my dog eats grass?" she queried.

I so much wanted to tell her to make an appointment and we'd discuss the matter further, when I could get paid for my advice. But that would have come across as rude. And mercenary. Plus, I'd already been accused of being "only concerned about money" just that afternoon. I maintained my plastered-on smile and prepared to deliver my ten-minute dissertation on the various theories as to why dogs ate grass.

"Well, there are a lot of ideas as to why—"

"What's the best thing for fleas?" another guy interrupted.

Great. Another ten-minute discussion. "I'm afraid there's not a simple answer. Flea control requires treating the environment as well as—"

"How much do you charge to spay a dog?" came another enquiry.

I turned toward the third interrupter. "The cost goes by the weight of the dog and whether or not she's in heat—"

Jack grabbed me by the elbow. "Excuse us, I'm starving." He steered me straight ahead and the little mob parted, allowing us an escape.

"Thank you," I breathed, as we headed toward the refreshment table.

"That's what I'm here for. To protect you from your adoring fans."

I snickered. "I suppose there are worse things."

As we made our way through the food line, a man behind us tapped me on the shoulder. "Do you treat rabbits?"

I turned around. "Yes, we see rabbits in our practice."

"Do you know what would cause a rabbit to start pulling out its fur?"

I attempted to spoon some salsa over my tortilla chips. "Uh, well, there are several possibilities. We really should see the bunny—"

He shook his head. "Couldn't you just tell me what shampoo to try?"

I missed my plate because I glanced up to look at him, and dribbled salsa over the white tablecloth. I shouldn't have tried to do two things at once. "Um, not really without—"

"That's okay. I'll just pick something up at the pet store."

I smiled and turned back to my plate, trying to move ahead so as not to hold up the line. Besides, it was no secret that the clerks at the pet store knew a lot more about treating animal diseases than the highly-educated animal doctors.

"After all, I only paid five bucks for the rabbit."

How was I supposed to respond to *that* logic? *Oh, well, if you had paid* ten *bucks it might be worth taking him to the vet. Recoup your large investment.* I hoped he didn't have kids. Weren't they free? I hastily snatched half of a cut submarine sandwich and exited the line.

Jack followed me to an empty table and offered to get drinks. I had just taken a big bite of my sandwich when an older lady plopped down next to me.

"I heard you're a vet," she said, by way of introduction. "My daughter wants to be a vet. Could she come to your clinic sometime and observe?"

I quickly chewed and swallowed the under-masticated bolus of food in my mouth. I could feel the large wad make a slow, painful descent down my esophagus. "She would have to ask the owner, Dr. Spangle." My words came out a bit strangled.

The woman's face dropped. "Oh. I don't like him. He killed our cat." With that, she got up and left.

Another woman immediately took her place. "Do you know what my vet charged to spay my dog? Fifty dollars! Don't you think that's outrageous?"

I wiped my mouth on my napkin. "I really can't—"

"You'd think with all the unwanted animals in the world, vets would do their part to try to help control the surplus population. But no. All they care about is money."

I wished Jack would hurry back with the drinks. My throat was dry from having swallowed an almost intact bite of sandwich.

"There are low-cost spay/neuter clinics available," I managed to choke out. "You don't even have to be a low-income client to use their services."

She frowned at me. "I would *never* take my dog to a horrible place like that. I want the job done right, not by some butcher."

You just don't want to pay for it. I nodded, but refrained from, once again, defending our audacity to charge for our services. It never seemed to register with people like this when I tried to compare the cost of a canine ovariohysterectomy to the cost of the same procedure in a human.

A young man took up the seat across the table from the overcharged woman. "If I brought in three dogs at once, could I get a discount?"

Sure, because it takes infinitely less time to examine three dogs at once than it does to examine three dogs separately. In fact, it was usually just the opposite. Trying to examine one dog with two others running around getting into everything tended to distract me. Not to mention trying to remember what I found on each pet. I smiled, thinly, and shook my head. "I'm sorry, Dr. Spangle doesn't give multiple pet discounts." Thank goodness I could place the blame for a lot of things I didn't want to deal with on the boss.

The man's face registered his disappointment, and he left. The woman next to me, however, was not finished with me.

"Why don't you vets get together and try to organize some low-cost spays?"

"Well, actually, we do—"

"I would think you vets would want to help control the overpopulation of animals," she stated, again.

Jack, mercifully, returned, carrying two drinks. I shot him a "help me" look. Fortunately, he got it.

"Honey, there's someone I want you to meet," he said. He turned to the woman. "Please excuse us." I hastily snatched the cup from his hand and gulped down a huge swallow.

"Thank you again," I whispered, as he hauled me off from the table. The woman still sat, glowering.

"Boy, you weren't kidding," he said.

"By the way, who is it you want me to meet?"

He laughed. "I don't know. I guess I'll have to find someone." He stopped about half-way across the room and struck up a conversation with a couple we knew from church.

"Excuse me," a middle-aged woman cut in and stood in front of me. "Are you the vet?"

I smiled and hoped it didn't come across as a grimace. "Yes."

She placed a proprietary hand on my arm. "Oh, I just had to talk to you. I know you'll appreciate this story. We have a miniature schnauzer, Fritz, and he does the funniest thing. I've never seen a dog do this before."

I kept up my smile and zoned out as she rambled on and on about the funny thing that Fritz did, which, on further introspection was not all that funny or unusual.

"Did you ever hear of such a thing?" she giggled.

I jumped, realizing she had asked me a question to which she expected a reply. "Oh . . . my. He sounds like quite a character." I brayed a laugh that even to my ears sounded fake.

She kept her hand on my arm, and I desperately wanted to yank it from her grasp. "We go to Dr. Watson. He's a wonderful vet. He always knows exactly what's wrong with Fritz, and he's such a nice man. Do you know Dr. Watson?"

I had met the man at a couple of veterinary meetings, and on first, and then second impression, I found him to be a rather arrogant, uncouth boor. "Uh, yes, I believe I know who he is."

She closed her eyes. "Such a dear man. Oh! Let me tell you about the time he saved the life of our other dog, Patches." She launched into another long-winded story while I shifted my weight from one aching foot to the other, unable to move away from her strong, immobilizing grip. My plight went unheeded by my fiancé, deep in conversation with the other couple.

She finally paused for breath and I butted in with, "Would you please excuse me? I need to use the ladies' room." Without waiting for a reply, I forcefully wrenched my arm free and bolted into the sweet solitude of the restroom, where I locked myself into a stall. I would have stayed there until the party broke up, but I was afraid Jack would eventually miss me and send a search party. Then I might be trapped in here with goodness only knew how many people—well, women, anyway—wanting to entertain me with their animal stories.

I finally emerged, but there was no sign of Jack. I started to head back to our table and finish my sandwich, but the pet overpopulation lady still occupied the seat next to mine, so I turned and moved toward the bar to get another soda. Before I could get far, another young man interceded me.

"Jill, the vet, right?"

I drew in a deep breath through my nose and blew it out slowly through my puckered lips.

"Maybe you can help me. My dog's had diarrhea for several weeks now and my vet can't seem to figure out what's wrong with him. Do you have any suggestions as to what I might try?"

I squared my shoulders and faced the young man. "Honestly, without knowing what's already been tried—"

"Well, what do you think could be causing it?"

"There are a lot of things that can cause diarrhea. I would really have to—"

"Never mind. I just thought you might be able to tell me something simple to do. I've already spent a lot of money." He turned and walked off.

Jack, where are you? My eyes scoured the room for my MIA fiancé.

"Oh, Jill," came a voice behind me. "I wanted to ask your advice."

I turned and looked into another eager face, this one belonging to an older lady with her dark hair pulled back into a tight bun.

"My daughter's cat has a runny eye and I have some eye drops left over from when my dog had an eye infection. Do you think it would be all right to use them in her cat?"

At least with this question, I was on solid footing and could give clear, concise advice.

"You should never use eye drops in your pet without having your veterinarian examine it first. Some eye drops can make things worse if used for the wrong condition."

The woman drew her fretting brows together. "But she can't really afford to take him to the vet. She's just a college student, you know, and doesn't have much money."

"Still, she shouldn't use the medication unless her vet okays it."

"Why? What could happen?"

I greatly resisted the temptation to let out a beleaguered sigh. "Worst case scenario is that she uses the wrong medication and causes the cornea to rupture, which would most likely cause permanent blindness or loss of the eye."

The woman pondered my answer for a moment, then came to a decision. "Oh, I don't think it's all that bad. I'm just going to give her my drops and see what happens."

I stared at her, speechless. *Well, thank you for soliciting my advice and discarding it. If you were going to do what you wanted anyway, why bother asking?* Poor cat. His own two-footed grandmother obviously didn't care enough about the risk of blinding him to subsidize a veterinary visit for him.

"Thank you for your help," she said, as she walked off.

Of course. Any time you want to ignore advice, feel free.

I finally spotted Jack in a circle of people and made a beeline for him. "Jack, I'm sorry, but I really need to be going," I apologized to the group.

He gave me a knowing look and excused himself. As we proceeded rapidly toward the exit, one of the people in the group called out, "Oh wait! I need to ask Jill about my iguana."

We pretended not to hear.

ELLEN FANNON

Chapter 19

I knelt and placed my stethoscope against the huge chest of the largest dog I had ever seen, but instead of the expected *lub-dub, lub-dub* I heard a sound like rolling thunder.

Uh-oh, hearts aren't supposed to sound like this. Then it hit me. The noise traveling into my earpieces from the massive beast's thorax didn't originate in his heart, but rather, in his throat. To confirm my suspicions, I glanced toward the front end of the animal. The brute's enormous block head had turned ever so slightly toward me and there was just the slightest curl of his top lip over menacing, white fangs. His black eyes penetrated mine with an intimidating challenge.

I scooted back quickly, ending up on my rump. Scrambling to my feet, I positioned myself behind the exam table, placing it between myself and my patient.

"Oh, Rocky's just talking. He doesn't mean any harm," laughed his owner, Mr. Nettlesmith.

I risked another direct look at the huge animal before me, whose unblinking stare assured me he meant business.

"He may be just talking, but I don't like what he's saying," I replied. "I'm going to need to muzzle him before I can proceed with the examination."

Mr. Nettlesmith rolled his eyes. "I don't know why everybody's so afraid of ole' Rocky. He wouldn't hurt a flea."

Maybe Rocky wouldn't hurt a flea. In his mind, however, I believed veterinarians were fair game. I left to retrieve a muzzle, hoping we had one large enough for the behemoth in exam room one. With a growling dog who outweighed me by a hundred pounds, I wasn't going to take any chances.

I fished through our basket of muzzles and finally came up with one I thought would work. Fortunately, Myra had just come out of the next room, and I pressed her into service.

"I may need your help. I've got a big dog in room one who's growling at me."

For once she didn't cop an attitude with me. She peeked through the window into the exam room and hissed, "Holy cow! That's Rocky! You didn't go in there by yourself, did you?"

Sensing she knew something I didn't, I replied, "Well, yes. Was I not supposed to?"

"That dog's psycho! We have to sedate him to do anything to him."

My heart began thumping erratically against my ribcage. "How was I supposed to know that? There's nothing on his chart!" Righteous indignation mixed with horror sent a tingling sensation through my entire body. I could have been mauled to death in that room! By a dog who wouldn't hurt a flea, but with no qualms against assaulting humans.

She snatched the chart from the box on the door and scanned it. I peeked over her shoulder just to be sure I hadn't overlooked the obvious. Sure enough, there was no "caution" or "needs muzzle" or *any* warning written on his record that indicated working with Rocky required extra precaution.

"Well," she sputtered, "everybody knows Rocky."

"No, Myra, everybody doesn't!" I grabbed the chart from her hand and wrote in big red letters across the top, *MUZZLE!!!!* I added extra exclamation points for emphasis, and then underlined the word several times. "Not only that, but Mr. Nettlesmith never said a word. In fact, he told me Rocky wouldn't hurt a flea."

She snorted. "I don't know about fleas, but he's done a number on people. Rocky's been fired from two other veterinary clinics."

"That's just great! Mr. Nettlesmith failed to mention that little fact to me." White, hot rage simmered just below the surface of my barely controlled facade of a professional woman holding back hysteria.

"Of course not. He blames the veterinarians for not being able to handle Rocky."

I took in a deep, calming breath and blew it out slowly through my nose.

"What's he here for, anyway?" Myra asked.

"Just his yearly exam."

"Thank goodness. We can probably just do a 'shoot and scoot.'"

"A 'shoot and scoot' works for me, providing we can even accomplish that." Theoretically, each patient walking through our doors deserved a thorough physical exam. We were taught in veterinary school that not conducting a complete physical exam on each pet constituted a huge disservice, if not downright malpractice. What if we just gave the animal a rabies shot and missed the huge abdominal tumor or the putrid ear infection because we didn't take the time to do a complete exam? What if the animal had a high fever and we missed it because we didn't bother to check its temperature before proceeding with a vaccination that could potentially make the pet sicker?

Nevertheless, with Rocky, I was willing to take the risk. I even had the nasty little subconscious thought that if I did end up killing Rocky with a rabies shot—which was highly unlikely—because I had skimped on his exam, it would be no loss to society, let alone Spangle Animal Clinic.

"All right, let's see if we can get this over with." Myra barged into the room ahead of me, and I semi-cowered behind her larger frame. Rocky took one look at the reinforcements and lunged for us.

Mr. Nettlesmith barely hung on to the end of the leash and laughed. "Now, Rocky, that's no way to be." It struck me, then, that Mr. Nettlesmith was a rather small, scrawny man, who most likely had been tormented as a child for his lack of physical prowess. I wondered if, subconsciously or otherwise, having a dog with the machismo of Rocky somehow bolstered the man's self-esteem.

Myra threw the muzzle at him. "You'll need to put this on Rocky before we can give him his shots."

The owner pursed his lips. "What a lot of poppycock," he muttered. "Rocky hates being muzzled."

I found my inner bravado and stepped out from behind Myra. "And we hate being bitten. If we're injured, we can't work. If we can't work, we can't take care of our patients, nor can we pay our bills."

Mr. Nettlesmith dismissed us with a wave of his hand. "Such silliness. Rocky would never bite anyone." Rocky flat out demonstrated his owner's untruthfulness by snapping at him when he tried to place the muzzle.

"Here now! Stop that!" Mr. Nettlesmith grumbled. "It's this blasted muzzle. It's upsetting him."

Myra folded her arms across her chest and fixed Mr. Nettlesmith with a no-nonsense glare. After making a few feeble attempts at muzzling Rocky, the owner finally managed to slide the muzzle over Rocky's nose. Before we could blink, Rocky brought up a huge paw and ripped it off.

"It's no use. He's not having it," declared the owner, the muzzle dangling from his hand.

I, on the other hand, *was* having it. In fact, I'd had it with both of them. "Give me that thing!" I barked. If there was anything that made me madder than a client who deliberately did not divulge the less-than-sterling behavior of his pet, putting me or the staff in unnecessary danger, it was an owner who half-heartedly went about placing a muzzle.

With the adrenaline pumping through my veins, my brain temporarily took leave of its good sense. I jerked the muzzle from Mr. Nettlesmith's hand, and with one swift motion, crammed it over Rocky's nose and snapping mouth before the beast could react. Myra immediately sprang into action and yanked the strap up behind the dog's ears, snugging it down tightly. Rocky tossed his rock-hard head knocking both of us into the wall behind us. His growling escalated in volume and ferocity, while large shoestrings of drool dripped from his compressed lips. He never once blinked.

"Now look!" chided the owner. "You're scaring him!"

The dog lunged at us, again, with his owner doing little to control him. I peeled myself off the wall, reached for the vaccines, and rammed my body into Rocky's with supernatural strength fueled by pure adrenaline, pinning him against the door. Myra threw her body against his head, and I quickly administered the injections. Both of us fell back, panting heavily, while the big dog continued to snarl.

"Take him out and put him in the car before you remove the muzzle," Myra ordered.

"And before we can see Rocky again, you will need to give him a tranquilizer an hour before your appointment," I added.

"Come on, Rocky," the unhappy owner said, dragging the struggling animal from the room. "Poor fella, no wonder you hate the vets." He turned and shot one last comment at us. "You'd think you people would know how to handle animals so they're not so traumatized every time they come in."

"Idiot," Myra mumbled under her breath before she walked off.

"Thank you," I called after her. If nothing else, in a pinch, Myra was one heck of an animal wrangler. As the adrenaline drained from my body, I found myself weak-kneed and shaking all over. It took several minutes before I was able to continue my appointments.

~

For some reason, when people learn you're a veterinarian, they seem to get this image in their head of someone who spends their entire day surrounded by adorable, cuddly puppies and kittens. *Healthy*, adorable, cuddly puppies and kittens. Pets like Rocky never cross their radars. Fortunately, big vicious dogs like Rocky were the extreme, but not a day went by in which I barely escaped with all my fingers intact.

Some of the worst offenders were the little land sharks, like Angel. I learned, over the years, that if a pet presented with the name of Angel, Precious, or Sweetie, watch out. Angel was a little Pekingese with a squashed-in face that couldn't be muzzled. Hence, working with her involved being faster than her snapping jaws. I couldn't even restrain her properly with one arm under her neck, as she invariably turned blue due to the messed-up anatomy typical of her breed which didn't allow for the simple necessity of breathing.

The first time I met Angel, her owner, Mrs. Farris, informed me Angel was mean because she had been "abused as a puppy." Since then, I wish I had a nickel for every mean dog who was abused as a puppy. I'd certainly be rich and able to retire comfortably. The problem with that theory is it didn't explain all the sweet dogs who truly *were* abused as puppies.

"I'm so sorry to hear about Angel's difficult beginnings," I commiserated. "How old was she when you rescued her?"

"Six weeks," Mrs. Farris replied.

There must have been a heck of a lot of abuse in Angel's first, short, six weeks of life to constitute a lifetime of PTSD. Certainly, Mrs. Farris had made up for it ever since. I doubt Angel's feet had ever touched the floor. Her owner carried her everywhere, except during the times I saw Angel being pushed in a stroller. Angel also sported quite the wardrobe. I never saw her in the same outfit twice. Despite my scolding concerning Angel's diet every time Mrs. Farris brought her in, the animal continued to be fed choice beef and chicken, with rice and fresh vegetables. I wished I could have eaten at Mrs. Farris' table. Her dog ate better than I did.

"Angel simply refuses to eat dog food," Mrs. Farris always protested.

"I wouldn't eat dog food either if I had a choice of beef and chicken," I told her. "However, it is nearly impossible to properly balance Angel's nutritional needs with home cooked meals unless you are working closely with a veterinary nutritionist."

"But I've tried feeding her dog food. She just leaves it in her bowl." The woman looked at me earnestly, pleading with me to understand her difficult position. "I can't just let her starve."

I knew my advice fell on deaf ears; nevertheless, I felt obligated to share my fount of professional knowledge with Angel's well-intended, but misguided owner.

"Mrs. Farris, I assure you I have never seen a dog skeleton next to a full bowl of dog food."

She shook her head. "You just don't know my Angel."

Oh, I knew her Angel, all right. Angel had Mrs. Farris exactly where she wanted her. It was obvious who called the shots in that household. And as if it weren't bad enough that Mrs. Farris spoiled the dog to the point of ridiculousness, Angel was also a hypochondriac. Or, to be more accurate, Mrs. Farris was a hypochondriac on Angel's behalf.

I always resisted a groan when I saw Angel's name on the schedule, which was fairly often. I fervently wished there were some way to convert Mrs. Farris into a "Dr. Spangle only" client, but alas, for some unexplainable reason, she liked me. I don't know why, as I had certainly never encouraged her. In fact, it seemed I did my best to drive home the point she was killing her pet with kindness. Since she never took my advice on anything, I wondered why she spent so much money obtaining it.

Today was no different. Angel had an appointment to check a "spot." I sighed, picked up her chart and called Angel and her owner back into a room.

"Oh, Dr. Bennet, thank heavens Heather was able to get us in today. I'm so worried about Angel," Mrs. Farris kept up a running monologue down the hall and into exam room two. As usual, she had Angel crushed against her large bosom. "I can't imagine what this terrible thing is. I hope it's not something serious."

"Well, let's have a look," I said. "When did you notice it?"

"Just this morning. I was so upset I called right away, but Heather said the earliest appointment wasn't until eleven thirty."

Angel peered at me over the top of her owner's arms and bared her misshapen little Peke teeth.

"Can you show me where this spot is?" I asked, making a reach for the now snarling little beast.

"It's right back by her tail. Oh, you will be gentle with her, won't you?" Mrs. Farris fretted. "You know how sensitive she is. Please don't hurt her."

I managed to snake one arm under the front legs of the rotund little dog without getting bitten, but unfortunately not without inadvertently groping her owner who still mashed the dog firmly against her chest. For a moment Mrs. Farris and I played tug-of-war with Angel.

"Let me have her," I instructed, in my most patient, professional voice.

Reluctantly, Mrs. Farris conceded the battle and allowed me to remove the Velcro-attached beast from her body. I now had a snapping, wriggling, butterball under my arm and I dared not let go.

Placing Angel on the exam table, I kept my death grip around her middle, while my free hand searched frantically for the "spot." There was no hair loss, no scab, no sore, no mass. Nothing.

"I'm afraid I'm not finding the spot," I said. "Could you show me where it is?"

Mrs. Farris tore herself away from Angel's growling front end, where she had been murmuring, "It's okay, baby, Mommy's here," and ran her hand down the dog's back. It took her an agonizing few minutes, during which time I struggled with the writhing canine. Just when I started to suggest she might have been mistaken about the "spot," Mrs. Farris triumphantly proclaimed, "Here! It's right here."

I felt around where she indicated, but still didn't feel anything. "I'm sorry, I'm still not finding it."

She guided my hand to a miniscule, little bump. I one-handedly parted the hair around the area—as best I could with a squirming, snarling, snapping, eighteen-pound dog under my arm who wanted to eat me alive—and said, "It's just a tiny wart, Mrs. Farris. Nothing to be worried about." With that, I heaved Angel back into her owner's arms, as my left arm had gone numb.

"A wart?" The woman repeated the diagnosis in a voice that held all the dismay of my having pronounced a terminal disease in her beloved pet.

"Yes. Warts are very common in dogs, particularly as they get older. They rarely cause any problems unless they grow so big they get caught on things or the animal chews them."

"A wart! Oh, how dreadful." Mrs. Farris snuggled Angel tighter, if that were possible. "My poor, poor Angel."

"Angel has gained more weight," I said, glancing at her chart. "We've discussed how detrimental all this excess weight is to her health. She needs to get more exercise and you need to cut back on her food."

"Oh, I couldn't possibly do that. She would hate me."

Well, we certainly couldn't have *that* now, could we? "Okay, well then, I'll walk you up to the front desk."

"You're sure this . . . *wart* is not cancerous."

"I'm sure. But I can always remove it if it bothers you."

The color drained from Mrs. Farris' face. "You mean surgery?"

I nodded. "It's very minor."

"Oh, no, I could never put Angel through that." She bent her head and kissed the still growling dog on the top of the skull, leaving a bright red lipstick imprint. "If you say not to worry, then that's good enough for me. Thank you for putting my mind at ease."

"You're very welcome." I rubbed my arm, trying to restore circulation.

I picked up the next record, a new client, and called her back into room one. At first, I didn't see my tiny new patient, a chi-hua-hua, snuggled inside the woman's jacket. Chi-hua-huas are a breed that many veterinarians dislike because of their nasty dispositions. I am one of the few veterinarians who actually like the little buggers, having grown up with several, and although they tend to be "one-person" type dogs, I usually found I was able to win them over. So, I didn't think anything about reaching my hand out to pet Lovey, until she bit me on the index finger. I grabbed a gauze and pressed it to my rapidly oozing wound.

Instead of expressing any sort of chagrin over her dog's behavior, the owner, Miss Garby, a tall, thin, schoolmarmish-looking older woman tightened her lips into a thin line. "Lovey obviously doesn't like you," she declared, in a voice dripping with disapproval, as if it were *my* fault.

Yeah, well, back at her, I was tempted to reply, but managed to restrain myself. "Excuse me for a minute. I need to disinfect this bite." I made a hasty exit before I could further embarrass myself from the dual humiliation of not only being disliked by the dog, but having let my guard down enough to allow it to bite me. This insult to injury, on the heels of just having to deal with Angel Farris, was just too much. There should be some unwritten rule that a vet should not have to see two nasty pets in a row.

As I stood at the sink rinsing away the blood and scrubbing the wound vigorously with antiseptic soap, my boss appeared.

"What happened?" he demanded.

"The dog in room one bit me. It was my own fault for not taking more care with a new patient before reaching out to pet her."

"Nonsense," he argued. "The client should have disclosed that information up front. I'll handle this."

I made a half-hearted attempt to stop him, but knew it was futile. He stormed into room one and I could hear a heated exchange between him and the new client, who likely, after today, would seek veterinary care elsewhere. Not that I would be heartbroken if she did.

"Madam, you should have informed Dr. Bennet your dog would bite."

"Lovey has never bitten anyone before. That young woman should know better than to reach for a dog in a threatening manner. Is she even a doctor?"

"Yes, I assure you, Dr. Bennet is an excellent veterinarian. She knows how to properly handle animals."

I pressed against the door, eavesdropping, a tiny frisson of exhilaration warming my core from my boss' unexpected and rare praise. My bandaged finger throbbed.

"Nevertheless, I prefer someone with more experience."

"Very well, I will be happy to see to . . ." As usual, he had not bothered to look at the pet's name, a sin of monumental proportions in the eyes of many owners, second only to calling the animal by the wrong sex.

"Lovey," the woman supplied, in a sour voice, that projected her lack of confidence in *his* professional capacity simply because he hadn't had her treasured pet's name readily on his tongue.

"Yes, of course. And what are we seeing Lovely for today?"

Ooh! Not good! I winced.

"It's 'Lovey', not 'Lovely'," I heard the woman snap.

I could tell Miss Garby and my boss were not going to mesh. Sure enough, the next sound I heard was an impatient sigh from Dr. Spangle, followed by, "Whatever! What's he here for?"

Oh, Dr. Spangle! Not two faux pax in a row! I shook my head in disbelief.

"*Her* problem is an infected ear." I could tell the woman spoke through clenched teeth, although I didn't have a visual.

"All right, let me have a look."

What followed was a melee of epic proportions. I have rarely heard such unearthly noise emanating from such a small creature. To add to the commotion, my boss' voice bellowed with unintelligible words, while Miss Garby's indignant protests peppered the charged air in the small room.

I shrank back from the door just as my boss came barreling out into the hallway. There was no way I was going to ask what happened. Besides, I had a fairly good idea, especially as the first thing he did was thrust his bleeding hand under the faucet.

"Myra!" he bawled. "Get me a small muzzle."

Unfortunately, I was unable to see the outcome, as Heather informed me there were two clients waiting. Praying the next patients were docile, I moved on. But I was strangely buoyed by the fact that apparently it wasn't only me that Lovey disliked. Just that knowledge alone boosted my fragile self-esteem.

Chapter 20

"Have you ever seen anything like this, Doc?" The concerned middle-aged, balding client wrung his hands as he hovered over his little balding West Highland white terrier, who sat trembling on the exam table.

I bit my tongue from the flippant reply just waiting to be voiced. *Only about ten times a day.* Nobody liked to be told their pet had a common disease, just like everyone else's pet. Owners wanted something rare and exotic so they could brag to their friends about how special their fur baby was. For some reason, I only received this question for the routine problems, not the bonified rare and mysterious ones that had me scratching my head in bewilderment.

Fortunately, though both patient and owner were balding, the reason was not the same. Marcus, the Westie, suffered from typical flea bite allergy, compounded by the fact he had the misfortune to be born a Westie, who undoubtedly suffered from a plethora of other allergies, as well. If you look up allergies in a veterinary dermatology book, I guarantee the poster child will be a Westie. It's the bad luck of the breed.

"Yes, Mr. Vincent, I'm afraid Marcus has flea allergies." The hair loss over the back half of the poor dog's body was classic, as well as the obvious self-trauma from chewing and scratching that had left large, inflamed areas on his bare skin.

I waited for the expected flea-nial response and was not disappointed. "Fleas? But Marcus doesn't have fleas."

I rolled Marcus over to expose his belly and pointed out two fleas scurrying for cover to his skeptical owner. At least Mr. Vincent had the good grace not to blame our veterinary clinic as the source of the nasty little parasites.

"Oh my! I just gave him a bath yesterday."

"Flea shampoo only kills the fleas that are on the dog at the time of the bath. Once the shampoo's rinsed off, there is no residual protection. You will need to follow the bath with a dip that stays on the skin, as well as treat the environment."

"But I never see more than one or two fleas on him," Mr. Vincent objected.

"That's all it takes if you have a pet who's highly allergic to fleas." The client still regarded me with a doubtful eye, so I went on. "Think about people with peanut allergies. Just the hint of a peanut product can send them into a life-threatening allergic reaction."

The light seemed to come on. "Yes, I see what you mean."

"That's why you have to stay on top of flea control in these patients."

Mr. Vincent shook his head. "I thought I had been. But I guess what I'm doing is not enough."

"I'll write everything down that you need to do. It won't be easy. Fleas are a big problem in Florida, and you can't afford to let your guard down or you'll be overrun with them in no time."

"Thanks, Doc. Is there anything you can do to help stop Marcus' itching? He's miserable, and he keeps me awake at night scratching."

"Yes. I'll give him some steroids and a topical spray that should help."

"Thank you, Doc," said the relieved owner, as I left the room to write detailed instructions for flea control for the umpteenth time that day. I had written these same instructions so many times, I could write them in my sleep. My brain went to its default mode of autopilot and my hand did the rest.

By rote, I scribbled down a list of do's and don'ts while my mind wandered. Man, I was sick of fleas. I was sick of seeing fleas. I was sick of talking about fleas. I was sick of writing down instructions for getting rid of fleas. I was sick of the client, who at the end of the appointment for some other issue, while I was mentally moving on to the next patient, brought up, "By the way, what can I do about the fleas?" This question led to another ten minutes of unallotted appointment time, because, of course, there was no simple answer.

I am immensely grateful that flea control has come a long way since I first started in practice, and there are some wonderful, easy-to-use products available now. But back then, fleas were a constant battle and source of aggravation—for clients, pets, and me. Besides having limited access to effective forms of flea control, I also did not have a copy machine, let alone a computer, with which to churn out copies of my flea control instructions; hence, each patient required a new, handwritten, personally prepared set.

~

I suppose I couldn't blame clients for some of the questions they asked, such as whether or not I had ever seen a certain condition like flea allergy dermatitis. After all, it was my job to answer questions, and most of the time I felt I did a pretty good job. If I didn't know the answer to a particular question, I could always look it up or ask someone more knowledgeable. But there were a few questions that, no matter how many times I heard them, always left me at a loss for words—at least words I could say to a client whom I wished to retain as a client.

Take my first encounter with Mrs. Westermeyer asking if I knew anything about puppies, for example. This wasn't the first or the last time I had heard the question, "Do you know anything about" (fill in the blank). Puppies? Anesthesia in Afghans? Breeding English bulldogs? Heart problems in Maine Coon cats? This question always left me fumbling for a response. I mean, I *did* manage to graduate from veterinary school. I have a diploma that says so. Therefore, I must know *something* about whatever condition the client asked about. As a matter of fact, I know something about a lot of things—airplanes, for instance. I know they have wings and a tail and an engine, and they fly, though it's probably best if I'm not asked to pilot one. But for some reason, the way the question is worded just begs for a sarcastic answer, with which I can't respond if I know what's good for me. And every time I hear a question that starts with, "do you know anything about," my stunned brain doesn't churn out any reasonable reply. So, I just stare, like a deer in the headlights, waiting for my neurons to warm up and send an appropriate message to my mouth.

A question I heard all too often was, "Do you have to go to school to be a veterinarian?" Aside from Jack's misguided attempt to ascertain my age on our first date, this question boggled my mind. I could only imagine what these people thought about my professional ability. Not much, obviously. Perhaps they thought veterinarians took a correspondence course for which they studied during reruns of Gilligan's Island, sent in the required forms, and received a mail-order certificate to practice veterinary medicine. Or maybe we just apprenticed for a few months under an experienced veterinarian before going solo. But since animal doctors were not *real* doctors, after all, I suppose the question seemed a valid one to many people.

All too frequently during emergency calls, I was asked, "Can it wait until tomorrow?" As tempted as I always was to make a snarky comment about the current state of my crystal ball—especially if it were 2 a.m. or Mrs. Pryner—I somehow always managed to refrain. I suppose I should have been flattered that people believed that I, the person who may or may not have actually gone to school to become a veterinarian, had the exceptional superpower to diagnose and treat vague symptoms over the phone. As well as predict life and death.

But the one question I will never forget came late one Saturday evening when I was enjoying a game of rummy with Jack. I wasn't on call and I was winning, something that rarely happened. Still, that didn't stop the answering service from interrupting my night off.

Strangely enough, the caller to whom they patched me through was another vet.

"Sorry to bother you," Dr. McMillan said when we were connected. Dr. McMillan, a veterinarian about my age, worked at a clinic across town. I had seen him a couple of times at a local veterinary meeting. "I've got some clients of yours here. They couldn't get in touch with Dr. Spangle, so the answering service called me."

That was odd. I couldn't understand why the answering service hadn't called *me*. That is, until I heard who it was.

"Their name is Flutterjohn, and their dog, Polly, had surgery for a bladder stone a couple days ago. I think the bladder incision has dehisced. I'm sure there's urine leaking into the abdomen."

Polly Flutterjohn. Another Dr. Spangle *only* patient.

"I remember," I said. "But I don't know why Dr. Spangle isn't answering his calls."

"The answering service said they have been trying to reach him for a couple hours. When they couldn't, they called me. Polly needs immediate surgery."

"Yes, of course she does," I agreed. "Go ahead and do what needs to be done."

There was a slight pause. "Well, that's just the thing. They don't want me to do the surgery. They only want Dr. Spangle, and nobody can locate him."

"Oh." That sounded like the Flutterjohns. "Did the service try his home number?"

"Yes, there's no answer. And he's not answering his pager, either. I don't know what to do. They refuse to let me do the surgery."

I sucked in a deep breath. "They're Dr. Spangle's clients. They won't want me, either."

After another long pause, Dr. McMillan suggested, "Do you think I should ask them?"

Mentally cursing Dr. Spangle for not being where he was supposed to be and putting me in this position, I replied, "Sure, you can try." I had been beating Jack at rummy and wanted to finish the game. The sounds coming from the telephone receiver became muffled as Dr. McMillan carried on a conversation with the Flutterjohns, his hand over the phone. A mirthless smile curled my lips as I imagined what was transpiring at the other end of the phone.

Finally, Dr. McMillan uncovered the receiver. "They asked if you would see them at your clinic."

Somewhat surprised, as well as a little irritated, I said, "All right. Tell them I'll meet them in twenty minutes."

"Will do. Again, I'm sorry to bother you when you're not on call. I know how that is."

"It's okay. There wasn't anything else you could do."

I hung up and shot a doleful look at Jack.

"I know. I heard," he said. He gathered up the cards.

"Wait! I was winning."

He grinned. "Yeah, I know. Oh, well." He stuffed the cards into the box. "Come on, I'll go with you."

"Jack, you really don't have to—"

"Yes, I do. It's late."

"I know, but I'll be fine. It's a little old couple and unless they're packing a piece, I think I can take them if they become violent."

"You might need help."

Yes, I might. Especially if I had to do surgery, which looked very likely unless I could locate the elusive Dr. Spangle in the next forty-five minutes or so.

We made the short drive to the clinic and found the Flutterjohns waiting anxiously at the entrance. From the bright porch light, I could see Polly, their beloved shih tzu, wrapped in a dark-colored towel, hugged tight to the wife's chest.

I unlocked the clinic door and ushered the worried clients into an exam room. "Excuse me for a moment," I said, after settling them into the room, "I just need to check something."

They nodded absently as I slipped from the room into Dr. Spangle's office. There, resting in its charger on his desk, sat the pager. A slow burn started in my gut and worked its way outward. He *knew* he had call tonight. Why didn't he at least ask me to cover emergencies if he couldn't? In the past, he never minded dumping his calls on me. I picked up his phone and punched in his home number. To my surprise, his wife, Patty, answered.

"Jill, hi, what can I do for you?"

"Uh . . . I'm looking for your husband."

She laughed. "Oh, I imagine Drew is tied up with some emergency, like he always is. He wasn't here when I came home. I just got in from visiting my sister in Georgia. I was supposed to stay the weekend, but her electricity went out. They're having the worst storms up there, you know." Patty continued to rattle on about the weather in wherever it was her sister lived, but I had more or less tuned out. "Anyway, after several hours with no electricity, I just came on home."

Should I tell Patty that her husband wasn't tied up with some emergency? No, I didn't want to worry her.

"Should I have him call you when he gets in?" Patty asked.

"Uh . . . no, that's okay. It's not important. Thanks, Patty." I replaced the receiver, pocketed the beeper, and returned to the Flutterjohns and Polly.

"I'm sorry, I just tried to reach Dr. Spangle again," I told them. "Nobody knows where he is, and he seems to have forgotten to take the pager with him."

They didn't reply for a moment, then Mr. Flutterjohn pushed Polly toward me. "She was straining to urinate after the surgery. We called yesterday and Dr. Spangle told us not to worry, said it was normal. But she hasn't urinated in almost twenty-four hours and we got worried."

"Then she got very depressed and wouldn't eat all day," Mrs. Flutterjohn picked up the story where her husband left off. "We called the answering service, but they couldn't reach Dr. Spangle, so they offered to call Dr. McMillan. He said her bladder incision is leaking."

She must have left out the part where the service offered to call me first, but they declined—preferring to take their chances with an unfamiliar vet, then changing their minds. While they were talking, I casually palpated the little dog's slightly distended belly in search of a bladder. I could feel a very small, thickened mass in the back part of her abdomen. This could mean that the surgical site had, indeed, broken open, releasing urine into the abdomen, or it could be something as simple as the fact that Polly's bladder was empty.

"Dr. McMillan said Polly needed surgery right away," the husband said, "but . . . well . . . we don't really know him."

"And we don't want someone we don't know operating on our Polly," Mrs. Flutterjohn added. Her worry lines deepened, and unshed tears glistened in her eyes. I reached for the tissue box on top of the cabinet behind me and handed it to her. She plucked out two tissues and gave me a feeble smile.

"Okay, let me have Polly for a moment. I want to verify Dr. McMillan's findings." Without waiting for further discussion, I tucked the little dog under my arm and headed for the treatment room. Jack, bless his heart, who always waited unobtrusively out of the way, recognized this as his cue, and came to assist me.

As Jack held Polly on the treatment table, I said softly, "I need to stick a needle into her abdomen and see if there's urine."

Back then, I didn't have the luxury of ultrasound to confirm the presence of free fluid in the belly. I could have done a radiograph with contrast material, but that would have required sedation and a lot more time. Pulling a urine sample from the abdomen was the fastest way to validate what I was pretty sure I already knew.

Polly's hair was already shaved from the surgery, so I did a quick swab of her belly behind her umbilicus and directed the needle straight through the slightly rounded abdominal wall, hopefully away from anything important. As I applied suction to the syringe, I was rewarded with a syringeful of clear, yellow fluid. I withdrew the needle, and just to be sure, squirted some of the liquid onto a gauze square. A deep sniff confirmed my diagnosis. Urine.

I returned Polly to the exam room with the news. "Dr. McMillan is right. Polly does have urine leaking into her belly. She needs surgery right away."

The couple exchanged horrified glances. Then Mrs. Flutterjohn wailed, "Well *who* is going to do the surgery?"

There it was. The question. I had to restrain myself with every fiber of my being from turning around and searching the room for an elusive surgeon, and from answering with a smart-aleck reply. *Since I can't wave a magic wand and produce Dr. Spangle, who, by the way, got us into this mess in the first place and then mysteriously disappeared, leaving us all in this impossible situation, perhaps I can call in the janitor to see if he'll do it.* I discarded my first thought. And the one after that, and the one after that.

We stared at each other, at an obvious impasse for several minutes, while I ordered my brain to come up with a more appropriate and acceptable response for the distraught owners.

I took a deep breath, then gently explained the situation. "I'm afraid we don't have many options. I can send her back to Dr. McMillan—"

"No!" they cried in unison.

At my astonished look, Mr. Flutterjohn explained, "We don't have anything against the young man, mind you, it's just that we don't know him."

I watched, helplessly, as tears streamed down Mrs. Flutterjohn's wrinkled cheeks. I tried again. "I could refer you to the university—"

Mr. Flutterjohn shook his head. "We just can't make that long trip."

I found myself picking at my cuticle and willed myself to stop. I forced the words I knew they didn't want to hear past my lips. "I'm afraid we can't wait until we locate Dr. Spangle. Your only other option is to allow me to do the surgery."

The elderly couple again shot worried glances at each other. "Well . . ." Mrs. Flutterjohn hesitated. "Have you ever done this surgery before?"

Now this wasn't the first time I had heard *this* question, either, and in all fairness, it was a perfectly reasonable question. But the devil in me always wanted to reply in a chirpy manner, "No, but there's a first time for everything."

Due to the direness of the circumstances, however, I managed not to, reminding myself of how worried the Flutterjohns were—not to mention that Polly had a life-threatening condition that needed immediate attention.

"Yes," I assured them. "Besides, we really don't have a choice."

The old lady's shoulders sagged. "All right then. Just take care of our Polly." Mrs. Flutterjohn hugged the little dog tightly against her chest, and I thought for a minute she had changed her mind and was not going to relinquish Polly without a fight. But after a long moment, her husband gently pried the animal out of her grasp and handed Polly to me.

"I'll do my best," I promised.

They turned and left, bent and broken, and, I was sure, with the notion they would never see their beloved pet alive again.

Mercifully, the surgery went well. I could see where Dr. Spangle's suture line in the bladder wall had broken down—perhaps due to Polly's excessive straining. These things happened from time to time, and it was not his fault. What *was* his fault was not being available when a complication arose. I repaired the defect, flushed the abdomen thoroughly with warm saline to clean out all the urine, and placed a urinary catheter to relieve pressure on the bladder wall for a few days to give it a chance to heal. I kept Polly over the weekend, monitoring her closely.

On Monday morning, I related the story to Dr. Spangle, with a certain degree of annoyance at having been placed in that awkward position. He offered no adequate explanation, nor, in my opinion, an appropriate apology.

"I had to go out of town," he informed me. "I forgot I was on call."

He grilled me relentlessly on what had happened and how I handled the situation. When the Flutterjohns came to pick up Polly that afternoon, he profusely apologized, assured them his absence had been unavoidable, and, surprisingly—since he rarely said anything good about me— told them Polly had been in good hands and he had the utmost confidence in me. And, of course, he would personally see to everything relating to Polly's aftercare.

"Oh, thank you, Doctor!" Mrs. Flutterjohn fell all over herself with gratitude. To *him*.

~

It was time for Charley to pass over the Rainbow Bridge. His nine lives had been used up one or two lives ago, and his kidneys were shot. His owner, Betty Tate, held him in her lap, stroking the once lustrous orange fur, silent tears spilling down her cheeks.

"I want to stay with him," she sniffled, "but I just don't know if I can."

"That's okay," I assured her. "You don't have to."

"But I don't want him to think I've abandoned him." A quiet sob escaped her lips. "Oh, I just don't know what to do." She dabbed at her face with a tissue.

"Some people elect to stay with their pet until it is sedated, and then leave before the final injection," I suggested. "Once Charley is asleep, he won't know if you're here or not."

She took a faltering breath and nodded. "Okay. That's what I'll do."

I drew up a large dose of sedative and administered it to the unresponsive old tomcat in her lap. Seeing his total lack of reaction to the shot, I knew this was the best decision. Charley had always been a scrapper, but the light in his lackluster, amber eyes had gone out. He just didn't care anymore. Putting a beloved pet to sleep is always difficult, mostly due to the emotional distress for the humans involved in the process. The actual procedure, itself, is generally quick and painless, and, as I tell upset owners, it is the final act of love we can provide for a suffering pet.

Many times, while waiting for the sedative to take effect, I try to engage the owner in reminiscing about happier times with their pet. This often helps take their mind off the last few moments of the animal's life, and brings them a little joy. But Betty wasn't in the mood to go down memory lane, so I gave her and Charley some privacy.

Charley had drifted off to a peaceful sleep when I checked back a few minutes later.

"He's asleep, Mrs. Tate," I said. "I can take him whenever you're ready."

The tears flowed copiously as the lady continued to caress her sedated pet. "I'm doing the right thing, aren't I?" She looked up at me, begging for affirmation.

"Yes, absolutely. Charley's in kidney failure and we can't fix that. He's had a long and happy life, and you have taken excellent care of him. Otherwise, he wouldn't have lived to be sixteen."

She took another shaky breath and blew it out audibly. "Okay. I guess you can take him."

As I reached for the sedated cat, she suddenly gripped his limp body. "He won't feel anything, will he?"

"No, he's completely asleep. He won't know anything."

Betty slowly handed Charley into my outstretched arms. As I turned to leave the room, she blurted out, "Promise me. You won't *experiment* on him, will you?"

DON'T BITE THE DOCTOR

Chapter 21

"Honestly, Jack, I can't even imagine what was going through the woman's mind. Do I look like a Dr. Franken-Bennet, the mild-mannered veterinarian by day and the mad scientist by night? Do people really think that once the last client is out the door, I pull down the shades and rush into my laboratory where I work into the wee hours of the morning attempting brain transplants between dogs and cats?"

He snorted. "No, you do something much more improbable. You abandon the advances of science to make a futile attempt at getting through an uninterrupted fifteen-minute dinner without the phone ringing."

I laughed. "Isn't that the truth?" As if on cue, my stomach rumbled. "Speaking of which, I'm starved."

"Me too!" came an exuberant little voice at my knees.

The voice belonged to Rebecca's three-year-old son, Matt. Somehow, Jack and I had managed to get talked into babysitting the little urchin for the day while Rebecca and her husband, Glen, spent "quality time" together. I didn't understand why Rebecca hadn't dumped Matt on his doting maternal grandmother, who continually reminded me that my biological clock was ticking—although I sincerely doubted she wanted a pre-wedding grandchild from Jack and me. Which I had no intention of providing. Despite the current culture and the sexual revolution, I firmly believed in the Biblical teaching in abstaining from sex before marriage. Call me old-fashioned, but my faith meant something to me, and I wasn't going to compromise. Fortunately, Jack, also a strong Christian, strongly agreed.

But I had the sneaking suspicion this unexpected childcare request may have been more than just an excuse to unload a three-year-old for the day. There seemed to be a hidden subterfuge to this whole arrangement, and I was beginning to smell a rat. I could just hear the plan hatched between Jack's mother and Rebecca. I suspected it went something like this:

"If Jill could just experience the joy a child brings, she would surely change her mind," my future mother-in-law said, in my imagined conversation.

"I know! I'll ask her and Jack to watch Matt for the day. Matty is such a delightful little boy. She won't be able to resist wanting babies after spending the day with Matty," my future sister-in-law replied, also in my imagination.

"Perfect! Let's do it!" My future mother-in-law clapped her hands together in unbridled glee.

Of course, I was not privy to this supposed conversation, but I was willing to bet I wasn't far off in my fanciful suspicions.

"We can't possibly take Matty Sunday," I told Rebecca. "I'm on call." There. That should quash any notions of turning me into a nanny on my day off. I left out the part where I wanted to say, "Are you out of your mind? I'd rather walk barefoot over hot coals than watch a three-year-old on my day off!"

It wasn't that I disliked children, per se. Jack's mother's logic was right, in one aspect. Being an only child, I had never been around children. I had never even babysat as a teenager. But I also didn't have a strong maternal desire to breed. Children made me nervous, especially when they came into the clinic with their parents and acted like impossible brats. With practice, I had found the perfect solution to dealing with parents who wouldn't control their monstrous offspring while I was trying to take care of the well-behaved members of the family, namely the pets. The louder and more obnoxious the children became, the softer I spoke. This required the parents to listen more closely, which often brought about the desired result of them *doing something* to rein in their unruly children.

The few times this didn't work, I threatened to give the kids a rabies shot and lock them in a cage. Then I laughed. Ha ha, just kidding, of course. But this was usually enough to shock the parents into doing something. And if this tactic still failed to shut the little brats up, I pointedly said to the misbehaving miscreants, "You'll have to be quiet so I can talk to your parents." Being spoken to by an authoritative adult often worked wonders in children who had never experienced an adult in charge.

Now I don't mean to sound like a Scrooge where children are concerned. And certainly, there were many well-behaved children who graced our exam rooms, eager to see what happened at the animal doctor; some even asked intelligent questions. These children were always a pleasure, and I enjoyed seeing them. Still, that didn't mean I *wanted* one.

Unfortunately, Matty wasn't one of those delightful children. Despite his adoring mother's and grandmother's opinions to the contrary, Matty was a horrible, spoiled brat. Being the first grandchild, and a boy, to boot, had given the impossible urchin privileged, untouchable status.

"Oh, that won't be a problem. Matty loves animals," Rebecca assured me, despite the fact she refused to get him a dirty, germ-infested pet.

"Rebecca, I can't take a three-year-old to the clinic. There are too many dangerous things he could get into. And I can't be responsible for watching him when I'm working."

"Oh, Matty won't be any trouble at all," she argued. "Besides, Jack can watch him."

I shot Jack a helpless look. *Get us out of this!*

"Becky—"

"I'll drop him off at one. You'll be out of church by then. It'll be fun!"

It quickly became apparent that Rebecca's idea of fun and my idea of fun were two entirely different things.

The minute she dropped Matty off, he terrorized Bitsy and Delilah, who took up residence in the back of my bedroom closet.

"Matty!" I chided. "Stop chasing the dogs. You're scaring them." My tone may have been a tiny bit harsh, but I couldn't stand to see children tormenting innocent animals.

The child threw himself on the ground, kicking and screaming. *"I want them to play with me!"*

"Matt, buddy," said Jack, "you can play with the dogs later. I promise."

My jaw clenched. "Doesn't he need to take a nap or something? Don't little kids take naps in the afternoon?"

Matt stopped wailing and shot me a look of pure disgust. "I don't *take* naps. I'm not a *baby!*" He sat up, the waterworks abruptly cut off, and announced, "I'm hungry!"

"Didn't your mom feed you lunch before you came over?" I asked.

"No. She said *you* would." Matt pulled himself up from the floor.

Thanks again, Rebecca, I owe you one. Did I really want this manipulative woman for my future sister-in-law? I sighed. Jack and I had finished eating my famous grilled-cheese sandwiches, and I had just cleaned up the kitchen. "Okay, I'll make you a grilled-cheese sandwich."

"I don't *want* a grilled-cheese sandwich! I *hate* grilled-cheese sandwiches!" The brat glared at me as if I had insulted his mother. Maybe he had read my mind.

"How about a peanut butter sandwich?" Jack offered.

"*No!* I want chicken nuggets." Matt thrust out his chin.

"I don't have chicken nuggets," I said, through gritted teeth. "I have grilled-cheese, peanut butter, and ham. That's it. Take your pick."

"I don't *want* any of that ole' junk! I *want* chicken nuggets!" He stomped his little Nike-clad foot.

The child had been with us exactly fifteen minutes and I was more than ready for Rebecca to come collect him. I narrowed my eyes. Would Rebecca object if I whacked the little monster on the one place where he couldn't sit down for a week? Subconsciously, I flexed my fingers.

"We'll go out," Jack said, quickly.

I glared at him. "Jack, there's no fast-food restaurant around here."

"There's a McDonald's in Hanson." He refused to meet my reproving eyes.

"Hanson's thirty minutes away," I pointed out. "What if I get a call?"

"I want to go to McDonald's! *I want to go to McDonald's! I want to go to McDonald's!*" The kid set up an endless loop.

Jack shot me a helpless look. I shot him a defiant one back. "Jack, I *can't* be thirty minutes away when I'm on call."

"*I want to go to McDonald's! I want to go to McDonald's! I want to go to McDonald's!*" The chanting became louder.

"Why don't you go without me?" I suggested a little loudly, as it was difficult to hear over the din.

"*I want to go to McDonald's! I want to go to McDonald's! I want to go to McDonald's!*"

"I don't want to go without you, Jill. Please?" Jack's eyes beseeched me.

Coward. You don't want to be alone with the brat.

"If I get a call—"

"We'll come back right away. I promise."

"Besides, we already ate lunch," I objected.

"So, we'll just order a drink or something. Please?"

"*I want to go to McDonald's! I want to go to McDonald's! I want to go to McDonald's!*"

I glared at the impossible little moppet, whose brattiness, once again, paid off. "We shouldn't give in to tantrums," I grumbled. "How is he ever going to learn that he can't always have his own way?"

"That's Becky's problem," Jack said. "Right now, I just want to shut him up."

I heaved a huge sigh and gave up. At least taking Matt to McDonald's in Hanson would give the poor dogs a short reprieve. "But if I get a call—"

"We'll come right back." The corners of Jack's lips curled into a grateful, lopsided smile and my resistance melted.

The half-hour drive to Hanson only seemed to last an hour, with Matt's nonstop prattle. Jack and I couldn't exchange two words without being interrupted.

"I have an idea," I said, proud of myself for my brilliance, "why don't we play the 'Quiet Game'?"

"What's the 'Quiet Game'?" Matt asked, his voice full of suspicion.

"We all have to be quiet. The first one who talks loses."

"That's a stupid game. I don't want to play."

"I think it sounds like fun," Jack offered, lamely.

"It's *stupid!* How much farther? Are we there yet?"

Are we there yet, indeed? My weary ears asked.

Finally, *finally,* we made it to the McDonald's in Hanson. Matt ordered his Happy Meal with chicken nuggets, and Jack and I ordered milkshakes. Big mistake.

"I want a milkshake, too," Matt declared.

"Your Happy Meal doesn't come with a milkshake," I stupidly explained.

"*I want a milkshake! I want a milkshake!*" Matt's stubborn little face turned red as he beat his fists against the counter.

"That's okay, we'll order an extra milkshake," Jack said, while I scowled at him.

We took our food and sat next to the play area.

"Hey!" Matt cried, pulling his toy from his Happy Meal bag. "I wanted a race car. I don't want this stupid toy!"

Jack reached over and took the plastic bag from his nephew. "But, Matty, this is really cool. It's a top." He tore open the bag, placed the top on the table, and gave it a spin. "See?"

"It's *stupid!* I wanted a race car."

"I don't think they're giving away race cars this week."

"I *want* a race car! On TV they showed race cars. I *want* a race car!"

"Miss?" Jack beckoned to a teenager wiping down the next table. "Is this the only toy you're giving away this week?"

The young girl nodded. "We ran out of race cars last week. They were very popular."

"Sorry, buddy," Jack said. "That's all they have."

Matt's face puckered. "I don't *want* this stupid toy!" He flung the top across the room, narrowly missing a young mother's head. The startled woman looked around for the source of the flying object. Matt sat back and folded his little arms across his heaving chest.

"Matty! You almost hit that lady!" Jack cried. "You go pick up that toy and tell her you're sorry."

"No!" Matt's chin shot up and his lower lip protruded.

"Yes!" Jack demanded. He took hold of Matt's unyielding arm and tugged.

"No! No! No! Let go of me! You're hurting me!" the child screeched. The whole dining room grew silent as the drama played out before the stunned eyes of the patrons.

I wanted to disappear into the floor. "It's not our kid," I explained, certain that would absolve us of judgment. Just then, my pager went off. "Jack, I've got to find a phone." I scurried out, leaving Jack to deal with his nephew.

A few minutes later, I returned. I didn't know what had ensued while I took the phone call, and I didn't want to know. "We've got to go," I said, noting that Matt hadn't touched his lunch.

"No!" Matt yelled. "I'm not done. And I want to play!"

"You haven't even started eating," Jack said. "Jill has to go see a sick animal. You can bring your lunch with you." He stuffed the food back into the bag and picked up Matty's milkshake.

Without further discussion, Jack and I started toward the door. Matt sat obstinately for a moment, then apparently realizing the show was over, decided he'd better follow us, rather than be left behind.

Jack buckled Matt into the car seat, as I fretted about the long drive back to the clinic. The patient was having difficulty breathing—not one I wanted to wait thirty minutes to see. We pulled out of the parking lot in tense silence, that is, until Matt dropped his milkshake.

"My milkshake! I dropped my milkshake!" he bawled.

Cringing, I took a surreptitious glance into the backseat, then cringed even more. The strawberry shake had bounced off the seat, popped its plastic top, and landed on the floor, spilling its sticky contents everywhere.

"How bad is it?" asked Jack.

"You don't want to know," I assured him.

Matt howled for the next thirty minutes, but neither Jack nor I gave in to the child's demands to relinquish our own milkshakes to replace his. Ordinarily, I would have readily handed over my unwanted milkshake, as my stomach churned with anxiety over my patient. But as a matter of principle, I forced myself to slurp up the last drop, where it sat in a cold, heavy blob in the bottom of my stomach.

Arriving at the clinic, I left Jack to fend for himself with Matt, as I hurriedly admitted the Sandersons and their aging pug, Moose, who clearly struggled to catch his next breath. His grayish gums only confirmed the seriousness of his condition. I listened to his chest, hearing muffled heart sounds, and hustled him away for oxygen and a chest X-ray. A short time later, I told the Sandersons what I suspected, based on the basketball shape of the cardiac silhouette on the radiograph. Moose had fluid around his heart, which prevented the heart from pumping effectively. Unfortunately, I did not have ultrasound in those days to confirm my diagnosis.

"I'm going to have to stick a needle into the sac around his heart and drain off the fluid," I explained to the worried owners.

"Is that dangerous?" Mrs. Sanderson asked.

"There is some risk," I admitted, "but if I can relieve the pressure against Moose's heart, he will feel much better."

"I guess we don't have any choice," Mr. Sanderson agreed. "We'll leave him with you."

I ushered them out and called for Jack to help me. A pericardiocentesis (sticking a needle into the heart sac) was a precarious procedure—even more so in those days before I had ultrasound available—and the patient needed to be held very still. Jack rose to the occasion, as he did so often, cradling Moose gently against his chest, while I clipped up a patch of hair over the dog's thorax. My own heart thudded anxiously because I had to perform this procedure blind, or by feel. The potential to cause more damage weighed heavily on my mind, and I willed my hands not to shake as I prepped the skin. I injected a bleb of lidocaine to numb the skin and underlying muscle and readied my needle.

A huge sense of relief washed over me as the needle found its mark, and blood-tinged fluid issued forth from the hub of the needle. Just as I attached a line and a syringe with which to pull out the fluid, Matt, whom I'd completely forgotten about, announced, "I gotta' go potty."

I froze. "Not now," I said through gritted teeth.

"But I gotta go *now!*" came the belligerent reply.

"Matty, the bathroom is just down the hall. You can go by yourself," Jack told him.

"No! I need help!" Matt pushed deliberately into Jack, which caused him to jostle my patient—who had a needle sticking into his chest a fraction of an inch from his heart.

"Matty," I growled under my breath, not wanting to disturb Moose any more than he was already being disturbed, "you can wait. But if you bump Uncle Jack again while he's holding this very sick dog, I will give you a rabies shot and lock you in a cage!"

I didn't look at the kid, since all my attention was focused on Moose, but I acutely felt the sting of each dagger Matt shot my way. The expression "if looks could kill" became a reality for me.

It didn't take long to remove the fluid from Moose's heart sac, and, thankfully, Moose was breathing a lot better. "Okay," I told Jack. "You can take Matt to the bathroom now."

"Uh, I think it's too late." Jack indicated the puddle surrounding his nephew.

"I *told* you I had to go." Matt's defiant little face dared me to contradict him.

"Now what?" I groaned. "Did Rebecca leave a change of clothes?"

"I think so. But it's back at the house."

I sighed. "Let me finish up with Moose. Grab a towel from the kennel area."

We managed to get Matt home, the truck now reeking of strawberry milkshake and urine, and changed him into clean clothes, after hosing him down (under much protest) in the shower. I tossed the soiled garments into the washing machine and collapsed onto the sofa.

"There's nothing to *do* around here," Matt complained, plopping down next to me.

"Didn't your mother send you some toys to play with?" I asked.

"I don't want to play with them. They're stupid."

"Fine. Watch TV." I grabbed the remote and channel surfed until I found cartoons.

"I don't like this show."

"Tough. Watch it anyway." I left him there and went to check on my poor dogs, who still huddled in the back of my closet.

Mercifully, Matt fell asleep, and Jack and I had an entire hour to ourselves, during which I relayed the story of Charley's owner asking me if I was going to experiment on him. I hadn't heard Matt wake up until he announced he was hungry. I'm sure he was, since most of his lunch was strewn all over the backseat of Jack's truck.

Due to the late hour, I informed the child I was making sandwiches here. No arguments. He started to object, but just then, the doorbell rang.

Matt raced to the door, opened it wide, and cried, "Mommy!"

At that wonderful word, I felt like a ten-ton weight had lifted from my shoulders. It was over! This horrible day with Jack's miserable nephew was finally over!

"Mommy, I just woke up," Matt announced, as Rebecca entered the living room. "I'm hungry!"

Rebecca frowned. "It's almost seven o'clock. You haven't had dinner yet?"

"No, Mommy, and I'm *starving!*"

Rebecca shot Jack and me a look of pure incredulity. "Why didn't you feed him dinner?"

"We were just going to get something to eat," I explained. "He just woke up from his nap."

She shook her head in disbelief. "Why did you let him nap at this hour? I'll never get him to sleep tonight."

Self-preservation? Pure desperation? "He fell asleep watching TV," Jack said, "he must have been tired from the long day he had."

"Mommy, Jill said she was going to give me a rabies shot and lock me in a cage!" Matt tattled.

Rebecca's eyes widened.

"I was just kidding," I said. "It was a joke." *Sort of.* I forced out a brittle laugh.

The horrified expression on my future sister-in-law's face said otherwise. "And honestly, Jack, you couldn't find something more worthwhile to do with your only nephew than watch TV?"

"Oh!" I remembered Matt's clothes in the dryer. "I've got Matty's clothes. They should be dry by now."

"Dry? What happened?" Rebecca's accusing eyes bored into mine.

"He had a little accident, that's all." *Seriously, lighten up, Rebecca, or I'm going to give* you *a rabies shot and lock* you *in a cage. Or perhaps a nice sedative.*

"What?" Rebecca looked reproachfully at us. "Matty *never* wets his pants. He's been potty trained for almost a year."

Matt tugged at his mother's shirt. "I *told* them I had to go, Mommy, but they said I had to wait."

I wanted to slap my hand over the little tattletale's mouth before he could blurt out any more indiscretions. I explained, in a futile attempt to defend ourselves. "Well, you see, Rebecca, Jack and I were in the middle of a delicate procedure on a very sick dog when Matt had to go."

She rolled her eyes. "Really, Jill, even *you* should understand that when small children say they need to go, they *need to go now.*"

And really, Rebecca, even you *should understand that when I tell you I was in the middle of a life-and-death situation, I could not drop everything to take a three-year-old to the potty. Which I* tried *to tell you when you dumped him on us that such might be the case.*

Rebecca pursed her lips. "I'm beginning to rethink the wisdom of leaving Matty with you."

Oh, please, rethink it. To the point that you'll never do it again.

"Becky, don't get so worked up. Everything's fine," Jack assured his sister. "We had a great time, didn't we, buddy?" He reached down and tousled Matt's nappy dark hair.

Shut up, Jack, before I hurt you.

"Yeah, I had fun," Matt agreed. "Mommy, can I stay with Uncle Jack and Aunt Jill next weekend?"

DON'T BITE THE DOCTOR

Chapter 22

"**He was coughing**, and I thought he had bronchitis, so I gave him 500 milligrams of amoxicillin twice a day. But it didn't help. Then I put my stethoscope on his chest and heard a heart murmur, so I figured he had congestive heart failure and started him on digoxin 0.125 milligrams. Now he's vomiting and not eating."

I listened, while trying not to grimace, as Dr. Frost described, in excruciating detail, his diagnosis and treatment of his Jack Russell terrier, Huey. There was only one problem—well, several, actually. Dr. Frost was not a veterinarian. He was a dermatologist. A human dermatologist. Not that he was a human who was a dermatologist . . . well, he was that, also, but he was a dermatologist for people. As in, real doctor, or R.D., as I called them.

Physicians often made the worst veterinarians. As medical professionals, they believed themselves perfectly capable of something so mundane as treating an animal. After all, a dog was simply a small person in a fur coat, right? This was back in the day before Dr. Google reared his ugly head, so even semi-educated guesses gleaned from the internet were not possible. It was sometimes difficult to make physicians understand that we lowly, inferior animal doctors might somehow know a bit more about veterinary medicine than they did. And having physicians for clients often required a certain degree of special handling so as not to tarnish their God-complexes.

"Bronchitis is certainly a reasonable assumption," I concurred with my medical colleague, "given the acute onset and nature of Huey's cough." Plus, the fact that when I palpated the dog's trachea, he honked like a goose. "But bronchitis in dogs usually responds better to tetracycline or trimethoprim-sulfa." I left out the fact that the amoxicillin was overdosed at least five times. Fortunately, amoxicillin is usually well tolerated.

"Is that right!" It wasn't phrased as a question. The good doctor seemed utterly astounded that I would know such a thing.

"As far as the heart murmur, well, I really don't hear any evidence of lung congestion. I'll take a thoracic radiograph to rule out congestive heart failure, of course, but many older, small dogs have heart murmurs that aren't symptomatic."

"So, you don't think the digoxin is necessary?" The older doctor peered myopically at me through thin wire-rimmed spectacles.

"No, I don't think Huey's to that point, yet."

He nodded his head, thoughtfully, as if weighing my opinion.

Now came the time for delicate finesse. "In fact, Dr. Frost, although I will confirm my suspicion with a blood test, I believe Huey is suffering from digoxin toxicity." *From the fact that you massively overdosed him.*

The man's bushy eyebrows met in a frown across his forehead. "Really?"

I plowed on. "Yes. As I'm sure you know, there is a fine line between the therapeutic and toxic blood level of digoxin."

He looked surprised, but quickly recovered. "Oh, yes . . . yes, of course."

And seeing as how you prescribe so much heart medication for your skin patients, you would be acutely aware of that fact. I smiled. "I'll draw some blood from Huey and get him started on some IV fluids and something for nausea."

Dr. Frost rubbed his chin thoughtfully between his thumb and forefinger. "Yes, I agree. I believe that's a reasonable course of action." He patted the animal absently on the head, then turned briskly back to me. "If there's anything I can do to help—"

"Thank you, but I think I can take it from here." *You've done* more *than enough.* I smiled at him before rescuing Huey from any more attempts on the part of his owner to practice veterinary medicine without a license.

~

"Do *not, do not, DO NOT* digitalize a heart murmur," Dr. Ainsworth lectured. "Should you digitalize a heart murmur? No, no, *no, no, NO!*"

I liked Dr. Ainsworth. He was one of my favorite professors, but I felt rather punchy today sitting in the lecture hall for the seventh straight hour, so I wrote in the margin of my notes, "Do *not, do not, DO NOT* digitalize a heart murmur." I underlined the words multiple times to be sure I didn't fail to grasp their significance. As if I would. At the time, sophomore year in veterinary school, sitting in one lecture after another without touching a real live animal, this information seemed so remotely far away that I despaired I would ever have the opportunity to actually use it. I glanced over at my best friend, Carlie, who had written, "Should you digitalize a heart murmur? No, no, no, no, no, NO!"

I nudged her and snickered under my breath, trying very hard not to create a disturbance. Dr. Ainsworth continued on about starting digoxin *only* when the animal began to display symptoms of congestive heart failure. Okay, I got it, already. Little would I realize how much until I stood across the exam table from Dr. Frost, R.D., a few years later.

But vet school was a charmed time, in many ways, especially once we started clinical rotations junior year. We had all the advantages of being on the cutting edge of veterinary medicine at its best—even if we students were mostly relegated to the role of human retractors and gofers—without the responsibility of having to make the hard decisions. In our cocooned little world, the worst that could happen was that we would highly embarrass ourselves in front of our fellow classmates or instructors by our lack of knowledge or expertise. We were kept on tight leashes—no pun intended—lest we do any real harm. The instructors were always there to catch us before we fell. Yes, the hours were long, tedious, and often overwhelming, but particularly in my small animal medicine rotations, I had fun.

One slow day in clinics, Carlie and I slipped into the ECG lab and hooked her up to the electrocardiograph machine. We recorded a tracing of her heart rhythm, ripped off the printout, and, giggling, went to find Dr. Ainsworth.

Dr. Ainsworth was one of those rare people who was not only incredibly brilliant, but also a great teacher and clinician. Only a few years older than the students he taught, he had already achieved head of the small animal medicine department, with a boarded specialty in both cardiology, and, we suspected, because he had nothing else to do one weekend, sat for and passed his internal medicine board, as well.

We found him in his tiny cubicle of an office, distractedly sipping a cup of bad vending machine coffee, jotting down notes for his latest edition of his cardiology textbook.

"Dr. Ainsworth," we greeted, tossing the ECG strip onto the scarred and stained wooden desk, "can you tell us what's wrong with this dog?"

He picked up the paper, glanced at it for a second, then said, "Well, in the first place, it's a human, not a dog, and in the second place—"

My mind shut out everything after that, and my dropped jaw failed to shut, period. After barely a glimpse, he knew we were playing a prank, but nevertheless, he painstakingly evaluated and commented on the amplitude of the R waves and the width of the PR intervals, no doubt using this as a teaching opportunity. The man knew everything. One brief peek and he could tell the ECG was that of a human. I belatedly remembered to close my gaping jaw.

He looked up and met our eyes, handing back the incriminating ECG. "In other words, I believe one of you is perfectly normal. At least your heart is." He chuckled and turned back to his work, unruffled by our silliness.

~

It came as no surprise when Huey's digoxin level came back extremely elevated. I marveled that Dr. Frost hadn't killed his beloved pet in his attempt to play veterinarian. The words of Dr. Ainsworth echoed in my ears as I explained to Dr. Frost, once again, that simply because a dog had a heart murmur did not mean it was in congestive heart failure. Digoxin is not a drug we commonly use these days, as there are much better, safer medications available now; but in the early eighties, it was the mainstay for dogs with congestive heart failure.

After several days in the hospital, Huey's condition turned around. I sent him home with trimethoprim-sulfa and cough suppressants to treat the bronchitis, which had pretty much given up on its own, probably figuring the digoxin toxicity had already won the battle for making the animal sicker. Dr. Frost seemed mostly unfazed by the ordeal, including, thank goodness, the substantial bill.

Not too long after this, Dr. Tillman, a local OB-GYN, called to say his two-week old foal was leaking urine from its umbilical area. Aha! I knew exactly what the problem was, courtesy of a dreadful rotation in small animal surgery under Dr. George. The foal had a patent urachus. The urachus is the embryonic tube that carries the fetal urine from the fetus to the mother by way of the placenta during pregnancy. This tube normally closes off after birth, but in some cases, it fails to do so, allowing leakage of urine through the umbilicus. When this happens, it is necessary to surgically tie off the urachus where it exits the urinary bladder. But I didn't need to explain that to Dr. Tillman. He told me precisely what needed to be done.

I drove out to Dr. Tillman's ranch on a crisp, clear Saturday morning, which should have been my off Saturday. The appointment had been kindly scheduled in that time slot for me by my boss, so I could spend as much time as necessary without worrying about rushing back to the clinic to see patients. Although I should have been irritated at Dr. Spangle's presumptuous usurping of my day off, I didn't particularly mind. It was one of those rare, perfect spring days when simply being outside made me glad to be alive, and my heart swelled with joy as I drove into the country.

I suppose bringing human babies into the world did not adequately satisfy Dr. Tillman's thirst for reproduction, as he had built an impressive ranch on which he bred Quarter Horses. The ranch, in itself, was a full-time operation, the running of which was left mostly to a very knowledgeable and amiable foreman, Zach. Despite my youth and inexperience, Zach always treated me with the greatest degree of respect and deference whenever I was called out for a problem at the Tillman Ranch, although he probably knew much more than I did about equine husbandry.

I passed the freshly-painted, white wooden fence bordering the front of the property, and turned at the gravel road leading to the gate. As I got out to open the gate, I stopped, tipped my face upward, closed my eyes, and took in the sweet smell of hay, the gentle warmth of the morning sun on my face, and the soft nickering of contented horses enjoying themselves in the green pastures surrounding the stable. Even the fact that I had to work on my day off was not going to spoil my jubilant mood. There was nothing like being paid to be outside on a glorious day such as this, with the wispy white clouds floating lazily in the azure sky, and just the slightest nip in the air. It made up for all the other times when I had to be out tending patients in miserable weather. I drove through the gate, allowing it to close behind me, and continued crunching slowly up the path leading to the stable, keeping an eye out for Zach.

As I drew closer, instead of Zach's beat-up pick-up truck, I spied the gleaming, metallic gray Mercedes Benz of Dr. Tillman parked in the shade of a massive live oak tree, and my heart flip-flopped. I had rarely seen the doctor at his own ranch, but each time had been uncomfortable. His rather overbearing, superior attitude could be quite intimidating, especially when I had the nature of an easily-intimidated person in my early days of veterinary medicine. The soft warmth of the cheerful sun and sweet chirping of merry birds retreated into the background of my happy consciousness as sudden dread began working its way outward from my thudding heart.

Dr. Tillman emerged from a stall, glancing at his watch. "I expected you thirty minutes ago," he greeted. Despite being dressed in old, tattered jeans, a plaid, flannel shirt with the sleeves rolled up to his elbows, and manure-caked boots, an aura of indisputable authority permeated the air around him.

I swallowed down my annoyance and replied, "The appointment was for eight o'clock. It's five minutes till." I met his stare, briefly, then popped the lid to my trunk to retrieve my supplies.

He didn't answer, but turned and bellowed, "Seth! Bring out that colt! The vet's here."

A minute later, a pale young man came out of the same stall from which Dr. Tillman had just exited, leading a chestnut colt with a white blaze on his nose and four white stockings. My heart overflowed with joy at the sight of that beautiful baby, still a bit wobbly on his legs. I approached slowly and held out my hand to inspect the lovely little creature.

"He's fine except for the urine leakage," Dr. Tillman informed me.

I ran my hand down the animal's side and touched his mid-section. As Dr. Tillman had observed, it was wet with what appeared to be urine. I raised my hand to my nose and sniffed. If there is one thing I am good with, it's smells. I can often detect diabetes, kidney failure, and specific bacterial and yeast infections on the basis of my nose alone.

Wiping my hands on my coveralls, I concurred with the diagnosis—much to Dr. Tillman's irritation, I was sure, for not taking his word in the matter. I pulled my stethoscope from around my neck and proceeded to listen to the heart, but not before hearing a loud, dissatisfied sigh. After ascertaining for myself the heart was, indeed, sound, I settled my stethoscope back in its place.

As I reached toward the little muzzle to examine the gum color, the impatient doctor said, "I *told* you there's nothing wrong except the patent urachus. Can we get on with this?" Once again, he glanced pointedly at his watch.

I waffled between informing the real doctor that since the responsibility for ensuring the safety of anesthetizing and operating on my patient lay solely on my shoulders, I felt obligated to verify the health of the animal before proceeding, and caving in to the doctor's clinical assessment. I chickened out and caved. Starting a surgical procedure off with a battle of the wills would accomplish nothing, and I would likely lose. Besides, the foal appeared to be otherwise healthy, so I didn't push the issue.

However, I did feel the compulsion to outline the surgery, lest there be any mistaken impression of what to expect. "As you know," I said, "I will need to tie off the urachus where it exits the bladder in order to eliminate any pockets that might retain urine."

He shook his head. "No, no that's not necessary. You just need to cut around the umbilicus and ligate it there."

I stared at him, aghast. Surely, he knew better. He was a *doctor,* for crying out loud. *Tact, be tactful.* I cleared my throat. "But leaving a blind diverticulum where urine can accumulate can lead to chronic urinary tract infections."

"Nah, it'll be fine. Let's get this show on the road. I don't have all day."

I stood numbly, torn between doing what I knew was best for my patient, and doing what the owner wanted—or, more to the point, ordered. Once again, I pondered the question of just why Dr. Tillman needed *me*. He obviously had everything under control, down to, and including how to do the surgery. So *why* exactly was I here?

~

I stood miserably across the surgical table from Dr. George, as he swore a blue streak at the incompetence of his hapless colleague, who had made the colossal mistake of referring this dog to the university. Dr. George even insulted the referring veterinarian's mother, who I'm sure, had nothing to do with the original surgery on this dog's bladder. As usual, I couldn't see much, as Dr. Wolf, the resident next to me, had claimed the choice vantage spot. Besides, Dr. George was six foot six, and the surgery table was cranked up to my chin. My calves had finally given out from standing on my tiptoes, and they cramped in silent rebellion.

It was not unusual for Dr. George to disparage the reputation of other veterinarians. He did so constantly, including the other surgical clinicians in the veterinary teaching hospital. It had been my bad luck to wind up in his ward. Everyone said he was crazy, and that wasn't just a cliché. The man was literally a certifiable nut case. But he had tenure, so nothing could touch him. I suppose he may have been a competent surgeon—I don't really know—but his teaching skills were non-existent, unless one wanted to learn how to be an arrogant, egotistical bully.

The residents under his tutelage were either totally browbeaten, or else they completely blew him off. Dr. Wolf had started his residency late in his career, after being in private practice for a number of years. Usually after Dr. George had performed his "miracles" and left his underlings to close the surgery site, Dr. Wolf would regale us students with stories from the "real world," where ivory tower ideology didn't often mesh tidily with reality. We learned a lot more from Dr. Wolf than we ever learned from Dr. George.

"Hmph, look at all this wasted suture," Dr. Wolf chuckled. "The man has clearly never priced the stuff. He wouldn't last a week in private practice."

I had no doubts about that. Just that morning, on outpatients, Dr. George had been called in to evaluate a dog with mammary gland tumors as a potential surgical candidate.

"You should have spayed her before she came into heat," he berated the older, matronly owner, who stood wringing her hands while simultaneously clutching her little sheltie to her bosom. "It's *your* fault she has cancer now!"

"But I didn't know," the lady tearfully defended herself. "My veterinarian never told me."

"He should be sued!" declared the self-righteous demigod. "I've a good mind to file a complaint with the Board of Professional Regulations, myself!"

"Oh . . . oh, please don't do that!" begged the client. "Dr. Lawrence is the most wonderful man. He's taken care of our dogs for years."

"He's an *idiot!*" Dr. George informed her. "Now, not only do we have advanced mammary tumors to contend with, but we will have to perform an ovariohysterectomy, as well. Otherwise, her ovaries will continue to produce hormones that will feed the cancer. It will be a long and difficult surgery." His lips curled in what I could only imagine was an attempt at a smile, but looked more like a sneer. "But don't worry. Fortunately, you came in on *my* rotation, rather than one of the other so-called surgeons in this institution. I will take care of everything and Dixie will be good as new."

My eyes widened at this audacious statement. Mammary cancer in dogs is always potentially serious, and until the pathology report came back, we wouldn't know for sure how serious.

"Oh, *thank you*, Doctor," the woman cried. She added, timidly, "but her name is Dolly."

"Dixie, Dolly, who the bloody *&^%# cares?" bellowed the doctor. "You're missing the point, Madam!"

Well, I imagine the client cared, since she had probably named the dog and lived with her, and regarded her with enough worth to take the time and trouble to bring her to the university for a potentially expensive surgery. Besides, when Dolly was wheeled into the surgery suite, we wanted to be sure we were operating on Dolly and not Dixie.

The woman turned a stunned face to me. I reached over and patted her hand. "We'll take good care of Dolly," I assured her, which I'm sure irritated Dr. George. After all, one shouldn't coddle clients. The focus must always be on *us,* not *them.*

Her brow wrinkled in a frown, and she pulled her lower lip between her bottom teeth, scraping off the bright red lipstick from the middle. A tear escaped the corner of her right eye, and she reached an index finger to wipe it away before it slid down her lined cheek. "I hate to ask, but how much is this going to cost?" She raised hesitant eyes to Dr. George.

Without blinking an eye, he rattled off a figure, then crossed his arms over his chest, challenging her to complain.

The woman sucked in a breath. Then, she pulled her dog closer and began speaking to her in a high-pitched baby voice. "Why, Dolly, your surgery costs a lot more than your mommy's."

Dr. George's haughty eyebrows shot up in a rare look of surprise, as nothing generally fazed him. Then, in a condescending tone, he said, "Do you mean to tell me, Madam, that you had an ovariohysterectomy and a breast removed for less?"

The lady's face flushed crimson, and I could almost see steam emerging from her suddenly flared nostrils. "Certainly not!" she snapped, obviously highly offended. "I'm not talking about *myself*. I meant *the dog's* mother!" She pulled herself up to her full five feet and snorted in contempt, "The very idea!"

Dr. George, for once, didn't have anything more to say, and he abruptly turned on his heel and exited the room, leaving me to placate the upset woman.

I snickered under my breath as I recalled the great man completely putting his foot in his mouth that morning, and the client, finally having enough of his boorish manner, putting him in his place. While I ruminated on the incident, the great man burst back into the surgery room he had just vacated.

"And be sure you remove that diverticulum before you close that bladder!" he barked to Dr. Wolf.

Dr. Wolf nodded, then, in teaching mode, explained to me and the other student at the surgery table, "If you leave a diverticulum, or pouch, urine can accumulate in that area and stagnate, making it impossible to completely empty the bladder. This can lead to chronic urinary tract infections."

"Will you stop jabbering and finish the $@*(& surgery?" bellowed Dr. George. "Every idiot except the moron of a referring veterinarian knows that!" He stopped and fixed us students with a benevolent, yet, at the same time, malevolent gaze. How he managed to blend the two completely contrasting looks, I can't explain. I only know he did. "Let that be a lesson to you not to be idiots when you are unloosed in the world." Then under his breath, but loud enough for all to hear, "As if that were possible."

Dr. Wolf's eyes crinkled in amusement, and he gave us a wink. As soon as Dr. George left the room again, he said, "Heaven forbid we waste time teaching in a teaching hospital so we don't graduate idiot veterinarians."

~

Those two occurrences were truly the only things I remembered from my miserable three weeks in Dr. George's ward. He criticized, bullied, and badgered us underlings, but as far as teaching us anything practical, he completely missed the mark. But I did learn two things. First, if you're going to put your foot in your mouth, don't start off by being an arrogant jerk. Second, bladders should not have extraneous openings into which urine could become trapped. On further contemplation, I actually learned that second fact from Dr. Wolf, not Dr. George.

This point came to the forefront of my mind in the next few moments as I argued with Dr. Tillman. In the end, at his insistence, and against all I knew to be proper technique, I gave in to his demand, made a simple incision around the umbilicus, and ligated the urachus at its exit point. Today, faced with this same choice, I would simply refuse to do the surgery. But back then, I hadn't quite developed the backbone it took me forty years to acquire.

As I drove off, even the gorgeous day failed to lift my dark feeling of intense regret and sense of failure to my patient. In veterinary medicine, there is sometimes a fine line between satisfying a paying client and doing what's best for the animal. The two don't always mesh, and the choice sometimes becomes an internal, ethical struggle. I prayed the handsome little colt would not suffer long-term repercussions due to my inability to stand up for his welfare. I also vowed never to seek Dr. Tillman's professional services should I ever require the care of an OB-GYN.

~

Come to think of it, there were a number of doctors I met over the years in the capacity as doctor to their pets whom I would steer clear of, like the internal medicine doctor who, without consulting me, kept adjusting his cat's insulin dosage, resulting in either uncontrolled diabetes or life-threatening hypoglycemia. Why he refused to give the cat the dose I prescribed is anyone's guess, but I suppose he thought he knew best. Apparently, nobody told him that cats don't read the textbooks, nor do they follow the rules. There was also the cardiologist who adamantly refused to give his dog heartworm prevention, and the dentist who refused to have his dog's teeth cleaned, even though the dog's breath could stop a truck.

That's not to say I didn't develop a rewarding doctor-patient relationship with other real doctors. Many of my personal doctors were also clients. The difference was they didn't have to take *their* clothes off in *my* office, which I found inherently unfair.

On the flip side, there were some people who would just as soon utilize my medical services for themselves, as it saved them the time and expense of consulting with their physicians.

At the Griffin farm, I had just finished reading the TB tests on their small flock of goats, when old Mrs. Griffin waddled out to the yard. Mrs. Griffin, an extremely overweight woman, generally left the running of the farm to her husband, a jovial, ruddy-faced man with a fringe of white hair around his round, bald head. It was rare to encounter his wife, so I was somewhat curious when she flagged me down before I could reach my car.

"Doc, wait up. I've got somethin' I want ta show ya," she wheezed, as she toddled with great effort over the uneven, sandy ground.

I moved toward her to save her the additional steps. "Yes, Mrs. Griffin, what is it?"

Without further fanfare, she yanked up her dress, exposing a massive amount of fleshy folds overlapping her dingy, elastic-shot underwear. "I got this rash, right here." She pointed to something between two large creases of skin. "And it's drivin' me crazy!"

I wasn't about to make a closer inspection, but that didn't deter the woman, as she neared, pulling apart the layers of skin with one hand and jabbing toward the problem area with the other. "See, right here? What do ya think it is?"

It was like a car accident by the side of the road in which you don't want to look, but you can't help yourself. After staring way too long, I averted my eyes. "I'm sorry, Mrs. Griffin, but I really can't say. I'm not a physician."

"Well, surely ya knows somethin' about skin rashes," she argued.

"Yes, in *animals*. I'm afraid I don't know much about human rashes."

She mercifully dropped the skirt of her dress. "Well, what do ya think I should do about it?"

I took a deep breath and let it out slowly through my nose. "I think you need to discuss this with your doctor. I'm afraid I can't be of much help in this situation."

"Hmph," she snorted, clearly unconvinced. She gave me a look that said she knew I could help her if I wanted to and I was deliberately being difficult because all doctors stuck together. Without another word, she turned and waddled back into the house.

~

"Just write the prescription in *my* name instead of Rascal's," instructed Mr. Gillis. "That way my insurance will pay for it."

"Mr. Gillis, I'm afraid I cannot legally write a prescription for you. I am not a physician."

The man regarded me, unhappily. "But do you know how much this medicine *costs*?"

"Yes, it's a little expensive. But it's the best thing for Rascal."

"And it's a human medicine?"

"Yes, you can get it at any pharmacy."

Mr. Gillis shook his head. "I don't understand. If it's a human medicine, why can't you write the prescription in *my* name?"

I sighed. "Because my prescription pads all say 'doctor of veterinary medicine' on them. Not only is it illegal for me to write prescriptions for humans, the pharmacy would not fill a prescription for a human written by a veterinarian."

"You're just making me spend money when it isn't necessary," he accused.

"Mr. Gillis, I'm not going to lose my license to practice veterinary medicine because you don't want to spend a few dollars on your dog's medication. I won't circumvent the law."

He snatched the prescription from my hand and muttered obscenities all the way out the door.

A similar theme in that same thread was for people who wanted me to write prescriptions for *them* under their pets' names.

"You just write it for Buck. What I do with it is nobody's business," Mr. Willoughby, a recent widower winked at me.

To say I was completely taken aback by the elderly gentleman's request was an understatement. I could feel the heat infusing my face, and I suddenly did not want to be alone in the closed exam room with him.

"But Buck doesn't have a medical condition that requires Viagra, Mr. Willoughby. I can't write him a prescription for a medication without documentation in his records that he actually needs it for a medical condition."

"Well, can't you just make up something?"

"There are not many indications for the use of Viagra in dogs," I said. Besides, Buck was neutered.

The hopeful expression on Mr. Willoughby's face morphed into one of chagrin, as he reached down to buckle his dog's leash onto his collar. "Well, can't blame a guy for trying," he said. "Come on, Buck."

~

"I'm afraid Willie has ringworm," I told the family in exam room two, as the children allowed the contagious feline to rub all over their faces. "And ringworm can be transmitted to people. You should limit the children's exposure to him until it is cleared up, and everyone needs to wash their hands thoroughly after interacting with him."

"Oh, we can't possibly keep him from the children," Mrs. Doogle replied. "He's so attached to them and them to him."

"Wait," said the teenaged daughter, her face contorting in horror. "You mean we can catch what Willie has?"

"Yes," I answered. "That's why—"

"What's it look like in people?" the teenager interrupted.

"It usually starts out as an itchy bump, like a mosquito bite, then spreads outward in a circular fashion. Hence the name 'ringworm.' It's not really a worm, it's a fungal infection."

"You mean like *this*?" the young girl rolled up her sleeve, exposing a textbook example of human ringworm, in the form of a scaly, red, circular lesion.

"Oh, my goodness!" cried Mrs. Doogle. "Does Cathy have ringworm?" She grabbed her daughter's arm and thrust it closer to me, as if I couldn't see it in the short distance separating us by the exam table.

I hesitated. I knew the probability of the girl having ringworm was 99.9%. Still, I wasn't licensed to diagnose people conditions. "Well, it certainly looks suspicious," I hedged, "but you'll need to have Cathy seen by her own doctor to be sure."

"Can Cathy use Willie's medicine?" asked Mr. Doogle.

Yes, but I'm not authorized to tell you that. In fact, I had used the clinic's ointment on myself the couple of times I had acquired ringworm from a patient. "It would be better if Cathy sees her own doctor."

Two days later, the Doogles called, highly upset. It seemed Cathy did, indeed, have ringworm, and her doctor had prescribed the exact same medication Willie had, and if I had just told them that information in the first place, they could have saved $130.00.

Chapter 23

I generally enjoyed the practice of swine medicine. Once you got past the smell, there was just something satisfying about interacting with the highly intelligent creatures, and their owners were usually laid back and friendly. Most pigs were outgoing and low-maintenance, compared to some of their other food animal brethren. We only had a handful of pig farms in our area, small mom-and-pop operations, the pigs produced primarily for home consumption.

One thing I particularly prided myself on was pig obstetrics. Being a woman with small hands gave me a great advantage when trying to assess and correct difficulties during farrowing, and I had delivered a number of live, healthy piglets in my time.

So, as a rule, I liked working with pigs—just not so much on my wedding day. I had started out the morning, as I imagine most brides do, with a long shower and washing my hair. In my profession, I didn't often have the luxury of being overly feminine, so I had pulled out all the stops with scented soap, an expensive shampoo (which was probably no better than my usual el- cheapo off-brand), and finished by treating my entire body to a fragrant, skin moisturizing lotion. I had toyed with the idea of having my hair professionally done, but in the end, decided to stay with my simple style, as I wanted to appear natural in my wedding photos. I blew my hair dry, adding some volumizing mousse, and, standing back to survey myself in the mirror, was rather pleased with the results.

Taking particular care with my makeup, I leisurely applied eyeliner, mascara, foundation, powder, blush, and a hint of pale, pink lipstick. Then, as I still had plenty of time, I sat down and impulsively painted my nails—fingers and toes—a pretty shade of pink to match my lipstick. Suffice it to say that my short nails *never* sported polish. Beautifully manicured hands and my profession didn't mix well. But today, I wanted to look pretty.

Unlike many brides, I did not want to be surrounded by people fussing over me before the wedding, so I had sent my parents on ahead to the church to see to the last-minute preparations and the delivery of the flowers and the wedding cake. I even refused to let Rosemary, my only attendant, come over to help me get ready. Besides, I had been dressing myself for years. I really didn't need anyone hovering over me. I intended to drive myself to the church an hour or so before the ceremony and finish my minimal preparations there. People fussing over me made me nervous, and if there was one thing I didn't want to be today, it was nervous. The small church wedding, in and of itself, had mushroomed into more than I felt comfortable with, but there had been no choice. Jack and I both wanted to be married in the church. But even a small church wedding tended to snowball out of control when plans began to be made—particularly when mothers became involved.

With time to spare, I looked around the house to see if I had forgotten anything. My suitcase sat packed and ready to go for our short honeymoon in Orlando. I felt like a kid, anxious to see Disneyworld for the first time. Bitsy and Delilah knew something was up, as they insisted on trying to jump on me or crawl into my lap, but for once, I shooed them away. Selfish, I know, but just for today, I didn't want to smell like a dog.

Then the telephone rang. Figuring my parents or Rosemary had forgotten to take something to the church, I picked it up and blithely greeted, "What do you need me to bring?"

There was a pause. Then I heard the voice of Angela from the answering service. "Uh, Dr. Bennet?"

My heart slammed against my ribcage and for a moment I couldn't catch my breath. *No, no, no!* A call from the answering service is never a welcome intrusion, but today, of all days, it boded of disaster. For a split second, I fought the temptation to disguise my voice and pretend to be someone else—someone who didn't have a clue where Dr. Bennet was, or, for that matter, who Dr. Bennet even *was*. My mind raced frantically. What loose end had I failed to tie up? The adrenaline that had spiked at hearing Angela's voice began to recede, as I reasoned, *it's just a simple question about something. No need to panic.* Nevertheless, I noted my hand shaking as it gripped the receiver and my throat had closed up. Until I actually knew why Angela was calling me *on my wedding day, for crying out loud,* I couldn't *not* panic.

I knew it was no use denying to be myself. Angela had already heard my voice. I forced a squeaky, "Yes?" through my paralyzed vocal cords.

"Dr. Bennet, I'm sorry to bother you, but I can't reach Dr. Spangle."

A sense of unreality washed over me, and my whole body went numb. I couldn't speak. I didn't even ask the obvious questions, as to whether she had tried his pager, his home, and the clinic. This scenario had played out so many times over the past few months that I knew the answering service had frantically exhausted all avenues before resorting to calling me.

Angela plowed on, apparently taking my silence for permission to continue. "It's Harold Wyatt. He has a sow who's been in labor all morning and hasn't delivered a piglet."

My mouth and brain still hadn't connected, and Angela asked, "Dr. Bennet, are you still there?"

I made some kind of grunting noise in my throat.

"He's desperate. There are no other vets in the area who see pigs."

Where is Dr. Spangle? Where is that miserable, lousy . . . . I allowed a few profane names for my boss to flit through my consciousness.

Finally, I managed to find my voice. "Angela," I told the woman in a tight, no-nonsense tone, "I am *getting married in three hours!"*

"Oh!" came an astounded gasp. "Oh, Dr. Bennet . . . I'm so sorry. I . . . didn't realize. I never would have—"

All of a sudden, my voice took on a mind of its own, and I railed against the poor woman, "Dr. Spangle is on call. You will just have to keep trying to reach him." I slammed the phone down, shaking with rage.

Sinking into a chair, my fists clenched in anger, I pondered furiously at the unfairness of the situation. Somewhere, out on the Wyatt farm, a helpless, frightened sow struggled to give birth, and due to circumstances completely beyond her control, there was no one to come to her aid. Without intervention, she could die a prolonged, horrible death, and Mr. Wyatt could lose an entire litter of piglets.

It's not your problem, Jill, I told myself. If only I had gone to the church early to get ready, like every other bride. If only I hadn't picked up that blasted phone. If only caller ID had been invented then! Had I not known about Mr. Wyatt's sow, I would, right now, be blissfully unaware of the predicament, and therefore couldn't worry about it. But I did know. And, doggone it, I *was* worried. And I had the ability to do something about it. I just didn't want the inconvenience. But how could I go about my happy celebration while in the back of my mind I knew I had left an animal to needlessly suffer and possibly die? Hadn't I taken an oath? I knew I would never enjoy what should be the happiest day of my life with that dark cloud looming over my head.

Although I knew it would do no good, I punched in Dr. Spangle's number. The phone rang several times before Patty finally answered.

"Oh, Jill, hi. I just walked in the door," she greeted, breathlessly.

I cut right to the chase without the usual pleasantries. "Patty, is Dr. Spangle there?" Perhaps, by some miracle, the man had actually returned home to *take his own calls.*

"Oh, no, Drew went to Alabama for the weekend to go hunting," she told me, happily.

"Well, Patty, he is supposed to be on call."

"Oh." She laughed. "It probably just slipped his mind. You know how he is."

Boy did I. "I suppose it also slipped his mind that I'm getting married in three hours," I ground out, with a touch of hysteria. Geesh, after all, he and Patty had been invited to the wedding, and I had expected them to at least show up, out of some shred of loyalty.

"Oh, my goodness, is that *today?* I thought it was *next* week." Distress filled her voice.

"No, Patty, it's today," I said, flatly. "And Mr. Wyatt just called with a sow in labor."

"Can't another vet handle it?" she asked.

"Dr. Spangle and I are the only ones around here who treat pigs," I said, an edge to my voice.

"Jill, I am *so* sorry. Drew usually checks in at least once a day, but I doubt I'll hear from him until tonight. I will tell him to come straight home when he calls."

"I'm afraid that will be too late for Mr. Wyatt," I bit out, knowing I was taking my anger out on her. Softening, I added, "I suppose I'll have to go take care of it. Hopefully, I'll see you at the wedding."

"Oh, yes, of course—"

It was rude, but I hung up on her before she could finish. Then I felt a tinge of remorse. It wasn't Patty's fault, after all. I only worked with Dr. Spangle. Poor Patty was *married* to him.

I checked for a dial tone and called Angela back. "Please call Mr. Wyatt for me and tell him I'm on my way."

"But . . . but Dr. Bennet—"

"It's okay, Angela, but I need to get going. Please call him for me?"

"Uh, yes, of course, but . . ."

"Dr. Spangle is in Alabama. He probably won't be checking in with his wife until tonight. In the meantime, would you divert any other calls to another vet?"

She sighed. "Certainly, Dr. Bennet. Again, I'm so sorry. I didn't know." She added softly, "I hope you make it in time for your wedding."

"Thanks. I've got to run."

My heart had plummeted into the depths of my stomach during the past few moments, and now it set up an uncomfortable thumping, as the reality of my predicament hit me full force. I had to drive out to the Wyatt farm, deliver piglets, pray the sow would not need a C-section, get back home, clean up, and make it to my wedding on time. Perhaps I should call someone, just in case. I tried Jack's house and Rosemary's house. Nobody answered. I tried the church office, but that was a long shot, as I didn't expect anyone to answer on a Saturday. I tried the minister, but he wasn't home, either. Unfortunately, cell phones wouldn't be available for another twenty years or so.

Where was everybody? Was I the only one not already at the church?

Stuffing down a wave of hysteria, I flew to my bedroom, dug my coveralls out of the closet, and pulled them on over my shorts and T-shirt. I rummaged around for my boots, as I hadn't expected to need them anytime in the near future, finally locating them in the laundry room. Then I tied a bandana around my hair, praying it didn't flatten or frizz.

In fact, I did a lot of praying on my way to the Wyatt farm. I'm not sure I was all that articulate in what I said, other than, "Please, God, please, God," over and over. Fortunately, the farm lay just outside of town, about a twenty-minute drive, and before I knew it, I was bouncing my Camaro much too fast over the gravel driveway leading to the barn, spewing pebbles in my wake and trying not to think of the dings they inflicted on my red paint. Mr. Wyatt, a thin, hunched-back older gentleman, and his wife, a short, plump woman, huddled, expectantly, just inside the barn door.

"Dr. Bennet," cried Mrs. Wyatt, the moment I got out of my car, "I can't believe we got you out here on your *wedding day*." She wrung her hands in a nervous apology. Then she added, almost as an afterthought, "but you sure do look pretty."

I managed a thin smile. "Thank you." It struck me as funny to be complimented on my appearance under these circumstances. In fact, I couldn't remember any of my clients commenting on my appearance, let alone on a call to a pig farm.

Mr. Wyatt grabbed my manicured right hand between his thin, leathery ones and pumped it vigorously. "I can't tell you how much we appreciate this. It's Petunia. I had my hand in, but couldn't feel nothing. She's in a bad way."

"Well, let's have a look," I said, and as I stepped into the barn and saw the poor creature lying on her side like a great beached whale, straining and grunting pitifully with no results, time stood still. When confronted with an emergency involving a frightened, painful animal, I have the ability to block out everything else around me—my own weariness, hunger, discomfort, disappointment over spoiled plans, and yes, even my upcoming nuptials in a couple hours. My focus is entirely on my patient.

I knelt in the straw and gently scratched the sow's bristly head and back. She raised her head, briefly, her tiny, black eyes regarding me with a mixture of curiosity and pleading, then she flopped back down in exhaustion. "Okay, Petunia, let's see if we can figure out what the problem is."

I donned a plastic sleeve, liberally applied lubricating jelly, and lay belly down in the straw, behind the struggling pig. She strained and clamped down on my arm as I entered the birth canal searching for babies. I waited until the painful contraction was over (painful for me, anyway), then resumed my exploration. Ah! There, just beyond my fingertips, I brushed against a stuck piglet. I squirmed closer to the sow, my cheek pressed against her rump, and willed my arm to stretch further. After several missed attempts to get a greasy grip on the critter, I finally managed to snag its snout, hooking its sharp little needle teeth between my thumb and index finger. Now I could tell the piglet was stuck sideways, and it was just a matter of maneuvering it into proper position. I tried pushing it back toward the uterus in order to turn it, but the sow had other plans, as she heaved with another mighty contraction. I suppose she felt she had come this far and didn't want to lose even more ground by starting from scratch. Sweat trickled down my forehead and continued down my face, taking with it my carefully applied makeup. It became a battle of the wills, with both of us pushing, but I eventually managed to dislodge the piglet, pulling it out into the world, where it let out a lusty squeal.

"My word! Look at the size of that piglet!" boomed Mr. Wyatt, as I handed it off to him to rub down.

"No wonder she had so much trouble," sympathized his wife.

"It's a girl. I think we'll call her Big Bertha."

I took a minute to sit up, massaging my rubbery-feeling left arm—which I was sure now hung two inches longer than my right—and regarded the newborn.

"I sure hope the others aren't that big," I said, as visions of a C-section floated in my peripheral thoughts. Otherwise, when the organist played, "Here Comes the Bride," the bride would be elbow deep inside a sow's uterus. Sweat soaked the entire top of my coveralls, and I tried, ineffectively to wave a little of the hot, stagnant air in the suffocating little barn toward my face with my functioning right hand.

After catching my breath and wiping my face on the sleeve of my coveralls, I re-lubricated my arm and went back in for another feel. To my delight, I could feel two more piglets trying to make their way down the chute. With a little traction, I easily pulled the first, and then the second. The two newborns immediately made their way to the vast array of teats, found an acceptable one, and latched on with gusto. Their delay in entering the world caused by their enormous sibling blocking the way had no doubt made them hungry.

"I think Petunia will be able to deliver the rest," I said. "That first big piglet coming sideways obstructed the birth canal. But I'm going to give her a shot of oxytocin and wait for a little while to be sure."

I rose and headed back to the trunk of my car, where I drew up a dose of oxytocin from a big bottle in my tackle box, which served as my medical box. Petunia didn't even flinch when I administered the injection into her gluteal muscles. Then we stood back and waited. As I willed the injection to work its magic, I noted an odd pinkish mark on the pig's rump, and with a sense of comic dismay, realized it was my pink lipstick. I started to reach up to touch my lips, then thought better about the idea. Served me right for trying to be "girly."

Within twenty minutes, Petunia delivered three more piglets, one after the other in short succession, each as anxious to get to the milk dispensary as its earlier born littermates. Only then did I glance at my watch.

"Dr. Bennet, you should go," Mrs. Wyatt prodded. "You don't want your young man to think you've left him at the altar."

I smiled. If I failed to show up, Jack, bless him, would know something unavoidable related to my job had happened, and even better, would understand and forgive me. Even today. Still, I didn't particularly want to start our married life off on that note. So, I gathered up my soiled sleeves and lubricant and headed back toward my car.

"I think Petunia will be okay now," I told the couple, "but just in case, I'll give you a call in a few hours."

"Oh, no!" objected Mrs. Wyatt. "You just have a beautiful wedding and enjoy yourself."

"It's only a phone call," I said. "And if you need me, I will come back. My soon-to-be husband knows what he's getting into."

The two stared at me with incredulous looks on their faces before breaking out into huge grins.

"Thank you, kindly," said Mr. Wyatt. "We'll name one of the piglets after you."

I supposed I couldn't have asked for a nicer compliment. But my warm fuzzy lasted only a short time as I realized I would be cutting it very close to getting back to the church on time. I spun gravel as I hastily made my way back down the driveway, and toward town. Pressing beyond the speed limit and praying not to be pulled over (would a policeman be sympathetic to my plight?), my heart pounded painfully, and my stomach clenched with knots of apprehension. There wouldn't be time for a shower, so I would have to clean up the best I could and make do.

I pulled into the church parking lot with ten minutes to spare, and saw several well-dressed people leisurely entering the front door to the foyer outside the sanctuary. I quickly ran around to the back of the church, through the fellowship hall (which I briefly noted looked beautifully decorated), and into the bridal room off the women's restroom. No sooner had I shut the door and begun yanking off my coveralls, than Rosemary pushed the door open with a bang.

"Where have you been?" she shrieked. "Everyone has been frantic looking for you!" She stopped and took in my disheveled appearance. "And what, in the name of heaven, is that horrible smell?"

"You don't want to know," I said. "Help me get dressed." I tossed her the garment bag holding my wedding gown, which, thankfully, my parents had brought to the church, and hastened to the adjoining restroom to scrub down my arms. The fact that the nail polish on my left hand was now chipped registered briefly in my subconscious, as did the scratches and redness of my left arm, but there was little I could do about it. Thankfully, nobody else occupied the ladies' room, and I did my best to wash off the odor of Petunia. Then I rushed back into the bridal room, where Rosemary had removed my gown from its plastic bag.

I quickly shed my shorts and T-shirt and raised my arms for her to pull the dress over my head. As she zipped the back, I noticed her trying to sniff me unobtrusively.

"Is it still bad?" I asked.

She straightened. "Oh . . . no, it's fine, really."

I didn't believe her. Just then my mother burst into the room.

"Jill! Where have you been?" She wrinkled her nose. "And what is that *smell?*"

I took a step toward her, then suddenly realized I still wore my manure-caked boots. I sat quickly and pulled them off, as Rosemary frantically searched for my white heels in the garment bag.

"And what's that on your *head?*"

Reaching up, I remembered the bandana I had tied around my hair in a futile attempt to preserve its style. I yanked it off and regarded myself sadly in the mirror. My foundation and mascara had run, and my face sported large blotches of ruined makeup intermixed with heat-infused red splotches. My hair stuck up in a short frizzy mop. At least the volumizing mousse had worked. I groaned, ran back into the bathroom, and plunged my hands under cold water to wash off the damage to my face. Meanwhile, my mother had materialized at my side and scraped away at my recalcitrant hair with a bristle brush.

"Come on, come on!" urged Rosemary, holding up my wedding shoes. "It's time!"

I hurried out of the bathroom, wiping my face on a coarse brown paper towel, and donned the slippers.

Rebecca appeared breathless in the doorway, took in the scene with wide eyes, and announced, "Mrs. Bennet, you need to be out there. They're seating the mothers."

My mother kissed my still-damp cheek and hastened out the door.

Rosemary and I stood staring at each other, our chests heaving with the exertion of the last few minutes. She shook her head.

"Someday, you'll need to tell me about this. But not now."

"It was an emergency. I had to—"

"I said not now. Come on, we need to line up." She pulled me out the door into the foyer, where my father took one surprised look at me, and thrust the bridal bouquet into my hands, as the organist began to play Trumpet Voluntary for Rosemary's entrance.

My father moved next to me, scrutinized me for a moment, then, wisely, said nothing. Just before we made our entrance, he licked his thumb and reached up to wipe something from the side of my face. "You had a little smudge."

"Thanks, Daddy." I smiled at him and took his arm.

The organ music changed to the Bridal Chorus, and the ushers threw open the doors to the sanctuary.

"Um, honey," my dad whispered as we took our first step down the aisle, "I hate to say this, but something smells a little strange."

I gritted my teeth into a smile and plunged down the aisle, my eyes firmly fixed on Jack standing at the front with his best friend, Wes, and the minister. Nothing mattered at this point but the fact I had made it to my wedding on time and in a few minutes would become Jack's wife. Jack's face shone with pure joy as he watched us make our way to the front. And when he placed the wedding ring on my left hand, my chipped nail polish didn't seem to register with him; then again, he wasn't really looking at my hand. His loving eyes stayed fastened on mine, and I felt as though I could see into the very depths of his beautiful soul. I had never been so happy.

It seemed like no time at all before the ceremony ended, and we retreated up the aisle hand-in-hand, as husband and wife. Taking up our positions in the reception line in the foyer, Jack pulled me briefly toward him for another kiss. As he drew back, a wrinkle appeared in his brow.

"Honey?" he said. "Are you wearing a different brand of perfume?"

I laughed. "No, Jack, I just had to make a little detour on the way to the church by way of a pig farm."

He nodded. "Ah, that explains it. I didn't want to hurt your feelings, but I thought you should know the new fragrance doesn't particularly suit you."

Further conversation was cut short by the guests making their way through the receiving line. I pushed my offensive odor to the back of my mind as I greeted those who had come out to celebrate this day with us. So many of them sported body fragrances that I figured after several hugs, my unusual bridal smell would be somewhat camouflaged.

~

Ten days later, I walked into Dr. Spangle's office and tendered my resignation.

ELLEN FANNON

Chapter 24

Quitting my job had been a rather gutsy move, as I didn't have another one lined up. Moreover, jobs had been scarce when I first got out of school, and the situation hadn't much improved, compounded by the fact that Jack and I wanted to stay in the area.

Working for Dr. Spangle had been a miserable experience, to say the least, but blithely going out of town without notifying me—yet again—on my wedding day, constituted the final straw. When I gave him my letter of resignation, he made a perfunctory apology for "getting his dates mixed up," and seemed genuinely surprised and hurt that I had not been happy in his employ. After all, he told me, he had given me a chance as a new graduate, something that most established veterinarians were reluctant to do.

I assured him of my gratitude for all he had done for me; despite his taking advantage of me, I had learned a lot during my three years with him. Also, despite everything, he hadn't been an ogre the entire time I had worked for him. There had been times when he had offered mentoring and helpfulness. But I sometimes wondered if he might have an undiagnosed, untreated personality disorder, based on the way his moods switched so abruptly and unpredictably, and I never knew from one minute to the next what to expect.

Still, I might have been willing to overlook a lot of his faults if it hadn't been for Myra. I was tired of being disrespected and dismissed. It was hard enough being an insecure new veterinarian, and next to impossible to do a good job without having the support of the rest of the staff. I had also discovered that on many of the weekends when Dr. Spangle disappeared, Myra had also mysteriously taken a trip out of town. The uncomfortable thought that there might be a little hanky-panky going on had drifted through my subconscious for a long time. Then, just before Christmas, I had walked into the treatment area and caught them kissing. They had jumped apart at hearing my footsteps, but not quickly enough. I had laughed and made some lame comment about "where was the mistletoe," but my heart had curled inward on itself a little bit. It pained me every time I thought about his sweet wife, Patty, to think he was cheating on her, and my estimation of Dr. Spangle's character had dipped even lower.

It was easy to see Myra's motivation. If she could only displace Patty and become Mrs. Drew Spangle, she would have even more authority over the clinic than she already possessed. Not to mention that Dr. Spangle made a good living, and she would benefit nicely from her change in monetary, as well as social status. If and when that ever happened, I knew I didn't want to be anywhere near the two of them.

Still, now I was jobless. Jack's mother took this as a welcome sign that I would soon be pregnant and give up my foolish notion of a career. If nothing else, I had to get another job just to get her off my back about starting a family.

"Honey, you did the right thing," Jack reassured me for the hundredth time, the subject of my impending resignation having consumed a good part of our conversations during our honeymoon. The wedding fiasco had been bad enough—although I figured that over time it would morph into a really good story—but the fact I obsessed about it during the time when I *should* have devoted all my attention to my new husband upset me even more.

"But, Jack," I reminded *him* for the hundredth time, "I don't have a job."

He put his arms around me and pulled me close. "You will. And it's not as if we're going to starve. *I'm* still working."

"I know," I said, my words muffled against his shoulder, "but things would have to be pretty bad for you to quit *your* job." Working with his father did have its advantages.

He laughed. "I'd have to quit my family, too."

"But if I don't get a job soon, your mother is going to insist on a grandchild."

He laughed even harder. "I love my mom and all, but frankly, she doesn't get a say about that."

I sighed. "Tell that to *her*. She's even recruiting *my* mother, and my mom is the one who insisted a woman needs a career." I pulled away and looked at his sweet, unperturbed face. "I've been to all the clinics in town. I've even been to the couple in Hanson. Nobody's hiring."

"Just give it some time. Something will open up."

"But, Jack, I can't just sit at home. I'll go crazy."

"So, why don't you open your own clinic?"

The idea caused a tiny spark to ignite in my brain. My own clinic? Could I actually make such a bold move? I was only three years out of vet school and still learning how to be a vet. Could I take on learning to run a business? Unfortunately, vet school didn't prepare students for the business aspect of practice. Besides, opening a clinic meant a huge investment in both time and money. No, it was too scary.

I shook my head. "Do you know how much money it would cost to open a clinic?"

"No, do you?"

"I don't know. But a lot. Probably a lot more than we can afford."

He sat back and studied my face. "Exactly. You *don't* know how much it will cost. And we won't know until we check into it further."

I took a hesitant breath. "We just got married. I don't want to start our life together with a crushing load of debt."

"How do you know it will be a crushing load of debt?"

I bit my lip. Maybe I should just swallow my pride and beg Dr. Spangle for my job back. Maybe I could wait tables or see if the Piggly-Wiggly was hiring. Or get pregnant. The last thought caused me to gasp aloud. No matter how desperate my future, I was not quite ready for *that* scenario.

"Honey, everything we do in life has risks. Don't you think my dad took a risk by opening his own business?"

Of course, Jack was right. It was just that I had never taken such a huge risk before, and I would be dragging my new husband into the unknown.

"What if it doesn't work out? What if we go bankrupt? What if—"

"What if you get hit by a bus tomorrow?"

I looked at him, not comprehending what getting hit by a bus had to do with opening a business.

Jack chucked. "Okay, not the best example. My point is life is uncertain. But we claim to trust in God's guidance and provision, right?"

"Yes," I said, somewhat reluctantly, as, again, I knew Jack was right, and I had, once more, failed to take God's plan into account. I had a bad habit of striking out on my own, not wanting to bother God, as if I had everything under control and was sure He had more urgent matters to attend to.

"Then I suggest we pray about this and ask God to show us the way."

I nodded. If starting up my own clinic was God's will, He would open the necessary doors. I suddenly felt a huge weight lift from me. It was so freeing to lay the whole situation at God's feet and let Him do the work. Why didn't I leave my problems with Him more often? Why did I keep having to relearn this lesson?

"And just think," Jack went on. "You could run your clinic the way you want. You could maintain a Christian atmosphere and make it a place where people are happy to come to work. You could hire all the help you need so you don't have to be fending for yourself all the time." He took my hand. "I know how hard it's been for you at Spangle's."

I had probably complained more than I should have about my frustration at never having adequate support staff. But Jack had always been a willing listener and had more than made up for what I lacked at work by becoming an excellent after-hours technician. His persuasion was starting to rub off on me. Imagine, having help! I was so tired of having to do everything myself or with an untrained or begrudging assistant.

"Okay. We'll pray about it. This is a huge step, and just because there are some tempting reasons to move forward, I don't want to run ahead of God this time."

Jack's mother was visibly disappointed to learn of our tentative plans. But in the end, it was she who found the perfect location—a small vacant store in the same strip mall as her hairdresser.

"It's absolutely ideal. Just what you're looking for," she informed us, as we walked through the vacant space with the realtor.

I didn't know how she knew this place would be ideal, but I let her enthusiasm work its way into my hesitant mood.

"Look, over here you can put in the waiting room," she said, waving her arm in a majestic sweep toward the open area to the right of the door, "with the reception desk right there, and chairs all around the room." She walked further back into the empty space. "And Jack and his dad can put up a wall, here, then a hallway into the exam rooms. You should have at least three . . ."

We trailed after her, allowing her to dictate what should go where. "Jack and his father are quite handy and can do most of the remodeling. It won't cost that much. And you can get all kinds of used equipment at a fraction of the price for new . . ."

Stunned, I stared at her.

"I've been doing some checking around," she said, offhandedly. "There's a clinic over in Brewton that's selling an X-ray machine, and you know, you really should think about putting in a computer system; that's where businesses are headed today." She started walking briskly toward the back of the building, Jack and I trotting after her like willing puppies.

"And when you have children, you can make a nursery out of this room back here," she concluded. Before we could react, she continued, "Oh, and I know the nicest girl who would make a wonderful receptionist."

"Mom, Jill is hardly ready to start hiring employees," Jack pointed out.

She turned and smiled. "It won't take that long to get this place up and running."

"We haven't even talked to the bank yet about a loan," I said.

She patted my shoulder. "You just leave that to Jack's father and me. We have a little money set aside that we would like to put to good use."

For a moment I couldn't speak. Then my words found their way out of my befuddled brain to my mouth. "We couldn't let you do that! What if the business doesn't make it?"

She waved her hand in a dismissive gesture. "That's pure nonsense. Your clinic will do a thriving business. Jack says you're the best vet in town."

I smirked at my husband. "Well, Jack may be just a tad bit prejudiced."

"Be that as it may, I have no doubts you will do just fine." She moved on. "Now, I'm thinking that putting a window in over there would be a nice touch."

Jack and I looked at each other. "What do you think, honey?" he asked. "The price is right. The location is good."

I took a deep breath and felt a huge grin break out on my face. "Let's do it." I threw my arms around my mother-in-law's neck and hugged her. "Oh, Mom, thank you!"

~

With my handy husband and father-in-law working every evening and weekend, the renovations took no time at all. It helped to have family doing the work, rather than contractors whose timelines always seemed to lag behind promises, expectations, and cost. Even some of the members of my Sunday school class volunteered to help, and I found a tremendous amount of variable expertise from carpentry skills to laying tile, wiring, and a number of other abilities I never knew they possessed. My mother came down to help with the final touches—painting, organizing, and, of course, supervising. Between her and my mother-in-law, my preferences frequently got sidelined, but it didn't really matter. I was simply excited at the prospect of opening my own business. Excited, yet terrified.

The clinic wasn't big, especially compared to Spangle Animal Clinic, but it suited my needs perfectly. After all the remodeling, I had a small, but adequate reception area, three functional exam rooms (although I couldn't see the need for three, my mother-in-law insisted they would be needed in the future), a tiny lab area, separate dog and cat hospital wards (which *I* insisted on, at the expense of the non-functional nursery), a tiny kitchen, and a cubby-hole for my office. The décor displayed a heavy feminine touch, with pastel colors, pretty pictures, and other homey touches, like frilly curtains and potted plants. A built-in diffuser periodically sprayed scented lavender, which had the dual purpose of a calming agent, as well as covering up the inevitable kennel odors that would waft their way throughout the clinic. In addition, I had a sound system installed, from which I played soothing classical and Christian music. I wanted to project a softer, gentler environment than what was generally found in most veterinary practices in that day, and I was thrilled as the final touches came together.

    I hired the bookkeeper who handled the finances for Hill and Son Plumbing, and she turned out to be interested in taking on a larger role as an office manager. After placing ads for a receptionist/technician, I narrowed down the list of applicants to an experienced young woman named Kelly, who worked in a clinic about forty-five minutes away and wanted to be closer to home. Better still, she was a strong Christian, as I wanted to keep my work environment as God-honoring as possible. Hiring people made me feel like a grown-up, something I desperately needed, as I still harbored nagging doubts of my ability to make it on my own.

    Sometimes I would wake in the middle of the night, covered in cold sweat, my heart hammering erratically with a sense of impending doom. What had I gotten myself into? How was I going to keep from letting everyone who believed in me down? The panic would envelop me with its crippling grasp until I forced myself to get out of bed and down on my knees, pouring all my worries out to God. Then I would slip quietly back into bed, where my sweet husband would reach over in a half-awakened state and wrap his warm arms around me, filling my heart with indescribable peace. I just had to find a way to hang onto that peace—to keep it from disintegrating in the harsh light of day.

After several weeks, the open house was finally set for All God's Creatures Animal Clinic. Rosemary, heading up the refreshment committee composed of several other church ladies, presided over a huge punch bowl occupying center stage on the bountiful refreshment table pushed against the wall of the reception area. The church had graciously allowed me to borrow their silver fountain punch bowl, which poured several continuous streams of a red concoction mixed up by my mother-in-law. My church friends had insisted on contributing the food and had really outdone themselves with a dazzling array of hors d'oeuvres, once again shaming my naturally ungifted culinary skills. I was humbled and grateful.

My mother, the extrovert, appointed herself as tour guide through the tiny clinic, expertly chatting up every person who stepped foot through the door. In deference to my professional reputation, she did not discuss horses.

"Do you believe the number of people we've had through here?" I remarked to my husband, as the stream of the curious and the well-wishers just kept coming, crowding into the small space.

"Maybe they came for the free food," he joked.

I smacked him, playfully. "Let's hope not. All God's Creatures opens on Monday. It's time for this place to start earning its keep."

He put his arm around me and pulled me close. "It will. I have every confidence in you."

His confidence in me filled me with strength, and I basked in the hugely successful turnout, as people continued to traipse in. I only hoped some of these people would turn out to be clients.

I turned as the door opened and in came another couple, bearing a gift-wrapped box. My face lit up when I saw who it was.

"It's the Wyatts!" I cried, happily, dragging Jack by the hand to the front door.

I greeted them as they stood just inside the door. "Welcome. Thank you so much for coming."

"The place looks mighty nice," said Mr. Wyatt, looking around.

"And this must be your new husband," gushed Mrs. Wyatt, as she thrust the package into Mr. Wyatt's hands and threw her arms around my surprised spouse.

"Yes, this is Jack. Jack, Mr. and Mrs. Wyatt."

Mrs. Wyatt released my husband and stood back, still holding onto his arm. "We just want to tell you how grateful we were for you sharing your wife with us. On your *wedding day*, no less!" Her shining eyes peered merrily up into Jack's face.

Recognition dawned on Jack's face. "Oh, so *you're* the ones."

Mr. Wyatt made a polite cough. "Yep, if it weren't for little Doc Bennet, here, we'd 'a lost Petunia and her whole litter."

"Oh, you should see them now!" Mrs. Wyatt exclaimed. She let go of Jack's arm and dug through her massive pocketbook, withdrawing an envelope containing photographs. She extracted the pictures, one by one, narrating each one.

"This one's Jill, the pig we named after you," she informed me.

As I studied the photo, I couldn't help but feel honored. I'm not sure I'd ever had anything named after me.

"Jill's quite the porker," laughed Mr. Wyatt.

I chose to take that as a compliment. "Petunia sure has a lovely family. Thank you for sharing these pictures." It sent a warm fuzzy through my body to hear everything had turned out so well for Petunia and her babies. Often times vets don't hear about the good outcomes. We only hear if things go wrong. I started to hand the envelope back.

Mrs. Wyatt pushed away my hand. "Oh, no, those are for you." Then, as almost an afterthought, she said, "Oh! This is for you, too." She snatched the wrapped gift Mr. Wyatt still held and handed it to me. "It's a little wedding present. Or an office-warming present, whichever you'd like."

"Thank you," I replied, truly touched. "Should we open it now?"

The couple nodded enthusiastically, obviously eager to see our reaction to their thoughtfulness.

I looked at Jack. "Go ahead, honey," he said.

Grinning, I ripped off the paper, then laughed as I saw what was inside. "It's a cookie jar in the shape of a pig!" I held the box up for Jack to see.

Jack smiled. "It's perfect. Thank you both so much."

"You're welcome," Mrs. Wyatt said. "We wanted you to have a wedding present to remember us by."

I snickered. "I don't think there's any possibility of forgetting you." I gave her, then her husband a hug. "If you don't mind, I think I'll keep this up front and fill it with dog treats."

"By all means," Mrs. Wyatt agreed. "Now then, we'd like to see your new place."

ELLEN FANNON

Chapter 25

On Monday morning, Kelly and I sat in my gleaming and empty new clinic willing the phone to ring.

"Don't worry," she said, for the umpteenth time. "It takes time for new businesses to become established."

"I know," I replied, glumly. "I just had such high hopes after the success of the open house."

"People know you're here. They'll come."

I sighed. "I'll be in my office if you need me." *Hah! Need me for what?* I ambled back into my pigeonhole of an office and squeezed myself behind my cheap, second-hand metal desk. Now what?

My mind wandered to the chaotic days I'd spent at Spangle Animal Clinic, and I wondered, not for the first time, if I had made a big mistake. At Dr. Spangle's clinic we never sat around waiting for the phone to ring. Most days I wished it would stop.

Dr. Spangle had wasted no time in hiring another new graduate to replace me. In some ways, I wished I'd had the opportunity to warn the dewy-eyed newcomer before he went down the same road I had traveled. Still, this time Dr. Spangle had hired a young man. Perhaps Myra would be more respectful and helpful toward him. On a positive note, I had managed to make connections with other veterinarians in our area, and they graciously allowed me to become part of their on-call rotation schedule. Other than

Dr. Spangle, who didn't trust anyone not to steal his clients, the other veterinarians in our area took turns taking after-hour emergencies for each other, which spread that burden out to once every ten to twelve days, rather than every other day. This took a load off my shoulders, as there was no way I could work all day and then take all my own emergency calls.

The phone rang, startling me. My heart rate picked up. A client? An appointment? I couldn't hear Kelly's muffled end of the conversation. I forced myself to wait until I heard her hang up before bolting out of the office.

"Well?" I leaned expectantly over the reception desk.

She looked up, apologetically. "Sorry. Just one of your church friends wanting to come by and pick up a plate she forgot to take home from the open house."

"Oh." My spirits sank. I gazed at the beautiful bouquet of flowers from Jack sitting to the side of the piggy cookie jar. The card read, "Congratulations on your first day. I'm so proud of you." I wondered how proud he'd be when my business bankrupted us.

~

"Four dollars," I moaned to Jack that evening. "I made a whole four dollars today on a toenail trim."

Jack stopped stirring something on the stove that smelled magnificent and wrapped his arms around me. "That's great, honey, your first client!"

I extricated myself from his embrace and gave him a stony glare. "At this rate I'll have to let Kelly go."

He turned back to the stove. "At least give her two weeks' notice."

"Jack! This isn't funny!" I wailed. "I'm scared."

He twisted back around to hug me again. "Honey, it's only the first day. You've got to be patient."

"Patience is a vastly overrated virtue," I muttered against his shoulder.

~

I sat in the reception area watching the hands of the clock move at a snail's pace while Kelly rearranged the desk, yet again. The ringing of the phone caused us both to jump.

"All God's Creatures Animal Clinic, Kelly speaking," answered my professional assistant.

I tried not to get my hopes up. It was probably my mother.

"No, I'm sorry, Dr. Bennet can't come to the phone right now. She's with a client."

My eyes popped dangerously close to dislodging themselves from my skull. I waved frantically to get her attention.

Kelly ignored me. "No, I'm afraid she'll have to see your dog before she can advise you."

I tried hard to control my breathing before I became oxygen deprived.

"Hmm. Let me see." Kelly paused a long, agonizing moment. "Oh! It looks like we have a cancellation for eleven-thirty this morning. I could probably squeeze you in there." She waited another minute. "No, I'm sorry, that's all I have available." More conversation ensued on the other end of the phone to which I was not privy. "Okay, I'll pencil you in. Please be here ten minutes early to fill out paperwork."

My over-wrought emotions boiled over as she hung up. "What are you doing?" I shrieked. "What if they couldn't come at eleven-thirty?"

Kelly turned to me, a study in complete composure. "You don't want people to think you're just sitting here twiddling your thumbs waiting for them to call, do you?"

I threw up my hands. "Well, why not? It's the truth!"

She held out a restraining hand. "Be that as it may, we don't want to give the appearance of desperation. Trust me. I know what I'm doing."

I blew out a shaky breath and decided to tackle the stack of ignored medical journals piling up on my desk.

I just knew Kelly's ruse would be exposed when my eleven-thirty appointment showed up to an empty waiting room. But, bless the dear woman, she didn't seem to give any indication that it was unusual being the only client in the building, particularly after being "squeezed in" to my overloaded agenda. She had been referred by someone who worked with Rebecca's husband, so even Rebecca had come through for me. My new client's little shih tzu had a small hot spot, an area that he had repeatedly chewed until it was raw. After clipping and cleaning the area, an injection of cortisone, and educating her on better methods of flea control, she expressed her gratitude at being able to get in that morning, paid her bill without complaint, and left, still apparently unfazed by the lack of other clients all vying for my time.

Kelly shot me a grin as the door closed behind my second client. "I've booked another patient for two o'clock. A new puppy wellness exam."

I couldn't help the smile I felt spreading from ear to ear.

~

Little by little, clients began to trickle in, and, although I never solicited them, I even had a few people who followed me from Spangle Animal Clinic.

"I'm so glad we found you," exclaimed Mrs. Jordan, as she presented her boxer, Lily, for her yearly. "Dr. Spangle said he didn't know where you'd gone."

What? I did a slow burn. Dr. Spangle knew very well where I'd gone. In fact, he'd had his lawyer verify that I hadn't violated my non-compete clause in my employment contract with him. I'm sure he was highly disappointed he couldn't put me out of business before I had even opened my doors, but I had made sure my location was well outside the specified ten-mile radius from his clinic before beginning my venture.

DON'T BITE THE DOCTOR

I suppose I shouldn't have expected anything different from my rather unscrupulous old boss, but it still stung that he wouldn't even tell people where I was. Although not the first veterinarian to leave his employ, I was the only one who insisted on remaining in the area. But it boggled my mind that he would perceive me as a threat to his thriving business. Besides, it made him look ridiculous and petty; we lived in a small town, after all, so how could he not know where I had set up practice?

"Lily has always loved you and you've always been so good with her," Mrs. Jordan went on. "Dr. Spangle's a good enough vet, but he doesn't have your bedside manner."

I glowed under her praise, and I knew what she said was true. What I lacked in experience, I more than made up for by a gentle and caring manner. I also went above and beyond for my clients. Colossians 3:23 had always been my life's endeavor: *"Whatever you do, work at it with all your heart, as working for the Lord, not for men." (NIV)*

Then, one day, several months after opening All God's Creatures, I glanced at the appointment book and did a double-take. No, it couldn't be! It had to be someone else with the same name. But how many Westermeyers could there be in Pineville? With dogs named Taffy? On top of that, the appointment was for a second opinion.

I called to Kelly who was just coming through the door with the mail. "Kelly, this appointment for Westermeyer. Did she say what the second opinion was for?"

Kelly frowned for a moment in concentration. "Oh, *that* woman. No, she refused to say. Said she would discuss the problem with you when she got here. She was rather curt. Do you know her?"

I nodded slowly. "Yes, but I can't imagine her wanting to see *me*. She is one of Dr. Spangle's most dedicated clients."

Kelly hmphed. "Apparently not anymore."

I didn't know whether to be apprehensive or flattered. Although intensely curious as to why Mrs. Westermeyer sought a second opinion apart from her trusted, could-do-no-wrong, long-time veterinarian—and a second opinion from *me*, no less—did I *really* want this woman for a client?

My stomach twisted in knots as I waited for her to make her grand appearance, which, true to character, she did, by way of announcing her arrival in such a way to Kelly that left no doubt as to the urgency and importance of her business. In her usual fashion, Mrs. Westermeyer conveyed her air of superiority and expectation of deferential treatment as she presented herself at the front desk.

I peeked through the door as Kelly handed her a stack of paperwork to fill out.

"That won't be necessary," she informed Kelly, waving the forms away. "I have all my records with me." She thrust a large manila envelope at Kelly and took a seat in the small waiting room, after brushing off the chair, and placed Taffy on her lap. "And would you please let Dr. Bennet know we're here? This is a rather pressing situation."

I watched, unobserved, for a moment as the woman took in her surroundings. Surprisingly, she didn't wrinkle her nose. Kelly yanked open the door leading to the exam rooms and I nearly fell into the waiting room.

"What are you . . ." started Kelly. Then, realizing what I had been doing, she grinned. "Mrs. Westermeyer is here."

Of course, Mrs. Westermeyer had looked up as I stumbled into the waiting room. Since I was busted, I tried to recover my professional dignity.

"Mrs. Westermeyer, I was just coming to get you. How nice to see you again." I crossed the small space and extended my hand, which, this time, she took. "What can I do for you?"

The woman stood, Taffy under her arm, and shot a look toward Kelly. "If you don't mind, I'd rather discuss this privately."

"Oh. Yes, certainly. Please come on back." I stepped aside and allowed her to precede me into the narrow hallway leading to the exam rooms.

She paused, briefly, craning her neck to look around. "This is a rather pretty clinic. I like the soft, feminine touch."

"Thank you," I said, caught somewhat off-guard. I think that was the first time I had ever heard anything remotely complimentary come from her mouth in regard to me. "Would you like a tour?"

Her no-nonsense persona returned. "Perhaps another time. We have a *huge* problem that needs immediate attention."

I indicated for her to enter the first room, and I closed the door behind us.

"Has this table been disinfected?"

"Yes, but I'll do it again." I liberally re-sprayed the cleaner and wiped it away with a paper towel.

She set Taffy on the table. The happy dog wagged her stumpy tail and attempted to give me a kiss with her long, sloppy pink tongue. I patted her head, fondly.

"It's good to see you, Taffy." Then I turned my attention to her owner. "I understand you want a second opinion. What's the problem?"

Mrs. Westermeyer shook her head and bit her lip. "It's just too terrible! Dr. Spangle says Taffy has a venereal disease."

I blinked. I was dying to jump in and ask questions, but that's not the way appointments worked with Mrs. Westermeyer. I waited for her to go on.

She took a jagged breath and continued. "I want to breed Taffy with a new stud. Sir Bartholomew Huddleston of the House of Langston. He lives in Virginia. He just finished his national championship." She dug around in her purse and produced a picture of a handsome, blond cocker spaniel. The dog's name was bigger than he was. I made a mental note to check Taffy's full registered name, as I knew it couldn't be something as simple as "Taffy," and I didn't recall ever having heard it.

I made the appropriate comments and returned the photo to her.

"Anyway," she sniffed, "even though I am having chilled semen shipped for an artificial insemination rather than a natural breeding, Sir Bartholomew's owner insisted that Taffy be tested for Brucellosis."

I nodded. "It's not a bad idea."

Her fretful eyes searched mine. "Yes, I didn't find the request unreasonable. So, I asked Dr. Spangle to check Taffy. I nearly fainted dead away when he told me the result was positive."

My heart squeezed with this news. A Brucellosis infection would not only eliminate Taffy from being a show dog and a breeder, but since canine Brucellosis can be passed to humans, it might mean her life, as well, should Mrs. Westermeyer elect not to take the risk by treating Taffy. I glanced at the beautiful, happy dog before me, who gave the appearance of not having a care in the world.

"Tell me, did Dr. Spangle do the test in the clinic?" I asked.

"Yes, it took about ten minutes. I demanded he repeat it. Both times were positive." Her lower lip quivered ever so slightly. "I just can't believe it." She ran a hand along the length of her dog's body. Taffy responded with more enthusiastic wagging, her whole rear end wiggling in ecstasy.

"What else did Dr. Spangle say?"

She averted her eyes. "He said Taffy could not be bred again. He also said it might be best to put her down as she could be infectious to the other dogs. And to me." She looked up and to my amazement, I saw tears glistening in her eyes. Up to this time, I never credited the woman with a feeling heart.

I reached for a tissue box on the treatment shelf and handed it to her. She took her time wiping her eyes and blew her nose, noisily. "I just don't understand. Taffy has never had trouble conceiving, nor has she ever aborted any puppies. All her puppies have always been healthy."

"That does seem unusual," I agreed. Something nibbled at my subconscious. Something I had read recently about canine Brucellosis. "Would you excuse me for a minute? I think I have a journal article about this very situation."

I didn't wait for a response, but bolted from the room, a flicker of hope igniting what had begun as a small spark into a blazing flame. I raced to my office and hastily tore through the stacks of journals waiting to be read and filed. Where was it? I *knew* I had just read something about the canine Brucellosis test. After a brief panic, I located the article and quickly scanned the content. *Yes! This was it!*

I lost my professional facade in my optimistic enthusiasm, as I tore back to the exam room. Laying the open journal on the table, I spit out, "Look! I found it!"

Mrs. Westermeyer appeared startled. She tried to follow the print I had shoved under her nose, but finally said, "I'm sorry, I don't understand. What's this mean?"

"It says that the rapid slide agglutination test—that's the one we do in the clinic—is just a screening test. You can use it to rule *out* Brucellosis. If the test is negative, we can say the dog doesn't have Brucellosis. But it can sometimes show false positives. If the test is positive, you need to do additional testing to confirm it."

Her eyes grew wide. "So, you're saying Taffy may not have this disease, after all?"

I couldn't help the huge grin on my face. "That's right. I need to pull some blood and send it to the university for a more specialized test."

Her color paled. "Why didn't Dr. Spangle tell me about this other test?"

"He may not have known. This study just came out." I showed her the date on the journal, which was this month's.

For once, Mrs. Westermeyer seemed at a loss for words. She stood stroking her dog and stared off into space for a long time. "He told me it would be best to put her down," she finally whispered.

I touched her hand. "Let's not be premature. I think there's a good chance Taffy is just fine."

Her face crumpled and she began to weep copious silent tears. I had never seen her lose her composure, and knew she felt as uncomfortable as I did. I shoved the box of tissues into her hand, picked up Taffy, and called for Kelly to help me draw blood in the treatment area, giving Mrs. Westermeyer some privacy.

When I returned Taffy to her owner, Mrs. Westermeyer had composed herself. In fact, she was back to her old, normal self.

"I don't mind telling you I have found over the last few months that Dr. Spangle's service has been less than satisfactory," she told me, "but this is unacceptable! Just unacceptable!"

I let her rant, which she did for the next several minutes. Then something she said caused me to perk up my ears.

"And that . . . that *assistant!* What's her name? Myrna? Moira?"

"Myra," I supplied.

Mrs. Westermeyer sniffed. "There's a young woman who doesn't know her place. Always giving herself airs of authority and trouncing around as if she owns the clinic. I never cared for her, but she's gotten so much worse since Dr. Spangle's divorce. Way too big for her britches."

What? Divorce?

"If you ask me, I think she has her eye on Dr. Spangle." She gave me a conspiratorial, knowing look. "Not that I think he's foolish enough to fall for that little tart's scheming, but one never knows what a man will do when a brazen hussy throws herself at him."

A pall of sadness settled heavily in my heart. It shouldn't have come as a shock, but nevertheless, the news of my boss' divorce from his sweet wife rocked me. I had been gone less than a year, so the break-up of the marriage had happened fairly quickly. Fortunately, there were no children involved. But I still mourned for Patty's sake. I wondered how she was doing and made a mental note to give her a call.

"I've taken up enough of your time," Mrs. Westermeyer said, uncharacteristically. "You will let me know the minute you get the results of the test?"

"Yes, of course. I've asked for a phone call so we don't have to wait for the results in the mail."

She took a deep breath, and the quivering started again in her bottom lip. "Thank you." Then she gathered up Taffy and left.

A warm glow washed over me that I had finally been able to win Mrs. Westermeyer's trust and respect. I prayed the results of the second test would be negative.

A few days later I breathed a huge sigh of relief when the lab called to confirm the test was, indeed, negative. I immediately called Mrs. Westermeyer, who was thrilled, although her reaction was decidedly low-key and back to her normal stoic manner.

"It's too late to breed Taffy, now, of course, but I will expect you to be available to perform the artificial insemination on her next heat cycle."

"I would be happy to," I assured her. Although I had come out on top in this situation, I knew it would only be a matter of time before my performance failed to meet her high standards and expectations. But for now, I would take what I could get.

~

The practice continued to pick up, with new patients being booked every day. Several months later, on a particularly hectic Friday, I had just ushered the last client out the door, when a young, distraught-looking man walked in without an animal.

"Can I help you?" I asked.

"Are you Dr. Bennet?" he asked.

"Yes. What can I do for you?" I took in the dark circles under his eyes and his stooped shoulders and wondered what had beaten him down so badly.

"I'm Brad Owens," he replied. "Dr. Owens. Could I talk to you for a moment?"

Dr. Owens? Oh, now I remembered. He was the new vet who had replaced me at Spangle Animal Clinic. Well, I supposed he wasn't so new anymore. But although he had been working with Dr. Spangle for a year, I hadn't met him at any of the veterinary meetings. Dr. Spangle must have instilled in him the deep distrust for other area veterinarians, as he had done to me.

"Of course, come on back." I led him into my little office and offered him the folding chair in front of my desk. He sat, his head down, his hands fidgeting between his knees.

"I apologize for barging in when you're just closing up." He raised his head and offered a thin smile.

"That's okay. I'm glad to finally meet you." I waited, as he seemed to gather his courage.

Finally, he spoke. "I know it's a long shot, but I was wondering if you would be interested in hiring an associate. I can't stay at Spangle's and I really don't want to leave the area. My parents live here and my dad is not in good health."

"I'm sorry to hear that," I offered.

His admission released a torrent of words. "I don't know how you stood that place for three years. My contract is almost up and I can't last another minute." He continued to describe how difficult and stressful the past year had been.

I was sorry to hear the working conditions were not any better for this unfortunate young man than they had been for me. Although not surprised, I had hoped that perhaps, as a man, he would be treated with more respect. "I guess things haven't changed, then."

He shook his head. "It's intolerable. And that technician! Now that she and Dr. Spangle are engaged, she's insufferable."

Engaged! Oh, good grief! I felt the blood drain from my face.

"I take it you hadn't heard." The corners of his mouth turned up in a sad smile that didn't reach his eyes.

"No. I haven't really kept up with the clinic news since I left."

"That's understandable. But Heather and Tess say nothing but good things about you. They say you're a great veterinarian and a good Christian. It's hard being a Christian in that environment." He caught my eye, briefly, then glanced back down at his hands. "Anyway, I thought it was worth a shot reaching out to you. I know jobs are hard to come by around here."

I nodded, deep in thought. "Look," I finally said. "Let me run this by my husband. I can't promise you anything, but I'll see what we might be able to work out. The clinic has become pretty busy, lately."

A huge smile lit up his face. "Thank you!" He stood, stumbling over his own feet in the tiny space, and held out his hand. "I look forward to hearing from you."

I smiled back. "Leave me your number and I'll get back to you in a day or so."

~

That night I broached the subject of taking on some additional help with Jack.

"But, honey," he objected, "you're just now getting on your feet with the clinic. I'm not sure you can afford to hire another veterinarian at this point."

"I know, Jack, but I'm not talking about full-time. I'm thinking I might be able to give him some part-time work and scale back a little on my workload."

"But I thought you loved your job." His concerned eyes searched my face.

"I do. But down the road I'm going to have to cut back a little and take some time off."

"What? Why?"

I laughed. "Maternity leave, papa."

Jack's eyes widened and his jaw dropped. "Are you saying—"

I nodded. "We're about to make your mother very happy."

"But . . . but, what about *you?* Your job? We weren't even trying! You always said . . ." His voice trailed off.

I pulled him into a hug. "God works in mysterious ways," I murmured against his shoulder. "Everything will work out according to His plan."

He held me at arm's length and his whole face lit up. "It always does," he replied, before pulling me back for a long kiss.

THANK YOU, DEAR READER

If you enjoyed reading this book, the best thing you can do to help the author is to tell others about it. Ellen would also greatly appreciate you rating her book and leaving a brief review at amazon.com and goodreads.com. Simply type in the name of the book and the author. When the website comes up, click on the picture of the book, scroll down, and there will be a button to click to leave a rating and a review. A review doesn't have to be long—a sentence or two telling what you liked about the book. Was it interesting, humorous, informative, thought-provoking, etc.? Thank you so much for your support.

Ellen would love for you to visit her website: https://ellenfannonauthor.com and subscribe to follow her weekly blog, *Good for a Laugh.*

ELLEN FANNON

SAVE THE DATE

Read on for a sample from another novel by Ellen Fannon

CHAPTER 1

"Save the date for our twenty-fifth Belmore High School Reunion," read the beautifully engraved invitation in Hannah's hand. The enclosed sheet listed the reunion's schedule of events and locations of each one.

Twenty-five years! The raised gold lettering on the embossed card plunged Hannah back in time, dredging up the memories and emotions of her eighteen-year-old self.

"Hmmm," she mused. "Should I even think about going?"

On one hand, who didn't fantasize about attending one's high school reunion and discovering that the stuck-up head cheerleader had gained two hundred pounds? Or that the star athlete who cast aside used girlfriends like snotty tissues had finally worked his way up to assistant manager at Burger Boy? Or—her eyes narrowed with malicious glee—the four "i's" (Suzi, Shelli, Jacki, and Barbi) had married four pig-farming brothers who chewed tobacco with their few remaining teeth, and lived on adjacent plots of land in Possum Snout Tennessee, population seven hundred and forty two (soon to be seven hundred and forty three when Jacki Martin Coon popped out her sixth child); because, as everyone knew, the four "i's" were joined at the hip. How miserable those four had made her life during junior high and high school.

No sooner had that image popped into her head than she found herself horrified. *Hannah Jensen! You should be ashamed of yourself!* She searched her heart for a smidgen of leftover bitterness that may have leaked to the surface. The truth was she hadn't really given those mean girls much more than a passing thought since high school. She had moved on and left them in the past where they belonged. Hadn't she? Had the reunion invitation opened up old wounds? That was the last thing she wanted. But had she ever consciously acknowledged forgiveness toward them? Surely she had. Or maybe somewhere along the way during the past twenty-five years it hadn't seemed relevant.

Remember what Mom always says, "If you can't say (or think) something nice about someone, don't say anything at all." Okay, let's think of some nice *scenarios.*

She recalled poor Marvin Peabody—the scrawny nerd who wore coke-bottle glasses and the butt of all the cool kids' jokes throughout his four painful years of high school. He would be at the reunion, as the CEO and owner of Universal Software, second only to Microsoft in terms of billions of dollars. Oh, and on his arm would be a former Miss America, now Mrs. Felicia Peabody. Marvin, in his spare time, had become a body builder, recently gracing the cover of *Sports Illustrated.*

"Good for you, Marvin," she said aloud, the corners of her mouth turning up slightly.

And how about poor Lynnette Frump, the mousy wallflower collectively ignored by all the cool dudes, who was now a super model?

"You go, girl," she cheered. This fantasizing could be fun, provided she didn't let her imagination run too wild, or too unkind.

And then there was her—Hannah Jensen, formerly Hannah Skinner. What about her? She dropped the mail on the kitchen table and headed for the bathroom mirror to survey her assets and liabilities. Hmmm. Well, on the assets side, she still weighed exactly the same as she did when she graduated from high school, albeit the weight distributed itself a little differently these days. Still, with some strong spandex and her little black dress, she could pull off a fairly good figure.

But what about her mousy brown hair—forever the bane of her existence, with its natural frizz and a mind of its own? She could always wear a wig and tell people she had experienced a makeover disaster at the hands of a new stylist who lured her in with the promise of a twenty percent discount. But, no . . . that would be just asking the good Lord to strike her with a fatal disease for lying, and then where would her poor fatherless daughter be? Okay, deal with the hair later. Maybe she would even have it professionally done if she could make an appointment with a salon back in her hometown.

Now on to her naturally, emerald eyes, the color usually found only in tinted contacts. Some fine lines radiated from the corners of her eyes, but with good makeup and dim lighting, they were over all acceptable.

Her nose was . . . average. Besides, noses weren't usually critiqued unless they took up a person's whole face to the point other people couldn't do anything but stare.

Her mouth . . . hmmm. Hannah puckered her lips, pressed them into a firm line, and worked them into a smile. They weren't the full, sensual rosebuds of romance novels, but they weren't paper thin either. Altogether a draw.

Her face . . . no disfiguring moles, scars, or warts.

Those frown lines, though . . . ugh. But nothing a little Botox couldn't fix. The thought immediately appalled her. She would absolutely *not* resort to Botox. She would not go to her high school class reunion looking like a plastic mannequin, unable to move her face. Or worse yet, what if the procedure went wrong, leaving her with droopy eyelids? Or, worse, just *one* droopy eyelid. Her classmates would think she was either inebriated or had suffered a stroke.

As she turned to examine her shoulders, and adjusted her posture, she heard the kitchen door slam.

"Blair, is that you?" she called, jolting from her reverie.

"Yes, Mother, who did you think it was? An axe murderer? If I *were* an axe murderer, I wouldn't have answered, right? I would just, like, hack you to death." Blair briefly paused her tirade before admonishing, "You really should keep the doors locked."

Hannah emerged from the bathroom to find her almost fifteen-year old daughter foraging through the refrigerator. Blair, having recently developed a health kick, complained, "Don't we have *anything* non-fattening in here?"

"I bought some yogurt just yesterday. And there are apples."

Blair turned and held up a carton of yogurt. "Mo-*ther*, hello! What is this?"

Hannah blinked. "Um, yogurt?" Why was the obvious not always obvious to a teenager? Somehow, she had messed up again, but for the life of her, she could not fathom what she had done wrong—other than breathe regularly, which embarrassed her daughter to no end. Not to worry, though, Hannah knew Blair would enlighten her.

Blair rolled her eyes, the way only teenagers can do effectively. "It's not *Greek,* Mother. *And* it's not lite. Look at the calorie count on this small container. There's, like, two hundred!"

Who knew? "Sorry, I didn't realize there was a

difference."

Blair huffed and slammed the refrigerator door. "I'll be in my room texting Samantha."

"Didn't you just see Samantha at school?" *Ah, shoot, did it again. Spoke common sense to a teenager.*

Blair shook her head and disappeared.

In spite of herself, Hannah grinned. Sometimes she wondered why God allowed parents to suffer through teenagers, but figured it must have something to do with original sin. Why couldn't He just put them into hibernation around age twelve and wake them up at twenty-one? Or better yet, thirty? Still, her daughter was growing into a beautiful young woman, who resembled her father more and more the older she got. It was bittersweet to see Alex's dark brown hair, strong jawline, and sapphire blue eyes in Blair. What *she* had contributed to her daughter's DNA, she didn't know. Blair was all Alex. Alex, the love of her life, had had the audacity to die and leave her a single parent—of a teenager, no less. The coward.

She sighed and pushed her thoughts of Alex to the back corner of her brain, where although he constantly hovered, he couldn't fill her whole being with the wrenching, aching, numbing pain that put her heart in danger of stopping altogether. Sometimes thoughts of Alex intruded in the strangest moments. But she couldn't dwell on him now or she would leave herself once again vulnerable to dying with him, as she had done in the beginning. She'd walked around dead for months, only her heart hadn't gotten the message to stop beating.

Shaking her head to clear it of Alex—difficult as that was to do with his carbon copy living in her house—she set out to make a nutritious and low-calorie dinner. She opened the refrigerator and pulled out a head of lettuce, carrots, radishes, cucumbers, tomatoes, baby spinach, and some low-fat shredded cheddar. Putting together a salad constituted busy work guaranteed to give her brain a reprieve from conscious thought, provided she paid close enough attention to keep from chopping off a finger or two. She took the two skinless chicken breasts she'd thawed earlier, and lightly sautéed them with low-fat butter.

Blair wandered into the kitchen just as Hannah finished arranging the chicken strips on top of the salad. "What is *that?*" she shrieked.

Hannah looked up. "Chicken," she answered, a hint of sarcasm in her tone.

"Mo-*ther*! How many times do I have to tell you I'm *vegan* now? I don't eat things that like, once had a heartbeat!" Blair glared at Hannah as though she had just desecrated a sacred shrine.

"I thought that was last week." Hannah couldn't keep up.

"Mo-*ther*, becoming vegan isn't like, something you do for a week! It's, like a whole life-style change. And is that *cheese?*"

"It's low-fat," Hannah offered lamely, wondering again when she had become "Mo-*ther*" instead of "Mom."

Blair continued her huff. "I can't eat this! You've like, totally *ruined* it!"

"Okay," Hannah shrugged. "Feel free to make your own. Leaves more for me." She picked up a fork and dug in.

Blair snorted an angry, rather un-ladylike burst of air, blowing her bangs from her forehead. "*Fine!* I'll do it myself!"

It must be about that time of the month. Whatever you do, don't dare even suggest it. Hannah remembered her own blossoming (more like beastly, betraying) hormones around Blair's age, and graciously chose to ignore her.

"What's this?" Blair's tone conveyed less antagonism and more curiosity. She picked up Hannah's class reunion invitation and looked it over.

"It's an invitation to my twenty-fifth high school

reunion. It came in the mail today."

"Are you like, actually going?" her daughter asked, incredulous.

"I haven't decided yet. Why?" *And, like, could you speak one complete sentence without using the word "like?"*

Another eye roll. Seriously, if the child didn't stop rolling her eyes, they'd end up permanently pointing toward the ceiling. She would have to bend her whole body in order to look down.

"It's just, like so lame, a bunch of old people sitting around and reminiscing about the 'good old days.'"

"Just wait. Your turn will come. I wasn't born this old, you know."

Blair snorted again. Hannah realized that like most teenagers, Blair never envisioned herself reaching the ripe old age of thirty. She would forever live in perpetual youth. She and Peter Pan. Sure, Hannah had been there too. Now *forty* was in her rear-view mirror.

"Like I said, I haven't decided yet. It's an awfully long way to go."

"Whatever. But don't, like think about dragging me with you." Blair finished tossing together her rabbit food, left her mess on the kitchen counter, and announced, "I'm eating in my room. I have homework."

Hannah sighed. Ordinarily she would have insisted Blair eat in the kitchen, and preferably with her. Even though it was just the two of them, they were a family. But sitting at the table with a surly teenager who didn't want to be in the same room with her tended to spoil her appetite. She wasn't sure why Blair was so churlish tonight, other than the fact that she was almost fifteen, which, in and of itself, was reason enough. She finished her delicious salad (with chicken and cheese), along with enough full calorie ranch dressing to clog her aging arteries, and rinsed her bowl. Then she wrapped the fresh produce left on the counter and put it away.

Hannah could hear Blair's music (if one could call the noise emanating from the child's room "music") from behind her closed bedroom door. She was grateful it wasn't played at deafening decibels, so she could easily block it out when she would retreat to her own bedroom and close the door, as she intended to do.

Grabbing the stepladder from the utility closet, Hannah hauled it into her bedroom closet and climbed to the top step so she could retrieve her high school yearbook from the top shelf. The dust stirred up in the process tickled her nose and made her sneeze several times. She wiped the cover of the book with her sleeve and climbed down gingerly, so as to not break her fragile, elderly neck and render her daughter an orphan.

How long has it been since I've looked through these pages? Hannah wondered. She couldn't remember. Propped against the soft pillows on her bed, Hannah opened the yearbook and leafed through each page, one page at a time. A strangely comforting, musty smell wafted from the old pages.

Gracious! Did we really wear those ridiculous clothes back then? And the hair styles! Even the teachers look ludicrous, and they were the adult role models. Hannah thumbed through the senior portraits seeing how many people she remembered. There was Gerald Adams, the first senior in alphabetical order, staring out from a haughty expression, despite the fact he sported a monstrous Afro on his white head. She could swear she'd never seen that kid in her life. Someone named Carol had written on this page: *"To a sweet girl in my English class. Stay as you are and you will go far."* Little hearts bookended the signature. Carol. Carol who? Hannah scanned the page for someone named Carol. Two girls caught her eye, Carol Bainbridge and Carol Carson. She didn't recognize either one of them. But she recognized the next face: Suzi Cabrezzi, with her smug little smile and her perfectly, long, straight, blonde hair. Suzi, who had been her friend during their elementary years—even spending the night occasionally—had morphed into an intolerable "cool kid" when she hit puberty, leaving anything and anybody uncool—such as Hannah—in her dust.

Hannah sighed and flipped to the next page. Oh great. Shelli Delgado, with her sleek dark hair and her thinly plucked eyebrows, colored in with thick black pencil, staring out at her. Shelli's face wasn't wearing its usual evil smile, but rather an arrogant, "I'm cool, therefore, I rule," look. And right across from her Hannah spotted Barbi Flores. Suffice it to say, Barbi lived up to her name.

Ick. Why had Hannah started down this memory lane? As though no time had passed, she felt the rejection of the four "i's" overcome her—the betrayals, the hurt, the humiliation, the longing to fit in, and the complete dismissal of her as a person. She'd actually befriended Barbi when she transferred to Hudson Junior High from some place down south and didn't know anybody. Barbi used her until she got in tight with the other three, then ignored her like she was yesterday's trash. Would it have hurt the girl to say "hi" in the hallway once in a while instead of looking past her as though she didn't exist? Barbi had cried on Hannah's shoulder when she first moved, when the other three "i's" ganged up on her because of her crush on Danny Kolinsky, accusing her of leading him on. And Danny Kolinsky, of all people? What a doofus. Still, for some reason, he tipped to the cool side of the scale by junior high, although Hannah never understood why. Just the thought of him still made her shake her head in bewilderment.

She refused to look at the last of the "i's," Jacki Martin. The label for the four "i's" came from Hannah's painful snubbing from the group and stood for the "Ins." Also, for some reason, when the four hit the monstrous stage between the ages of twelve and thirteen, they all changed their names. Susan became Suzi, Michelle became Shelli, Barbara became Barbi, and Jackie dropped her "e." Apparently, one could only be cool if one's name ended in an "i." A number of fringers, anxious to get in on the coolness trend, followed. Melissa Jones became Missi, Amanda Perkins became Mandi, Joan Tate became Joani, and even Peggy McAllister changed her "y" to an "i," which looked rather dopey in writing. But what could one do with a name like Hannah? Hanni? Nope, didn't flow.

Hannah flipped to another page, and right there, poor Annabel Lee Pott's picture in the upper left corner touched a raw spot in her heart. She hadn't thought of that girl in years. Chubby, and cursed with a mother who not only saddled her with the horrible name—apparently a fan of Edgar Allan Poe—but also subjected her to home perms and wouldn't let her shave her legs, making the child the brunt of adolescent cruelty. Her legs, covered in thick, dark hair, stood out like those of a hairy ape because of Mrs. Pott's refusal to allow Annabel Lee to wear hose until she turned sixteen. On top of that, Annabel Lee sported a unibrow. As if those problems weren't bad enough, her mother held the post of permanent president of the PTA, so she was *always* at school.

The mean, cool kids took great delight in torturing Annabel Lee by calling her "Annabelly" and "Potty." Hannah tried to befriend her the best she could, but Annabel Lee's micromanaging, over-controlling mother made life difficult for everyone; her child's friends included. Plus, Annabel Lee seemed to have no social awareness. None! So, hanging around with her meant Hannah's chances of ever becoming part of the cool kids' groups decreased exponentially. Still, she felt sorry for Annabel Lee, and as the two class outcasts, Hannah often looked after her and refused to join in the shunning, regardless of what the others thought.

DON'T BITE THE DOCTOR

When Hannah first saw that reunion invitation, she thought it might be fun to see how some people turned out, despite her initial pig farm fantasy. She really didn't wish miserable lives on anyone, not even the four "i's." Not that being a pig farmer meant misery—except perhaps to snooty city girls. But what if the four "i's" behaved just as horribly as ever and made the reunion unpleasant for her? What if Annabel Lee Pott and Marvin Peabody and Lynnette Frump still garnered disdain? Did people really grow up and move past their adolescent idiocies? Then an uncomfortable thought took her by surprise. *Have I?* Surely she had. And even if her former nemeses hadn't changed, *she* could still be an adult.

You are forty-two years old, Hannah. Those girls . . . well, women, now, can't do anything to make you feel insignificant. You can rise above anything petty they dish out. And while you're at it, what makes you think they'll dish out anything petty? She mentally presented all her ill-founded trepidations to herself and tried to reason that certainly those women had changed from the mean-spirited teenagers they once were. So why had she allowed these unwelcome feelings to resurface simply by looking at her old yearbook? It was slightly unnerving.

Then Hannah's eyes fell on the photo of *him,* and her breath caught in her throat. It was Dayne Harrelson, her high school boyfriend of three years. How had she forgotten about him, her first true love? He wasn't just a crush or puppy love. They had a true, mutual, deep, heart-squeezing, happily-ever-after love—until he dumped her and broke her heart. Of course, she hadn't *forgotten* him, exactly. Twenty-five years of life had intervened.

"Mom!" Blair burst through her bedroom door without knocking. "I need my red shirt for tomorrow."

Hannah looked up, jolted back to the present. "It's in the laundry, honey."

"In the laundry?" Blair shrieked. "You *know* I need it

for—"

"Don't get your knickers in a knot," Hannah replied, calmly. "I meant it's hanging in the laundry room."

The wind dropped from Blair's sails. Then she spied the yearbook. "Is that like, your yearbook? Oh my gosh, it totally is! Let me see!" She grabbed the book from Hannah and began flipping through it, squealing with laughter. "Where's your picture? I want to see you!"

"It's under 'S.'"

"Oh, right, I forgot." Blair found her mother's senior class picture and tried to hold back her snort. "It's ... like ... really not *that* bad."

"Gee thanks."

"I mean, it's ... just ... like your ... *hair...*"

"I'll have you know that was the style back then. I worked hard to make my hair look that good."

Blair stared at her as though she had two heads.

"Styles come and go, Blair. Your kids will probably think you looked pretty silly when they look at your high school yearbook."

"No way. I'm never having kids."

Switching gears, Blair announced, "Remember I'm sleeping over at Samantha's tomorrow."

"Will her parents be there the whole night?"

"Of course, Mother," Blair responded with a dramatic eye roll.

"Who else will be there?"

"Nobody. And you know her parents. They don't conduct séances or sacrifice goats in their backyard."

"And you'll text me at least twice?"

"If I have to."

"You have to. And you remember I'm meeting that friend of Aunt Laura's for coffee tomorrow night."

"Gah! A *date?* Aren't you a little old for that, Mother?" Blair's normally pretty face contorted with disdain.

"It's *not* a date!"

"It *is* a date! And set up by Aunt Laura, for heaven's sake! I think I'm going to barf."

"She didn't actually set it up. The man happens to be a friend of her brother-in-law's."

"Eew. That's even worse. He probably, like lives with his mother and sells drugs to grade school kids."

"Blair! He's been thoroughly checked out. He's not a serial killer, doesn't hoard cats, and the best part is *he doesn't have children!*"

Blair failed to get the dig. "Hmmph. He's probably, like one of those old dudes who, like, has a gray ponytail and drives a little sports car."

"Enough. I have a right to a life, young lady."

"With some old geezer? Can he even, like walk without a cane?"

"He's forty-four."

"Like I said . . ." Blair left her statement unfinished and floated out of the room, leaving the door open. "Night, Mom."

"Good night, Blair. I love you."

"Love you, too, Mom." Hannah heard her walk down the hall, then shout back, "He probably kidnaps people and chains them up in his basement!"

Hannah closed her yearbook and set it aside. It was *not* a date. Even so, she looked forward to the meeting with all the anticipation of an income tax audit. She knew, without a shadow of a doubt, that she would never find another man who could make her heart flutter like Alex could. Plus, she was still very much in love with Alex, even if he was inconveniently dead. But a dead husband didn't make for lively conversation or keep her warm in bed on cold winter nights. She was lonely, blast it. And God hadn't seen fit to drop husband number two on her doorstep. But a blind date? Yuck! Wait, no, it wasn't a *date*. It was a blind meeting. Even worse. Blair was probably right. The guy was probably creepy or wacko or—something. Otherwise, he wouldn't be single and having to be set up with strange women. Still, she'd had to kiss a few frogs before she'd found Alex. Maybe there was another prince out there for her.

Goliath wandered into her room, climbed onto her bed, and laid his massive black head on her thighs, cutting off her circulation. Goliath, bless his doggy heart, had never quite grasped the concept he wasn't a teacup poodle. As his name implied, he was an enormous beast. The best she could figure, his heritage consisted of a mixture between a Newfoundland and a Wooly Mammoth. He had an immense body, outweighing her by at least seventy-five pounds and a long, slightly curly, black coat, which made it difficult to tell his front end from his back end. He also had the sweetest, most gentle disposition ever seen in a beast his size. She brushed his shaggy hair out of his eyes—she would never resort to putting his bangs in a ponytail or hair clip, empathizing with his perpetually bad hair days—and patted his rock-hard head before attempting to shove it off her legs, a feat easier said than done, as his head alone had to weigh at least fifty pounds. He let out a discontented moan at being pushed aside, and settled down next to her. Thank goodness for a king-sized bed, even if Goliath did take up three-quarters of it.

"What do you think, Goliath? Should I go to this reunion?"

As usual, he didn't answer.

Hannah sighed and scratched Goliath's head. "I'll have to think about it." She reached to switch off the bedside lamp and snuggled under the covers, trying to claim a small piece of the bed for herself.

Sign up for Forget Me Not Romances newsletter and receive a special gift compiled from Forget Me Not Authors!

Join our FB pages to keep up on our most current news!

Forget Me Not Romances Readers and Authors

Take Me Away Books

Winged Publications

Soaring Beyond

Fiction and Science Fiction